Ian Davey is born, raised and still living in Harrogate, he has always been fascinated by the many myths and legends of his home town and its surrounding areas that are plentiful! With a fascination for true history, legend and myth, Ian blends all these ingredients together to produce something almost believable in our modern and cynical world. He is also a musical composer for both orchestra and voice. Ian is passionate about reaching the heart through imagination in both music and word and it has always been his hope that others will enjoy his works.

To my wife and family for supporting and believing in me and my vision for this book.

Ian Davey

Book One of a Trilogy – A Stitch in Time

John Twigg's Childhood and His Family

Austin Macauley Publishers

London * Cambridge * New York * Sharjah

Copyright © Ian Davey 2023

The right of Ian Davey to be identified as author of this work has been asserted by the author in accordance with sections 77 and 78 of the Copyright, Designs and Patents Act 1988.

All rights reserved. No part of this publication may be reproduced, stored in a retrieval system, or transmitted in any form or by any means, electronic, mechanical, photocopying, recording, or otherwise, without the prior permission of the publishers.

Any person who commits any unauthorised act in relation to this publication may be liable to criminal prosecution and civil claims for damages.

This is a work of fiction. Names, characters, businesses, places, events, locales, and incidents are either the products of the author's imagination or used in a fictitious manner. Any resemblance to actual persons, living or dead, or actual events is purely coincidental.

A CIP catalogue record for this title is available from the British Library.

ISBN 9781035804092 (Paperback)
ISBN 9781035804108 (Hardback)
ISBN 9781035804122 (ePub e-book)
ISBN 9781035804115 (Audiobook)

www.austinmacauley.com

First Published 2023
Austin Macauley Publishers Ltd®
1 Canada Square
Canary Wharf
London
E14 5AA

My grateful thanks to The Sealed Knot Society, Sir Thomas Ingleby of Ripley, Harrogate, Betty's Tearooms of Harrogate and Samuel Smith's brewery for allowing me to reference them in this fictional work.

Table of Contents

John Twigg's Birth	11
Helen and Michael	21
John Starts School	26
The Wishing Stone (Part 1)	40
Sunday Lunch with Nanna And Grandpa	47
The Wishing Stone (Part 2)	57
Hampsthwaite	65
Subpoena Duces Tecum	75
The Picnic at Hampsthwaite	79
Nocturnal Ramblings	90
A Timely Break	102
The Siege Of Ripley Castle	109
Time Marches On	130
Past Tense, Future Perfect	139
Bitter-Sweet	150
Union of Differences	158
The Final Straw	171
The Strange Occurrence at Little Almscliff	181
Rendezvous	187
The Colours of an Actress	199

University	212
Success	231
Fate and Human Falter	236
Cruel Transportation	249

John Twigg's Birth

John Twigg drew his first breath at 6:20 AM, on the 28 June 1975, at Harrogate General Hospital, in North Yorkshire. His father Michael, had been sent home earlier that evening by the nurse, who had told him quite categorically, "Mrs Twigg will go her full term! There's no point you hanging around here, go and get yourself some sleep!"

But it wasn't too many hours later before the telephone rang at his home and the message was to come back to the hospital as soon as possible, as 'Mrs Twigg was in the final stages of labour'. He jumped into his car and rushed to the hospital. Still in his pyjamas, his heart was thumping and he could scarcely think of anything else, he even found it difficult to stay to the 30mph speed limit as he made his way down Knaresborough Road.

At that time of the morning, there was very little traffic about, so he chanced it and put his foot down! As the cobwebs of his broken sleep started to leave him, the absolute realisation of what was about to happen, hit him. The broadest grin came over his face and he yelled out "Yahoo!" at the top of his voice, much to the curiosity of a little old dear walking on the footpath with her old Jack Russell dog, tottering slowly behind her on its lead.

"I'm gonna be a daddy!" he bellowed at her through his open car window as he passed. The poor old lass turned to watch as the car sped past and heaven knows what she was thinking, as this 40-year-old man, with greying hair that had not seen a comb and looking like a scarecrow, whizzed by!

Gently shaking her head as if in despair, she turned and walked on with her dog in tow and muttered to herself, "I dunno. Youth of today! Tut-tut!"

He screeched to a halt in the car park of the hospital, right in the middle of two car parking spaces and jumped out of his car, forgetting to wind up the window or even lock it. Running up to the entrance of the hospital, he passed a jolly-faced ambulance driver chap, who, with his obvious experience, recognised the exuberance for what it was and as Michael passed him, puffing and panting, he said, "Congratulations, lad! All the best to you!"

"Oh, thank you, thank you, thank you!" said Michael, as he briefly grabbed the hand of the ambulance man and shook it as if it were a water pump. Passing the reception desk, he tried to compose himself slightly, as the receptionist looked over her glasses at him and fixed a firm glare. Then her face softened, as she looked at this man with hair all over the place, pyjamas buttoned up wrong and a pair of slippers that were in the design of a couple of racing cars, bought years ago for him as a bit of a joke by his brother John.

"I presume you know where you're going, by your demeanour and apparel?" she said with mock solemnity. "I wouldn't want you going off to occupational therapy with your pyjamas buttoned up incorrectly, they do have standards down there!" she said with an impish grin.

"Oh, God, lass!" Michael shouted, in the absolute silence of the reception area, "know where ah'm goin'? I have pictured this moment fer months, luv, an' what's more, ah will leave this place wi' a grin so large, it'll tek two firemen an' an osteopath to remove it!"

And then, like someone demented or a drunken and giddy man, he clicked his racing cars together and ran without another word up the corridor towards the midwifery department. The receptionist smiled, remembering her own husband at the birth of their baby 20 years before and the similarity of the scene she had just witnessed. Then, with her smile broadening still further, a smile that she could not suppress, she resumed her duties with a happy, heavy sigh.

Michael flew up the long, inclining corridor. Passing the antenatal department, his thoughts briefly took him back to the antenatal sessions, for mums and dads-to-be, where he sat in with his wife Helen and several other happy, but anxious-faced couples, stretching on the floor or doing mock breathing exercises or discussing birthing techniques or other acquaintances babies arrivals and the torments and joys of birth.

"Now remember to time the contractions," he vaguely recalled, "and if the waters break, here's the symptom and here's what you do—"

By the cringe, ah'm pleased ah'm past that bit o' t' proceedin's, he thought to himself, as he passed the cafeteria area and steadied into a more moderate pace. Then, darker thoughts entered his head, all of a sudden. *What if t' bairn's malformed?* he thought gloomily. *What if Helen can't do it right, like? What if she has to 'ave one o' these 'epesioptamics' things?*

He was now approaching the room that Helen was in on the labour ward and heard her and the nurse talking softly and calmly. For a moment, he listened, hardly daring to interrupt, in case he missed any vital piece of information that would confirm or alleviate his fears.

"Oh, you shouldn't be too much longer, Mrs Twigg, you are 7 centimetres dilated and baby is fully in position now, just try to relax until your husband arrives, he shouldn't be too long now, I know that reception gave him a buzz about 15 minutes ago. Just take the gas and air if you find the—"

"Here I am, swee'pea!" said Michael, bursting through the door, like the star performer at the London Palladium! "I got 'ere soon as ah could! How's it goin'? Are they lookin' after ya, lass? When's it due like? What have ah got to do to help?"

"Michael, Michael, calm down," said Helen smiling at him, "everything's just fine and dandy!"

"Oh!" said the startled nurse, "Mr Twigg! Helen is just fine. Just sit yourself down and relax. Everything's going just fine! Would you like a cup of tea? Baby may be just a little while yet."

"Yeah, yeah, that'd be grand, luv," he said to the nurse, who appreciating that a few moments alone, would be apropos for the expectant couple. Michael took Helen's hand, almost as if to propose marriage all over again and looked adoringly at her, her raven black hair soaked with perspiration from her exertions. But her eyes were bright as fire and full of life and love at seeing Michael and the thought of the two of them being three very soon.

"Are you alright, lass? Is there owt I can do to help?"

"Michael!" she said with a weary laugh. "I'm not ill! I'm not an invalid you know! We're going to have a baby! Our baby—soon—ohh, ohhhh." Helen's face changed slightly as the pains of a contraction started. "Pass me that mask, Mike," she said, pointing at the face mask that provided the gas and air.

Panicking, Michael fumbled around to get the mask, at the same time shouting, "Nurse, nurse, where are you? It's gonna be alright, love," stuttered Michael.

"Yes, I know!" said Helen through gritted teeth.

"It'll be just fine and dandy, Helen. I'm right here with ya, pet!"

"Yes, I know—I'm—" Helen held her breath as the urge to push took control of her and with screwed-up eyes, she started to go red in the face.

"NURSE, NURSE, where the hell are you!" screamed Michael, taking hold of Helen's hand and she squeezed his, almost bloodless. "NURSE!" he bellowed at the top of his voice, much to the shock of the poor midwife who by this time was standing right next to him. "Help her, she's stopped breathin'!"

"Calm down, Mr Twigg," said the midwife, having collected her composure, "everything's fine!"

At the same moment, Helen gave out a huge gasp as she exhaled, then started to pant, as she got her breath.

"You daft bat!" she said, still panting and forcing a smile, "I'm not ill. I told you, I'm having a baby!"

All the while, the midwife was checking the monitor next to the bed and timing the contractions.

"I think baby is nearly ready to meet you both," said the midwife, smiling at them. "Your contractions are rapid and regular and your waters broke 25 minutes ago—yes, I think we're just about ready to see your little addition!"

It wasn't too long before the moment started in earnest. The midwife gowned and gloved, Helen in birthing position, panting and occasionally holding her breath and screwing her eyes up tightly.

"Michael," she said through gritted teeth, "Give me your hand!"

Michael, who had been asked to sit down on a chair near the bed, was with her in an instant.

"Swee'pea, I'm here, I love you, I love you," he said through wide, dewy eyes and clasping her hand, he watched as baby's head started to appear. Not a word was said. The only noises were the sound of monitors and the cries and gasps coming from Helen as she pushed and the distant clatter of stainless steel and crockery, coming from way down the corridor as the kitchen were preparing to serve breakfast.

The shoulders came and he watched the midwife, who was as cool as a cucumber all the while, cupping baby's head in one hand and watching Helen closely. Then, with a gargantuan effort, Helen let out a huge cry of exertion and release, as the baby slipped into the world.

"By the cringe!" shouted Michael. "Oh, my godfathers! That were just amazin'. Helen, Helen, it's a baby!" he said with mock relief.

The midwife gave him a swift look that he could not have misconstrued for anything other than 'shut up'. Then, she put a clip on the umbilical cord and then held the baby upside down and put an aspirator into its airways. As she did this, all three of them saw that they were blessed with a perfectly beautiful little boy.

Removing the aspirator, the baby didn't need any encouragement to let out his first cry! The midwife carefully wiped baby's face with a soft tissue, then wrapped him gently in a soft blanket and gave him to Helen, who by this time, was in floods of tears at the exertion and sheer emotion of the whole experience. Michael wasn't far behind her and started to sob uncontrollably.

"Are you alright, Mr Twigg?" said the midwife, with a look of concern.

"Yeah, fine, luv," he blurted out. "Can ah try some o' that gas an' air, d'ya think?"

The midwife smiled and said softly to Michael, "I will leave you alone for a few moments and then we need to sort Helen out with other things, Mr Twigg."

"Like what?" said Michael, with a look of panic.

"Oh, just little things that follow a baby's birth, you know. Nothing to worry about, just bits and pieces that will not be of interest to you. When I return, it might be a good idea for you to go for a nice cup of tea and sit yourself down. I will call you again when we have finished."

She removed her latex gloves and gown and put them into a bin next to her. "There now!" she said with a look of satisfaction. "Another little miracle!"

With that, she turned to walk out and left the proud mum and dad alone. But as if having a second thought, she popped her head back around the door and said,

"Congratulations to you both!" then she disappeared down the corridor to leave them to their special moment.

She returned just two or three minutes later and said, "Right, Mr Twigg, it's time for me to see to Helen and baby now. I have ordered you a nice cup of tea down in the cafeteria. Just pop down and say who you are. There's some nice chocolate biscuits this morning too or hot toasted muffins if you'd like some. Go on, they're free to you!"

Michael looked wistfully at Helen, who, still starry-eyed at the little bundle with the big lungs, still in her arms, said gently, "Go on, love, go for a cuppa and relax. I'm fine. Let the midwife see to me now."

Michael needed no more prompting. Happy that he'd seen his little boy born and confident that his wife was in the best hands, he found his appetite and left the room and followed the sounds mentioned before, down the corridor, promising food and coffee!

Sure enough, as he entered the little cafeteria, the smell of cooking hit him. Prior to the birth and for a day or so before, food was the last thing on his mind. But now, the smell of bacon and eggs, toast, coffee and the whole breakfast experience hit his nostrils as if he'd not eaten in weeks.

"Good morning, sir!" came the cheery welcome from the pretty young serving girl. "What can I tempt you with this morning?"

"Oh, god, erm, yes, it does look good, lass. I'm a bit befuddled y'know! Ah've just seen me baby born! What d'ya recommend?"

"Well," said the girl, "The omelettes are top-notch today, fancy that? Or I could do boiled egg an' toast soldiers? Maybe a nice bowl of cornflakes?"

"Aw fer god's sake, lass, gi'e us sausage, bacon, egg, fried bread, fried tomato, button mushrooms, beans, black puddin' an' toast! Ah'm starved!"

The girl looked him up and down, noticing his pyjamas, still buttoned up wrongly and, lifting herself onto tip-toe to peer over the counter and, looking downwards to his racing car slippers, she said kindly, "Ah, a new daddy, eh? You only qualify for a toasted muffin or coffee and biscuits!"

"Aw, do us a favour, lass!" said Michael, "Ah'm famished!"

"We have rules here, sir, that we have to stick to! All this food is chargeable and if you want what you're asking for, it'll be £1.20!"

"Typical!" said Michael. "Here I am, starvin' to death, an' all YOU can think abaht is food!"

He was still drooling over the breakfast foods that were calling to him from under the heat-lamps on the other side of the servery.

"OK!" he said, "give us the works! Ah'm worth it! Me missus is worth it! An' by the cringe, me new baby's worth it! Bring it on lass!"

The girl smiled, with a knowing sort of a smile and selected all the things he had requested.

"God, that looks scrummy!" he said with his tongue nearly out of his head. "Don't be tight on t' bacon, lass, ah need the salt!"

The huge, calorie-ridden breakfast was served to him, including the buttered toast and coffee.

"That'll be £1.20 please, sir," said the girl.

"Hey, no problem!" said Michael, fumbling around his buttocks, where normally his wallet would have been in his trousers. "Yeah, it's a bargain at that price!" he continued, as his fumblings started to become more urgent. "Oh, erm, yeah, ah seem to be in a bit of an embarrasin' situation 'ere, lass," he said, turning the colour of the cranberry juice in the jug next to him, "Erm, I forgot that ah'm still in me jim-jams! Can I put it on a tab?"

"Sir, this is not a public house!" said the girl, "This is a hospital!"

"Aw, piggin' 'eck," said Michael, give us a coffee an' a muffin then."

The girl, who all the while was trying to suppress a secret, said, "Oh, don't worry, sir, your wife had already pre-empted this and paid for it in advance! Your breakfast was on the cards as surely as the birth of your own baby! I know that you are Mr Twigg!"

"Oh, by the mess, bless you, lass!" said Michael. "Gi'e us it before I starve t' death!"

So Michael sat himself down at a table, in his dishevelled pyjamas, racing car slippers and hair like a Christmas tree and the girl set his breakfast before him, which he set to like his very life depended on it! As he attacked his sausages, he glanced at his watch and remembered the time of his little boy's birth. 6:20 in the morning.

After his mammoth breakfast, Michael smacked his lips and rocked back onto two legs of his chair, smacked his belly with both hands and shouted over to the girl behind the counter, "That was just perfect, lass! The brahn sauce weren't too clever mind, but me egg were just as I like 'em, nice runny yolk! I can't do wi' these eggs y'get sometimes, wi' t' yolk like a bit o' rubber! And yer toast were just great! Toast 'as got to be almost burnt, good an' brahn, an' left just long enough to cool, so's to just let the butter stay on t' edges wi'out meltin' too much!"

"Ha, you certainly are a connoisseur of breakfasts, aren't you, Mr Twigg?" said the girl, "but I do take it as a compliment! Will you have a word with my manager, I might get a pay rise this side of the millennium!" she said with a broad grin.

"Gi's another cup o' coffee, lass," he said, happy in the knowledge he'd said the right things to her, "an' ah promise that if meet up wi' yer manager, ah'll tell 'er that without you cookin' 'ere, the 'ospital would no daht close dahn! Ha!"

"Get away with you!" said the girl blushing crimson and turning away to get him some more coffee.

As this happy discourse was progressing, one or two people started to amble into the cafeteria. A couple of weary doctors, still in their white coats, one with a stethoscope still around his neck, slumped into a huge, worn, but comfy leather sofa at the edge of the eating area.

"Morning, Doctor Bains; morning, Doctor Peters!" said the girl, "Coffees?"

"Oh god, yes!" said Dr Peters, "It's been a busy night! Make them strong and black!"

"Coming up," said the girl. She came out with a tray with the drinks on and put Michael's coffee down before him first.

"How much do I owe you, lass?" said Michael.

"Well, seeing as you have no money and seeing as you have nothing to offer in way of payment, I will pay for this for you. It's on me, with my compliments and best wishes for you and your new family! I know it's not much, but until you have that word with my line manager, it's all I have!" she said in a mock poverty speech, with suitably pulled face and eyebrows at near 45 degrees.

"Aw, you're a star, lass, a real star! My thanks to ya'!" he said, jumping up and giving her a hug and a kiss on her cheek, nearly knocking the tray out of her hands and much to the embarrassment of the girl, but to the infinite delight of the doctors observing this and relishing the humorous moment as they looked at Michael, still dressed as described before and, as doctor Bains looked Michael up and down and saw his racing car slippers, roared with laughter.

"Eighup!" said Michael to the doctor, with a grin, "haven't ya seen a friendly hug before now?"

"No no, not with a passion that only a couple of formula Fords could muster!" said the doctor playfully.

The general mirth was caught by all within the cafeteria, including some porters and other visitors, who were now coming in for an early breakfast or cup of tea. General hilarity erupted, much to the delight of the now weary, but happy Michael.

"I s'pose ah better see 'ow me lass is doin'," he half joking, half seriously said to his audience, who were all in good humour, early as the hour was, by this lovable fool. But, seeing the freshly made coffee that was made for him by the girl, he set to that first, closing his eyes at each sip and started to realise the happy gravity of what was happening to him, his wife and their lovely new baby boy.

"By the cringe!" he said to himself, "it's actually 'appened! Ah'm a dad! Ah'm a success! All me bits work!"

With this and after finishing his drink, he realised that as the morning was progressing and that he *did* look a proper plonker, so he thought it prudent to see Helen as soon as possible and vacate the hospital whilst he still had a shred of credibility.

Arriving back at the room where he had left Helen, he was shocked to see the room empty. Panic set in for a moment, thinking that she maybe had to be taken somewhere else, because of a problem. Turning down an adjacent corridor and looking earnestly to left and right, he noticed the nurse who was with Helen when he first arrived at the hospital.

"Ah, Mr Twigg!" she said cheerily. "Helen and baby are just down here in ward 7. What a gorgeous little boy you both have! Did the midwife tell you he weighs in at 7lbs 6oz?"

"Erm, no, I don't think so," said Michael, trying to recall his thoughts. Just a few paces down the corridor, they entered ward 7. Helen was lying on a bed, looking radiantly happy, hair combed and with a pretty pink nighty on, with little blue bows around the neck and cuffs. In her arms, was the baby, wrapped in a warm soft white shawl, fast asleep.

"Oh, Helen!" he said as he rapidly went to the chair waiting for him at her bedside. "Are you alright? How's the baby? Did they tek good care of ya? I was worried when ah got back t' the delivery room an' found you gone! What did they do to you?"

"Woah! Hold your horses," laughed Helen, "the midwife gave me an injection, which helps to discharge the bits that the baby was attached to inside me. She checked all my bits and bobs 'down there' and then made me comfortable. Then she attended to the baby for a while and weighed him. He's 7lbs 6oz you know!"

"Yeah, I know, the nurse told me," said Michael, who, all the while, was staring at the baby with a mixture of awe and wonder.

"Here!" said Helen, realising that he wasn't really concentrating on what she was saying, "Come closer and have a hold of your son, don't be frightened, that's right, remember your ante natal training, 'How to hold your baby'?

That's it," she said as Michael carefully took the baby and cradled him in his arms for the very first time.

Michael said not a word. Helen looked at him, with a beaming smile of pride and happiness, as Michael gently rocked the little bundle, very amateurishly and staring at the baby's little face. He eyed his son lovingly, wondering at his tiny fingers and perfectly formed little ears. This beautiful moment seemed to last for ages and Helen relished this precious, tender moment, a moment that would be etched into her memory for the rest of her days.

At length, she gently rubbed Michael on the side of his leg and said, "Hey, remember all the dozens of names we thought of over these past weeks? We can forget half of them now, eh? Ha ha!"

"Aye, luv," said Michael, "that we can!"

"Have we decided on his name yet then?" she said.

"Well," said Michael, "we said if it were a boy, we'd stick to keepin' family names in, din't we; well, we both liked 'John', din't we? What d'ya think o' that?"

Helen looked at the baby dotingly and said, "Mmm. Yeah! Yes, he does suit that! Yes. JOHN TWIGG!" she said out loud. "John Twigg, welcome to the world!"

"Well, it's my middle name and mi' brother's first name an' all! Ay, he'll be fair chuffed when 'e finds aht!" said Michael, grinning from ear to ear.

And so it was, that John Twigg was born, to a loving and doting couple, who inwardly vowed to love and care for him, with all their might and main, for the rest of their lives.

Helen and Michael

Michael was a big, strong, athletically built man. 6ft 4" of muscle, good looks and wicked sense of humour. His looks belied his 40 years. He had youthful skin and a full moustache that partly covered his top lip, but not a 'gaucho' type and he had a full head of wavy hair. Apart from his hair greying somewhat, most people would not have put him past 30. Indeed, he was still a member of the local 'old boys' rugby union team, where, because of his size and strength, he was the obvious choice for the 'prop' position.

He had been a miner and spent many years 'dahn't' pit', at Grimethorpe colliery, just northeast of Barnsley, in South Yorkshire. Grimethorpe was one of the deepest pits in Britain and, with mergers with Houghton Main and Dearne Valley Collieries, employed some 6000 men in its heyday. Michael and Helen left the poverty-stricken village of Grimethorpe early in 1971, after coming up lucky on the football pools, where they'd won the staggering sum of £50,249. Enough today, but a phenomenal amount in those days!

Helen was a secondary school teacher at Willowgarth School, in Barnsley, but with such an amount of money being won and as much as she adored her job at the school, she agreed with Michael that a new life and new horizons beckoned to them. That windfall gave them that opportunity to break away from the muck and coal dust forever.

They loved Yorkshire and didn't want to move abroad or even far away from their roots. Just somewhere nice and pretty, with all the outdoor beauties and activities they could get their hands on. They loved the fresh air and solitude of the countryside. After some weeks of researching towns around North Yorkshire, they settled on the spa town of Harrogate. With all its historical association, from Agatha Christie, who wrote many of her Poirot and Miss Marple stories there and regularly resided at the Old Swan Hotel, to the famous Sir Edward Elgar, the composer, who loved Harrogate and penned many of his compositions there.

Despite the pools win, they purchased a comparatively modest 3 bedroom semi-detached house in the north of Harrogate, at 54 Hill Top Way, but it did have a huge back garden and a big double garage, which was Michael's 'den', in which he was able to indulge in several of his hobbies, of which he had many. The house was immaculate, inside and out, mainly due to their own efforts. Both he and Helen were avid DIYers and had transformed the place.

Helen enjoyed decorating and indeed, could have put many professionals to shame! She was no shrinking violet, even to the most intimidating of DIY tasks, like papering a ceiling or building a stone wishing well in the garden, that doubled up as a barbeque. She even designed it herself!

Michael's father had been an artificer in the Royal Navy during WW2 and as such was a veritable gold-mine of engineering and maintenance skills, skills that the young Michael learned eagerly from his dad, who he had the utmost respect and admiration for, right up to the present day, for he was still very much alive and kicking and living with his wife, Michael's mum, in the little village of Clayton, not far from Grimethorpe.

Michael could turn his practical hands to almost anything. When he set his mind to something, he just sat down, gave it a good deal of thought, made a few plans and a little arithmetic and he would build it! Now semi-retired after their good fortune with the pools, Michael did not need to work, but was one of these chaps who just could not sit down and relax. He often would consider working for some kind of charity, but no, that all seemed to be shop work or supervising.

No, his skills were with his huge hands and having completely gutted and renovated their house, Michael was at a loss of things he could do next. After much discussion with Helen, he tentatively started a little business, making traditional wooden toys from his 'den' which was equipped with every tool imaginable, from wood and metal turning lathes, to routing machines and cross-cut saws.

He designed and made wooden toy soldiers that were popular when he himself was a little boy. Wooden trains and carriages. Ducks that could be pushed along by a dowel stick and had little leather feet on its wheels, that made a 'plapping' sound on each revolution. He made marble-runs and jig-saw puzzles out of 3/8" plywood, cup-and-ball, (a toy going back to the Middle Ages!) and a host of other, brightly hand-painted toys for small children to play with. With a little research and experimentation, he even perfected the making of Swanee whistles and bamboo 'recorders'.

For starters, he had just approached one or two local toyshops, (when he had produced enough stock) and made some non-too binding verbal deals with the shopkeepers, on a 'sale or return' basis. The money that came back to him, helped to buy the new raw materials he needed. Amazingly, the little enterprise took off and he started to get repeat orders for more and more. Because he didn't have to keep up with the 'supply and demand' of a normal business venture, he just kept up production at his own sweet pace.

Much as he enjoyed making wooden toys, Michael loved metalworking too. He was already in the process of building his brother, John, a fully working, miniature traction engine as a Christmas present, which was his own design and built from absolute 'scratch'. From sheet metal, he cut out and welded, with his MIG welder, the firebox, boiler and tender; on his lathe, the smoke funnel, axles and a host of other components.

Helen often wondered at this big man, who belied his outward appearance and had such a gentle and loving attitude and demeanour to her, his hobbies and the world in general; a world which in the past, had been so cruel to him through struggle and hardships as a child and physically, in the dark dusty mines at Grimethorpe.

A letter arrived for him one day, from the proprietor of one of the toyshops he'd been supplying, basically saying, "I have contacts in the USA, who are crying out for genuine, traditional, handmade toys, such as the ones you are producing. What you are doing is comparatively unique and there is a huge opportunity here for you. I can certainly help you here and for a small remuneration—"

Michael smiled and tore the letter up and held it, for no reason, in his right hand, screwed up.

"Eighup, Helen," he shouted as he ran out of his den, "ah've bin offered a job! What does't tha' think o' that?"

"Wow!" she retorted, with a beaming smile that crinkled her forehead, "Where? What? Doing what?"

"Back dahn't' pit, lass!" Her face fell like a ton of bricks.

"You're joshing, aren't you?"

"No! Why should ah' be joshin'? he said with affected indignance. "Ah' got many a talent that they need dahn t' pit and on t' pit 'ead, they want me back to work wit' management like! Aren't ya pleased for me? An' it's fer quite a few shillin' more than ah' were on when ah' left! After all t' years ah did movin' coal like, don't ya think ah' should gi'e it another chance wi' t' big knobs an' t' managers?"

"Oh, Michael, tell me you are mocking me here," she said, close to tears by now.

"By the cringe, lass; of course, ah piggin' well am!" he shouted picking her up from under her arms and throwing her into the air as easily as if she were a toddler, then with a huge belly laugh, caught her again as she fell back into his arms, as easily and gently as that toddler and he kissed her lovingly and gave her a cuddle, as a child would to a teddy bear.

"Course am', jokin', ya daft bat," he softly said, with a huge grin on his face, that was now buried into the nape of her neck—and her dangling off the ground in his left arm, like a big rag doll and with his right hand still free and holding the torn up bits of the letter from the toyshop proprietor, he let them go into the breeze, to flutter amongst the bumble bees and butterflies, flitting around their garden.

As already mentioned, Helen was a secondary school teacher. She had loved her job with a passion. She loved the challenge, not just of the teaching itself, but the visual transformation of the children, becoming young men and women, with all the hormonal episodes that go with it.

She felt nostalgic about the way the children would start the school at 11 years old and with the majority of them, looking like what they were, 11-year-old kids, in brand new uniforms, the boys in their blazers and the girls in their regulation length skirts and blouses, then almost in the blink of an eye, watching them leave at the other end, at 15 or 16 years old, (as many did in those days) and going into the wide world, equipped hopefully, with what they would need to get them through their lives and in securing a career.

Helen was eight years younger than Michael. An extremely attractive lady, with hazel brown eyes, raven black hair, that grew straight and to the middle of her back. She was slender, but not willowy and stood, in her stocking feet, at 5ft 2". She would often wear devil-red lipstick and nail polish, which perfectly set with her black hair and fair skin. Michael absolutely loved that! He would often say to her, as they were preparing to go out for dinner or to a concert, "D'ya know, lass, ah could eat yer alive when you put that lippy an' nail varnish on! Y'know it drives us wild!"

Of course, Helen knew perfectly well the power she had over him with this simple combination and she relished it just as much as he did!

"Oh?" she would say with affected oblivion to the fact, "What is it that 'does it' for you then?" pouting at him and pushing her hand through her hair and looking at him with 'come hither' eyes. Many and many a time, this little scenario lead them to be considerably late for dates with friends, cinema, meals or the theatre and so many times, they would have to make people stand up, so they could get to their seats in the auditorium, which would invariably be right in the centre of a row and naturally, right in the 'quiet bit' of the performance!

Helen was the soothing influence in their marriage, although they rarely rowed or argued. They never had spats about the big things in life, even before the pools win. If they ever had words at all, it was always over silly little things.

"Mike, be a love and don't squeeze the toothpaste from the middle of the tube, you know it gets my goat!" or, "Helen, ah've lost me Swiss army knife like! Ah left it on' t' sideboard! Yer allus tidyin' away, an' ah can't find nowt when you've bin on one o' yer blitzin' sessions!"

But when Michael was unhappy or worried for his job or a situation when he worked at Grimethorpe colliery, Helen would soothe and calm him and the big, 'battle hardened' miner became a soft, even child-like character.

So, this is Mr and Mrs Michael Twigg. Recently blessed with a bouncing baby boy and the most wonderful thing that had ever happened to them in their lives. Little John Twigg, the apple of his daddy's eye. Michael was total putty in Helen's hands, but even more so at one look into the eyes of his little boy!

John Starts School

John Twigg was a good boy. A really good little boy. Throughout his babyhood, he only ever cried when he was sleepy, as all babies do or when he hurt himself and needed a kiss and a cuddle from mummy or daddy. Even when he was teething, he was as good as gold and better. As for sleeping, it was very rare indeed that he didn't sleep the whole night through and when he did wake, he just 'goooed' and 'gaaad' to himself, but it was always enough to wake mummy up and go to change and feed him.

Michael soon became the model dad. He helped with all the housework. He cooked, washed, ironed, did the shopping and became quite adept at bottle feeding and nappy changing! He also became a bit of an icon at the local shops, inasmuch as, on a normal 'workaday' for the majority of people in Harrogate, his huge frame was seen above all the little old biddies and housewives doing their 'shop' for the day at the butchers, supermarket or chemists. Michael often enjoyed the fact he was almost out of place. He was taken for granted in the bowels of the earth as a miner, now, he almost had celebrity status!

"Isn't he such a charming young man?" said Mrs Brewer to her partner-in-gossip Mrs Piper, who had, like herself, recently lost her husband for various reasons.

"What a doting dad! Isn't his little boy just the image of him? I wonder if he'll grow up to be as big as daddy?" she said with slight innuendo, as he passed by them. Michael gave no heed to them, but smiled, at the thought he might be still attractive to the opposite sex, at what he considered himself to be, an 'old man'!

By the time John was four, he was extremely circumspect. Nothing passed him. He asked questions way above his years.

"Daddy, the man on the telly said it's going to snow tomorrow? Who'll bring the snow? Do you have to pay for it, Daddy? Can we play with it when it comes?" to which Michael grinned from ear to ear and looked at his little lad with wonder.

"Eighup, Helen, John's askin' if ah've got t' buy the snow, forecast fer t'morra! Tell thi' wot, swee'pea, that comes from your genes, not mine lass!"

"Don't ever talk to me about mines again you!" came the voice above the noise of the telly and the cooker hood in the kitchen as Helen was preparing the supper.

"Ya plonker, ah said nowt about mines! Ah said YOUR GENES, NOT MINE," he shouted, smiling at the fact that Helen hadn't heard him correctly.

Little John, not getting the joke, looked at his dad as if to say, "Did I say something wrong, Daddy?"

When the day came for John to start school, he was very eager! He had been eager for weeks. All his mates from playschool were going to Bilton Grange County Primary School, about half a mile from their home. Helen had bought him his school uniform, which he loved and, had had some nice photos taken, some days before, in their back garden.

"Please will you save a picture for Nanna and Grandpa?" John asked earnestly. "Can we take it 'round to their house soon, Mum?"

"Of course, we can!" said Helen, smiling at the picture. "I'm so proud of you! You look so grown up in your new uniform! Your Nanna and Grandpa won't even recognise you!"

That made John's face light up! The thought of visiting his Nanna and Grandpa! He loved their house; it had a smell all of its own. Not a nasty smell, it was a welcoming odour that he could not put his finger on, just a lovely, warm, welcoming smell, especially in the 'cubby-hole' under the stairs, where Grandpa kept his air guns. Oh, how John loved to secretly go into that place, the smell of leather boots and shoes, gun-oil and the big plastic box that Nanna kept all her boot polishes and brushes in.

Just at that moment, Michael came bounding down the stairs, having just washed and shaved and wearing an aftershave that both Helen and John loved. Straightening his polo-shirt collar, he said,

"Mornin', you two! What's fer breakfast? Eighup, John lad, ya do look posh in yer new uniform!" and picked the little lad up into the air and gave him a hug. "By the mess, it tek's me back to when ah were a lad!"

"Did you cry on your first day at school, Daddy?" asked John.

"Me? Cry?" said his dad, "Me? Ah bawled me eyes aht! Ha ha! You won't cry though, lad! Ya got more about ya than that!" he said, tweaking his cheek playfully.

"Come and sit down, you two!" shouted Helen, who had gone into the kitchen to finish preparing the breakfast she had started a little while earlier.

"Boiled eggs and toast soldiers!"

"Great! Scran!" said Michael to John, "Ah'll race thi', lad!" and they both ran to the kitchen, where they were greeted by the delicious smell of toast and coffee.

"Ay, ah do love boiled eggs an' toast soldiers, don't you, John lad? Ah, remember when mi mam used to do 'em for us as kids." He continued, as he dunked a soldier into his egg, "Ah tell ya, when ah got to dunkin', ya needed yer sou' wester an' leggin's on! Ha Ha! Or when me mam would mek' us egg banjos of a Sat'day afternoon! Aye, they were the days!"

"What's an egg banjo, Daddy?" enquired John with a puzzled look.

Michael nearly spat out his mouthful of food with laughter at that. Even Helen was close to tears in that split second. Laughter is contagious and they all laughed until they cried! It took a bit of time for things to calm down, but when it did, John once again asked, "What's an egg banjo, Dad?" The laughter started all over again, but this time, Michael responded and drying his eyes, he explained.

"Well, John, y'know what a fried egg is, don'tcha? Well, it's a fried egg sarnie, a sandwich wi' a fried egg in it like. And if t' yolk ain't popped, an' ya take a bite out o' it, it runs all dahn yer front, so ya have ta hold yer sarnie in one 'and, an' wipe the yolk off wi' yer other 'and like you were playin' a banjo."

And he demonstrated what he meant, strumming up and down on his chest, as if to remove spilt yolk, whilst holding the sandwich with his other hand, about where a banjo's fret-board would be. Helen was nearly on the floor in tears with laughter and had to cross her legs in case she wet herself! John imitated what his dad had just shown him, enjoying the laugh too! And to cap the whole hilarious scene, Michael dunked his toast soldier into his egg and withdrawing it, took it up to his mouth to eat it and still giggling, looked at Helen for a second.

In that second, his runny yolk ran off his toast soldier and went right down his front, just as he had talked about. That was it! They were all totally helpless with uncontrollable laughter! Helen wasn't even making a noise as she laughed, she had run out of air! Only after a long pause, she inhaled deeply and with a crimson face, screamed with laughter and holding her sides, she panted.

"Oh, oh god—oh—oh—god," she spluttered. "I'm going to PEE myself!"

Her eyes were red and bloodshot with laughing and the three of them were in hopeless hysterics for ages, in fact, by the time they had regained their composure, their breakfast was nearly cold!

A little while later, after Michael changed his polo shirt and Helen had put the washing up into the dishwasher and then tended to her, 'ahem', personal needs after the previous episode, all was ready for the big moment, to take John to school for the very first time.

John was champing at the bit to go. Helen got John's lunchbox and checked that he had everything; sandwich orange, biscuit and a banana. Grabbing his new satchel, John was first to the car and waited for his dad to open it up. Then they all clambered into the car and made their way, the half a mile or so to the school. Normally, they would have walked, but as it was a special day and as Helen and Michael planned to do a bit of shopping straight after seeing John go into his classroom, they thought it a good idea to take the car.

"Are ya ready fer this then, John lad?" said Michael, looking at him in the rear-view mirror, "Hey, first day o' school, eh? Remember to be polite, an' don't ask t' teacher too many questions like! You've plenty o' time ta be askin' questions! Yer a right bright lad, an' ah don't want thi' to embarrass thissen wi' confusin' t' teacher! Ah, wouldn't want yer ta get egg on yer face now would ah?"

Helen grinned at that remark and Michael glanced at her, with an equally broad grin, as they both thought of the episode in the kitchen a short while before. John didn't get it and pursed his lips and bent his brow, trying to fathom out the joke.

Within a couple of minutes, they had arrived. The roads around the school were very busy and it took them a few more minutes to find somewhere to park. Getting out of the car, John straight away saw one of his friends walking up Bilton Lane, past St. John's church, with his mother.

"Hiya, Luke!" shouted John, to which a slightly embarrassed Luke waved back to him and tried to disengage his other hand from his mothers, as she was busy chatting to another woman, walking up the road with her. His mother reasserted her grip on the little boy's hand instinctively, not even considering why Luke was trying to take his hand from hers. He wanted to look 'independent' and a bit more 'grown up'.

Luke was dressed the same as John, in his smart little uniform of red jumper, with the school logo on the left hand side of the chest, dark grey trousers and a white shirt. It wasn't long before all the mums and dads were waiting with their children, in the rear playground of the school. Only minutes to go and the bell would ring.

"Now mind yer p's an' 'q's lad! Enjoy yersen now! We'll be thinkin' 'bout ya!" said Michael, trying to bolster John, who although excited, gave in to the general wailing and tearful examples he was seeing from some of the other children and especially from some of the mothers, who were filled with emotions at their little offspring, now at this unforgettable time, their first day of school.

The memories came flooding back to so many mums and dads, looking wistfully and slightly embarrassedly at each other. Others were as happy as crickets and were waving frantically to their children and blowing kisses, from a little way off, as they nattered to friends and neighbours.

"Have you got a hanky in your pocket, John?" said Helen, as she looked down at him, his eyes filling slightly, but trying to remember what his dad had said about 'being made of stout stuff'.

"Yes, Mummy," he said pulling the hanky out of his pocket to show her, then the neatly ironed hanky came up to his eyes and he dabbed at them, trying hard not to burst into floods of tears. At the sight of this, Helen wasn't far behind him. Michael just looked on, smiling at John, but said nothing. He couldn't, without giving away the fact he was close to tears too! Suddenly, the *di-ding, di-ding, di-ding* of the hand-held school bell split the low hubbub of everyone around. That sound jolted everybody into a different mindset. The mood changed completely.

Last minute hugs and kisses were exchanged, affected smiles and laughter from the red-eyed mums to their children, who, in the main were skipping for joy at the thought they were going into school for the very first time. Only one or two children were clinging to their parents, sobbing uncontrollably, making it agony for the parents to let them go.

But, after a minute or two of licence from the cheery teachers, who were all about, they were blithely clapping their hands and shouting, "Come along now, children, get into two straight lines now, girls to the left-hand door and boys to the right! Come along quickly now please!" and the children were scrambling to get to their places in their respective queues. John's face had changed from tearful, to exuberant.

"Bye mum, bye dad," he shouted from the queue. Helen and Michael stood there, hand in hand, waving to John, as the queue slowly proceeded into the school.

When they had all gone inside and the doors closed, the mums and dads ambled away, mostly silently, presumably with their thoughts. Helen and Michael were no exception to this and they said nothing to each other until they got back into their car.

At length, Michael said to Helen, "Y'all right, lass?" taking her hand in his, as they drove along King's Road and into the town centre.

"Yes, of course—" she said after a long intake of breath through her nostrils. "It just doesn't seem like five minutes since he was born, does it?" she said, looking at him with a sad smile.

"By the cringe, yer right, luv! Time is a fleetin' thing alright! Ah can even see me dad's eyes in me own bairns' lately!" he said, lightening the mood. "D'ya fancy a cuppa when we get into tahn before we do t'shops?"

"Yes, that would be great," said Helen, "just promise me you won't order any damned eggs!"

They parked just outside of the main shopping area and strolled into the town. Amongst other things, they wanted to get some copies of the photograph of John in his school uniform, to send to family and friends. Having placed the order with a very helpful assistant in a photographer's on Albert Street, they decided to get their cup of tea first.

So, ambling through the town, they strolled down West Park, to the Cenotaph, then onto Cambridge Street, Oxford Street and then Commercial Street, where they knew of a café that did a sterling pot of tea for two and stupendous scones and strawberry jam. They entered the café and sat at a window table for two. Almost immediately, a young serving girl, dressed in typically teashop style, i.e. in black dress, cut just below the knee, a white 'pinny' and a little white lace head 'tiara', came over to ask what they would like.

"Oh, tea for two and a pot of hot water on the side please," said Helen.

"Certainly, madam," was the polite reply.

"We normally have a couple o' scones too, as y'know, but our lass did us quite a big breakfast this mornin'!" said Michael to the girl. The girl wrote the order down on a small notepad and smiling courteously at them, made her way to the kitchen to get their order.

"John particularly wanted mum and dad to have one of his photos," said Helen, after a long silence. "Should we get one framed, do you think? I'm sure John would be thrilled! It's your dad's 71 birthday next Sunday, remember?"

"By mi' whiskers!" said Michael, "ah *had* forgotten y'know! Good idea. Let's sort that aht today. We'll have t'get a card an' all like, an' best get 'im a big box o' sugared almonds! He loves them y' know! Yeah, ah'm sure they'd both like a picture o' our John fer their mantelpiece."

Along came the tea. Perfect Twinings breakfast tea. Helen poured.

"God, that's good!" she said, relishing the first sip.

And after a not-too-rude slurp from Michael's cup, he also stated, "Do ya' know, that's t' best cuppa char ah've had in ages, lass. Hey, yours is just t' dog's bits, but ya can't beat it here, can ya, lass?"

Helen laughed at Michael's vernacular.

"Only a wife could love it!" she said smiling. "My tea is compared to the 'dog's bits'!"

"Oh—well, lass—ah didn't mean t' be rude like, it's just that—"

"Oh shut up, you big numpty!" she said, smacking his leg under the table, "I love you despite yourself!"

"By the cringe, lass," he replied, "there's not many lasses this side o' Rotherham that would put up wi' me like you do, swee'pea," half embarrassed at his own accent and approach and half embarrassed at his slurping. "Do y'know, lass," he said, looking at her and taking her hand under the table, "You are the angel of my heart's desire. Ah'll never know what yer ever saw in me!"

"Take a good look in the mirror!" she replied tenderly, "and you will forever have your answer!"

After their tea, they made their way into Harrogate's centre. Harrogate is a fairly large town, but it is its catchment that makes it seem large. The shopping centre was and still is, compact and busy, but it is not exhaustive. Going up the main street, they went into all the familiar shops that every town had at that time. Marks & Spencer, Littlewoods, Woolworths, W.H. Smith's. They managed to find all the bits and bobs they needed, including the sugared almonds and some wonderful 'Fat Rascals' from Betty's tea shop on Parliament Street.

"Eighup, lass, it's mah turn t' cook tonight," said Michael, "we've got some lovely pork loin steaks, what say ah do 'em up in a lovely onion gravy, slow cooked wi' carrots, cheesy mash, mushrooms an' leeks? An' ah could do spotty dick an' custard fer afters?"

"Mmm, that sounds good!" Helen replied, "but we got some fat rascals, don't you remember?" she said enquiringly.

"By the gods, yer right!" said Michael. "Sorry, lass, ah'm just thinking abaht mi lad when 'e comes 'ome. He'll be famished like!"

"Yes, he will be, the poor little sausage!" she said, remembering John. "Yes, do yer spotty dick an' custard then, lad!" she said, playfully mocking his accent.

"By the cringe, ah' will!" Michael said, pulling her arm and heading out of Boots the chemists.

Slightly running, to keep up with his huge strides, Helen said, "We can take the fat rascals to mum and dad's at the weekend! They love them too and it's been ages since we took them any!"

"Well aye, lass," said Michael, they're a bit calorific anyroad, an' ah could do wi' losin' a pound or two!" he said in jest, remembering what he would normally consume in a day to support his huge frame.

As it got closer to 3:30 in the afternoon, both Helen and Michael were getting almost nervous. Helen was watering her plants around the house and Michael was peeling the carrots for tea.

"Best be pickin' John up soon, lass," said Michael.

"Yes, we must! Shall we walk up now, do you think?" said Helen, biting her bottom lip in thought.

"Ah guess so, said Michael, wiping his hands on his apron, which incidentally, was again bought by his brother John, as a bit of fun. It was fashioned in such a way that when it was worn, it displayed a female form, with stockings, suspenders and a humungous pair of breasts! On Michael's huge frame, it looked even funnier! Helen put on her shoes and tidied her hair, as Michael took off his apron.

"It's a grand afternoon, an' yer dead right, let's stroll up to t' school!" said Michael.

"Yes, good idea! I'm sure John will be full of it and want to tell us all his news, so a walk will give him the opportunity to do that," Helen replied. With that, they both set off for the school. "How's the traction engine coming on?" said Helen. "I daren't come into your den when you're creating or inventing something, especially when I hear you cursing and swearing at something that's gone wrong!" she said with a grin.

"Oh, it's comin' on a treat! I ordered the wheels for it from a place in Norfolk. Ah saw an ad in mi 'model maker' magazine. They come to ya rough cast like, all ya got to do is skim and polish 'em. Ah thought it'd tek some of the work aht of it, an' save on t' cussin' an' swearin' like! Bit o' good news for you then lass, eh? Ha ha."

They walked up Crab Lane, to join Bilton Lane and only a hundred or so yards to the school, Helen said, "Has John said anything to you about the nightmare he's been having lately?"

"Why, no lass, ah can't say that he has! Why? What's up? All kids get bad dreams! Ah sometimes dream ah'm back dahn t' pit!"

"No, listen," said Helen, with a bit more seriousness in her voice. "He has woken up on several occasions, shouting for help and I've gone to him, to see him really panicking and sweating and saying that he 'can't find his way out' and that 'it's so dark in here,' and when I'm able to calm him down, he doesn't seem to remember it—it fades, then he's alright and he snuggles down again. On the first few times, I thought nothing of it, but it's happened a dozen times or so this last month."

"As ah've said, kids do 'ave nightmares, luv', don't worry abaht it! Why 'aven't ya mentioned it to me before?"

"Well, as you say, I just thought it was just one of those things—and—"

"And so it is, Helen!" said Michael, slipping his arm around her waist, pulling her to him and giving her a peck on the cheek. "So it is!"

They reached the school playground and what a difference in the moods and demeanours of all the mums and dads now! Everyone was excited and chattering away to each other. The insular little groups and conversations of that morning had gone and there was a general feeling of happiness that seemed to pull strangers together and tenuous friendships were cemented within this blissfully happy hubbub.

"Do you know, I thought I recognised you when I saw you this morning!" said one woman to another, "You went to Granby Park School, didn't you?

How are you?" And in another half-done conversation was heard, "Well it's been really nice to talk to you, I had no idea that our wives worked together! You must come round for a drink one evening—!"

Then, without warning, the *'di-ding, di-ding, di-ding'* of the school bell was heard and the hubbub got louder with the anticipation and within a couple of minutes, out poured the children, all grinning from ear to ear, skipping out the cloakrooms, clutching their satchels and lunch boxes. There were frantic cries of, "MUMMY! DADDY!" and "COO-OOH! We're over here, Peter!"

All the kids were totally animated, not letting mum or dad get a word in edgeways, telling them all about their days. "—and then we got these big books with dinosaurs in and then she gave us crayons and pencils and then we had playtime and then we did some counting and then—" Such was this happy reunion all around. John and Luke were almost last to emerge from the cloakroom and they were deep in conversation with each other.

"Wow! Your dad's a genius if he can make toys! Wow, a traction engine! My big brother has one, but my uncle Wilf and auntie Margaret bought it for him for Christmas. I've got a Scalextric set! Would you like to come round and play with it sometime?"

"Wow, yes, please! I'll ask my mum and dad if I can come around sometime—"

"Eighup, John lad!" Michael interrupted, "how's it goin'?"

Instantly, John's conversation and attention was taken from his friend Luke, likewise, Luke saw his parents and ran off in that direction. Throwing himself into his dad's arms, John shouted, "Hello, Dad! Hello, Mum!" as he then hugged Helen.

Taking their hands, he walked in the middle and gave the whole day's events, but every now and then shouting, "See you!" to friends old and new, as they too made their way home.

By the time they got home, John was still enthusing about his day. As Helen opened up the front door, they could hear the telephone ringing, so they all got in as quickly as they could and Michael rushed to the phone before it stopped.

Meantime, Helen said to John, "Why don't you pop upstairs and get washed and changed out of your school clothes? There are clean jeans and T-shirts at the bottom of your bed that I haven't had time to put away yet, just get some from there—and don't throw your school clothes all over the place, fold them up neatly and hang them up—and put your school shirt into the washing basket! There's a good lad!"

"OK, Mum," said John from his bedroom.

As John was coming back down the stairs, Michael shouted, "John? Are ya there, lad?" from the living room, where he was still on the phone, "It's yer grandpa! He's phoned up to see how you faired today at school! D'ya wanna have a word!"

"Oh, yes please!" said John, taking the phone from his dad.

But Michael pulled the phone away from John's ear, just as he was about to speak and said, "Ah'll catch yer later, Dad—" and Michael could hear from the earpiece, *OK, son, see you later!*

"Hiya, grandpa!" said John excitedly as he grabbed the phone, "How are you?"

How are YOU is more to the point, my young buck! Did you enjoy your first day at school? Your Nanna and I were thinking about you all day!

"Oh, fine, thank you! We did all sorts of things! We were given all sorts of textbooks and books to write in and we had some stories read by the teacher and we met the Headmaster and we had to write our names on our books and we did some colouring and we had our lunch and we played some games in the hall and we said prayers and we sang some songs and the teacher played the piano and then it was time to go home and my mummy and daddy were waiting for me in the playground and then we went home."

Ha ha! You sound like you've had a busy day! So you're looking forward to going back tomorrow then?

"Oh yes, Grandpa! I've made lots of new friends and my friend Luke sits next to me in class and my other friend Kevin Gibb is in our class and so is Sally Lyntell who lives over the road."

Oh, that sounds great, lad! We're looking forward to seeing you and you can tell us all about it again! Would you like to come down and see us at the weekend? I've just been talking to your dad about it, it's my birthday you see and your Nanna wondered if you'd like a Sunday roast?

"Oh, yes please!" said John excitedly. Then he paused and thought for a second, then shouted at the top of his voice, "Mu-um! Did you and daddy get that photo of me for my nanna and grandpa—?" then stopped in his tracks, as he realised he had let slip his secret present for them.

Then at the same time, he heard his mother shouting back to him, "No, sweetie, we only put the negative into the photographer this morning, it won't be ready until Friday," and his grandpa saying on the phone, *Oh John, that sounds interesting, what is it a photo of?*

Realising he couldn't backtrack, he said in an embarrassed tone, "Erm, it's a photograph of me in my new school uniform."

Splendid! We really look forward to seeing it then! Will you hand me back to your dad please, John, I just need to talk to him briefly again!

"OK, Grandpa, look forward to seeing you—love you—bye—bye—DAD! GRANDPA WANTS TO TALK TO YOU AGAIN!" John bellowed at the top of his voice. Michael came back through from the kitchen, with his apron on again and took the phone from John.

"Away an' play ah'tside fer a bit lad while ah talk to yer grandpa."

Michael eventually put the phone down and with a happy smile, announced to Helen that Sunday was sorted out and that a roast beef dinner, of which his mother was famous in the family for, especially her Yorkshire puddings, that were to die for, would be waiting for them when they arrived.

"John'll be cock-a-hoop when 'e hears we're definitely off t' see 'em!" he said. "Na'then, ah'd best get on wi' mi cookin' or else we won't get owt t' eat this side o' breakfast! Giz abaht half an hour, Helen, then get our John ready fer his tea will ya?"

"Of course, love, I'm just on with a bit of ironing, then I'll round him up."

"Giz a snog before ya go though, lass," he said and got the reward he had asked for. So, John was playing in the back garden, Helen doing some ironing and Michael, in the kitchen, tending to his cooking.

Helen smiled, as she heard him, in between the clatter of pots and pans, singing out loud to himself, *They—asked mi 'ow ah knew—mah true luv were troooo—*" (Clatter, bang, slam,) *"ah, of course, replied—summat, summat summat—smoke gets in yer eyes—*oh piggin' 'eck," he said as he dropped something.

"What a guy!" Helen said to herself.

Presently, the drone of the warm afternoon was interrupted by Michael.

"Grub up, you two!" he shouted. "It's on t' table!"

In rushed John, who didn't need asking twice. "Want a glass o' wine wi' it, Helen?" asked Michael.

"God, yes," she replied. "Is the Pope religious?"

Dinner was a huge success and not a scrap was left on any plate. Helen and John had said all the way through it, how tasty it was and what a good cook he was. Michael humbly shook it off with, "Nowt o' t' sort! No, no no—ah'm not gonna disagree wi' ya! But ah do admire yer honesty like! Now, 'ands up fer a puddin'?"

Helen and John put both of their hands in the air.

"What's for afters, Dad?" said John.

"Ah! Spotty Dick an' lashins' o' custard!" came the reply.

"Yippee!" said John.

"Drool drool!" said Helen.

Pudding didn't last long. After they had cleaned their plates and all were suitably full, Michael announced that he had confirmed the invitation to Clayton, to see Nanna and Grandpa. John was beside himself with happiness.

"Will my photo be ready?" he said.

"I'm sure it should be," replied Helen, reassuringly.

"Do ya know, John, yer Grandpa is 71 this birthday?" said Michael. "So it'll be nice fer him to get yer photo. We got 'im some fat rascals from Betty's up town, an' some nice sugared almonds that 'e likes. Can't stick 'em missen', but to each 'is own ah guess!"

The rest of the week was full of very much the same as described. John is happy at school, Helen and Michael enjoying life in and out of the house. More toys were created in the 'den' and the weather stayed pleasant. Many times throughout their days, they truly appreciated that they had been blessed with their good fortune.

Everything was perfect. They just wanted an ordinary life and prayed, in their own small way, that this good fortune would be inherited by their son John. They often dreamed with each other what John would become, what he would eventually aspire to. Would he marry? Would they be grandparents one day? Would he go into a trade? A profession? An entrepreneur?

Michael was not a religious man. On the other hand, he was not an exactly an atheist, more agnostic really. He believed that there must be something more than him and that when he died, he felt that something might be there, deciding what happened to him next—if there was indeed a 'next'. Many was the time that he and Helen, who was a little more tending towards Christianity than him, would discuss the subject of faith, religion and the whole issue.

Helen kept an open mind, but religion was never an arguing point. Indeed, Michael loved to go to church at Christmas time, even from a child and enjoyed singing carols and the sight of the Christingles and papier-mâché angels with golden wings, that he himself had often created, under the guidance of the schoolteachers all those years ago, in the depths of the coal mining industries' poorest villages in South Yorkshire, when his father was an engineer, working on the pit head winding gearing and lift shaft constructional safety.

Michael often recalled Christmases in those places, with a tired moon at 3 o'clock in the afternoon, dimly shining through haze and coal dust in the atmosphere, onto the blackened terraced houses of these mining villages. It was surreal and had an almost ghostly or magical appearance, with the air heavy with a soot and a sulphurous odour.

The Wishing Stone (Part 1)

As promised to John, Helen popped into the town on the bus to collect the photographs. She admired the one in the frame that they had chosen.

John should be pleased with that, she thought to herself, as she put her change into her purse from the purchase.

"Thank you! Please call again!" said the assistant in the photographer's shop, as Helen turned to walk out. She thought of Michael as she walked up Station Parade. "It's only a couple of weeks until his birthday too! Gosh, he'll be 45!" she said to herself, "I'd better think of something to get him!"

She went into a jewellers shop and browsed at the display cabinets. Yes, there were lots of lovely things for sale, but she didn't see anything that she considered would really 'do it' for Michael. He was big and a little rough-handed and the jewellery was delicate and dainty. Then, she saw a display of rustic jewellery, made from less dainty materials. There was a boars tooth, set in a pewter base, with a large 'eye' for a leather band, for wearing around the neck.

Also, there were pewter rings, with cabalistic inscriptions on. Some of them were very large and to be honest, quite ostentatious! They reminded her of those gold rings with sovereigns set in them. She hated them! There were, however, natural granite and basalt stones, with a hole in the middle, again, on a pewter base and a leather band for wearing around the neck. There was every type of crystal and semi-precious stone. Some of the stones were the size of an orange, split in half to expose the crystals inside, of deep purples, pinks and blues.

She was strangely attracted to this display and spent some time admiring them. The jeweller had been watching her all the while and when he had given her what he considered an appropriate amount of time to look at the display, he walked across to her and said, "Good morning, madam, can I be of any assistance?"

"Oh, erm, I don't know really, I'm just browsing," Helen replied. Having been in his trade for many years, the jeweller could read a customer like a book and knew when to approach them, knew when to wait and when to go for 'the sale'.

"Are you looking for a gift for a lady or gentleman? Or for yourself perhaps?" he enquired.

"Well, yes, it's for my husband actually. Apart from his wedding ring, he has precious little in the way of jewellery and I was looking for something a bit unusual—"

"Ah! I'm sure we have just the type of things you are looking for, madam!" he said with expert observation of Helen's reticence and uncomfortable body language.

"Look at these genuine hand carved Peruvian gemstones," he enthused, showing her a display she hadn't looked at yet. The spotlights that were specifically directed at the display of gems, showed them off to perfection. They absolutely gleamed with radiant colours and as the rotating display turned slowly around, her eye alighted on a large citrine stone that momentarily mesmerised her.

The jeweller followed her gaze to the stone and instantly stopped the carousel from turning. Unlocking the glass front, he reached inside and took out the citrine, which was quite large, about the size of a walnut shell. With affected ignorance of the fact he'd already seen her stare at it, he continued, "Oh, now this is a beautiful citrine stone. Over three and a half million years old, hidden inside the earth, only to be unearthed by an ancient civilisation perhaps and brought across the seas, maybe on a galleon trader ship centuries ago! Who knows?"

He was, in fairness, semi tongue-in-cheek with his little sales speech, but nonetheless, it did stir Helen's imagination!

"What's it for?" she asked simply.

"Oh! We have a comprehensive write-up on all of our stones. Some are for good luck, others are for healing. Yet more are to attract positive vibrations and influences and others ward away negative and evil influences. Here!" he said, offering her a little booklet on all the stones and their supposed 'properties'. "Take this, it gives you a good insight into all these particular gems that we stock."

He had, during this conversation, placed the citrine in her hand and she stared at it, admiring its beautiful yellow-orange colour. Instinctively, she clasped her fingers around it and closed her eyes for a second.

"What does this one do?" she asked.

"Amongst other things, it is sometimes called the 'wishing stone'," he said. "If the heart is true and pure and the request is honest and not aimed at wealth or material gain, the stone is said to grant one wish—one wish only, to the owner."

"A bit like a genie in a bottle then, eh? Ha ha!" joked Helen.

"That's to be seen by the owner, I suppose," smiled the jeweller in reply.

"But how do you wear it? What do you do with it?" asked Helen.

"It's up to you, but many people keep them in their pockets, others keep them under their pillows. They are purported to have properties similar to the Red Indian's 'dream catcher'," he replied. "It soothes the nocturnal hours and captures bad dreams."

At this, Helen's face changed slightly and she looked out of the shop window.

"Are you alright, madam?" enquired the jeweller.

"Oh, yes, I'm sorry, yes, I'm fine! How much is it?" said Helen.

Taken aback by the speed of her decision, the jeweller said, "Well, er, yes, that particular stone is £8.25, but I can gift wrap it for you if you would like—"

"No, that won't be necessary. I'll take it!" said Helen.

In 1980, that amount of money was not paltry. But Helen's face told the jeweller, that either he had done his job correctly in selling the stone to her or else, she was just so bowled over by its beauty, that she didn't care about the cost and the stone had sold itself to her. Either way, the jeweller was happy that the stone was off his stock and that of course, is what business is all about.

Wrapping the stone in some tissue, then putting it into a little paper gift bag with a small carrying string on it, he took Helen's money, gave her change, a receipt and the stone. She thanked the jeweller for his help then she walked out of the shop, smiling broadly. As she walked down past the Victoria monument, she was still smiling. Back in the jewellers, when she had the faraway look and had stared out of the window, she indeed was deep in thought.

The jeweller had said the stone was invaluable for soothing the sleeping hours and proof against bad dreams and nightmares. Her thoughts at that moment had switched from Michael's birthday, to John's wellbeing. He had

had such horrid dreams, she just wondered in that split second, if it would, could, even remotely, offer him some relief from them. She laughed at her own silliness and at length, she said, "Silly cow!" to herself as she walked down Beulah Street. But, she could not help but acknowledge the strange feeling she felt as she grasped the stone.

She had experienced a tremendous feeling of peace, well-being and calm. She mocked herself for it, but she just could not dispel the feeling. What she found a little disconcerting, was that fact that she had tendencies towards Christian thoughts and ways and she reproached herself a little in the thought that she had bought something, nay, subscribed to something that was decidedly pagan in fact and deed.

She comforted herself in the knowledge that the act at least was selfless and was done with her son's well-being at heart. She still felt decidedly uneasy. As she walked on in the sunshine, she wondered if she had done something very wrong. She even considered taking the stone back to the jewellers for a refund, but the feeling she had experienced there prevailed. At length, she resolved to hide the stone away for now and just 'see what happened'.

Helen strolled home, as it was such a beautiful afternoon. Looking at her watch, she realised that it wouldn't be too long before John would be coming out of school. Michael had already said earlier that he would pick John up at 4 o'clock.

It'll be nice for John if we were both there again to see him out of school, she thought, increasing her pace a little. She couldn't help thinking about the stone and the strange effect it had on her. It was not a nasty or frightening experience, but quite profound. She wondered where she could hide it.

"Where is there a place that Michael or John wouldn't dream of going to?" she mused. "I know! My undies drawer! They'd never go there, they have no need to! That's where I'll hide it!"

Still smiling, she reached the top of Bilton Lane and could see the other mums and dads through the playground railings, waiting for their children. Perfect timing! Helen entered through the gate as the school bell started to ring. She made her way to the rear playground, where she crept up behind Michael and dug him in both sides of his ribs with her index fingers.

"Eighup lass!" Michael said turning around and with a beaming smile and a hug for her, he said, "Ah wasn't expectin' ta see yer 'til a bit later!"

"Oh, I got the things I wanted and it just worked out nicely! Have you enjoyed your afternoon?" she said.

"Oh, yes ta!" he managed to say before John, who had come out of the cloakrooms and had seen them, ran at full speed up to Michael and wrapped his arms around his legs. "Oof!" blurted Michael on the impact.

"Hey, lad! That were a good tackle! Ah'll be makin' a scrum 'alf out o' ya yet, ha ha!"

Immediately, John turned to his mum and giving her the most perfunctory of pecks on her check, he excitedly asked if she had got the framed photo.

"Yes, yes, calm down, calm down!" she said smiling at him.

"Can I see please?" he asked eagerly.

"Let's just wait until we get home, eh?" Helen said kindly. "How was your day today?"

Of course, that took John's mind off the photo and he gabbled away about his day, scarcely taking a breath and certainly not allowing any questions or further interruptions from his mum or dad, all the way home! That suited them!

Washed, changed and eating their tea, general conversation ensued. Lots more from John, who told them he had made a papier-mâché balloon.

"We had to blow a balloon up, then we got this bowl of glue stuff and dipped bits of old newspaper in it, then stuck all the bits onto the balloon until it was covered and then we let the balloons dry for a bit while Miss Foster read a story about a teddy bear that only had one ear and then we put some more gooey paper all over our balloons and then we had lunch and then we put MORE gooey paper on and—"

"Ha ha, we get the picture, John!" said Helen. "What are you going to do with them when they dry?"

"Oh, we're going to paint faces on them and they're going to be displayed in the school hall!" came the reply.

"Ah remember doin' summat like that when ah were a nipper!" said Michael. "We used oranges instead o' balloons like, an' then when they were dry, we cut the oranges aht, an' sealed the globe back up wi' more papier-mâché. 'Next day, we cut a little 'ole in 'em, an' put some dried peas inside, an' put a little stick in one end, an' hey presto, we all 'ad a maraca a piece! That were just before Chrimbo, so ah gev it t' me mam an' dad as a prezzie! Ee, they were right chuffed wi' that!"

"Ha ha, how Christmas week must have just flown by with merriment and dancing!" Helen teased, looking at him with her hands on her hips, then adopting a pose as if she was a flamenco dancer.

"Cheeky bugger!" said Michael, slapping her playfully on her bottom.

"Talking of presents!" said John. "Can I see the photo now please?"

Helen left the dining room, carrying some of the plates and cutlery back into the kitchen. "Just give me a hand with the washing up, you two and then I'll get the photos."

That done and the washing in the dishwasher, they all sat down in the living room and Helen brought out a large brown paper bag from the side of her chair. John's eyes lit up. Helen slowly pulled out the contents, while John rushed over to her chair.

"Ta-da!" she said with a smile to John.

"Oh, Mummy, they're wonderful!" John said as he eyed the first, smaller photo. Next came some larger prints and at the bottom of the pile, was the framed photo John had been waiting for all week.

"There now!" said Helen. "How's that? Do you like the frame we chose?"

"Oh yes, Mum, it looks great! Thank you so much! I hope Nanna and Grandpa will like it!" said John, not taking his eyes off it.

"I'm sure they will!" said Helen reassuringly.

"Mummy, what's that?" John said as he pointed at the little bag that contained the citrine stone. Colouring up, Helen tried to fudge the moment.

"Oh, erm, it's nothing, darling, it's just something I bought on the spur of the moment, I don't know why I bought it, just a little bit of nonsense that caught my eye."

"Can I see it?" asked John.

"Eighup, secrets, eh?" said Michael.

"Well, er, not exactly," she said, trying to give Michael a significant stare as if to say 'shut up!' "It was just a bit of jewellery that caught my eye—it's nothing really."

"Oh PLEASE, MUM!" pleaded John,

"Yeah, c'mon, lass!" said Michael. Slightly annoyed that Michael hadn't caught her meaning,

Helen sighed and said, "Alright then! It won't mean anything to you both though!" and she unwrapped the citrine stone. Helen gazed at it in admiration. John and Michael just gawped at it.

"Is that all it is?" said Michael.

John hardly gave it a second look, but knowing that his mum obviously liked it, he just said, "That's nice mum!" and he ran upstairs clutching his framed photo.

"Why all the cloak an' dagger like?" said Michael smiling. "If yer wanna buy yersen summat from t' shops, yer don't need ta be coy abaht it!" and he also walked off, humming to himself. Helen breathed a sigh of relief and closed her fingers once again around the stone, to which she again, felt that unexplainable feeling of well-being and tranquillity.

Sunday Lunch with Nanna and Grandpa

Sunday came and John was up with the lark. A beautiful fresh, sunny morning smiled down on Harrogate. Helen was tidying the last of the breakfast things away and Michael was in the bathroom, having a shave, singing to himself as he applied the razor, *Since yer got ta go—OHH, yer betta GO nah—go nah, go nah— GO nahhhhh—*

Then with a final rinse with water, he dried his face and applied some aftershave. "Ooohh, ah-ahh, ooohh," he said as he patted it around his face.

"You sound like a monkey, Dad!" John laughed from his bedroom.

"Ah'll monkey YOU yer little tinker!" Michael snapped back in mock annoyance. They only had a slice of toast a piece for breakfast, to keep body and soul together, as they all knew that lunch would be substantial.

"Best be not 'avin' too much you two, 'cos yer Nanna does serve up big portions!" Michael said with a smile.

"Ohhhh—GOOD!" smiled Helen back to him.

All done and dusted, they were on their way to see Nanna and Grandpa. John had his photo next to him, on the back seat of the car, all wrapped up in some nice, appropriate gift wrap. Next to that was the sugared almonds and a beautifully produced box, with a thin blue ribbon around it, containing the fat rascals from Betty's tea shop.

"I just can't wait to see Nanna and Grandpa!" came the voice from the back seat.

"Nah, me neither!" said Michael. "Ah hope yer good an' hungry, ya know yer Nanna does flippin' big dinners!" he laughed. Helen grabbed Michael's hand and looked at him. He turned to look at her, whilst still negotiating the road and he smiled. "D'ya know, ah'm starved!" he said. "Just as well, 'cos me mam doesn't scimp on t' grub!" he said quietly to Helen. "Ya know me mam's Yorkshire puddin's!"

Helen smiled. She knew that the day would be just perfect in the company of her mum and dad-in-law. She loved them both dearly.

They came down the A1, then through South Emsall and taking the Doncaster Road south, they turned off for Frickley. Reaching Clayton, they then turned left onto Common Lane, Hall Brig, Churchfield Road, then left onto Tan Pit Lane. They past Tea Pot Corner, (a name that always amused Michael, ever since his parents moved to Clayton,) then to the very end of Tan Pit Lane.

There was a dirt track at the end of the lane, veering to the right and Michael's parents had a cottage at the corner of the track. Their timing was impeccable. Grandpa was in the front garden, putting up the big sun parasol over the garden table as they arrived. 'Bee-beep!' went the horn from Michael's car as he approached.

Grandpa raised his hand in greeting. Nanna had heard the sound and came out of the house, wiping her hands on her apron as they pulled up. What a scene to warm the cockles of the heart! As soon as the car engine was turned off, John was out of the back seat and racing towards his grandparents as fast as his little feet would carry him!

"Nanna!" cried John, throwing himself into her arms. "Grandpa!" he said with equal gusto and hugging his grandpa with a grip like a stranglehold!

"Oh! Ha! John, my boy!" Grandpa said, stroking John's head and smiling down at him. "It's good to see you! Welcome, welcome, ha!"

John was beside himself at seeing his grandparents. He loved everything about them and their house.

"Mike lad! Good to see you!"

"You too, Dad, It's bin' long enough, ain't it? Happy birthday to ya!" he said shaking his dad's hand.

"Yes, happy birthday, Dad," said Helen, embracing him fondly. Michael and his dad hugged each other and clapped each other on the back.

"Helen, my dear! It's so good to see you!" said Nanna, hugging her, "My, how John has grown! Come in! Come in and sit yourselves down! Dinner should be about a couple of hours. Are you all getting hungry?"

"By the mess, mam, 'course we are! We 'ad 'ardly any brekky deliberately!" said Michael.

"Can't wait, Nanna!" followed John.

"How about a nice cup of tea?" said Nanna, looking at the four of them stood there in the sunshine.

"That would be lovely! I'll come and help you," said Helen.

"Wait, mother!" said Grandpa, "how's about a nice cold beer Mike boy?" he said to Michael.

"By the cringe, Dad, that'd be welcome!" he replied.

"Come and sit out in the garden with me and let the lasses natter and catch up, eh?"

"Sounds good to me, Dad!" said Michael.

"Two beers coming up!" shouted Helen, as she and Nanna went into the house.

"Can I have some pop please?" John was heard to say, as he followed his mum and Nanna inside. Presently, Helen came out with two ice-cold beers, in Bavarian steins, with lids and handles.

"I thought these would keep the wasps out!" she said smiling and setting the two beers before them.

"Oh, cheers, pet," said Michael.

"Prost!" Michael and his dad said to each other, as they clinked their steins together and took a deep draught.

Michael and his dad sat in the garden, under the shade of the huge parasol of the garden table. The aspect was delightful and the sumptuous aroma of Sunday lunch wafted in the air, making them hungry. They leaned back in their chairs and chatted about all and sundry. His dad was nut brown, from weeks working in his garden and greenhouse and the white, short-sleeved shirt he was wearing, showed off his tan to best advantage.

All was peace and quiet. The only sounds apart from the occasional clatter of utensils or laughter from the kitchen, was the lovely sound of the summer itself. Blue-tits and song thrushes, warbling their Creator's praise. Magpies unmistakable clacking and the drone of bumble-bees, visiting all the flowers that Grandpa had so lovingly tended. All was radiant and beautiful.

"So are you enjoying retirement then, son? Are you exploiting all your pent-up talents and hobbies then?"

"Hey, you betcha, Dad!" said Michael, lowering his stein from his lips and licking his moustache. "Some days, ah don't know where to start first! When ah worked dahn't' pit, it were automatic. Clock in, clock aht like. But nah that ah don't *have* ta get out o' bed of a mornin', it's become the very reason FOR me gettin' up good an' early! Ah've so much t' do, an' so much ah *wanna* do, there's just not enough hours in a day!"

His dad laughed, "Aye, I'm still like that and I've been retired six year! Tell me, have you heard from your brother John lately?"

"Oh yeah, Ah got a phone call from him abaht 10 days ago. Y'know he's wit' t' Sealed Knot Society, doin' these battle re-enactments? Well he's been promoted or summat like that, to a Parliamentarian officer, an' he were saying he's got a big, powerful war-horse to ride! They're coming up to Ripley castle near 'Arragut to do some kind o' battle, an' said it would be nice to meet up!"

"That sounds like fun, Mike, will he be staying with you and Helen?"

"Nah!" came the reply, as Michael was taking another sip of his beer, "They all live in tents! Ha ha! We did offer like! Ah can only 'ope it don't piddle it dahn wi' rain!" They both roared with laughter at that.

"John would have loved to have come today, but he was away on business in Paris," said Grandpa.

"Serves 'im right fer being self-employed like!" joked Michael.

Michael looked at his father with admiration, as the elderly but sprightly man picked up his newspaper to find and article he had seen earlier, that he thought would be of interest to Michael. As he was doing this, Michael's thoughts went back to the Second World War, when he and his brother were sent into the countryside for safety during the blitz. Michael was only five years old when he boarded a train from their home in the centre of Sheffield.

Michael ended up with a family in the heart of the South Yorkshire countryside and his brother John, went to Derby. There had been some confusion in the evacuation of many of the children and some of them had been split up, much to the distress and horror of the parents and the children alike! But it was a necessary thing and it all ended happily for everyone, thank God! Michael's father was born and raised in Buckinghamshire and his mother hailed from Lincolnshire, where his brother John was born too. Michael was a bit of a 'cuckoo in the nest'.

First of all, he didn't really look like his mother or father, but he did look like his grandfather on his father's side. John, on the other hand, was the image of his mother. In accents, they all sounded completely different from each other. Michael's strong South Yorkshire accent was the result of the wartime years and his job as a miner at Grimethorpe Colliery.

Meanwhile, the ladies were busy setting table and chatting away to each other, getting and receiving their respective gossip and news as they did so. Putting the finishing touches to the table, Nanna said,

"Right then! That's us done. Shall we go out and join the boys?"

"Good idea!" came the reply. So replenishing their tea, Nanna took off her apron and the pair of them went out into the sunshine.

"Hello, you two!" said Nanna. "Where's John?"

"Dunno, mam?" said Michael. "You didn't see him, did ya, Dad?"

"Why, no, I can't say I've seen him since you all arrived!"

"Maybe he's in the loo?" said Helen, I'll just go and see if he's alright." And with that, she stood up to go and find him. She didn't need to. Out ran John from the house, with a big smile on his face.

"Where have YOU been all this time?" Helen asked,

"Oh. Erm, nowhere special—"

"Come on—what you been up to, young man?" pressed Helen. John reached up to whisper into his mother's ear. He pulled at his mother's arm to get her a little further out of earshot from the others. He cupped his hand against her ear and whispered,

"I've been in the cubby-hole under the stairs looking at Grandpa's air guns! Please don't tell me off, I didn't do any harm! You won't tell Nanna and Grandpa, will you?"

"You silly sausage!" Helen said laughing at the worried look on John's face, "They won't mind!" Helen took John's hand and led him into the garden, where everyone greeted him and asked where he'd been. John looked at his mother and bit his bottom lip, not knowing what to say for the best.

"He's been in your cubby-hole, looking at your air guns, Dad!" she said with a sigh in her voice, but a big smile on her face.

"Sorry, Grandpa, I didn't load one or set one off or do any damage or touch your pellets or—"

"Hey, lad, that's perfectly alright! I'm glad you like my guns! I was just the same as you when I was your age. Here I am at 71 and I still love them, so why not you? 'Tell you what! Next time you come to visit us, why don't we go into the woods behind our house and you and I can do some 'pot-shotting' at some tin cans? How does that sound?"

John's face completely lit up and he threw his arms around his Grandpa and gave him a kiss on the cheek.

"There you are now!" said Nanna. "You've quite made your Grandpa's day! We'll never get him out of the wood, ha ha!"

After about a half an hour of pleasant conversation all round, Nanna got up and said, "It's time to serve! Helen, would you help me get the veg ready and I need to relax the roast beef before it's served."

The three men-folk were positively drooling and as Helen and Nanna walked into the house, the boys started jabbering about anything that would take their minds off food!

"'Ow's ya vegetable marra's comin' on, Dad? 'an ah'll bet yer tomatoes are comin' on a treat, eh?"

"Oh, we went for a super pizza the other night, Grandpa—"

"Your mother made the most superb mushroom chowder a couple of weeks ago, with freshly baked buttered crusty bread and—" The one track conversation was interrupted by Helen, who shouted from the door that dinner was nearly served.

"Get yourselves ready, it's nearly time to eat! Mike, Dad, would you like wine or another beer to go with your meal?" Both of them replied that the wine would be nice. "Red or white?" came the response.

"What would you prefer, son?" Grandpa asked, gently holding his son's elbow.

"Helen!" Michael shouted, "Get that bottle o' claret we brought dahn fer me, Dad!" Once again, Michael hugged his farther and said, "Happy birthday to ya dad, an' many, many more of 'em!"

They all sat down to dinner. The roast beef of old England was brought in on a huge silver platter, ready to be carved by the man of the house. It looked and smelled absolutely divine! As it was allowed to relax, the exalted Yorkshire pudding was brought in to eat first, as is tradition in old Yorkshire. A healthy portion was served up for all by Nanna and copious amounts of gravy, made from the stock and goodness from the roasted rib of beef, was lashed on all plates.

All were slavering, but Nanna said, "Wait a moment everyone, two things we must observe! Firstly, we must say grace," to which everybody bowed their heads and clasped their fingers together.

"Dear Lord, for what we are about to receive, may we be truly thankful. Amen!" and they all repeated, "Amen."

"Next," she continued, "A toast to your Grandpa, my dear husband!" she said turning and looking at him with deep affection and moist eyes, "Happy Birthday to you!"

"Happy birthday, dear dad!" they all shouted in their own ways and pitch of voices. Then they all started to sing *Happy birthday to you*—

So dinner commenced, with the traditional starter, of Yorkshire pudding and gravy. Praises were said all around the table for the sumptuous taste and the quality of the superb Yorkshires. Michael uncorked the Bordeaux and poured four glasses and some cola for John. Then silence. As good food does, it robs conversation, until all was eaten.

Once again, Nanna was heartened to hear so many praises about her cooking. "That were absolutely gorgeous, Mum!" said Michael.

"Yes, it was mum!" agreed Helen.

They all had something to say. Smiling, Nanna got up and went into the kitchen, followed by Helen, to get the vegetables and roasted potatoes. On their return, Grandpa uncovered the piece of tin foil that had been placed over the meat and he stood to carve it. In time honoured way, he sharpened the carving knife on the steel, while they all watched eagerly. He served up good generous portions of the roast and arranged them on all the plates, leaving room for all the veg and potatoes.

Apart from the roast, there were roasted parsnips, broccoli, carrots, cabbage and homemade horseradish sauce. More Yorkshire pudding was offered and eagerly accepted by all. They all helped themselves to the other things on offer on the table, including lashings more gravy. What a feast! The general conversations started up again as dinner was being eaten and it took a good half an hour to get to empty plates. But when the last of it was gone, Nanna asked for all the plates, which were duly passed round to her. She stacked them up, ready to go into the kitchen for washing up.

"Everyone go and sit down and let that settle before dessert!" Nanna said.

"I'll help with clearing," said Helen and proceeded to do just that. The men-folk went into the living room and flopped into arm chairs, still smacking their lips and resorted to using tooth-picks. John followed their example with a grin.

A few minutes later, the ladies came in and sat down too. Fanning herself with a magazine, Nanna said, "With it being such a hot day, I thought that a nice fruit salad and cream would be a bit more welcome that a hot pudding for sweet. Is that alright with everyone?"

Of course, the general response was immediately affirmative.

The fruit salad was duly eaten and applauded. Everyone lent a hand to the clearing away, including John, who by this time was getting impatient to give Grandpa his gift. He had been told to say nothing about it until after dinner and then, only when his mum and dad gave him the nod to do so. That moment came when they were all sat in the garden again. John was watching the fishes in Grandpa's fish pond and the adults were just enjoying the sun and the peace and quiet.

Michael said to John, "Eighup our John, Ha'n't ya got summat fer yer Grandpa?"

John was on his feet in a second and raced into the house. He knew just where the photo was and grabbing it in both hands, he ran out again shouting, "Happy birthday, Grandpa!" and gave him the present.

"Oh! Now, what's this then?" he said enthusiastically.

"I hope you like it, Grandpa!" John said with a typical little boy smile. Grandpa put on his spectacles and carefully unwrapped the present and savoured the moment, drawing it out as long as he could and kept the wrapping face up, having undone all the sticky tape from underneath. Then he slowly pulled the photo away from the wrapping and looked at it.

"Oh John, It's a photograph of you! And my, what a lovely frame! Thank you so much! Nanna, have a look at it!" he said, leaning across and showing it to her.

Meanwhile, John was grinning and had gone all coy and had that 'not knowing what to do with his hands' sort of posture, that only children can do. His grandparents said as one, how lovely and grown up he looked in his new uniform and they beckoned him to them for a huge hug. All of this, of course, naturally got onto the subject of his school and what he had done in his first week.

So poor Helen and Michael looked at each other, with an 'Oh no, here we go again!' sort of look, as John reiterated his week in tiny detail, word for word as he had done to them all week long. After a speech of some half an hour of his week, his grandparents congratulated him on all his achievements. Once again, John had that silly grin and wrung his hands through the bottom of his T-shirt, as kids do when a little embarrassed.

"This will take pride of place on the telly, John," said Grandpa. "Nanna, you'll have to find somewhere else for your China dolphins now, ha ha!"

The afternoon wore on and by about 5 o'clock, Nanna asked if anyone was getting peckish? Everybody patted their stomachs and said that their dinner was still settling, but Michael said, "Tell ya what we *have* got for ya both, some of those lovely fat rascals from Betty's tea shop in 'Arragut! Maybe's ya wanna keep 'em fer yer supper, eh?"

"Oh thank you!" said Nanna, "We love them! Yes, we'll enjoy those with a nice cuppa later."

"Yes, I like mine buttered!" said Grandpa.

"No, you should have them as they come!" said Nanna.

"Buttered!" said Grandpa.

"Plain!"

"Buttered!"

"Plain!" and they both grinned at each other.

By 6:30, Helen said, "Right you two, it's time we were leaving mum and dad in peace, plus it's back to school for you tomorrow, young man!" she said to John. "By the time we get you home, washed and jim-jammed, it'll be bedtime," she said, playfully patting him on his bottom.

"Yes, ah guess it's time we med' a move," Michael said in agreement. And they all got up from their loungers, stretched and started moving into the house, taking with them the odd tea cup, plate, beer stein and newspaper. Michael gave the fat rascals to his dad and said in a subdued tone (but really designed to be heard by his mum as well), "You put butter on yer fat rascals if ya wan' it dad, don't listen to 'er!" he laughed, surreptitiously pointing at his mother.

"I heard that, YOU!" she said laughing at him. Presently, all was ready for them to leave, but Helen gave Grandpa another wrapped up present and, rattling the box she said, "No guesses to what THIS is! Happy birthday once again, Dad and enjoy the rest of your day."

"Oh, yes, my sugared almond radar has already zoomed in on them! Thank you very much indeed!" And with hugs and kisses all round, Michael, Helen and John clambered into the car. Last minute waves, blown kisses and everyone shouting, "Bye!" they turned onto Tarn Pit lane and slowly drove away, hands still waving from the car windows. One last *'beep'* from the car horn and they were gone.

On the way home, Michael said to John, "Did ya hear me talkin' ta yer Grandpa about yer uncle John comin' up ta 'Arragut wit' t' Sealed Knot Society soon?"

"No daddy?" said John.

"Well, ya DO know what they do, 'cos ah've shown ya pictures 'aven't ah? Well, they're comin' ta Ripley Castle to do some kind o' battle. Would ya fancy goin' along ta see it like?"

"Oh YES!" said John excitedly. "When is it?"

"Can't remember exactly when, but ah'll find aht, an' we can make an afternoon of it! 'You fancy that Helen?" said Michael.

"Yes, I do actually, we don't see John very often and it would be a good entertaining afternoon!"

"What do they actually do?" said John, with great interest, "How do they fight?"

"Well," continued Michael, "They 'ave cannons an' muskets, an' they 'ave pikes an' such."

"Does anyone really get hurt, Daddy?" asked John.

"Well, ha ha, they're not supposed ta, but ah guess some of 'em must get hurt, 'cos even though they're not firing live bullets or cannon balls, there's lots of men pushin' an' shovin' abaht, an' ah guess they must hit each other accidentally from time ta time like!"

"That would be wonderful to see, Daddy! I love Uncle John! We don't see him very often!" said John.

"Right then, ah'll get that firmed up then!" said Michael.

The Wishing Stone (Part 2)

Back home again and all of them were tired but happy. The kettle was put on straight away for a cuppa for Helen and Michael and a nice mug of hot chocolate for John. John had a shower, helped by his mum, then into fresh pyjamas and down the stairs to enjoy his chocolate. They all sat sipping their drinks and discussing the day, when a deep booming of distant thunder was heard.

Looking out the back window, Michael could see the ominous black cloud, heading towards them, although it was still quite sunny over them. It was extremely muggy and Helen and Michael both agreed that a good storm was necessary to clear the air and as it had been some considerable time since it had rained at all, the grass was well in need of some water! It got darker and darker. The thunder grew louder by the peel. John wasn't too keen on thunderstorms; he took after his Nanna there.

Michael remarked to Helen, "Hey, if this lot travels dahn-country, mi mam will be in t' cubby-hole under t' stairs, wit' cat, 'cos t' cat dun't like thunder either! Ha Ha! Hey, John lad, you could keep 'er company an' play wi' yer Grandpa's airguns at t' same time!"

John tried to smile, but the storm was getting closer—and so was his bedtime! Within 10 minutes the wind had sprung up and the storm threatened to break over them in earnest. It hadn't started to rain yet, but it became as black as night. The birds had stopped singing and gone to their roosts. Michael went outdoors, to check that all was secure before the deluge.

No sooner was he back in through the kitchen door, than a bolt of lightning spit the gloom and hit a poplar tree in the garden but one to their house. The thunder was instantaneous and deafening and almost as if the thunder had been a signal, the rain came down in torrents. It rained so hard, the garden could not be seen, as it was bouncing off the grass and produced a 'fog' of water some 2 feet high.

Michael nearly jumped out of his skin as the thunderbolt hit and shouted, "What the f—" the word being drowned by the deafening roar of the thunder. Even Helen shouted, "Oh my GOD!" at that same moment. John screamed aloud and continued to scream in terror.

Michael shut the back door and rushed into the living room. They were hard pressed to calm John down before the next frightful flash and ear-splitting crash came. John buried his face into his mother's chest and clung on for dear life, whimpering and crying uncontrollably. Roar after roar, of thunder came in quick succession. It was so violent; Helen and Michael looked at each other significantly. It was, for several minutes, almost as if Armageddon itself had started over Harrogate.

By and by, the storm abated. Helen and Michael were extremely shaken, but did their best to show at least some degree of nonchalantness of the storm and tried to laugh it off for John's sake. John was absolutely terrified and trembling with fear in his mother's arms, whimpering piteously and would not let go his grip from her.

Again, Helen and Michael looked at each other, wondering what to do next for the best. Michael took the initiative and as the thunder was still crashing alarmingly around them, although growing less and less in ferocity with each crash, Michael scooped John up into his strong, all protecting arms and started to sing to him jovially,

"10 green bottles, 'angin' on a wall, 10 green bottles, 'angin' on a wall, an' if one green bottle should—"

"STOP IT! STOP IT, DADDY!" screamed John.

"Calm down, lad, it's all over nah!" he said kissing him on his cheek, while still holding him in his arms. "It's all OK, lad, it were just a storm! It's natural an' 'appens from time ta time! Don't be afeart of it, it's yer friend! It waters t' gardens, gives t' dicky birds summat ta drink, meks us flowers grow, an'—"

"DADDY! Please stop!" screamed John. "The thunder was calling my name!" sobbed John. "It was calling MY NAME in a horrid deep voice and it scared me—it scared me, Daddy—" and he sobbed uncontrollably.

Michael gently saying, "Shhh, hush now, lad, it's all OK now, yer wi' yer mum an' dad, nowt's gonna hurt ya, lad, shhh—"

But Helen and Michael were looking at each other all the while, with great misgivings.

John would not let go of his father and he trembled in his arms and sobbed his heart out, but said not another word. Michael just rocked him gently in his arms and hummed lullabies to him. At length, Helen and Michael mouthed things to each other, to the effect, "Let's get him up to bed now and see if he'll settle."

John was all but asleep, just the occasional deep intake of breath, as the last of his sobbing died away. The storm had all but passed; just the occasional growl of thunder was heard in the distance. They both gently put him onto his bed, but didn't cover him with his duvet, as it was still so hot and humid. They opened his window to allow more fresh air into his bedroom and a lovely smell of wet grass and earth came wafting in, a comforting aroma after such an alarming episode.

The lone sound of a blackbird was heard, singing in the now still and calm of the evening and beyond the black clouds on the horizon, a sunset smiled down over the western sky. Happy that John had fallen asleep and that the storm had now passed, they both gently kissed him on his forehead and went back downstairs.

"By the cringe, lass, that were a cracker, weren't it!" said Michael, who was afraid of nothing usually, least of all a thunderstorm. As a child, he would often watch a storm from his bedroom window at the dead of night and not bat an eyelid. Helen agreed with his comment.

"I haven't seen anything like that since I was a child. We went to the Dominican Republic on a family holiday and a tropical storm came over. The locals just loved it and we were all petrified! I remember one young local lad, running out of the hotel and lying on his back on the lawn of the hotel, laughing his head off! He disappeared under the ferocity of the rain! But the LIGHTNING and thunder was just amazing! But what we have just experience was getting very close to the intensity of that storm.

'Tell ya what, lass, ah weren't ready fer it when t' first flash came, it nigh on scared me aht me undercrackers!"

They were still a little shaken but they were at least able to laugh at it now.

"Talk about the 'smell o' fear 'eh lass, ha ha!" Helen snuggled up to Michael on their big, soft white leather sofa, with their almost-cold cups of tea and spent a few precious moments together, of peace and quiet. The evening was wearing on and Helen at last gave in to the arms of Morpheus.

Michael wasn't far behind her and said, "C'mon, pumpkin, let's hit the sack, shall we?"

So they sleepily tidied a few things away, closed the living room window, checked the doors and headed up the stairs, Helen first, then Michael. He playfully cupped her buttocks in his hands as he followed her.

"Oh, you're JOKING, Michael!" Helen laughed as they got to the top of the stairs, "You're not really wanting—"

"Daft bat!" he said. "Ah just love looking' at yer bum! Finest bum in t' world, yours! Ah just couldn't resist it like. It's like watchin' a couple o' ferrets trying ta get out o' a sack!"

"Cheeky bugger!" she said, spinning round and playfully smacking his face.

"Eighup! Eighup! Grievous bodily 'arm!" he laughed.

"Seriously," she said, running her index finger down his chest, "if you do fancy—er—"

"Ah were only joshin', lass, yer safe toneet! Ah'm bushed, an' a dead sparrah can't fall out o' its nest can it!"

"There's nothing dead about YOU, Michael Twigg!" she whispered into his ear and nibbling his earlobe.

"Mind yer don't push us too far pumpkin," he said with a broadening smile, "ya just might be opening Pandora's Box wi' a super-stud like me!"

"Come and take me, tiger!" she said, licking her lips at him.

"That's it! By the cringe, ah warned ya, get yer kit off!"

"You smooth talking lady killer! How can I resist you!" she said in a girlie voice. A smack on her bottom confirmed that there were no dead sparrows when it came to Michael!

A hot night. Windows open. A gentle breeze cooling hot bodies. Close to the end of their love making, an ear-splitting scream came from John's room.

"Jaysus! What's goin' on?" Michael said as he disengaged from her.

"Oh my God!" shouted Helen.

"What's wrong!" Michael swiftly put on his pyjama bottoms to hide his modesty and flew into John's room, swiftly followed by Helen, who was close to panic.

"John lad, John! What's up? Shush, hey, ev'rythin's alraight, lad! Calm yersen'," John was absolutely hysterical.

"I can't get out! I'm trapped! Daddy, help me PLEASE! I can't get out of this cubby-hole!" and he sobbed and sobbed his heart out. Helen took John in her arms and cuddled him. She was in tears by this time at seeing her son so distraught. With pleading eyes, she looked at Michael for some kind of resolve. Anything to stop the torment John was obviously experiencing.

Michael took hold of John and said calmly, but firmly to him, "Tell yer dad what ya see, lad, what is it that scares ya like? Ya can tell yer dad, what is it that ya can see?"

John rubbed his eyes and after a moment and still sobbing, he said, "I can't see anything, Daddy. It's a cubby-hole."

Helen and Michael looked at each other significantly.

"Is it yer Grandpa's cubby-hole John?"

"No," came the reply after a moment or two, "it's cold and dark. It's like a little box and I'm lying in it. There isn't much room. I can't stretch my arms and legs. There is some wood above my head. There isn't any light and I can't find my way out! Oh daddy, I'm frightened!"

Helen looked at Michael, as if hit with an idea.

"I'll just be a moment," she said to him, rushing out of the bedroom. Michael just looked as she went, dumbfounded. She returned after a few seconds, with something in her hand, wrapped in tissue.

"What ya got?" asked Michael.

"It's just that stone I showed you a few days ago," said Helen.

"What the hell ya gonna do wi' THAT?" he asked with an annoyed tone in his voice.

"Look, just shut up and humour me!" she snapped back at him. Her look left no mistake in Michael's mind; she wasn't to be argued with. "Call me stupid, but this stone is supposed to help people with sleeping difficulties and bad dreams."

"WHAT the hell are you talkin' abaht, Helen?" Michael said as he sprang up from John's bedside, "What claptrap is this then? The lads had a bad dream! Nowt more or less! What the hell ya gonna do with a piggin' stone fer God's sake?"

"Look, I know it seems a bit odd, but this stone is supposed to—"

"Supposed to WHAT?" snapped Michael. "Send lad ta sleep? Stop 'im from 'avin' nightmares?" John, who all the while was listening to them arguing, burst into tears again. Their attention was then drawn to him and they tried to soothe him all over again.

"Nah nah, John, don't be upset, yer mam an' me were just talkin' abaht summat else! It weren't owt ta do wi' you like!" But John couldn't be pacified.

"There's something here with me! There's something in my room that talks to me and makes me frightened!" said a tearful John. Michael and Helen just stared at each other.

"What—is here with ya, lad?" said Michael, with a very concerned look, but John's eyes were slowly closing with tiredness and he soon made no sense at all. He seemed to calm all of a sudden. The stone was right next to his head, as Helen was still clutching it next to him.

This wasn't lost on Michael, who, suppressing anger said, "Get that thing near 'im then, an' do whatever ya 'ave ta to wi' it ta keep t' little lad peaceful! Ah'm goin' t' bed! Goodnight!"

Helen was extremely unhappy and tearful by Michael's words. He rarely lost his temper, but he seemed particularly rattled by this stone. It seemed ironic that she had a leaning to Christianity and him agnosticism or even paganism and she was the one endorsing a pagan stone to help her son, whilst Michael was dead against it!

Helen stayed with John way into the small hours and beyond. John never stirred. Helen heard Michael snoring and with heavy eyelids, she looked at John's beside clock, that said 2.25 am. John was sleeping peacefully. Helen had held the citrine stone all the while and felt the same calm she had felt earlier.

Instinctively, she put the stone under John's pillow and kissed him on his forehead. She popped to the loo and then crawled into bed next to Michael, who was by this time, totally oblivious of her. She was absolutely shattered, but had a 'busy' head and just could not switch off from the day's events. Eventually, as she started to doze, she heard a deep growl of thunder in the distance and she muttered, "Piss off!" to herself, as she closed her eyes.

The next day, John was up with the lark and singing to himself. He was singing one of the songs he had been taught at school the previous week. Michael was already up and making a pot of tea and some buttered toast. Helen slowly came-to and for a few moments, wondered if the whole of the last night's proceedings really happened at all! The smell of the toast roused her further.

"John?" she shouted, still lying in bed.

"Yes, Mum?" came the reply,

"Are you alright, sweetie?"

"Yep! I'm just playing with my action man!" Helen sank back into her pillow. It was as if she had had a bad dream and nothing more.

"Michael?" she continued, "Are you OK, love?" she said raising her voice a little to carry to the kitchen,

Ah'm t' dogs bits! Just doin' some toast an' marmite fer a bit o' a starter! she heard him say over John's singing and the sound of the radio that was blaring in the kitchen.

"Be a love and bring me a cuppa up, would you?" she asked meekly.

"Ah'm just bringin' yer one up now, ya silly cow!" he said happily and with a spring in his step, he came through the bedroom door. "D'ya think ah would leave ya tea-less on a smashin' mornin' like this?" he said with a beaming smile. "Here! Get yer lips wrapped 'round that!" he laughed as he put the tea on her bedside cabinet.

"Saucy!" she said, as he was leaving the bedroom. He put his hands on his hips and wiggled his bottom at her and with a wink, he went back downstairs. Helen propped herself up on her pillow and sipped at her tea. John was singing a little song in his bedroom.

Downstairs, Michael was singing too, to the radio, *Skip t' last fandango-oo.—sendin' cog wheels 'cross t' floo-oor—*

It was as if nothing had ever happened the night before. Helen did not dare ask about it and nothing was offered. They had breakfast and did the usual morning duties. John packed his satchel and Helen made his sandwich and put his orange squash into his lunchbox. Michael was as chipper as a cricket and displayed no signs of worry or discomfort from the previous night.

As they were mulling about at the breakfast table, John came up to his mum and said, "Thank you for letting me use your stone, Mummy, I need to return it to you now."

"Why! That's alright, dear," she said, taken aback, "what do you mean by that? I just had it in my hand at the time and forgot to take it out of your bedroom!" she said desperately trying to think of a reason for it being there.

"Oh, it told me that you had done it for me and that you wanted me to sleep and that you loved the stone and that it loved you too and that it would keep me safe."

Michael heard that, but said nothing. They all got up from the breakfast table and all was as normal as could be, although Michael had looked long and hard and most significantly at Helen throughout breakfast.

Hampsthwaite

John at school and with it being another bright and fresh morning after the previous evening's storm, they decided to go to a little village not far from Harrogate, in fact, part of Harrogate's outer perimeters. Hampsthwaite, a delightful little village, about a couple of miles north-west of the centre of town, had been recommended to them by friends as the perfect spot for a picnic. A very 'olde worlde' picturesque sort of place, that didn't take too much imagination to visualise what it may have looked like in mediaeval times.

Parking their car by the village green, they strolled down the road, admiring the beautifully kept little cottages, with their trim gardens and trees, shrubs and flowers everywhere. A very welcoming pub to their left, which they made a mental note of, a village shop, selling all and sundry, from newspapers to safety pins, food, to bags of kindling sticks. There was a tea room and one or two other little shops, even a garage, selling motor cars! They went into the first shop on the street corner and browsed a while.

"Good morning!" came the cheery welcome from the lady shopkeeper. "Can I help you?"

"Well, erm, yes, ah think so," said Michael and turning to Helen, he said, "Do ya fancy owt, Helen?"

"Oh, I tell you what would be nice, those Danish pastries look gorgeous! Fancy one of those a piece?"

"By the mess, they do look good, don't they, luv," he said. "Two o' yer Danish pastries an' a couple o' cans o' cola please, oh, an' ah'll tek this newspaper too," he continued, putting a tabloid on the counter.

The shopkeeper carefully took the pastries from the glass shelf with tongs and put them into a paper bag and span the bag round, to make 'ears' at the corners, to make a seal. She then got the colas out of a large bespoke fridge and put them next to the pastries and paper.

"Thank you, sir, that'll be £2.35 please," she said as she popped the things into a carrier bag. Michael gave her a fiver and she rang it into her till and gave him his change.

"Can you tell us where t' church is, luv?" he asked,

"Oh yes, of course! Go straight down the road here," she said pointing in the direction they needed, "and go past the garage, the road forks just past there, you need to take the right hand road and the church is on your left, only a couple of hundred yards. You can't miss it! Are you new to the area?" she asked Helen.

"Well, we've been here about seven years. We live in Bilton, but I'm ashamed to say we've never been here before! You know what it's like!"

"Ah well, I hope you enjoy your visit here! All the local villages have their own special charms and points of interest!"

"Thanks fer that, luv, we'll do us best ta get to 'em very soon! Thanks nah, see yer later!" Michael said as they walked out of the shop.

"Oh, do come and see our wonderful village display of scarecrows—it's an annual thing you know!" the shop-keeper shouted after them. "It's colourful and great for kids—" she tried to add as they walked down the high street.

As they strolled down the village, chatting to each other, they noticed one or two of the cottages had the dates that they were built, above the front doors.

"God, some o' these are old, aren't they?" said Michael.

"They certainly are indeed!" replied Helen.

"1609, this one 'ere!" he said,

"Gosh, yes and that one, 1596!" she replied, pointing at another.

They ambled down past the garage and stayed right on the road. Soon, they saw the church, boasting the name of "St Thomas a' Becket Church", a beautiful church, set in a very picturesque position, right next to the river Nidd. They opened the church gate and went into the beautifully kept graveyard, with its willows overhanging the headstones and producing shafts of sunlight down on the immaculately clipped grass. Cypress trees and a magnificent oak also spread their branches, as if revelling in the protection and solitude of this lovely place.

They tried the church door, which opened smoothly and silently. They entered and even though there was nobody else there, they instinctively lowered their voices to almost a whisper. It was deathly quiet in there and they slowly walked down the aisle and up to the altar. They studied all the stained glass windows and the exquisite carvings of the oaken pews and beams. After some time thus occupied, the door opened again and in walked the vicar, to collect some paperwork he had forgotten from the previous day's service.

"Ah, good morning!" he said in a deep and resonant voice.

"Mornin' vicar," said Michael, "ah do 'ope we're not disturbin' ya like?"

"No, no, not at all! Is there something I can help you with?" he said kindly.

"Oh, no," said Helen, "we're just visiting the village and the church was recommended to us as a must-see!"

"Oh, that's nice to hear! Are you from out of town then?" the vicar asked.

"Well, we have lived in Harrogate for several years, but we have never visited Hampsthwaite until today," she replied.

"I do beg your pardon," said the vicar earnestly, "I'm not looking to my manners here, my name is Philip Whittaker, I have the honour of being the senior vicar of the Parish," he said offering his hand. Michael took it instantly and introduced Helen and himself.

"Yes, it is a lovely church, probably the best and certainly the most handsome church I have served at. There is a little leaflet on the history and a description of the church in a box at the doorway, if you would care to take one, I'm sure you will find it interesting! The present church was built on the site of a much older one, some 190 years ago and an even older church, of which some of the foundations and the gravestones still survive from, dating back almost four and a half centuries! Anyway, I do hope you enjoy your visit and perhaps you will join us at our services sometime! Good day to you!"

And with a wave, he disappeared into a little office. Helen did pick up the leaflet that was recommended to them and they felt obliged to put a little money into an old coin box, made for the express purpose of receiving donations.

They walked outside and looked at some of the gravestones and sure enough, some of them were very old indeed. In fact, some were so old and the inscriptions so badly worn and decayed, that they were unreadable. As they walked out of the churchyard, the church clock struck eleven. Quite a nice, singular sound to it, the type of chime that has a quarter past, half past, quarter to and on the hour precursor chime before striking the hour itself.

They went over the bridge, across the river Nidd. Just on the far side of the bridge and to the left, there was a large 5-bar gate. As there was no 'keep out' signs and only a small, rusty hook holding the gate closed, they opened the gate up and strolled down by the river and sat on a grassy hillock overlooking the river and with a broadside view of the church, only about thirty or forty feet from them. Out came the Danish pastries and the cola. What a lovely, relaxing spot. A true beauty spot indeed!

Having refreshed themselves, they lay back on the soft grass and listened to the sound of the river, as it danced over its rocky bed, flowed under the bridge to the left of them and away through the countryside to Knaresborough. Michael pulled a wild barley stalk from the ground and put it in his mouth, rolling it from one side to the other. Helen had her eyes closed, but she was smiling all the while at this lovely, peaceful spot.

"How's your traction engine coming on, Mike?" she asked with a genuine interest.

"Fair to middlin'," came the sullen response.

She detected the uneasiness in his voice, but tried to win the moment with, "I'm sure your brother will be bowled over when he sees what you have made for him, he has always loved traction engines! Do you know, he respects you so much, I think he envies you sometimes! You are such a talented man you know," she said, digging him in his side with her finger, "and what's more, you can certainly keep THIS girl happy with some of your—talents!"

It was lost on him. He stared at the sky with a far-away look.

"Hey look! I found a four leaf clover!" she said picking at two clovers and making a three into a four. He didn't even look at it.

"I got your favourite sausages for tea, by the way, real German bratwursts with all the trimmings? I thought you and John would like that?" Michael didn't respond. She knew that she was in for some kind of talking-to. It came at length.

"Helen, ah need ta ask yer a question. What's with all this claptrap abaht stones an' such? What were it abaht t' thunderstorm last neet? Yeah, ah know it were a bleedin' bad 'un like, but what's wi' all this stone, an' 'im, givin' it yer back this mornin', wi' some shite abaht 'it 'ad med 'im feel berrer', an' that 'e were givin' yer it back like, an' that it were talkin' ta 'im like? What bollocks is this?"

Helen was struck dumb. "Well, answer me, fer God's sake!" he shouted. She was still searching for words. "Yer not turnin' inta a friggin' witch, are ya, lass?" he shouted at her. That was it. She spun round and slapped his face very hard. He instantly grabbed her hand with a vice-like grip that made her wince and said, "That one were fer free! The next one, ye'll pay dearly for, that ah do promise!"

"Don't you EVER talk to me like that again!" she shouted.

"Likewise!" he said in a louder voice than hers. She got up and stormed off towards the gate.

"Where d'ya think your goin' then?" he shouted after her.

"HOME!" she sobbed and she made her way out of the gate and headed back over the bridge towards the village.

"Good afternoon!" came the salutation from an elderly gent on his bicycle as he rode over the bridge.

"Yes, I'm sure it bloody well is!" Helen shouted back at him.

Poor chap stopped on his bike, lifted his flat cap and scratched his head as she stormed by. Michael was adamant he wasn't in the wrong and sat on the riverbank for some considerable time. But eventually, he started to succumb to the feelings of guilt, if not guilt, then perhaps sorrow that he'd been so hard on her. He tried to justify himself in his own mind.

At length, he sprang up from the hillock and, realising that Helen wasn't for coming back, he picked up the carrier bag containing the newspaper and empty tin cans and walked towards the gate and then onto the road back to the village. There was no sign of Helen anywhere.

He embarrassedly called her name from time to time, "Helen? Are ya there lass?" and he stared into the garage and little shops previously described, in case she was inside one of them.

His face grew longer and longer at the thought that Helen had indeed gone home. It was a sobering moment. All of a sudden, he felt very alone. Very vulnerable. Helen had been by his side, through thick and thin for 10 years. He almost felt sick that this spat had caused so much damage. He went up the main street, still calling her name, but in vain. He approached the car, but she wasn't in it or anywhere to be seen. Michael's eyes started to fill.

"Cuss me an' mi big gob!" he sobbed, as he started the engine. "Ah've allus bin me own worst enemy wi' mi big gob!" he said to himself, drying his eyes. As he started up the lane towards Otley road, he tried to give himself courage in his own convictions. *Ah needed ta ask that question, din't ah? Bugger me, if t' boot were on t' other foot, Helen would 'ave asked me as much wouldn't she? Oh, Helen, ah do love ya lass, wi' all me 'eart ah do!*

He looked for her all the way through Killinghall and all the way back down Ripon Road, but to no avail. Still sobbing, he passed a grocer's shop at the top of King Edward's Drive and stopped to buy a huge bouquet of flowers. "How can a dumb old git like me say the kind o' sorry that ah needs ta say to her?" he said to himself as he paid for the flowers. The girl behind the counter could see that he was distraught and as he was about to leave, she grabbed hold of his hand and with a sensitive look to him she offered him a red rose.

"I know it's none of my business, sir, but take this for your lass, give it after the bouquet and tell her you love her." She looked around the shop, to see if her boss might be lurking around and then said, "Go on, it's for free! Good luck!"

"Bless yer gentle 'eart, lass," he said with gratitude.

Michael reversed the car into their driveway and stopped the engine. His heart was thumping. As he got out of the car, he could smell the early signs of tea cooking from the extractor fan from the kitchen. He didn't know what to do or say. He felt sick.

"How can ah tell 'er ah'm sorry?" he hesitated for a moment, then picked up the flowers and the red rose, then locked the car. As he went to the front door of the house, it opened, to reveal Helen, wiping her hands on her apron. There was a hugely pregnant pause. They stared at each other for several moments, he with his flowers in his hand and her in her apron. As one, they flew into each other's arms. He dropped the flowers in the instant. They hugged and cried.

"Ah'm sorry lass, please forgive us!" he sobbed, as she was equally exclaiming sorrow, saying, "I am too, honey, I should have talked to you sooner, oh how I need to talk to you, you don't understand, I'm not a bad person, I'm not a witch, I'm not a—" her words were taken away from her by Michael, who pressed his lips against hers and kissed her like it was their very last. The bouquet and red rose were forgotten and left on the driveway, for the moment at least.

As the afternoon wore on, they had made up a degree of their differences and were more relaxed. It was evident that a lot more dialogue would be needed. But the happy thought that John would need picking up from school lifted their spirits and they both agreed to say no more on the subject. They grinned and gave each other a smacking kiss, then leaving the dinner to its own devices in the oven, they opened the front door, to see the flowers on the driveway.

"You daft bat!" she said and smiled at him.

"YOU daft bat!" he said back to her. "Tek 'em in' t' 'ouse and we'll tend to 'em later," he said. She smiled broadly and did as she was asked.

After tea, John was, as usual enthusing at what he'd done at school. Michael, however, was secretly still brooding over the previous night's issues. John grew tired at length and after brushing his teeth and doing all the usual 'goodnights' and bedtime routine, Helen said to Michael, "I'm just going to get John to bed and tuck him in Mike."

"Oh, right lass, ah'll be there in a mo!" Michael had thought about this moment all afternoon. He heard the loo flushing, telling him that John was indeed ready to go to bed.

"Erm, ah'll tuck 'im in, Helen," he said. "You've worked 'ard enough this aft! Come an' get yer cuppa before it goes cold!" With that, he went up the stairs, two at a time, to see Helen at John's bedroom door.

"Oh, well that's good of you, thanks Mike!" she said with a look of tired relief on her face. "I'll go down and see you in five, eh?" she said.

"Aye, lass," he replied dryly, but corrected himself by saying, "Oh, an' yes, we got a Perry Mason ta watch later, ah love mi Perry Masons tha knoas!"

"Nah then John lad! All ready fer bed? Let's get yer tucked up an' comfy like. It's a lot cooler t'night, an' there's a full moon lookin' after ya!"

"Thank you, Daddy," said John smiling up at his dad, "I'll sleep well, Daddy."

"Tell me son, what was it yo' were dreamin' abaht that scared ya last night? An' what were yer mam an' you talkin' abaht wi' t' stone she gev ya?" John's face dropped and Michael could see he was treading on thin ice. "Oh, don't look worried, lad!" he laughed. "It's just that ah don't really know about such things, an' ah were just interested. Can't ya tell yer ol' dad abaht it too?"

"Well," said John hesitating a little, "I sometimes get this dream—"

"Tell me abaht it lad." Michael said softly, as he stroked John's hair,

"Well—it starts with me walking. I'm looking at my own feet, but I'm wearing funny shoes and clothes and I'm walking very fast. My shoes are squeaking. They're black, with square toes and they have buckles on them, silver square buckles—"

"Go on, lad."

"Well, my clothes are black too. I have black stockings on but my trousers only go to my knees!" John laughed at that bit, so did his dad, just to humour him.

"What else do you see, John?"

"Well. I'm walking very fast. I don't know why and I'm talking to myself, but with words I don't understand."

"Can ya remember any of the words?" asked Michael.

"Well—I remember saying, 'I hate the witch!' or something, then as I'm walking, still looking at my feet, I can hear my heart beating very loudly and I remember saying some foreign words that I don't know or understand!"

"Can ya repeat the words, John?"

John laughed at the thought he would sound ridiculous and he became all coy and silly.

"Oh, go on, tell us what ya said!" Michael encouraged John, "Ah promise ah won't laugh!"

"Well," John went on, trying to recall the exact words, "It doesn't make sense, but I say 'Supeena duces tekem'," and he started giggling all over again.

Michael made a fuss of John, then asked again, "Is there owt else in yer dream ya can tell us about?"

"Well, the next thing I remember is being in a cubby-hole, but not like ours or Nanna and Grandpa's, I'm lying on by back and it's very cold and I feel like I'm going backwards, like when you sometimes play that little game with me and give me a ride on your back at bedtime and say, 'I'm the wind and you're a little feather' and spin me round on your back and then hold me in your arms and lower me onto my bed, it feels a bit like I'm being lowered down, but it's black! There's no light!"

Michael could see John was getting upset and he calmed him.

"It's all right, John, it's only a dream and dreams can't hurt ya. Shhhh," he said stroking his hair.

Helen, meanwhile, came up the stairs to find out what all the talking was about. She sat on the other side of the bed and gave Michael a significant look, as if to say 'what have you been saying! No more now!' then she kissed John, who was very sleepy by this time. Michael did similar and they both stood up, said goodnight to John and turned his bedside light out.

"Ah'll leave yer door open, John, an' ah'll leave the landin' light on too. Yer mam an' me won't be long fer bed oursens."

"Night!"

"Night!" came the reply. They went back downstairs in silence. Helen put the kettle on and Michael sat in his armchair and brooded.

Helen brought in the tea and sat on the sofa, looking at Michael. It was quite a few minutes before either of them spoke. At length, he said, "Ah wonder if we oughtn't tek John ta see a doctor wi' these bad dreams, Helen?"

Helen pondered this, but then said, "It's like you said yourself Mike, all kids have bad dreams. John's no exception."

Michael sipped his tea and was deep in thought. "What's with this stone then?" he asked calmly.

"Look Mike, I don't want to row over this again. It was a bit of silliness on my part! I bought it on a whim! I thought it was pretty. I actually bought it for *you* for your birthday and was going to have it set so's you could wear it around your neck, but I had second thoughts and was going to take it back to the shop for a refund."

Michael looked down, a little embarrassed at that, but he continued, "Why gi'e it ta the lad though? Ah don't understand!"

Helen remembered the leaflet that the jeweller had given her and she went into her handbag to get it. As she was doing this, she started to tell him of the 'supposed' power or influence the stone was purported to have. Michael read the leaflet and listened to Helen's story.

"Load o' rubbish if ya ask me!" he said with more than a little trepidation in his voice. "That's hocus pocus, in't it, lass?"

"Well, no more hocus pocus in an emergency than rubbing a dock leaf on a nettle rash, when there's nothing else around to ease the sting or putting honey on a wound or graze if you've no antiseptic to hand? John was very distraught and I had nothing to comfort him with! He wouldn't, couldn't listen to reason and the stone came to mind! I had nothing to lose by trying it!" her voice was beginning to raise and he could tell she was getting frustrated and angry.

"I just thought it would help, don't' you see? I just thought it might fucking HELP!" and she burst into tears. Michael felt dreadful, as a huge realisation came over him.

"Oh Helen luv, please forgive me? Ah—ah'm sorry lass, ah'm truly sorry. Ah didn't realise—ah didn't understand—"

"And you called me a fucking WITCH!"

"Yes, yes, ah know, oh Helen, ah'm so sorry." And he too started to cry and tried to put his hand on her shoulder.

She pulled sharply away and said, "Just leave me alone!"

Michael knew he had overstepped the mark and that trying to pacify her was useless. He went upstairs and into their bedroom and sat on his side of their bed. They both sobbed audibly in their respective 'rooms'. They needed their own space at that moment to reflect on themselves and each other, but everything would be alright now. The storm had past.

The following day, Helen and Michael were very subdued with each other, but very polite. Breakfast was not an easy affair for either of them, but they both knew in their heart's that the other was feeling just the same. John didn't seem any the wiser of the last evening's 'words' and he ate his breakfast with gusto. Michael thought it was time to make the first move.

"Eighup, John, while you were at school yesterday, me an' yer mam spent the afternoon at a lovely little place just outside o' 'Arragut, called 'Ampsthwaite. It were right pleasant, an' a smashin' place fer a picnic! Would yer fancy goin' there this Sat'day?" and he looked at Helen with a smile as he finished the sentence.

"There's a lovely church an' there's a river right next to it! Yer mam an' me sat on t' riverbank fer a while, an' it were a lovely spot!"

Helen picked up on what Michael was saying and continued, "Yes, it was lovely! AND," she said, "there's a little shop we can get ice-creams and pop!" John clapped his hands with excitement and said that he would love to go there.

"Right then! That's settled!" said Michael, but looking straight into Helen's eyes. They both smiled gently at each other.

"Yep, That's settled!" said Michael.

Subpoena Duces Tecum

A few days passed by and all seemed back to normal with Michael and Helen. One evening, having got John washed and up to bed, Michael was watching his favourite programme, Perry Mason, whilst Helen was sat on the sofa reading a book. During the dialogue of the programme, he heard Perry mention a word that rang a bell with him. The word came again and Michael grabbed a pen and wrote it on the back of the newspaper, that was lying on the carpet next to his chair.

His face had a stern look on it and Helen looked up over her book and said, "You alright, love?"

"Yeah, Shhh—" and continued to write something down. Helen smiled and continued with her book. *Part time sleuth!* she thought to herself. He then reached for the dictionary that was on a shelf in an alcove next to the chimneybreast. He thumbed the pages.

"What is it, love?" Helen asked again.

"Oh, it were a word ah just 'eard on telly, it reminded me o' one o' t' words our John said that he'd said in his dream."

"What word is it?" asked Helen curiously.

"Sounds like 'supeena', ah'm just lookin' it up like.

"Isn't that a law term that's got something to do with either arresting someone or making them go to court?"

"Dunno—" said Michael. He was still looking in the dictionary. "S—U—P—"

"Try another possible spelling—maybe it's S.U.B or something?" she said with interest.

"Subordinate—Suborn—Subpoena—HERE IT IS! Ah' fahnd it! SUBPOENA, pronounced *'supena'*—a written order requiring a person to appear in a court of law—to summon with a subpoena! Bingo! Nah then, what was the other words 'e used—"

Michael searched his memory for the words, "Subpoena duces tekem!" he said, "that were it, subpoena duces tekem!" He looked up 'duces'. "*Duce*—leader, as used of Mussolini—Mmm, ah don't think so. Let's see—*Deuce*—, the two on playing cards or dice. Mmmm, *Deuce*—dated American colloquial, in exclamations of annoyance, THE DEVIL. BAD LUCK!"

They both looked at each other and agreed they didn't like that at all! "No," he said after several more minutes perusing the dictionary, "there's nowt at all like tekem, tekum, tecam or 'owt like that ah can find."

"Well, maybe those other words are law-terms too?" said Helen. "I know, I'll phone my friend Sophie! Do you remember her? She came to our wedding? It was her husband that got a bit merry and tripped over on the dance floor and nearly knocked our wedding cake off the table? Ha ha! We went to university together, she studied law and now works in London for a solicitors company. I'll give her a buzz! What time is it?"

"Quart' t' nine," came the reply. She got out her diary and went to the back pages, where her phone contacts were. She went into the hallway and sat on the bottom stair and dialled the number. *Brr—brrrr. Brr—brrr. Brr—brrr.*

Hello? Came a ladies voice.

"Oh, Sophie? It's Helen! Helen Twigg?"

Oh, Helen! How lovely to hear from you! Goodness me, it's ages since we spoke to each other!

"Yes it is isn't it! I'm not disturbing you, am I? I know it's getting a bit late—"

No, not at all! Brian's out tonight with some of his cronies! They're planning a canoeing weekend up in Scotland and of course, it all has to be thrashed out over a few beers! So I'm on my own, I was just doing some ironing! You've saved me from the rest of the mountain! she said happily.

As it had been quite some time since they had last talked, they spent a good half an hour just chatting and catching up. Michael got back to his telly, but kept an ear on what was being said. Eventually, Helen got to the point and as casually as she could, she said, "Oh, 'tell you what, if I gave you a law-term, could you tell me what it meant?"

Why, yes of course! What is it? You're not in trouble, are you? Ha ha!

"No no, nothing like that, it was just something that came into a conversation with a couple of friends and this term came up and no-one knew exactly what it meant. I thought to myself, 'I know just the person to ask!'"

Fire away! said Sophie.

"It sounds like, 'supeena duces tekem' or something like that," said Helen.

Oh yes, That's 'subpoena duces tecum' Helen. It's a subpoena for production of evidence. A court summons ordering a named party to appear before the court with documentary evidence for something.

"Oh I see!" said Helen. "Well, how interesting! It always sounds a lot more impressive in Latin, doesn't it?"

Ha ha, yes, it does I suppose, but it's tradition, pretty much like in music, it won't say 'fast and lively,' it will say, 'allegro spiritoso' on the sheet music! Similarly, every plant and drug will have its 'true' name from derivatives of Latin or Greek. I found it quite hard to grasp Latin at school and into higher education—hic, hac, hoc, ha ha!

"What does the 'duces tecum' bit mean then?"

Oh well, literally translated, it means, well, let me see, 'duces', to command, I command, 'tecum', to come to, it means 'I command you to come to me at my house or at this place'! she said.

All the while, Michael had been listening intently to this conversation and it made him feel uneasy, if not a little scared. After another hour and a half of chatting, Helen managed to end the conversation with Sophie. After promising to keep in touch and get some dates together for a 'meet-up', they said their goodbyes and Helen put the phone down.

"God!" she said in exasperation. She went into the kitchen to put the kettle on. "Did you catch the gist?" she said to Michael.

"Yeah, ah did. How the hell would John know such words as those? Ah've never 'eard 'em before, 'ave you?"

"Well yes, the word subpoena rang a bell like I said earlier, from the likes of your television programmes, but I didn't know the *exact* meaning."

She made the tea and they sat down on the sofa to drink it. They both sat in silence, staring at nothing for quite some time.

Helen looked with sleepy eyes at the clock on the mantelpiece, which said midnight. Michael was still very much in thought.

"What's up, honey?" said Helen.

"Ah still can't get me 'ead 'rahnd wot John said the other neet, 'e said summat abaht t' thunder callin' 'is name and that summat were in t' room wi' 'im!"

"Michael!" Helen said, putting her hand on his shoulder. "Enough! Let's go to bed! He's a child. Children often exaggerate. They often have invisible friends or enemies! It doesn't mean that our John is any different from any other kid. Just let it go! You'll see, John will grow out of it soon, I promise!"

"Yeah, ah guess so. But how do you explain the Latin words then?"

"I can't answer that, Mike. Memory genes? I just don't know, love. Come on, let's go to bed," she said softly and she took Michael's cup from him and put it onto the coffee table, she took his hand and lead him upstairs to bed.

The Picnic at Hampsthwaite

So after a stormy week, in more ways than the one, a beautiful sunrise rose over Harrogate, early on Saturday morning. Up with the lark, they all busied themselves with the preparations for the picnic. They all had a light breakfast and now, John was helping his mum pack the sandwiches into a big wicker picnic hamper. Michael had raked around in the top of the linen cupboard to find a huge tartan woollen blanket that they often used to sit on, on occasions like this.

The car was opened up and in went all the needs for the picnic, including a couple of badminton racquets and shuttlecocks, a frisbee, a tennis ball, a fishing net on a bamboo cane and a tin sea-side bucket, in case John caught any tiddlers! In went the hamper, a huge tartan flask with tea in it, a few magazines and a book or two. After a moment or two, thinking to themselves about possible omissions to the list of things they needed for the day, they set off for Hampsthwaite.

They had all agreed to take a bit of a spin around the outer villages of Harrogate first, as it was such a lovely morning, so equipped with a map of the area on her lap, Helen had the job of navigator. They set off in the opposite direction of Hampsthwaite and headed through Starbeck and up the hill towards Knaresborough, famous for its beautiful riverside walks, quaint tea shops and its castle, of which the majestic ruins keep a stern watch over the river Nidd from its high, rocky position.

As they went over the bridge, they noticed the entrance to the famous Mother Shipton's cave and the dropping well. The former being a renowned witch or supposed witch, who was born in a cave right next to the dropping well, one stormy night in the year 1488 and who eventually was to have made some of the most profound predictions ever made, the latter being a small cliff in the rocks, right next to the river, where water constantly drips.

Teddy bears, gum-boots and top hats, all sorts of articles are hung on strings at the top of the cliff face, (which is only some 15 feet high) and the water drips on and around them. The water is high in calcium, sodium and magnesium and after a period of time, these minerals solidify around the object and eventually turn it into stone! It is sometimes known as the 'petrifying well'. On through Knaresborough, to Bond End, they took a left and up a steep hill out of the town and onto the country road.

The little village of Scotton came up next, where Guy Fawkes, famous of the gunpowder plot, had spent much of his childhood. Next, the even smaller village of Nidd and then on to Ripley, with its magnificent castle. Ripley castle, the seat on the Ingleby family for centuries, boasts the most breath-taking parklands and gardens, lakes and follies and the flavour of each century and era can be felt everywhere, from the battlements on top of its hoary walls, to the quaint horseshoe shaped weir that is crossed by a little bridge on the nature trail which winds through the adjoining woodlands.

They parked the car just a little way out of the main part of the village and walked the rest of the way. Helen, Michael and John stared with wonder at this place and admired the history, architecture and ambience of the whole area. As they walked along the main road, they passed a stone statue of a wild boar, semi sat, but with its front legs on the ground as if just about to get up from a lying position or else in the last moments of life and about to collapse and expire.

"Ah tell ya what, you two, aren't we lucky ta be livin' in such a beautiful area as this?" said Michael.

"We most certainly are!" replied Helen. "The whole area has an almost magical feeling about it doesn't it? Hey, look!" she interrupted herself, "Look at the stocks on the village square!"

Michael and John followed her gaze and sure enough, an ancient set of stocks was there, at the bottom of the steps of a small stone cross.

"Eighup! We'd best be gettin' some photos of us all in them stocks, don't ya think?"

"Great idea!" agreed Helen and John. Michael got his camera and they all strolled over to the stocks.

"Me first!" shouted John as he raced up to the ancient timbers of the long-past punishment. He put his feet through the holes and folded his arms.

"How's this, Dad?" he shouted with a slightly embarrassed grin.

"Just a mo, ah'm just settin' t' camera," Michael replied and he proceeded to make the adjustments he needed.

As John was waiting for his dad to finish what he was doing, a group of tourists came walking by, all speaking a foreign language and carrying travel brochures, cameras and all the paraphernalia that tourists carry. Many of them stopped and looked at John and had a good laugh. John squirmed with embarrassment and asked his dad if he could get out of the stocks.

"Hang abaht a minute, ah've nearly done, stay there!" John went from crimson to purple as his dad got down into a crouch position with his camera.

Helen, meanwhile was secretly laughing at John, who had gone from the brave to the bashful in just a few seconds. Some of the tourists saw Michael taking the photo of John, so they started to copy his example and aimed their cameras at John too.

"Hey, you do big smile for camera, yes?" said one of the tourist ladies to John.

"That's the ticket, John!" said his dad who was busy snapping away too. "Yer famous nah!" he said to John with a grin.

Soon, the tourists moved on and down towards the entrance to the castle. John ran up to his mum and hugged her, still acutely embarrassed, as he watched the last of the tourists disappear through the castle's gateway.

"My turn next!" said Helen, who did the same as John had done and put her feet through the holes in the stocks. It was John's turn to have a good laugh and he did so with exaggerated intensity, trying to justify his own embarrassment in his own little way. But after laughing so ridiculously loud for a minute or so, Michael was obliged to calm him down with a significant look and a point of the finger, "That's enough nah!"

John immediately fell into line and calmed down. Michael took several snaps of Helen, the last of which, he said to her as he was pointing the camera, "Lean back, wi' yer hands behind ya—yeah that's right, nah face this way," he said as he zoomed in from the side of her, "Nah pout, baby, pout!" he smiled.

She did and a photograph was taken, that remained on their dressing table for the rest of their lives.

They walked down to the weir and looked for just a short while at the outside of the castle, then into the courtyard and at the beautiful old church, right opposite the entrance to the castle. They all agreed that they needed to come here again very soon to explore in more detail. Helen reminded them that this is where the battle was to be re-enacted by the Sealed Knot Society, so it was a definite date in the diary for them.

With that, they went back to the car and set off, out of the village and rejoined the main Ripon to Harrogate Road. They entered the larger village of Killinghall and took a right onto the Otley Road. Not far along, was the right hand turn to Hampsthwaite and down a leafy lane into the village. They drove down the main street and over the bridge, they found a little natural lay-by just past the five bar gate.

Everyone jumped out of the car and all were designated things to carry. Michael opened the gate and let his family through. Closing the gate behind them, they all walked down to the riverside, to the exact spot they had stopped at the last time. The big tartan blanket was set on the grass and all the things they had brought with them were unpacked and ready for the day's shenanigans.

Oh what a glorious day, glorious aspect and setting for a picnic! The sound of the river, babbling over its rocky bed in the shallows, that were closest to where they were sat, the intriguing depths of it, to the further side, where the current was swift and washed the grassy bank that was in fact the edge of the church's graveyard. The trout could be seen jumping out of the water here and there and the calming, gentle sound of the church clock's bells, chiming the time, previously described.

John grabbed his fishing net and made his way to the edge of the river. It was shallow at this side and barely a few inches deep. In the middle of the river, only a few feet away, were a series of 'islands' that one could wade over to and climb onto. They were covered in soft grass and certainly inviting to a young pirate like John! In he went, having taken off his socks and shoes.

"Mind how you go now!" Helen shouted after him, as he went in, ankle deep and with his fishing net in hand.

John stepped into the cold, clear water and had to acclimatise himself to the temperature and he grimaced as his hot feet met the cold water, but within a few seconds, he was in and loving it. Michael took out a small, leather-clad radio from his jacket pocket, the type that was popular in the late '60s and early '70s. He turned it on and tuned into a station that they all liked the sound of.

While John was exploring the islands in the river, Helen and Michael sorted the contents of the picnic basket. Grabbing the cold drinks, which consisted of a few cans of lager, some cola and lemonade drinks, Michael took them down to the river and placed them into the water to keep them nice and cool for when they wanted them. All prepared, Helen and Michael lay back in the sunshine, on their tartan blanket, smiled at each other, then relaxed to enjoy this wonderful day.

An hour or more was enjoyed, with no interruption. Helen and Michael dozing in the warmth of the afternoon, listening to the radio and John from time to time shouting from the river, "I just caught another little fish!" or "Hey, there's another big trout just jumped out of the water near me!"

Helen actually dozed off, only to be awakened by the sound of a drink can being opened. 'Pshhweeee' went the sound and she opened her eyes to see Michael standing over her, with a can of lager in his hand.

"Eighup, lass, ah thought ya were asleep, an' ah didn't want ta disturb ya like! Do ya fancy a cold drink? It's flippin' 'ot, an' ah needed summat cold ta drink!"

Collecting her thoughts, she immediately said, "Oh, yes please, I'm parched! Can I have a cola?"

"No sooner said than done!" he said, pre-empting her request and presenting her with the drink. As this was happening, the church clock was sounding over the babbling sound of the river. 3 o'clock.

"Time fer a spot o' scran ah think?" said Michael, who started to unpack the food they had brought with them.

"John? John lad? Are ya hungry?"

"Starved!" came the reply from John, who was sitting on one of the grassy banks in the river and he came bounding across, like his life depended on it!

Helen served the food. Corned beef and pickle sandwiches, cheese sandwiches, little sausage rolls, scotch eggs, crisps, houmous dip and bread sticks and some flapjack for afters. They all attacked it with a vengeance! It didn't take long before there was nothing left but screwed up bits of tin foil and crisp packets! John went back to the river and his fishing, while Helen and Michael started to throw the frisbee at each other.

Seeing the fun going on the bank, he waded out of the river to join them. The frisbee soon gave way to the badminton racquets, then onto the tennis ball. At last, they all flopped onto the grass and declared that they were ALL the winners! Michael then suggested that they packed the things away and look around the church that John had heard about, but as yet had not seen.

They all agreed that it was a good idea. It was getting late in the afternoon and the sun was showing signs of maturing into a gold and red hue through the trees, although its warmth had by no means diminished.

They packed all the things away into the car and then made their way back over the bridge and into the church yard. The church basked in its serenity and loveliness, shafts of light filtering though the cypress trees and casting waving sunbeams onto the old headstones and the pristinely kept grass and hedges. They once again entered the church, but this time, they had the advantage of the camera.

Michael took several shots, here and there, of various points of interest, from the nave to the chancel and of the gorgeous, sumptuously carved pews and choir stalls. They all slowly strolled outside, closing the church door behind them as they did so and went back into the graveyard to have a look around. They all went their separate ways, for no reason at all, it was just the way it happened and looked at the headstones. Michael noticed that several of the stones had pentagrams inscribed onto them, which he thought very odd in a Christian churchyard. He continued to wander around, looking to left and right.

"Ee, thissun's an old 'un!" said Michael, turning round to see Helen, who was bent over, reading a similar legend on another stone. "Elspeth Critchley, born 1687, died 1709. She weren't too old then!"

"Yes, here's one too, how sad is this?" said Helen. "Peter Godfrey, dear son of Matthew and Mary, born 1705 and died 1707! Poor little soul!" said Helen. They compared a few of these piteous headstones and memorials, then a shriek came from John, who was at the side of the church.

"Mum! Dad! Come here! I have found my own grave!"

"Daft bat!" Michael shouted to John as he and Helen went to see what he meant.

They went hand in hand to the side of the church, where the oldest headstones seemed to be, presumably from when the oldest of the churches stood on this spot. John was stood directly opposite the side entrance of the church, where two tall trees were growing side by side and produced a natural archway of branches and thickly growing leaves. There was a little pathway between these trees and John was brushing away the dust and dead leaves from the inscription of a stone just at the foot of the left hand tree.

"Look, Daddy! It's got my name on it!" said John, jumping with excitement. Helen and Michael didn't share the enthusiasm, as they both looked at the weatherworn stone that John alluded to.

"By the cringe!" exclaimed Michael, as he got closer to the headstone and examined it. Sure enough, the legend did indeed say 'JOHN TWIGG. BORN 28 JUNE 1517. DIED 26 AUGUST 1566'. The stone was so old and worn, it was only by virtue of the fact that the sun was in exactly the right spot and angle, they could make it out at all!

"How come it has my name on it and he's got the same birthday as me!" asked John with a puzzled look.

"Daft bat!" Michael said again with a grin. "How can it be you? You're stood 'ere wi' us! Besides, this bloke were alive over 400 year ago!"

Helen chipped in too, "Yes, love, I admit it's a bit funny seeing your own name ANYWHERE, but on a headstone, how odd!"

"Especially wi' a surname like 'Twigg'! 'Can't say as ah recall any o' me ancestors ever livin' up 'ere, 'far as ah know, we're the first!" added Michael.

"But it IS such an unusual name, isn't it? I wonder if we could do a bit of research on it?" said Helen, pondering the thought.

"Let's see if there are any other headstones with 'Twigg' on them!" said John, who suddenly felt important and they all split up and searched the entire graveyard, but to no avail, the one they had found was the only one that bore the name of Twigg.

As luck would have it, the vicar they had met on their last visit to the church came through the church gate and was making his way to the main porch and he saw the three of them poking around the graveyard.

"Ah. Good afternoon to you! Goodness me, you really must love our church, mustn't you?"

Then a thought came into Michael's head on the instant.

"Oh, er, yes, good afternoon, vicar, 'nice ta see you again, we had come fer a picnic wi' our son 'ere," and he introduced John to the vicar.

John, having been brought up to show respect and manners at all times, looked up at the imposing size and height of the vicar and offered his hand. The vicar instantly bent down slightly to take John's hand and said, "Well, hello, my son. I'm very pleased to make your acquaintance!"

John went a bit coy again and grinned inanely. Michael continued, "Yes, we 'ad a nice picnic on t' other side o' t' river, an' we 'ad said to our lad 'ow nice the church were like, so we decided to show 'im arahnd a bit."

"Splendid!" said the vicar, "are you enjoying the church and its lovely grounds young man?" he asked.

"Oh yes, thank you, sir and guess what! I have found a gravestone with my name on it!"

The vicar roared with laughter, as they all did. Michael was one step ahead of events here, the conversation was going exactly the way he had hoped.

"Yes, it's a bit unusual ta say the least! We were wonderin' if you 'ad a record of all the burials 'ere or some kind o' register o' the families an' all that?"

"Why, yes, we do indeed! Show me the headstone in question," said the vicar. As they all proceeded to the side of the church, the vicar said, "Ah, now then, a lot of these stones date back to a couple of churches ago, so as to speak. Let me see the dates." And he stooped to peer at the inscription. "It's very worn with age, isn't it, but yes, I can just make it out, 'JOHN TWIGG. BORN 28 JUNE 1517. DIED 26 AUGUST 1566'. Yes, the problem is that records of burials weren't kept at this church until the year 1603, so this ancient stone tells you everything that there is to know about it! I'm sorry!" he said with a smile of consolation.

"Ah well, never mind," said Helen, "we'll just have to draw our own conclusions as to whether or not 'John Twigg' was one of our ancestors!"

"You may be able to find out more if you go to your local library?" said the vicar. "In fact, I do believe there are detailed registers and archives to be found in London somewhere, I can't recall who and where now, but I do wish you luck with your research! Do come back and let me know how you get on? Good day to you now!" he said with a cheery smile and a wave of his hand and he walked down the pathway next to the church and disappeared from sight around the front.

Michael went back to the grave with his camera and took several photographs of it, from different angles, to try and get a good image of the legend. That accomplished, they all agreed that it was time to head back to the car, so they slowly walked back over the bridge, where John picked up a stone and threw it into the river below him, *'Splooosh'* and he watched the circles on the water radiate in all directions.

"Come on, you!" shouted Helen, as they were getting into the car. "It's time to go!"

Back home again and they were all in high spirits. They all helped to unload the car and get the things into the house. John offered to take the playthings into the garage and Michael took the big tartan blanket back into the linen cupboard. As they had had quite a substantial picnic, nobody was what could be called 'starving', so Helen suggested hot dogs for supper. Naturally, Michael and John jumped at that, as they would, being 'lads'!

"Can I have cheese dogs, Mum?" John shouted.

"Eighup, worra good idea, me too!" said Michael.

"OK, you two, you've got about 15 minutes before they're ready!" she shouted to them both. Helen poured away the flask of tea that they didn't drink in the end and smiled that they had taken it anyway! She set the garden table, as it was still such a lovely evening and she got a nice bottle of cold Liebfraumilch from the fridge, for Michael and herself to enjoy with the hot dogs.

She found some individual little strawberry cheesecakes in the fridge and she thought that they would be nice after the strong flavour of the Frankfurter sausages. She hunted out brown and red sauce, mustard and put those onto the table. She had already rough cut an onion and that was sizzling in a little butter in a small saucepan. All was ready and she called them to 'come and get it'.

As the sun went down and having finished their supper, they watched the little pipistrelle bats flitting low over the garden, hunting for insects. The sky was slowly growing red-orange and reminded Helen of the colour of a 'Tequila Sunrise' drink. Nobody wanted to go back inside, but needs must and they had already given John extra licence for staying up, so reluctantly, Helen took John into the house for a quick shower and then bedtime.

"Can I say goodnight to daddy again when it's time for me to go to bed, Mum?" asked John.

"Of course, you can, sweetie!" replied Helen kindly and kissing him gently on his cheek.

"Now then my big boy, hands up for dumplings!" she said to him to get him to lift his arms, so she could get his T shirt off.

Meanwhile, Michael was still sat in the garden, relishing the gorgeous aspect of their garden at this fleeting time of the evening. He poured himself another glass of wine and sat back in his adjustable garden chair to soak in the moment. He could hear Helen and John laughing from time to time, through the open bathroom window. All seemed perfect and Michael closed his eyes for a moment and smiled to himself that the stresses of the past few days seem to have been ironed out and that normality had at last come back to their lives.

He reproached himself for his silly outbursts and comments to the woman he adored so much, his beautiful precious wife, his very best friend, his Helen. He got up out of his chair and went into the garage to get a couple of paraffin lamps. The sun was gone, but it wasn't dark yet, but soon would be. He also thought that the glow from the lamps would give a nice warming sort of feeling.

Soon, Helen brought John down to say goodnight to his dad.

"Night-night, lad!" said Michael, giving John a bear-hug and pressing his lips to his son's belly, blew a big 'raspberry' against his skin.

John giggled with delight and said, "Goodnight, Daddy, sweet dreams!"

"An' sweet dreams ta you too, poppet!" he said.

"Daddy, will you be the wind and me be a feather, like you used to do when I was little?"

"What? A big hunk like you, wantin' ta be a feather, an' carried up' t' stairs? Ya mean like this—" and without another word, he jumped up and whisked John off his feet and threw him onto his back.

John squealed with delight as his dad whirled round and round like someone demented, saying, all the while, "Ah'm the wind, an' you're the feather!"

Round and round he span, Helen howling with laughter all the while and they made their way into the house and up the stairs. Michael still making noises representing the 'whooshing' of the wind, they came into John's bedroom and then Michael grabbed John from his back and with his strong arms, lifted him into the air, as he did when John was a toddler and with silly guttural noises lowered him onto his bed, with a bump, just as he used to do all that time before.

John was panting and laughing and said, "Oh daddy, thank you!"

Michael was still making silly noises and placed his hands on his son's tummy, he bounced him up and down on the bed, like he was bouncing a ball and with the rhythm of the bounces, he playfully said, "Goodnight, goodnight, goodnight goodnight!"

John was positively glowing with happiness. Helen was still laughing at the scene and now it was Michael's turn to have the boyish, inane grin on his face.

Having got John settled, they went back into the garden. The paraffin lamps looked so inviting! But Helen shivered slightly as the cool night air hit her and she went back into the house to get a cardigan. They sat and talked about the day and the fact that John had been such a good boy, especially at Hampsthwaite, having found a headstone with his name on it!

Michael couldn't help himself but to admit that he still had misgivings about these events. Helen had to agree, but they both agreed to just wait and see what happened. The little pipistrelles flitted around about them. From their respective garden chairs, they held hands and enjoyed the last embers of the evening.

Nocturnal Ramblings

The night wore on and Helen and Michael were now ready for bed. The wine had helped their general feeling of well-being and they were a lot more comfortable in the knowledge that John seemed more relaxed too. So they headed upstairs and had a quick shower, brushed their teeth and turned in. Michael woke up at about three o'clock, to the sound of John talking to himself in his bedroom. He got out of bed, went to John's bedroom door and listened.

For a good minute, all was silent, then came some muffled talking, but Michael could not make out what John was saying.

"He's dreamin'! Daft bat!" said Michael to himself, but he lingered there, just to ensure all was well, especially after all had been said and done a few days ago.

Then he heard John shouting in a loud, imperious voice, "And I further put it to you that you DID NOT make such a journey and that you did instead make your way to the dwelling of Mary Randall and forcing your way in, you did steal the sum of one shilling and four pennies!"

There was a deafening silence and Michael could scarcely believe what he was hearing. Then John shouted again, "I SAY YOU DID!—Your Honour, I have no further questions. Your witness!"

By this time, Helen had heard the shouting and noticing that Michael was not next to her in bed and that perhaps he and John were having some kind of argument. She joined Michael on the landing, just outside of John's bedroom door. Michael instantly put his finger to his lips and Helen took the hint. They both listened, straining their ears. Nothing but silence.

Helen whispered, "What's going on?"

"Ah don't know, lass! Ah heard 'im talkin' to 'imsen like, an' just thought 'e were dreamin' but he's been comin' aht wi' some rayt gobbledygook, like 'e were in a law court or summat!"

"How bizarre!" whispered Helen, "he's obviously dreaming, but—"

She was interrupted by John shouting, "The King does indeed hold such practices in the highest abhorrence, Your Honour! I put it to you that you hexed Mistress Randall's rooster to death, making its flesh inedible!"

Silence again. Helen and Michael just looked at each other with their mouths open wide! There were no other sounds from John, except the sound of him breathing. They gently opened the bedroom door and stared at their son, who seemed to be sleeping peacefully. John stirred and was obviously conscious of their presence.

He opened his sleepy eyes and said in a tired voice, "Hello, Mummy, is everything OK? Why are you in my bedroom? Is it time to get up?" and he rubbed his eyes.

"Yes, everything's fine, sweet pea," she softly said. "We'd just come to say goodnight!"

The lie worked and John said, "Goodnight, Mum; goodnight, Dad!" and with a smile, he turned over and went straight back to sleep.

They closed John's door and went back into their bedroom. As they got back into bed, Michael said, "Ah'm worried abaht this, Helen, 'e were talkin' like an attorney or summat. Do ya think he needs a psychiatrist or summat?"

"No, no, I'm sure it's not that sort of thing, it's almost like he has memories! But of what and how? He's just a little boy!"

Michael thought for a while and then said, "Do ya believe in reincarnation like?"

"Well, I don't know, Mike. I really don't, but I DO believe that this must be a passing phase. John is a perfectly normal, healthy little boy. Do you have any memories from your dim distant past, Mike?"

"Well, me earliest memory is sittin' under t' kitchen table, while me mam were doin' t' spin-dryin' an' as ah were watchin' t' water comin' aht o' t' spin-dryer, ah remember havin' t' urge t' push, an' then crappin' me nappy like! Ha ha!"

Helen desperately tried to suppress her laughter so as not to wake John up again. They were both slowly coming to terms with the fact that their son was special at best, a little 'odd' at worst, but in a fascinating way.

"There's summat wrong though, Helen! Ah still reckon we ought ta tek 'im to a child psychiatrist or someone that can answer why he's speakin' abaht things 'e can't possibly 'ave any knowledge abaht! Ya do hear of things like 'possessions' an' such, an' it gives us the shivers!"

Helen reluctantly agreed that for their own peace of mind, they should investigate further. Helen got out of bed and went into her underwear drawer and got the citrine stone.

"Oh, don't start THAT agen, lass!" said Michael, as she unwrapped the stone from the tissue it was in.

"Michael! It cannot possibly do any harm! It did seem to help him the last time. Just humour me!"

Michael didn't argue and Helen went into John's bedroom and carefully put the stone under his pillow. When she returned, they talked and talked on the subject until the glow through the curtains told them that dawn wasn't far away, so they agreed to talk more on the subject when an appropriate moment came, when John wasn't around. Then they cuddled up and fell into a deep sleep.

The sun was streaming through a gap between the bedroom curtains and as Helen slowly surfaced, she heard the bedroom door, as it slid over the carpet and in came John, who was already up, washed and dressed and he brought in a tray with a couple of glasses of orange juice on it. He had been into the garden and picked some buttercups and had put them into an eggcup, next to the orange juice.

"Good morning, Mummy! Did you sleep well?" came the cheery welcome.

"Oh, erm, yes, I think so, darling."

"I brought you some orange. I thought you might like it!" said John, with a broad smile.

"Oh, bless you!" said Helen. "Michael, wake up! John has brought you a glass of orange juice!"

"Eh? What's that ya say?" said a very sleepy Michael, "what time is it?"

"It's 10 o'clock!" said John, "and I was getting hungry. Can we have breakfast soon please, Mummy?" he asked pleadingly.

"10 o'clock! By the cringe, Helen, why have you made me lie in fer so long?" said Michael digging Helen in her ribs.

"Cheeky bugger!" Helen said in response and squeezed his kneecap under the sheets.

John turned to walk out of the bedroom, but Michael said, "Just a minute, lad, how d'ya feel this mornin'? Did ya sleep alright like?"

"Yes, thank you, Daddy, but when I woke up, I found mummy's stone under my pillow. I didn't take it, honest!"

Michael and Helen looked at each other, not knowing what to say for the best.

"Don't be silly, sweetie, nobody said that you took it, that's fine, just forget about it! It was probably me, I maybe left it there when I was making your bed!"

"Oh, that's alright then, Mummy! I put it back in your knicker-drawer while you and daddy were still asleep!"

With that, he went back downstairs, humming to himself as he did so. They sipped at their orange juice, then after a moment or two, Helen said, "Just a minute, how did he know that I had hidden the stone there?"

She smiled at Michael, who was grinning from ear to ear at her.

"You've got a son with a knicker-fetish ah think!" he said.

Helen stood up, grabbed her pillow and playfully hit him with it, again and again.

"Whoa! GBH! Eighup! Gerroff! You just wait, ya little vixen!" he said, trying to protect himself from the blows. This completely relaxed the atmosphere and he grabbed the pillow from her hand, but before he could apply a similar punishment to her, she ran out of the bedroom shouting, "Last one to the bathroom's a rotten egg! And she bolted the door behind herself and smugly shouted, *'ner ner na ner ner!'* to him from the other side of the door.

"You just wait you!" said Michael as he went back into the bedroom. Helen smiled as she heard him mutter from the bedroom, "Just you wait! Ah'll be 'avin' YOU!"

Helen booked an appointment with the G.P. for John. She had to use the utmost tact and stealth of word to explain to John why she was taking him to the doctor.

"But I don't feel unwell, Mummy! Why are we going to see a doctor?" John asked.

"Well, it's not that you are unwell, love, but you often have bad dreams and your dad and I just wondered if the doctor could give you something to help you to sleep easier. Tell me, John, can you remember dreaming about anything last Saturday night, you know, the day that we went to Hampsthwaite for our picnic?"

John thought for a while, then said, "No, not really, but I do remember you and daddy coming into my room for something."

"Nothing else?" asked Helen.

"I remember finding your stone under my pillow, but I put it back where it belonged, but I tried not to wake you up though!"

"How did you know where the stone belonged, John? I don't ever remember telling you where I kept it!"

"Erm, I don't really know, I just sort of 'knew' it was there. Sometimes when I'm lying in my bed and you and daddy are downstairs watching the telly and I can hear you talking and laughing, I feel lonely and one night, I just felt that the stone was calling to me, I can't explain, I just knew it was there and it made me feel safe and it comforted me. It was almost like it was *your* voice telling me to go to it. I promise I didn't move it, I just unwrapped it and held it in my hands. It told me that everything was OK and that I should go back to bed and go to sleep, so I wrapped it back up again and put it back and went to bed."

Helen was quite alarmed by John's story and made mental notes of it all.

"This voice that you can hear, is it a lady or a man talking to you?"

"No, it's not a man or a lady, it's just sort of like when you are reading a book, as you read the words, you can hear them inside your head, but not a voice. Do you know what I mean? Sometimes I think that it might be your voice though, Mummy." And John smiled up at her, hoping that he had said the right things. She bent down and gave him a cuddle.

"There's my big boy!" said Helen, forcing a smile, but secretly feeling very uneasy.

Helen and John arrived at the doctor's surgery a good 10 minutes early. Having checked in with the receptionist, they sat down on a large brown sofa. Helen picked up a magazine and John found a big box of toys. Even though the toys were for slightly younger children than him, he busied himself with a little wooden jigsaw puzzle, the sort with very large pieces, for infants to play with.

Within just a few minutes Helen heard, "Mrs Twigg?" and Dr Forsythe was stood at his surgery door and he welcomed them both in.

Dr Forsythe was a very professional looking man of about fifty. He was of the 'old school' and with impeccable manners. He wore a black pin-striped suit, white shirt, black bow tie and beautiful gold cuff-links. He had receding grey hair and a pair of glasses that he invariably looked over as he was talking to someone as if they were a pair of pince-nez. He also had a lovely, soothing, gentle and mild Scottish accent.

"Hello, Mrs Twigg and hello to you, John, my how you have grown!" he said with a friendly smile. "Now then, how can I help you today?"

"Well," said Helen with a degree of uneasiness, "John has been suffering from some rather unpleasant dreams lately and I was wondering if you could just see if there was anything you could suggest or something you could give him to help him to sleep?"

"Oh dear! Bad dreams, eh, John? Well now, let's see. Can you tell me about them? Is it always the same dream? Tell me all about it."

John looked a bit worried and shy to respond to the doctor, so Helen helped by saying, "Why don't you tell Dr Forsythe what you told me and your daddy? Remember, about the cubby-hole?"

"Oh yes, I remember that," said John and he told the doctor all about that part of the dream. The doctor listened politely, making notes all the while.

"I see. Can you tell me how often you have these dreams?" he said looking to Helen as well.

"Oh, sometimes once or twice a week, other times, it may be many weeks until the next one," said Helen.

"Tell me, are you in the habit of having supper?"

"Well, yes, sometimes—" came the answer from Helen.

"Do you eat much cheese, say, on toast or anything fatty, like cream or the like? Does John like a cup of strong tea or coffee at bedtime?"

"No, not really, he likes hot chocolate or malty drinks before bed. Sometimes, we'll have cheese on toast as you've said, but it's not every time. Why, is that wrong?"

"Oh, goodness me, no!" said the doctor, "it's just that certain foods are a little harder to digest that others and they can have a distinct effect on what you dream about!" The doctor took some more notes down and then looked at Helen and said quite firmly, "John isn't on any form of medication is he? Anything at all?"

"No! Nothing at all, doctor!" The doctor took John's temperature and looked into his eyes, ears, nose and throat. He smiled at John and said, "Do you snore?"

John just went coy and giggled and said, "No!" in a silly voice.

They all laughed, as the doctor was still writing in his jotter. He then looked at John, smiling and with a kind and sincere face he said, "Always remember John that we all dream. All of us! Some are happy, some sad and some scary! But they *are* only dreams and they cannot harm you. Always think of happy things as you are going to sleep! Think about the nice things you did during the day, the things that make you laugh, the people you love, like your mum and dad! Tell yourself you are going to have happy dreams and there is no place for bad dreams in your head!"

John smiled at the doctor, who offered him a sweetie from a little white bag. John's eyes lit up and chose a toffee in a wrapper.

"I do hope that's OK, Mrs Twigg?" the doctor said significantly to Helen.

"Yes, of course!" she replied.

The doctor asked several more questions, the importance of which Helen could not see, but it was obviously important to the doctor. Then the doctor stood up and said, "John, there's some toys here in this box. Would you like to play with them? I just need to talk to your mummy for a minute or two, is that alright?"

"OK!" said John, who after seeing the toy-box, wasn't really bothered how long they talked for! Gesturing to Helen to go into a little side room, he asked her to sit down.

"What is it, doctor?" she said with a worried look on her face.

"Oh, don't be alarmed, I just needed a word with you out of earshot from John." He thought for a moment, as if choosing the words to say to Helen, but at length, he said, "John is just fine, I'm quite sure, so don't be alarmed. All children have nightmares or bad dreams, it's a very common thing. When it comes to certain pubescent girls for instance, all sorts of things can apparently happen! Have you heard of poltergeists?"

"Yes, I have! You're not saying that—"

"Calm yourself, calm yourself!" said the doctor, with a reassuring laugh. "I merely asked you that because there genuinely are things that medical science just does not understand yet, poltergeist activity is one of them. Children can literally overnight, speak a foreign language or be brilliant at mathematics. They can predict all manner of things that may happen in that day. I can remember a similar case many years ago, when a young mother, pretty much in your situation, came to me with her toddler daughter, who had developed some truly extraordinary, er, 'talents', shall we say.

I remember the mother saying that her little girl said to her one morning, "Mummy, doorbell!" The mother had heard nothing, but the next moment, the doorbell rang. A few days later, the little girl said, "Mummy, mirror fall!" and the next moment, a mirror that had hung on their dining room wall for years, crashed to the floor, breaking the glass and damaging the frame beyond repair.

Yet another story, the little girl was playing in her Wendy house, when all of a sudden, she burst out crying and said, "Nanna gone to sleep!" and she was inconsolable. The lady in question found out about a half an hour later that her mother-in-law had passed away at the precise time the little girl had said!"

"Fascinating!" said Helen with a forced smile.

"Look, Mrs Twigg, I am merely trying to show you that John is NOT unique and that this type of phenomenon does occur from time to time. As I have said, all because it may not be recognised throughout the realms of medicine or psychiatry, this type of thing does come about from time to time."

Helen seemed a little more comfortable with the doctor's explanations and encouragement.

"I'm sure everything will be just fine, Mrs Twigg. I do find John's case quite fascinating and I do assure you that I have his welfare well and truly in my focus. If you feel uncomfortable in any way, you must promise me that you will give me a phone call, day or night now and I will be with you to help, I assure you. I know that this must be quite an alarming thing for you all to be experiencing, but I feel confident that it will pass. There are of course, many avenues open to us, if the symptoms persist or get worse, but I feel confident that they will not Mrs Twigg!" and he held the back of her hand with a reassuring gesture.

"Thank you, doctor, that is indeed a relief and a comfort to know," said Helen. They left the little consultation room and went back into his surgery. John was still playing quietly with the contents of the toy-box.

"Hello!" he said cheerfully, while Helen sat back down and the doctor sat back at his desk. After writing for a while, the doctor took his spectacles off and said, "I'm going to prescribe you a mild sedative for John. Give him two teaspoons-full just before bedtime. Make sure you try to keep suppers bland, no cheese, no sauces or spicy food. I think this should do the trick young man!" he said ruffling John's hair.

As they were getting up to leave, the doctor said, "I don't think there's anything to worry about unduly, Mrs Twigg, many children go through a phase of bad dreams and nightmares. They are unpleasant, but they do invariably go given a little time. Finish the course of medicine I have prescribed for you and see what happens. Naturally, if there's no improvement, come back and see me again, but I hope that this will do the trick."

Most of this conversation was for John's benefit, so he was in the picture of 'what they had talked about' in the consulting room and Helen acknowledged the glance from Dr Forsythe.

"Thank you, Doctor," said Helen.

"Yes. Thank you, Doctor!" said John.

"Goodbye," said the doctor, as he saw them out of the surgery. With that, he called for his next patient and Helen and John left the practise. They popped along to the chemist shop just down the road from the doctor's surgery, to get the prescription made up.

Helen handed over the prescription document and the lady behind the counter said, "I'm afraid it may me about 20 minutes, we are extremely busy, I *am* sorry!"

"Oh, that's OK," said Helen. "I need to go to the butcher's anyway, John, so we can do that now! Would you like some sweeties?"

"Oh, yes please, Mummy!" came the eager reply and off they went to the local butcher, about 5 minutes walk from the chemist.

Helen asked John if he was alright and that he was happy with what the doctor had said. John was completely nonchalant about it and said, "Yes, I like Dr Forsythe, he's a nice man and he doesn't scare me and he doesn't make me want to cry."

"That's good!" said Helen. "And did you understand what the doctor was talking about when he was saying that dreams are not real and that they can't harm you?"

"I'm only frightened when I *have* the dreams, I'm not scared now!"

"That's the ticket!" said Helen, considering that as a good answer and it showed her that their counsel and that of the doctor, may just have worked.

"Mummy, could I please borrow your stone, so that I can have it near me at bedtimes, to stop the bad dreams coming?" John said very matter-of-factly.

"Why, yes! I don't see why not, do you think that it really helps then, John?" and again, John replied in the same way as before, "Oh, yes. You can have it back during the day."

"Oh, that's kind of you!" said Helen smiling. Helen got the meat she required and John was happy and smiling, clutching a little bag of jelly babies as they strolled back to the chemist's to collect the prescription. Having got John's medicine, they strolled home.

Back at the house, John ran as fast as his feet would carry him up the side of the house to Michael's den.

"Daddy, Daddy!" he shouted.

"Eighup! Na'then, big lad! How'd ya get on wi' t' doctor then?" said Michael, wiping his hands on a rag, then lifting John high into the air and giving him a kiss on his cheek.

"Oh, fine, thank you! I got some sweets, Dad! Would you like one?"

"Oh, no ta, ah've just 'ad missen a cup o' tea an' a sticky-bun abaht half an hour ago, ah won't be eatin' me tea if I 'ave owt more wi' sugar in it ha ha! Come an' see worram doin' in me den!" he said to John and led him by the hand into the garage.

"Hiya, Mike!" came the greeting from the kitchen door, as Helen was putting the meat into the fridge.

"Eighup, lass! Everything alright like?" he replied.

"Yep, I'll fill you in with the details later on!" said Helen with a tone in her voice that Michael could not mistake.

Helen made a simple meal of lamb chops, mashed potatoes, peas and some white cabbage with a little cracked black pepper and a nice onion sauce. As John had been off school that afternoon, his friend Luke came round to see if John wanted to play for a while. John was thrilled and asked pleadingly if it was OK with his mum and dad.

This had actually been arranged that morning, when they had taken John up to school. They had met Luke's mum in the playground and said that John would not be there in the afternoon and it was Helen's idea that Luke came round to play if he would like to, after tea. As Luke only lived three doors up the road, they thought it would give John the opportunity to forget about his visit to the doctor, as they didn't know at the time, what the outcome would be and that John may have felt a bit unhappy. Luke's mum also thought it was a great idea and had agreed whole-heartedly.

"Tell ya what, John, would ya like me ta get the seesaw aht that ah med for ya?" said Michael.

"Oh YES PLEASE!" came the reply from both boys. Michael had made John a seesaw that not only went up and down, but span around at the same time, like a round-about. Michael did just that and within a few minutes, the boys were whirling round and bobbing up and down on the seesaw.

"Mind ya don't mek yerselves sick bi goin' rahnd too fast, eh, lads!" laughed Michael. This little plan to get John out of the house and well away from earshot had worked a treat! John's attention was well and truly on his friend and he would not be coming in for a while.

They both sat on the sofa and Helen told a detailed account of what happened at the doctor's surgery. Michael listened with interest but still with a look and feelings of misgivings.

"What are you thinking, Mike?" she asked.

"I dunno really," said Michael heaving a deep sigh. "Ah just can't get me 'ead rahnd this at all! Ah expected the doctor ta come aht wi' summat a bit more positive like, y'know, send 'im to a psychiatrist fer kids or summat or a parapsychologist, ah dunno! Ah mean, POLTERGEISTS! What the piggin' eck's all that abaht? Is our lad 'aunted or summat? Bugger me, do we need ta get a priest ta exorcise 'im like?"

"Mike, calm down, love," said Helen gently and got out of her chair. She put her arm around his shoulder to comfort him. "The doctor knows what he is talking about dear, he hasn't made any haphazard decisions. You must remember that he has to explore all possibilities and make his judgements from them, one at a time. He has given us the utmost assurance that John is in no danger and he will grow out of it.

Put yourself in the doctors shoes, how would you feel if he went in from the other end and had said, *Oh yes, we'll send John down to the parapsychology department at Oxford University and perform all sorts of tests on him and eliminate all the possibilities,* just imagine how we would be feeling about that! Yes, I agree, it's extremely odd that we heard him talk in such a way, like a solicitor, but he may have even heard that from one of your television programmes that you enjoy, you know, like Perry Mason?"

"Nah, ah don't think so. 'E were talkin' abaht shillin's an' pennies. Perry Mason never said 'owt abaht shillin's! Plus the fact that John were speakin' in Queen's English, 'e weren't speakin' in an American accent, was 'e?"

Helen reflected on that, but determined to bolster Michael, she continued, "Yes, I hear what you're saying, but remember what the doctor had said? There are things that medical science just doesn't understand, YET! Think about leprosy. Once upon a time, it was a killer, a scourge and something that may have been dealt by the gods or devils! Today, it's almost eradicated from the face of the earth. Look at magnetism. You can't feel it or see it, but we now know what it is and how it comes about? Once something is understood, it is no longer a mystery or the doings of ghosts or demons? It becomes science fact from science fiction!"

She stared at him with pleading eyes, hoping that her words were ringing true with him. After a long silence, he looked at her and again gave a heavy sigh, but he smiled and said, "Yeah, ah guess you're right, lass. Why our lad though?"

"Because he's special!" Helen said placing her hand on his cheek and smiling sweetly at him.

"OK, we'll try this medicine aht wi' him an' see what 'appens."

A Timely Break

John and Luke played on the seesaw for an hour or more, before they ran into the house, tired, red-faced and sweating.

"Can we have something to drink, Mum?" asked John, still trying to catch his breath.

"'Course you can, love! What would you like?"

"Please may I have some cherry cola?"

"Of course, you can!" she said and she poured John a large tumbler-full of it and gave it to him. "Now, Luke, what would you like love?"

"Please may I have some orange?"

Helen smiled and said, "Of course, here you go!" and she poured him a tumbler-full of that. There was silence as the thirsty boys drank and it didn't take long! The glasses were handed back to Helen and they both thanked her and made their way back out into the garden to play again.

Helen shouted after them, "Remember, time is pushing on now, Luke will have to go home fairly soon!"

"OK!" shouted John from the garden. Helen thought she'd give them another half an hour or so before she wound things up.

Meanwhile, Michael had been pottering about in his den and was just tidying things away from his afternoons work. Helen went in with a cup of tea for him.

"Oh, cheers pet!" he said as he took the mug from her.

"And what has my lord and master been creating today then?" she said sidling up to him and slipping her arm around his waist.

"Oh, ah've been busy! Most o' t' mornin' ah were workin' on another batch o' wooden toys, 'cos the toyshops that ah supply say they can't get enough of 'em! Ha ha! 'Suits me ah guess! This afty, ah were workin' on the traction engine fer me brother, John, see? It's comin' on in't it?" and he showed her what he had achieved so far.

"God but you're talented aren't you?" she said with a loving grin.

"No, no, no, no, no, ah'm not gonna disagree wi' ya! Ha ha! But ah DO admire yer honesty like! Ha ha!"

"Talking of which, Mike, it's YOUR birthday next Friday and you haven't given me a clue as to what you would like as a prezzie!" she said.

"Aw, don't be so daft! The one an' only present ah'd like, is YOU! You are what ah fancy most lass, an' ya know it!"

"OK," said Helen with a wry smile, "how about stockings, suspenders or maybe a babydoll, devil-red lippy and nail varnish and perhaps a dab of Chanel No 5?"

"By the cringe, lass, that's the sort o' prezzie that's gets me sap risin'!" he said drooling at her and eyeing her up and down. She beckoned him to come closer and he responded immediately.

He was about to devour her as she leaned against his work bench, with a 'come-hither' look in her eyes, she immediately played the tease, which Michael absolutely adored and she said, "Uh-uh tiger! Wait until your birthday!"

Michael nibbled her neck and she loved it, but she said, "Steady on now, don't open your presents until your birthday, you naughty boy!"

Michael grinned and said, "Then don't open t' chocolate box wi'out offerin' one!"

They stared into one another's eyes for a moment and then she said, "Alright, big boy, just one—later, when John has gone to bed!"

After a tender kiss, Helen went back into the house and Michael finished tidying up his den. Soon, Helen shouted, "John! Luke! It's time to come in now! Luke, I'll walk you back home love."

"Coming, Mummy!" came John's reply, as he and Luke span around a few more times on the seesaw-come-roundabout. The boys at last came into the house, once again all hot and panting. Helen had pre-empted the request and gave them both the same drinks as before and they downed them in one.

Gasping for air, they both said as one, "Oh, thanks!" and put their glasses down on the kitchen work surface.

Helen smiled at them and was happy that John seemed to be so relaxed with his friend and especially after the visit to the doctor. All seemed calm. If not resolved, then calm.

"Right, Luke, come on now! John, say goodbye to Luke."

"Thanks for coming to play with me tonight, Luke, it was ace wasn't it!"

"Your dad is ace, John! My dad couldn't build a seesaw that's a roundabout too!"

"Yeah! My dad's the best dad in the whole world! He can make anything! He can make you a helicopter if you want one! He can make a ship! He can make you a—"

"Eighup, you two!" interrupted Michael, "ah'm not THAT good y'know! Ha ha! C'mon, yer mam's waitin' for ya t' tek Luke 'ome. Are ya ready to go, Luke? Got all yer bits and bats?"

"Yes, thank you, Mr Twigg, thank you for letting me play with John and letting me play on your seesaw! It's really wonderful!"

"Ha ha, nowt o' t' sort lad, ah'm glad ya like it!" said a humble Michael.

"Come on, you two," shouted Helen from the front door, "it's time to go," and the boys followed her out.

"Thank you again, Mr Twigg! You're brilliant!"

Michael smiled and repeated to himself what he had said out loud to Helen earlier in the evening, "Gosh! Ah won't disagree wi' ya, but ah do admire yer honesty, lad!" and he chuckled to himself.

Then, on reflection, he took some pride in Luke's remark, that something that he had produced with his own hands, had made someone, nay, a child happy.

Helen and John were back in a matter of minutes. When they opened the front door, they could hear Michael on the phone to someone. They kicked off their shoes and put on their carpet slippers.

"Can I watch some telly before bedtime, Mum?" said John.

"Well, not for too long, we need to get you showered and into bed soon."

Helen's words had not left her own lips, when she felt a shudder go through her—'bedtime soon!' Would the medicine work? Would he have more bad dreams? Would she have to resort to the citrine stone? Would Michael go crazy if she DID get the stone? What if John came out with strange oratings again? All these things came to her in that instant and she suddenly felt extremely uncomfortable. She tried to expel these feelings by making herself think of other things.

"What is there on telly that you fancy then, John?" she shouted from the kitchen to the living room, where John was already sat in his dad's chair and looking at the TV guide paper.

"Oh, Perry Mason is on in 10 minutes!" he shouted back.

"Oh GOD!" she murmured to herself, "it HAD to be THAT, didn't it!"

Meanwhile, Michael was talking to his brother John on the phone and they were arranging the details of the Sealed Knot's visit to Ripley Castle to do their re-enactment of the famous siege of the castle.

"Ah thought ya said it were in three weeks' time, lad?"

Helen heard him say. "Oh, no, that's OK, ah'm sure our John'll be pleased wi' that! What time 'ya comin' up like?" There was a few moments silence as Michael waited for an answer to his question, "That'd be great!" he said at length. "Ah'll talk to Helen, an' we can all get together an' 'ave a chin-wag! It'll be good ta see ya, lad, ah can't wait fer it! Yeah—yeah—OK—ta'ra fer now, see ya!" and Michael put the phone down and came into the living room.

"You sound in good spirits, Mike!" said Helen,

"Oh, aye! It were mi brother, an' ah've got some news for ya both, regardin' the battle o' Ripley Castle that we all talked abaht a few weeks ago at me dad's birthday, remember? Well, it's next Sat'day afternoon! Ah thought 'e said in abaht three weeks' time like! Are you two up fer it? D'ya fancy watchin' a real live battle?"

Both Helen and John were beside themselves. John instantly forgot about Perry Mason and said in an animated voice, "Daddy! Daddy! I can't wait to see uncle John in his uniform!"

Helen joined in and said, "Oh, yes! That will be great! We don't see much of John and to see him in 'action' will be just fantastic! Don't forget to take your camera Mike!"

"Hey, that ah won't, lass!" he said with real enthusiasm.

"Hey! That can be part of your birthday present too, big fella!" said Helen with a clap of her hands.

"Aye! Ah never thought o' it like that!"

Over tea they all sat and enthused about what Saturday would bring. John asked, "Are there children taking part too?"

"Ah guess so son, but ah don't know what they do like!" said Michael.

"I think I'd like to do that too!" said John, "I like the old fashioned guns and all the clothing and all the cannons and all the things we saw in the photographs that uncle John showed us last time he came to see us! I'm a bit too young to use a gun, but I could put the bullets in their guns for them and I could polish their leather boots and things like that!"

"Ha ha, steady on, lad!" laughed Michael. "They might 'ave people doin' those things already y'know!"

"Oh, but I love guns! I love my grandpa's airguns! He said we could play with them next time we go to their house, didn't he?"

"That he did!" said Helen, "And your grandpa will keep his word I promise you, John."

"One day, I want to be just like you, Daddy and I will make myself a gun that really works!"

"Eighup! 'Wanna be like me? D'ya wanna be a miner, an work dahn a pit, diggin' aht coal like?" laughed Michael.

"No, silly daddy! I want to be able to make things just like you and help you when you're very old and I can help you do the things that you'd be too old to do and I can use all your lathes and your drills and saws!" John said with a big silly grin.

"Ahh, that's ma boy! A chip off t' old block you are, lad! One day, all me tools will be yours, an' ya can make what ya like!" John's eyes lit up.

"When will that be, Daddy?" he asked with the enthusiasm that only a little boy of his age could do.

"Na'then! Steady on, lad! Ah'm not dead yet! Ye'll 'ave ta wait a while yet tha' knoas!"

They all roared with laughter and even John realised what he had said and laughed the loudest.

"Aren't I a silly bean, Daddy?" and he giggled like the little boy he truly was.

"Eighup, John, it's time fer bed! D'ya fancy being a feather, an' me the wind?"

"Oh, yes please, Daddy! I love it when you do that for me! WEEEEE!" John shouted.

Helen smiled and whispered in to Michael's ear, "You certainly WERE the wind last night *you*, I don't know what you'd been eating, but GOD! The duvet was on the wardrobe this morning!"

"Cheeky bugger!" he said as he grinned back at her, "an' ah s'pose women don't fart at all then eh?" and he slapped her bottom with a *'whoomp'* on the impact.

"Ouch! You sod!" she said laughing. "You do realise you've just forfeit your 'chocolate' you so fancied!"

Michael dealt her a little-boy-hurt look and stuck out his bottom lip.

"Oh yeah! Soz! Ah'll kiss it better then," and without another word, he grabbed her and bent her over his knee and blew a huge raspberry right on her buttocks.

Helen howled with laughter and tried to splutter out the words, "Get off—you silly sod—"

"What's that ya say, lass?" Gerroff? Ah'll show *you* gerroff!" and he spanked her like a naughty little girl across his knee.

John cried with laughter and shouted, "Mummy! You look so silly!"

"Eighup! This is yer mam's fault, ah nearly forgot abaht you, John lad!" and he pushed Helen off his knee and she landed on the rug in front of the settee.

"You PIG!" she shouted at him, still laughing.

"Oh! A pig now, am ah? Eighup John, tek note, 'ear an' listen ta what a poor bloke like me 'as ta put up wi'! Don't get married, lad! See what ah've gorra put up wi'?"

"MICHAEL TWIGG!" Helen shouted nearly breathless, "No chocolates for you at all!"

"Ahh, don't ya be threatenin' me wi' that, lass! Ah may just retaliate an' keep all me peanut brittle to missen! Two can play at THAT game tha' knoas!" They were all still in hysterics as Michael whisked John off his feet and threw him onto his back, ready for the ride upstairs.

"Ah'm the wind—an' you're the feather—" said Michael as he whirled around the living room, John squealing with delight all the while. Helen got to her feet and just looked at the pair of them, enjoying their silly but deep and personal bond, the bond of a loving father to his son.

Helen smiled and she said to herself, "Oh Michael, how I do love you. You are so special. You are truly one in a million."

Up the stairs they went, Michael still making *'whoooosh'* noises to John, who was still giggling as he enjoyed the ride.

"'Ere we go—dahn onto t' bed we go!" and he held John on his back in his big hands and lowered him onto his bed with a deliberate bump. John was laughing as his dad kept bumping him up and down on the bed, like a ball.

He was still laughing and trying to catch his breath as he heard Helen calling, "Come on now, time to brush your teeth."

John went into the bathroom and did just that and after getting showered and changed into his pyjamas and after being given two teaspoonfuls of the medicine he had been prescribed by Dr Forsythe, he was ready for bed. As with all children, there was a little bit of chatter, in an effort to stretch out the time that his mum and dad would stay with him, but encouraged to go to sleep with the promise of an exciting day at Ripley Castle next Saturday, John felt happy and nicely sleepy.

"Goodnight, Son," said Michael, kissing him on his forehead, "sleep tight!"

"I will, Daddy!" came the reply, through a very large yawn.

Helen also kissed John gently and said, "Yes, darling, sweet dreams," and she slipped the citrine stone under his pillow. John snuggled down and felt the stone and a broad smile came over his face, even though his eyes were now shut.

"Night, Mum," came the sleepy response. Helen smiled and looked at her son for a moment, as she left the bedroom and she hoped and prayed the medicine would do the trick, aided of course by the stone. Helen and Michael went back down the stairs and enjoyed a cup of tea and they chatted about all and sundry. Naturally, much of their conversation revolved around John and his situation, the medicine, the doctor, the words John had used, the whole issue.

As time wore on, Michael said, "Well, ah guess we should turn in too, lass, we've all 'ad busy days, eh?"

Helen agreed, but with a sultry smile she added, "Wanna open the box of chocolates then? I can't temp you with just one little nibble then?"

Michael grabbed her hand and pulling her up the stairs he said, "You bet yer sweet aspidistras, you can! Ah can't wait ta see what's on the menu, ah know ah'll be spoilt fer choice!" and they raced upstairs and took a shower, giggling and whispering nonsenses to each other.

John smiled to himself, only just conscious that his mum and dad were coming to bed and it comforted him. After a while, he heard them turn off the bathroom light and tiptoe across to their bedroom and close the door behind them.

The Siege of Ripley Castle

Saturday couldn't come quickly enough and John was up with the lark. Once again, he took some orange juice up to his mum and dad, in an effort to get them up! They were absolutely fast asleep when he went into their room, having politely tapped at the door, but got no response, so he gently opened the door to see them lying there, bedclothes half on, half off the bed. He saw that they were both naked and he became acutely embarrassed, so he tip-toed out again and went back downstairs.

He made as much noise as he could, in the vain hope of waking them up. As luck would have it for John, a bus had come down the street outside their house and couldn't get between two cars that had parked on opposite sides of the street and without much consideration to other road users. The bus could not get between them and had no option but to sound its horn. *'BEEEEEP—BEEEEEEP'*

The horn was sounded several times before anybody did anything about the obstruction, but after about five minutes of the beeping, the owner of one of the cars came outside, muttering and cursing to himself, still in his pyjama bottoms and moved his car a little further down the street. All this, of course, had awakened half of the street, including Helen and Michael! John heard his dad stir. Michael was cursing and swearing himself as he got up to go to the bathroom. This was John's cue to take the orange juice up again.

"Good morning, Mummy!" he said bright-eyed and bushy tailed, to which all he got in response was a very sleepy "What? Who? Oh, yes, good morning love, what time is it?"

"It's ten to seven!" came the enthusiastic answer.

"OHHHH—GOD!" said Helen, flopping back onto her pillow and covering herself up for decency. Michael had heard John and had wrapped a towel around his waist and came back into the bedroom.

"Eighup, John lad, what are ya doin' up at this time o' t' morning?"

"Have you forgotten, Daddy? We're going to see Uncle John at the battle today!"

"Cripes, yes! But not until 2 o'clock, ya daft bat!" he said with a smile.

"Eighup, Helen, the lad's brought us some orange ta drink! Thanks, John, we'll be gerrin' up soon, just let me an' yer mam wake up a bit an' we'll be wi' ya!"

"OK dad, see you soon," said John and he went back downstairs to watch some kid's programmes on the telly.

When the time came, they all set off for the day's special event. They approached Ripley, through Killinghall, on the main Ripon road. Even though they were an hour early for the opening of the pageant, the roads were crammed full with cars, parked randomly along the way, much to the disgust of Michael. He noted that the biggest and most ostentatious of the cars were parked, basically exactly where they pleased, breaking all the rules and laws and he commented on these huge petrol-guzzling monsters with the inevitable private registrations.

"Look at THAT thing!" he said, pointing at a huge 4 by 4, "Look at the illegal registration on it!" and they all noticed that indeed, the registration plates were contrived to spell someone's name.

"Sad gits!" said Michael. "It's one thing 'avin' wealth, but another shovin' it up the noses o' folk that don't!" he said. "Who are they tryin' to impress like? Themselves? Ah bet that *that* one's owned bi' one of these blonde bimbos that wears a pair o' sunspecs on 'er 'ead, but never wears 'em as sunspecs, just because it looks 'cool'!" he vociferated.

"Hey, steady, Mike!" said Helen. "We're out to enjoy ourselves! I know how you feel about these things, but hey, just let it drop?"

"Yeah, ah know, it just does me 'ead in when 'alf the world is starvin' ta death, an' we get brainless buggers like them who are obviously worrying themsen's ta death abaht the unemployed!"

"Mike! Enough! People are entitled to spend their money on exactly what they see fit! Some of these people may never have worked in their lives and they don't know any different!"

"Well, bloody good fer them! A couple o' weeks dahn a pit might just mek 'em see what true life us all abaht!"

"ENOUGH!" shouted Helen. "You are a wealthy man now and you need nothing! Why are you going on about this?"

Michael snapped back, "Because ah know what poverty is! Ah know what it's like ta 'ave nowt ta eat. Ah know what it's like ta 'ave me arse 'angin' aht me pants. So did me dad an' mam, an' by their own 'ard work an' sweat, they dragged themsens up an' aht o' t' gutter—sorry, lass," Michael said after a moment's reflection, "it just meks me blood boil when ah see such 'in yer face' arrogance o' such individuals wi' nowt ta do all day long but shove their wealth in other people's faces—people not as fortunate as you an' me lass. Ah promise ya, if ah 'ad a million quid, ah would still not do owt as smug an' gloatin' as that!"

Helen thought for a moment and could see in Michael's face and demeanour, what he actually meant. No silver spoon in his mouth at birth, yet with some of the motor cars around here, it was obvious that many had been born with a 100 piece solid silver dining set in theirs.

They eventually found a parking space, purely by luck, as a car pulled out from where it was parked. Michael swiftly reversed into it before he lost the chance to someone else. As the car's engine was turned off, they immediately heard the sound of military style drumming coming from the direction of the castle and occasional shouting, as if orders were being directed at soldiers. John was very excited and couldn't wait to get out of the car.

"Mind yourself, John!" said Helen, "There's lots of traffic here, mind you don't open the door onto the road! Get out onto the footpath!"

John unbuckled his seat belt and scrambled across the back seat to the near side of the car, just as his mother had asked him to do.

"Come on, Mum and Dad! Hurry! We might miss something!"

"Don't be daft!" laughed Michael. "It's only midday, an' things don't start until 2 o'clock!"

They all walked slowly towards the castle and the noises were getting louder and louder. Then a small band of men dressed in clothing of the period just about to be re-enacted, came strolling past. John eyed them up and down and he grinned. He admired their costumes, which were so foreign to his eyes.

They had woollen jerkins of serge, coloured in beiges and russets. They all had large white blouse collars and broad-brimmed hats (made of similar materials to their jerkins) and one or two of them had large silver buckles around them. All had broad leather belts around their waists and baldrics over their shoulders. One of them had a bugle hanging from his baldric, made from genuine horn. They wore knee-length breeches, buttoned just below the knee, dark grey hose and leather shoes, simply fashioned to be just pulled onto the feet.

As they approached, they saw John staring at them and one of them shouted, "We give you good day, young sir! Hast thou come to enjoy the marvellous spectacle about to ensue this day?" John grinned and coloured up and tried to hide behind his mother. "Pri'thee, do not be bashful!" said the man.

Michael said to John, "Answer the bloke, lad, 'es only askin' ya if yer ready ta see the battle later!"

"Erm—*yeah*—" said John in a silly and embarrassed voice.

"By my halidom, thou art a timorous bairn!" he said with a huge belly laugh. "Me thinks there are dainties and sweet-treats to enjoy in some of the tents on the green!" he said winking at John, who still stared at him with a silly grin.

Michael and Helen smiled at the man and thanked him for 'playing the part' for John. The man smiled back in acknowledgement, then said, "In good sooth, we must be off to ready ourselves to do battle! Fare thee well, friends!" he boomed and with a flourishing wave from his broad brimmed hat, which he had taken off to salute them, he bowed, one foot forward and swept the hat almost to the ground.

With that, the little troop of men carried on past them, laughing and generally saluting all and sundry that came their way.

"What a lovely thing for them to do!" said Helen.

"What a great way to welcome people as they arrive!" Michael agreed and felt a happy surge of confidence that today, would indeed be a wonderful day out.

As they approached the castle gates, they saw several women, dressed in costumes of the same period as the men they had just seen. The inner square of the castle courtyard had a few gaily striped tents, in reds, blues and whites. On top of each tent was a long narrow flag, fluttering in the breeze. Some of these women were selling all manner of souvenirs from the Sealed Knot Society, including programmes and little items of memorabilia, like miniature musket key rings and note pads and pens with their own logos on.

Others were busy making things as would have been in those days. Some were knitting or weaving; some were tatting or making cough remedies from herbs and plants. Helen, Michael and John all looked with fascination at what was going on. They bought their tickets and a programme of events for the afternoons entertainments and they made their way into the castle grounds and they all stood with open mouths at all the hustle and bustle of the actors.

There were mounted Parliamentarian soldiers on well caparisoned war horses, in their knee length riding boots and spurs, with helmets and face-guards, gauntlets, breastplates and white, broad collared blouses and leather under-jerkins. They thundered by, behind a safety cordon, all the way around the perimeters of where the battle would take place.

There were pike men and foot soldiers, as well as countless infantrymen. Officers from both camps, in their fineries and plumes in their felt hats were walking nobly around, as if surveying the territory. Little groups of rival soldiers were taunting each other with derogatory shouting across the grounds.

"A pox on your King!" came the gibe from a few Parliamentarian soldiers to a troop of Royalists.

"And may Cromwell rot in his own iniquitous venom!" came the retort.

There was time to take in all the exhibition tents, with all the other crafts and foods on offer, there was even a cook-tent, making the food that would have sustained the soldiers in the field of that time. Yet another tent had some officers in their smart uniforms, both Parliamentarian and Royalist, cordially inviting people to join up with or subscribe to, the Sealed Knot Society. There was a little shop near to where they stood, selling ice creams, so they all got into the queue and looked at the billboard with the varieties of ices for sale.

"What d' ya fancy, you two?" asked Michael. They all looked at the board.

"Please may I have a 99 with a flake, Daddy?"

"And I fancy a mivvy!" said Helen.

Michael ordered what they wanted when it came to his turn to be served and he chose a vanilla tub with a little wooden spoon for himself. Suitably supplied with the ice-creams, they wandered back to the main viewing area, in the field behind the castle.

A more picturesque setting or more convivial atmosphere could not have been hoped for! The sky was blue, fluffy white clouds here and there and the sounds of the drums and trumpets calling their respective men to arms, was enthralling. The crowd slowly made their way to the perimeter ropes, pushing and shoving to get the best vantage points. The Twigg family were quite lucky; they found a place at the centre of the 'arena' and well and truly staked their claim for the viewing point. John was totally in awe of what he was seeing and commented at this and that as it was happening.

"Look, there's a big cannon being brought in by a horse! Look! There's another one!" Helen and Michael were also watching with the same enthusiasm.

Dozens and dozens of men-at-arms came into the field. All the while, the deep and hypnotic sound of the war-drums was beating out rhythms to the troops. The braying horses instinctively knew that this was their time to 'show off'! The occasional shot of a pistol or musket was heard, presumably to heighten the enthusiasm of the huge crowd now gathering. The atmosphere became electric, almost as if a real battle was about to begin.

Through the din, Michael shouted to Helen, "Ah wonder where our John is? Ha ha, ah bet 'es in 'is element wi' this!"

Helen just nodded and smiled as the troops and officers came around on foot or horseback, looking exactly like they must have done over 300 years ago, right down to their accents and slight beards and moustaches. Things started to slow down, the troops and pike men assembled, the foot soldiers now in position, the cannons and halberdiers were waiting. Soon, all was silence. All that could be seen were rows and rows of pikes, soldiers, horses and the plumes and feathers on the hats of the officers, waving in the breeze.

Without a moment's notice, came an ear splitting *'BOOOM'* from one of the huge cannons at the far side of the field. It was answered by another *'BOOOM'* from the retaliating force at the other end of the field. Hundreds of people put their fingers in their ears. General consternation ensued. Parts of the audience laughed, some let out a cry of surprise at the deafening roar of the cannons. Children cried. Children laughed.

On the field, a forest of pikes was brought to a fighting position and a tremendous roar from all the men at arms was heard. The air was just full of the sounds and atmosphere of a battle that came straight out of the history books and it was right there before everyone's very eyes! John had his fingers well and truly stuck in his ears, but was none the worse for the noise of the cannons, the concussion of which, made your cheeks shudder and your skull vibrate!

There was mayhem on the field! Trumpets were blowing, cannons roared, muskets were being fired and shouting from the troops filled the whole area. The war horses thundered by the crowds and orders were being screamed in all directions. The gun-smoke from the cannons and muskets almost obliterated the scene from time to time and the heightened excitement from the watching crowd was almost palpable.

The foot soldiers, halberdiers and pike men all clashed together with realistic ferocity. Volley after volley came from the ranks of the musketeers. The smell of the hot sweating horses, here coming close to the crowd and there galloping into the middle of the skirmish. Everyone in the whole field was now transported back in time to a true battle between the Royalists and the Parliamentarians.

The crowd, including the Twiggs, were totally transfixed at the spectacle. There was so much to see all at the same time! Cameras were snapping away by this time all around the spectator area and Michael wasn't an exception! He was busy snapping here and there, smiling all of the while and John was completely in awe of everything, then out of the thick smoke, came a huge war horse, straight to where they were stood and towering over them, in all his Parliamentarian regalia, was uncle John, with sword in hand, his horse excited and its nostrils flaring and it whinnied loudly as he pulled the bit into its mouth to stop it where it was.

Michael recognised his brother instantly and took the most fantastic photograph of him in full action! The crowd absolutely loved this and they all vied for a position to get a photo of this truly magical sight.

"I give you good day, brother-mine, God willing, we shall overcome these scurvy knaves!" he shouted above the din.

"Ya can't lose, lad!" shouted Michael, with immense pride that the crowd around realised that this magnificent beast was indeed ridden by his own brother! Then John pulled at the bit of his horse and it whinnied loudly once again as it raised its huge body and front legs above the crowd to turn around, then John spurred the animal on and it galloped off back into the mêlée.

Oh, the pomp and majesty of the whole event was just breath-taking! The drums were beating all the while and the trumpets blasted signals to the troops. And when it all eventually came to a conclusion, the crowd were totally overcome and were clapping and cheering, some almost in tears with pure emotion at this fantastic event.

As the clapping was at its deafening height, the words "God save the King!" could be heard from a hundred voices of the Royalist soldiers. Then a salute of 20 or more muskets was fired simultaneously, to mark the end of the event. Again, the crowd went wild with delight and enthusiasm. There was a long period of continuous applause and the 'dead' here and there on the battlefield got up and collected their things like helmets, swords, hats and so on. They too gave a bow to the roaring spectators.

One or two 'casualties of war' came out of the field, with bloodied noses and black eyes, but all still smiling and clapping each other on their backs, which was a relief to the nearby crowds and a reminder that it *was* only a re-enactment!

Eventually, the crowd started to move away from the field. Over the public address speakers, that were all around the area, on high poles, came information about the castle itself and of the facilities on offer all around the area. Many people went into exhibitions within the castle, displaying magnificent collections of armour and weapons, like crossbows and longbows, swords and pistols, muskets and clothing. Others sat in the gardens and enjoyed a much needed cup of tea! Still more strolled about the lake or chatted enthusiastically with the all too eager soldiers about the re-enactment they had just witnessed.

Many younger people were asking dandy officers or muddied foot soldiers how they might join the Sealed Knot, having been so impressed with what they'd seen. Helen, Michael and John wandered outside the castle, to get some fresh air and allow their ears to stop ringing from the roar of the battle. All of them were absolutely full of the experience and they exchanged all sorts of comments of their favourite bits and saying to each other, "Did you see this or that bit!"

They passed the village stocks and walked over the cobbled square to an ice-cream shop. They had already had one a piece earlier, but with the weather still very warm and dry, they all felt the need for something cold. John fancied another cornet, but Helen and Michael bought a can of fizzy orange each. None of the above described lasted very long!

At length, Michael said, "Shall we see if we can get ta see our John?" to which Helen and John thought that was a great idea, although Helen said, "I would imagine he's got lots to do before he can socialise, Mike, he'll have his horse and all his riding equipment to sort out; plus, we'd be hard pressed to find him amongst all the others and I wouldn't imagine we'd not be allowed into the field where they are camping."

They strolled up through the village and then left, onto the Pateley Bridge road. They could hear the shouts and laughter of the actors in a field to the left hand side, not far away from where they were, so they carried on along the footpath. They saw a few people taking photographs from a five bar gate that overlooked the camp, so they too went to see what could be seen. When they arrived at the gate, they could see the size of the camp and hundreds of men, women and children, all dressed in the clothes of the time, milling around the gaily coloured round tents and marquees which constituted their camp for their stay at Ripley.

As luck would have it, they could see John about a hundred yards away, talking to another Parliamentarian officer. Michael cupped his hands to his mouth and shouted John's name, but John couldn't hear over the general noise of the camp. He shouted again, this time, John heard him and after a moment he had finished what he was saying to his friend. John came trudging across the field towards them, still in his uniform and regalia, but carrying his steel helmet under his arm.

"Eighup, John! That were quite summat else, lad!" said Michael as he offered his hand to his brother. John took off his gauntlet and took Michael's hand and shook it enthusiastically and then he leaned over the gate and kissed Helen on her cheek in greeting. He then bent down and put his hand through the gate to shake little John's hand.

"Hiya, Uncle John! You look wonderful in your costume! I watched you ride up to us and I could see your horse's teeth when it made those noises at us and I watched all the soldiers and all the men with long sticks and the men with the guns and the big cannons that went 'BANG!'," and he clapped his hands as the last word left his lips.

"Ha ha, I'm really pleased that you enjoyed it, John," said his uncle.

"We ALL thought it was marvellous, John!" said Helen, "and you coming out of the smoke like that towards us on your horse, was just like something from a film! It was incredible!"

Michael totally agreed and said, "Ah thought ya were gonna run us dahn lad! Ha ha, ah've never been that close to an' 'orses nostrils when they're fair flairin' like that! Ah cud 'ave shoved a pint pot up 'em an' not spilt a drop!"

"Ah, he's called Hercules! He's magnificent, isn't he?" said John, "But a more gentle creature you couldn't wish to see, but he's also a terrible show off, he's good looking and he knows it! He just loves playing to the gallery. He really comes to life when there's an audience!"

"Well, you both certainly put a show on fer us!" said Michael. "In fact, the whole thing were fantastic! Ah never thought it'd be like that! Are ya gettin' changed, nah? Do you all get into proper clothin' after a battle like?"

John put on his imperious Parliamentarian voice again and jokingly said, "Pri'thee upset me not, lest I should kick thee in the codpiece! These are indeed 'proper' clothes you impudent, scurvy knave!"

They all had a good laugh at that. Then Michael said, "Well, ah guess we ought ta be pushin' off an' let ya gerron wi' yer kit cleanin' an' such. Can we meet up fer a pint later, John?"

"Hey, that would be just great!" said John. "We all gather at the local pubs in Killinghall in the evening. We get there about 4:30ish. Why not come and join us all? I promise you a warm welcome from my comrades here!" he said with a knowing grin. "Get here if you can or have a mind to!"

"Ta lad, we just might do that!" and they shook hands again and John gave Helen another kiss on her cheek.

As they were about to walk away, little John shouted, "Uncle John, can I stay with you and play with some of the children I saw here? I promise I'll be good and I'll do whatever you say, but please, can I stay? Mum, Dad, can I stay for a little bit longer with Uncle John?" Helen smiled and thought for a moment, as did Michael.

"Oh, I'll be good, Mummy!" said John with such an earnest expression.

"Aw, what the heck! Is it alright wi' you, John?" Michael asked and Helen agreed with the sentiment, saying, "I'm sure he'd love to do that. Is it possible? Do you have rules about that sort of thing?"

"Well, no, I don't think there is and yes, it would be great to have my nephew see some of the 'behind the scenes' of Sealed Knot! Master John Twigg, thou art cordially welcomed into the realms of the victors of the mêlée of the said Ripley Castle! Would'st thou care to see the inside of the victorious camp of the Parliamentarian army?"

Little John didn't understand a single word of that, much to the delight of the three adults.

"Are you sure that's alright, John?" asked Helen, biting her bottom lip.

"Yes, of course!" came the reply. And without another word, little John was whisked up by his uncle, from under his arms and lifted over the five bar gate and into a world that existed hundreds of years ago.

Michael said, "OK, John and thanks fer that, we'll 'ave a bit of a wander and a fresh-up at 'ome, an' we'll see thi' abaht five-ish. Where 'ya gonna be?"

"We'll be at the Greyhounds Inn in Killinghall," said John, "that's where most of the Parliamentarians hang out. The Royalists go into the Three Horseshoes on the other side of the road. It will be fun for everyone, I promise! You can get a superb meal at the Greyhounds; they do the most amazing steak in ale pies!"

So waving, Helen and Michael turned to stroll back into Ripley and uncle and nephew walked into the Sealed Knot enclosure.

Little John was completely swept away with the sights and smells of the camp. The battle over, he was shown around all the tents of friends of big John and saw some of them in various states of undress, cleaning their clothing or polishing their weapons.

"Hi, Phil!" said big John to a musketeer, who was sat in his tent, jerkin off and just in his big baggy blouse and breeches on and, who seemed to be having problems with his musket.

"Oh, hi, John, how's it going? Good bash this afternoon, eh? The crowd seemed to enjoy it, didn't they? Hey, who's this then?" he said smiling at little John.

"Ah! Philip o' Wharram, allow me to present to you, my nephew, John the younger!" said big John, with a wave of greeting from the one to the other.

Picking up on the vernacular, Phil responded immediately and stood up to welcome his young visitor, "I give you good day, young master John! Verily, I welcome thee to our humble encampment! Pri'thee, do excuse the state of my habiliments, for in truth, I was rounded upon by the noxious enemy who have vexed my thoughts and have rendered my musket mute!"

Little John giggled and had his usual inane grin at a situation like this. Phil and big John exchanged a few comments about the afternoon's battle and congratulated each other on the performance.

All the while, little John was staring at Phil's musket and at length, asked, "Excuse me, sir, may I hold your firelock?"

Both Phil and big John stared at each other dumb for a second and then little John carried on, "I just want to see it for a minute? May I hold it?"

Both men could see no reason why not, but Phil said, "You do know it's not a toy and it does weigh quite a bit? How do you know the word 'firelock'?"

"Oh, I just know it!" said little John, who was not perturbed by this and held out his arms to receive the musket.

"It's bigger than you!" said big John, laughing at him. Little John held the musket on his knee and could scarcely lift it up, but he stared at the mechanism for a while and tried to cock the hammer. He didn't have the strength. Phil came to the rescue and cocked the weapon.

Little John looked intently at the mechanism and at length said, "You won't be able to fire this weapon, because the frizzen has been bent and the flint won't spark correctly and if the spark is weak, the powder in the pan won't be ignited!"

Phil and John just stared at each other in amazement.

"John?" said his uncle, "Tell me how you know so much about muskets! Have you learned about them at school or do you have a friend whose daddy might be with the Sealed Knot Society?"

John replied casually, "Oh, no, I just know somehow. I don't really know how. I remember dreaming about them when I was just a little boy!"

There was deafening silence for a good few seconds whilst Phil and big John tried to think of something to say to break this atmosphere. At last, Phil said, "Well, young man, we need new blood in our ranks and a cadet like you with such knowledge of firearms would be invaluable!"

"What does invaluable mean, sir?" John asked enquiringly.

Of course, that simple question just answered everything. He was just a little boy with a limited grasp on sophisticated words, so how on earth did he know about words that were associated to a weapon that has been redundant for nigh on three centuries?

As tea time approached, there was a stir around the camp for food! Some of the women were cooking on camp fires and some 'cheated' a bit and were cooking on paraffin or camping-gas stoves. The delicious aroma of bacon, fried onions, burgers and a whole mixture of cooking-smells filled the air. Both uncle and nephew John and Phil, were still deep in happy conversation about the Sealed Knot and it was only the whiff of cooking that brought them all to a sudden stop!

"What time is it, Phil?" asked big John.

"Erm, half past four," he said, looking at his twentieth-century watch from under the cuff of his seventeenth-century blouse.

"Right, John! That's our cue to meet up with your mum and dad!"

"Oh, goody!" said little John. "I'm getting hungry! I've only had two ice creams since breakfast time!"

"See you, Phil, I'll talk to you later," big John said, with a very significant look towards little John, who was busy admiring some of the other paraphernalia in Phil's tent.

"Yes, see you later!" said Phil, "It was nice to have met you, young John and thank you for showing me what was wrong with my musket!"

John just went all coy again and said, "Oh, that's alright, I hope you can fix it!"

With that, they walked out of Phil's tent and made their way to the gate and onto the footpath that lead them the mile and a half or so to Killinghall, for their rendezvous with Helen and Michael at the Greyhounds Inn.

The footpath along the main road to Killinghall, which normally would be almost empty of pedestrians, was a hubbub of the Sealed Knot members, walking both to and from Killinghall. They were all chatting animatedly to each other and shouting across the busy road, in greeting to friends on the other side. John held his uncle's hand all the while and felt quite important that he was being seen with all these strangely clad people.

It was a real treat for the motorists, who waved, sounded their horns and shouted greetings from their car windows at these ghost-like revellers. Trucks sounded their air-horns as they thundered by and even cyclists shouted such things as "Good luck!" as they went by. When they arrived at the Greyhounds Inn, there were all denominations of the Sealed Knot folk both inside and outside the establishment.

Foot soldiers, pike men, civilians, men and women, boys and girls, officers in all their finery, all mingling with each other, from both regiments. Some were sat on the cobbled area to the front of the Greyhounds, in full view of the public house directly opposite, the Three Horseshoes, where there were yet more of them sat out on the footpath right against the main Ripon to Harrogate road!

The atmosphere was friendly and happily uproarious, with mock taunts from both sides of the road, but not as to be considered a disturbance of the peace by any means. For the tourists and locals alike, the 'Sealed Knotters' wallowed with pride in their apparel and played to the gallery with their period accents.

"How likest thou the taste of steel true to the King, varlets?" one Royalist musketeer shouted across the road, raising his broad brimmed hat in condescending acknowledgement to a group of Parliamentarians on the other side.

"By my faith, beaten as you most soundly were, it is obvious that thou hast not lost thy sense of humour, ha ha!" shouted a Parliamentarian officer. Many a jovial taunt went back and forth in this way throughout the early evening.

The respective managers or landlords of these establishments were by no means sorry at the fact that they had been ascended upon by these unusual characters, quite the opposite in fact, there was not a seat or dining table left in either place and they were slowly drinking the cellars dry and the kitchens were hard pushed to meet the demand for their meals! Both pubs had run out of pint glasses and the actors were using their own leathern drinking mugs, which all added to the wonderful atmosphere.

Inside, Helen and Michael were waiting and had managed to get a table for four earlier on before the crowds started to come in from Ripley. Big John went in through the front entrance of the Greyhounds with little John, holding his hand. He smiled and chatted to left and right with his comrades. Michael had seen them come in and made his way to the bar, which was completely lost behind all these uniformed revellers. He beckoned to John to come to him at the bar, as trying to shout over the noise was futile.

"What d'ya fancy, John?"

"Oh, a pint of lager please, Mike," came the reply.

"And you John?" he said to his son.

"Please may I have some lemonade?" Drinks all round were bought and they made their way through the crowded lounge to the table where Helen was sat. She stood up to greet the two of them and hugged them both fondly.

"Cheers!" said Michael.

"CHEERS!" came the response from all and they clinked their glasses. Big John took a deep draught of his, after the afternoons events, he was thirsty and he nearly polished off the whole pint in one go!

"Hey, John, you were dead right abaht the steak pies, we've seen 'em come aht o' t' kitchen, an' they DO look grand! Ah think we'd best be 'avin' one o' those a piece, don't you, Helen?" and she immediately agreed.

They perused the menu anyway, just to see what else was on offer. Little John asked if he could have scampi, but the adults all agreed that the steak in ale pie, with chips and peas sounded just what was needed after a rumbustious day. Helen got up and ordered the food and bless her, she came back with another pint for big John, whose eyes lit up and he rubbed his hands as she put it on the table in front of him.

"There you go, big lad, another pint of 'neck-oil' as they say hereabouts."

"Ah Cheers sis'!" he said with a broad smile.

The general atmosphere was lively and convivial. The day had been enormously enjoyable for everyone, performers and spectators. The food was excellent and discussed by one and all in the pub. All the while, however, big John was still wondering at his nephew and how he knew so much about the musket. He resolved to tell Helen and Michael about it at a later date, but he just felt there was something wrong, if not wrong, then very strange about it, unless, of course, he really DID have some knowledge somehow about this ancient weapon. At length, their meals came.

"Here you go!" said the waitress, "three steak-in-ale pies and a scampi?" and she was accompanied by a young female helper.

"Would you like any sauces or accompaniments?" she asked.

"Oh, no, no, I don't think so," said Helen, "but what about you boys?"

"Daft bat!" said Michael, "Bring us some 'orseradish sauce, would ya, pet?"

"Of course!" said the girl and she turned to get it, then John shouted, "Please may I have some tartar sauce, miss?"

The girl smiled at them and wondered why they would want horseradish sauce with a steak pie! But 'hey-ho,' she thought to herself, 'that's life!'

After another hour or so, they all agreed it was time to be making a move, so they all stood up; Helen got her handbag and cardigan, big John got his leather bag which he normally wore over his shoulder and little John gathered some paper and colouring crayons that he'd been given by the publican to amuse himself after his meal, as the adult conversation was a bit boring to a five-year-old. No sooner had they stood up then a group of the revellers came surging forward to claim their seats. Big John laughed and said to one of them.

"Hello, Ned, would you pinch my grave as quickly, ha ha!"

"You're havin' a laugh, aren't you, John?" said Ned, "To say seats are at a premium in here is an understatement, lad! You could have SOLD yer bloody seat, let alone get up an' walk away from it ha ha!"

They all had a good laugh and as the four got up, six tried to push into the four seats. For those around who saw this, they too laughed at the hilarious sight of pushing and shoving, jostling and cursing!

"Mine, I think knave!"

"By Our Lady, you jest infidel, MINE!"

"You'll not even get your oversized breeches in there, Matthew!"

"You just watch and be amazed varlet! I only have a skinny little bum inside said breeches, ha ha!"

The Twigg family laughed at all this as they made their way to the rear entrance of the pub to get their car in the pub's car park and as they shouted their goodbyes to the general crowd, many of them saluted big John and his family with "God save the King!" and other votive exclamations and they flourished their hats and banged on the tables as the four of them walked out of the pub. As they were about to get into the car, they all said their goodbyes to each other and they all took turns to hug big John.

"Keep in touch, lad," said Michael. "An' ah'll get yer a copy of our photos, eh?"

"Thanks, Mike, that would be great! But I must get going now, we all leave tomorrow morning and we've all got to get packed and off the site by 11 o'clock, so 'bye everyone, 'bye!" he said as he walked out of the car park and headed back off in the direction of Ripley Castle.

"John! Do ya want a lift back?" shouted Michael,

"No no, I fancy the walk and it's such a lovely evening, I'll stroll back with some of my 'lot' walking up on the other side of the road, but thanks anyway! Cheers! And, oh, happy birthday Mike," he said, putting his hand into an inner pocket of his jerkin and producing a birthday card.

"Oh, ta lad, ah'd all but forgotten abaht it missen!" With that, big John joined some of his friends and walked up the footpath with them. They climbed into the car and made their way back home. When they got back to their house, they all flopped onto comfy chairs and they all laughed and discussed the events of the day. Helen went into the kitchen to pop the kettle on and then came back in to join them. John was full of it and he couldn't wait to tell his friends at school on Monday.

When the conversation calmed down a bit and they were quietly sipping their tea, Michael casually said, "Oh, yer uncle John were tellin' us at the bar that you saved the day by 'elpin' 'is mate Phil wi' 'is broken musket! That were clever of ya, lad! 'Ow did ya do that like?"

Helen was oblivious to this intelligence and her eyes met Michael's and he widened his to her. John coloured up a bit and didn't know what to say. Michael continued, "Oh, it's all reet, lad, ah aren't gonna tell ya off like, ah'm just curious as ta 'ow ya were able ta 'elp!"

John was still fumbling for words and his eyes started to fill. Helen laughed to lighten what was obviously a heavy moment for John.

"Oh, John! How clever of you! I didn't hear about this," she said looking at Michael again. "Tell me about the musket! Was it big? Did you like it? Did it smell like your grandpa's airguns?"

That did the trick, John came out of his shell a bit at the thought of his grandpa's guns and he smiled and said, "I love guns, Mum! I've not seen a real firelock before!"

"Then how do you know it was called a 'firelock' then, sweetie? Even I didn't know that was its name! I thought they were called muskets!"

"Oh, they are! But any weapon like that is called a firelock because of the way it works and how it sends the shot out of the gun!"

There was a pregnant pause.

"Ah'm really interested, John lad, ah don't know owt abaht these guns! Can you teach me, lad?"

John again sensed his dad's 'trap' and he clammed up.

Helen said, "Hey! I know what, John, if you would rather not talk about it, would you like to draw a firelock and you can *show* us how it works?"

John liked that idea and he picked up a blue crayon that he had brought home from the pub and turned a sheet of paper over, then proceeded to draw a very simple diagram of a musket and its firing mechanism. Helen and Michael just watched dumbstruck. When he had finished, he held it in front of his parents, holding it at the corners of the paper.

"Here! This is how a firelock works—I think." They stared at it for a moment.

"What do you mean *'you think'*, John?" Helen asked soothingly.

"Well, I have dreamed about it. I dreamed that I was making one of these and I somehow knew what all the parts were called and how they worked! I promise I haven't seen one before, please don't be angry with me, I just seem to know! It's just a dream, it probably wouldn't work because it was just a dream and I'm only a little boy and I might have just made it all up in my head, Mummy."

They stared at the drawing a little more. Michael eased the tension by laughing and saying, "Yeah, it were just a dream! Ah bet yer can't tell me what all these bits are called then!"

"Yes, I can!" said John,

"Can't!" said Michael,

"Can!" said John now smiling.

"Can't!"

"Can!"

"Can't!"

"Can!"

"Alreet then, clever clogs, tell us what they're called then! 'Tell ya what, tell us all abaht it, an' ah'll give yer an *'ah'm the wind an' you're the feather'* all arahnd the garden as well as goin' up t' stairs! 'Ow's that?"

John took the bait and squealed with delight at the prospect of a double helping of his favourite bedtime ride! So John put the paper on the table and sat on the sofa with them.

"Well," he said as he perused the drawing, "This is called the stock," and he pointed to that part of the gun, "and this is the barrel. That bit is called the trigger and that bit is the trigger guard."

Helen and Michael looked at each other, they were comfortable with this so far, as his Grandpa had shown him his airguns countless times and would have told John the names of these components. John continued, "and this is called the hammer and this is called the flint jaw, it's the bit that holds the flint. Then this bit is called the frizzen, it's the bit that the flint hits when the trigger is pulled. This bit's called the pan, it's where you put some gunpowder and this bit here is the frizzen spring."

John never once looked up during this oration and showed no signs of emotion or embarrassment, he just continued, calmly explaining, "And inside there is the mainspring for the hammer and there is a bit called the tumbler and a sear and a spring to make the sear work!"

Another pregnant pause and Helen and Michael were totally speechless, with their mouths literally hanging open. They just stared at each other. Michael desperately tried to think of something to say, but couldn't. Helen was the same.

At last, Helen said, "Can you write these words down for me, John?" to which John just giggled and said, "Silly, Mummy! I don't know how to spell them! We haven't done much spelling yet at school but I promise I will one day and will make you another drawing and I will put the words in and I can show my Grandpa and he might buy a firelock and he might let me play with it and I can polish it for him and he might let me oil it and keep it nice and shiny!"

As promised, when bedtime came, John got his reward. Helen brought him downstairs in his pyjamas, having had a nice bath and brushed his teeth. Michael had reflected on the earlier conversation with John and had come to the conclusion that it was what it was and whatever it was, it was here to stay and there didn't seem much that that could be done about it.

So, John came bounding into the living room and shouted, "Ready, Daddy! WEEEEEE!"

Michael grinned at John and did his usual things for his son. He whisked him up and whirled him around and then put him on his back, he span him round and round, making all the wind noises and silly sounds that John loved. He went through the kitchen and out into the garden, cavorting like a demented man and all the while, John was howling with delight!

Round the garden several times, under the apple trees that were heavy with fruit and down the side of the high privet hedge, then back into the house and up the stairs, two steps forward and one step back, much to John's delight. Then the ultimate joy, the big bumpy landing onto the bed! "BUMP! BUMP! BUMP!" said Michael, as he set John down with several bounces.

John was flushed and breathless with laughing and Helen, who had followed them all the while, laughed too, wondering where Michael got his limitless stamina from! Strong as he was, he was no longer a 'spring chicken'! Both Helen and Michael paid extra and special attention to John that evening. They wanted him to feel that there truly was nothing wrong and that he was loved so dearly.

As they were saying their last goodnights, Michael put his hand in his pocket and produced the citrine stone and showed it to John, who smiled and looked up at his dad lovingly and he said, "Thank you, Daddy! I love you. I'm sorry I'm such a silly bean. I'm so sorry that I make you worry for me. I know you think there's something wrong with me, but I'm OK daddy, honest and I promise I will try to not have any more bad dreams and I will try not to wake you and mummy up ever again."

Michael, who had previously been laughing with his son, listened to this speech and could not suppress his anguish and he scooped John up in his arms and pressed him to his chest and he wept out loud, saying, "John, oh mah John, 'ow ah do love ya too, lad! Ne'er forget it, son! Ah'll love ya until ah die. You're mah precious, bonny boy."

Helen melted to tears at the sight of this tender and truly heart rending moment and she had to leave the bedroom and she sat on the side of their own bed and she cried her heart out.

Michael did not leave John until he was sound asleep. Helen had gone back downstairs earlier and had fallen asleep on the sofa. Michael went downstairs and into the living room, where he saw Helen and he could see that she was well and truly asleep, so he gently picked her up, as easily as if she were John and put her arm around his neck. He carried her up to bed, gently took off her jeans and covered her up with the duvet and she only stirred slightly as her jeans slipped from her legs.

Michael went downstairs and into the garden. The moon was shining down brightly and the stars seemed particularly twinkly and magical. He put his hands over his face and slowly drew them down his cheeks, his eyes still moist and his heart nigh bursting.

He stared to the heavens and he shouted, "Why me an' mah poor little family?" to the massive outline of Orion in the sky above him.

"Can't ya leave mah little boy alone?" he shouted, as if to some entity or something, anything that could hear him. "Just leave us alone, will yer? He's just a boy!" and his voice became tremulous, "He's just a little bloody boy. DAMN YOU!" and he spread out his arms to the moon and stars as if begging the great unknown for help or clemency.

There was, of course, no reply, just the moon and stars shining down on him, as they had done to every living being since the birth of time. Silent; enigmatic; unchanging; cold; heartless. He fell to his knees in the middle of the lawn, with his arms still stretched in supplication to he knew not what and fell forwards, his head and arms now loosely on the dewy grass and he wept.

"You bastard!" he sobbed.

The moon and stars watched and kept the secret, but gave neither answer nor comfort to poor Michael. Only the high-pitched squeals of the pipistrelle bats and the approach of a curious domestic tabby-cat that came for a 'love' broke the intense passion of Michael. He remained there for some considerable time, his head a jumble of emotions and questions that could not be answered. The night was cold and unusually starry and Michael gazed in wonder at the heavens. It was deathly quiet, apart from the bats flitting by him from time to time.

In the distance, a lonely dog barked once or twice and this 'earthly' sound brought him back to reality. "Happy birthday, Mike lad," he said to himself. He took his handkerchief from his pocket and dried his eyes and he reproached himself for being so foolish and he told himself that he should be more pragmatic and level headed. He took a few deep breaths of the cold night air then he slowly walked into the house and locked the kitchen door behind him.

As he checked the house for security, he went into the living room and saw a small pile of birthday cards and presents, all gift wrapped and with words of love and joy for his birthday, from all his family and friends. He screwed up his eyes as he tried to suppress his tears once again and the love and affection that he knew was his, started to outweigh the cruel and awful things that seemed to have plagued his family for so long.

Time Marches On

With time, John became so used to his recurring dreams, that they eventually held no fear for him and that within itself, made them scarcer and a lot less frightening. He would go to bed almost defying the dreams and he stood up to them and controlled his own emotions. He mastered the art of being able to recognise the fact that he was actually dreaming and he could then control the outcome. He could wake himself up at will.

If he dreamed about the squeaking black leather shoes he'd say to them,

"Oh, not YOU again! Just GET LOST!" and they would just disappear. If he dreamed about the 'little cubby-hole', he would simply say to himself, "John, it's time to wake up," and he would.

The citrine stone was invaluable for a few years, but gradually, even that was consigned to a drawer somewhere and pretty much forgotten about.

John was always a bright little boy, but by the time he was of the age to go up to secondary school, he really did excel in many subjects. He was a very quick learner. Once shown, he seldom forgot anything that held his interest or imagination. Like his father, he loved practical projects and hobbies. In woodwork and metalwork, he was extremely competent and confident. Many a time, his mum and dad or Nanna and Grandpa would ask him what he would like to do when he grew up and his aspirations changed from week to week, depending on what project he was working on!

He'd be passionate about becoming a builder then he wanted to be a gunsmith, then an engine designer or maybe a soldier? Who knows? He was young and enthusiastic about most things and his attention to detail was equal to that of his father. He had helped his dad to make the fire-box for the traction engine which was completed and duly given to Uncle John as a Christmas present.

His love for guns never diminished and many was the time that they all went to visit Nanna and Grandpa and John spent hours with him shooting at tin cans and chalk figurines, the type that can be won at funfairs on the rifle ranges.

All through his secondary school years, John became more and more interested in history. He loved the sound of Latin words and if ever he got the opportunity to read it, he did. If he saw any Latin inscriptions, above the portal of an important governmental or council building for instance, he would copy it down on a piece of paper and he tried to translate what it said when he got home to his books.

With this, came an interest in law. He always remembered saying those Latin words years before in his dreams and he found it fascinating. Sometimes, he had the distinct feeling that fate was taking a hand in his future and he didn't resist it.

Then came the time that John's hormones hit him. His voice was breaking from alto to bass-baritone and even he saw the funny side of his own voice! All of a sudden, he discovered girls! Up to press, he didn't care too much for them. They were just 'girls'. Boys wore trousers and girls wore skirts. But all of a sudden, the girls were developing neat little figures.

They had shapely legs, that some of them would show off by shortening their skirts at every opportunity, by rolling them up at the waist, to show a little more thigh, of course, when they were safely far enough away from their mums and dads! They had pretty eyes and languishing eye-lashes. Boys and girls were becoming young men and women and just like a beautiful springtime, as the ripening seed is stirring in the earth, so too in the unconscious minds of the young people.

John couldn't wait for French lessons with Mrs Whittaker, because he had Lorna McCauley sat in front of him in class and he simply adored her! She was beautiful! She had the most delicious, soft Southern Irish accent and she had gorgeous nut-brown eyes and raven black hair that she tossed from side to side to get it from her eyes as she was studying her French text book and John could smell the perfume of her shampoo as it wafted towards him. He adored it. He would close his eyes and smell the air, with an inane grin on his face.

"TWIGG! What appears to be the matter with you?" came the booming voice of the cantankerous Mrs Whittaker, chalk in hand and walking towards him.

"Oh, nothing, Miss, I was just—"

"JUST WHAT!" she screamed at him. "If I see you dozing off again, I will send you down to the headmaster, do you hear me?"

"Yes, Miss!" said a bright-red faced John, embarrassed to the last degree that the object of his love had turned around and stared at him. She was grinning from ear to ear and she winked at him. All of a sudden, Mrs Whittaker's threats had about as much impact as cotton wool balls. The drone of the classroom faded away as he stared at Lorna's back and admired her as she occasionally flicked her hair and moved her bottom on her wooden seat to get more comfortable from time to time.

Lorna lived in a large caravan on a trailer park on the Knaresborough Road, between Harrogate and Knaresborough. Her father was a company representative for a large firm in Ireland and for the year or so he was working on the company's 'England' project, the McCauley family all lived over here, rather than be apart for such a long time. Poor Lorna and her younger brother, Sean, were often teased and taunted by some of the other school kids, who called them 'tinkers' and 'trailer trash'.

This only served to increase John's feelings towards Lorna. John contrived to make friends with Sean and thought it would be a way of getting closer to Lorna and Sean thought John was great! First of all, John was older than him by a year and secondly, he was impressed at what John could do! He was brilliant at woodwork and metalwork and some of John's projects were displayed in the schools foyer and reception area.

Very soon, John was invited back to the caravan for tea by Sean. John couldn't believe his luck! This was it! He would get to meet the family and maybe sit next to Lorna! As it happened, when John arrived, (in his 'coolest' clothes) only Mrs McCauley and Sean were there, Mr McCauley being away on business and Lorna, it transpired, was at ballet lessons and wouldn't be home until much later. Mrs McCauley was a very pleasant lady and John could see where Lorna got her looks from. They were so alike that they could almost have been sisters.

Mrs McCauley said, in her soft Southern Irish accent, "I've heard a lot about you, John, both Sean and Lorna speak very highly of you and it's nice to meet you at long last!"

John was encouraged by this and he returned the compliments, saying as many good things as he could think of about Sean and Lorna. He maybe laboured a bit too hard singing the praises of Lorna and there was a visible look of jealousy about Sean. The meal was simple, sausage, egg, chips and baked beans, but the boys polished the meal off in no time. John was able to get a good look at the interior of this 44 foot trailer. It was roomier than he had thought it would be and it was kept immaculately.

He could see Lorna in his mind's eye everywhere he looked and he hoped against hope that Lorna would come home before it was time for him to go. It didn't happen and John eventually conceded that he wasn't going to see her that night, so after several games of scrabble, John took his leave and thanked Mrs McCauley for inviting him for tea.

Mrs McCauley shook his hand and said, "Goodbye, John, it was nice to have met you and thank you for being so kind to my two all this time!"

John thought that was a strange thing to say but he didn't give it any more thought as he walked up to the bus stop.

John worshipped, as they say, at the altar of McCauley. Many was the time John would walk Lorna home, even though it was way out of his way, rain or shine, just hoping that she would give him the slightest sign that she was interested in him. He so desperately wanted her as his girlfriend and she knew it. She always called him 'Twigg' and never John, but on one, heavenly occasion, she linked little fingers with him as they were walking home and this became holding hands properly. John nearly died! His heart was beating out of his chest as he walked her up to her caravan.

"OK, see you, Twigg," she said, still holding his hand, "See you tomorrow."

John couldn't contain himself and he leaned forward to kiss her, she teasingly responded, by leaning towards him, lips almost touching his, then she just giggled and turned on her heels, looked back at him tauntingly and said, "See you, Twigg!"

With that, she went into the caravan and closed the door. John was totally gutted at having been so close to kissing the girl of his dreams and all the way home, which was about a mile and a half, he both swore at and blessed these precious moments with her. The rain started to fall and he only had a shirt on, no raincoat or any other protection.

He walked home starry eyed and his thoughts were wild and passionate or at least as much as could be with a 16 years old boy. He would write letters to her that she would never receive and he would dream about her all the time.

"Never in the whole wide world was there ever a girl as beautiful as she!" he often mused to himself.

When he eventually arrived home, Helen saw the drenched state he was in and asked, "Where the heck have you been! School finished ages ago!"

"Oh, nowhere special, Mum, I just walked home with a friend!"

"Where does your 'friend' live then? France?"

Helen laughed as she looked at her sodden son standing there looking like a drowned rat holding a soggy satchel! Michael ran in from his den, trying to avoid the downpour and looked at John as he opened the kitchen door.

"Eighup! What's this then? 'as yer mam just done t' washin' an' forgot ta tek yer aht o' yer school uniform like? Ha ha!"

"Oh HAR HAR!" said John sarcastically.

Michael smacked John's bottom playfully and said, "Yer not too piggin' big ta be put reyt an' in yer place, lad! Don't give ME yer petulant teenage lip!"

John smiled at his dad and realised that, yes, he needed to go upstairs and get out of his wet things and have a warm shower.

Then one day, Lorna didn't turn up for class. Nobody seemed to know where she was. She was a bit of a loner and she didn't have a 'best friend' as such, so John couldn't make any enquiries as to her whereabouts from any of the other pupils. Friday came and still no sign of her. He thought that she may be ill, so he got the most fantastic idea, to go and see her! He would take her some flowers and a small box of chocolates!

"Yes, that's it!" he thought to himself, "That will show her just how I feel about her!"

Saturday morning couldn't come too soon and John was up bright and early. He made a pot of tea and a plate full of toast for his mum and dad. The smell of the toast did the trick and brought a sleepy Helen and Michael out of their bedroom.

"Eighup, ah can smell summat ta eat! 'ave ya left owt fer us up 'ere, lad?"

"Of course!" said John "Do you want it up there?"

"Well, That'd be rayt decent of ya, lad! Helen, John's gonna bring us some toast and tea up! Worra good lad!" he said condescendingly.

Helen and Michael went back to their bedroom, having just visited the bathroom. John knew that it would be safe to go in and he went into their bedroom with a tray with the breakfast on it.

"There you go!" he said cheerfully.

"Thank you, John," said Helen smiling at him.

"Worra ya doin all ponced-up like? Goin' somewhere special? Eighup, Helen, it must be a lass 'es seein', 'cos 'es got half a bottle o' poo-foo on! Ha ha!"

Helen and Michael laughed, John just smiled, slightly embarrassed, because, of course, his dad was dead right! Inwardly, his mum and dad were very proud and happy that John at last had discovered the opposite sex.

"Right, I'll see you both later!" John shouted as he raced down the stairs. He grabbed a light fleece-jacket from the under stairs cupboard, shouted 'bye' once more as he left the house and made his way up to the bus stop. When he arrived at Harrogate bus station, he went straight to a florist that was just on the other side of the road, on Cheltenham Parade. The lady was just setting up a display stall as he bounded over.

"Hello, can I have a bunch of flowers please?"

The lady smiled and said, "My goodness, you're an early bird, aren't you? You want a 'bunch of flowers', eh? Well, you've come to the right place!"

"What do you recommend?" John asked innocently.

The lady could see what this was all about and said, "Well, if I were you, I would choose something with red in it! You DO love her, don't you?"

"Oh, yes! I certainly do!" John replied with gusto, before realising what he had said himself and he coloured up. The lady was sensitive to this and came to his rescue.

"Ah, I'm sure your girl will be delighted with these, fresh-cut this very morning. They have lovely reds and golds in amongst them. Aren't they pretty?"

"I'll take them!" said John, still a little embarrassed and looking from left to right all the while, in case he saw any of his mates.

"That'll be £2.50 please," she said and wrapped the flowers in pretty floral paper and secured it with sticky-tape. John fumbled in his pocket and brought out a £5 note. She thanked him and gave him his change.

Feeling a little conspicuous, but happy with his purchase, he walked up Beulah Street to a bespoke sweet shop. He stared at all the sumptuous chocolates and handmade confectionary on display. He walked into the shop and looked at yet more of the offerings under the glass-fronted counter.

"How can I help you, young man?" said the confectioner. "Are you looking for something special? I see you have a lovely bunch of flowers, would the chocolates be for a lady friend?"

"Yes, erm, yes, they are," said John, still a bit embarrassed.

"How about an individually made box of 6 chocolates of your choice, in a presentation box and gift wrapped?" asked the confectioner.

John thought that would be a lovely idea and he nodded to the man. John picked out 6 beautifully made chocolates and they were arranged expertly by the confectioner into a little cardboard tray. John watched intently as they were then gift wrapped and a little red ribbon tied and ornately bowed on the top.

"Would you like anything else?" asked the confectioner.

"No thank you, how much will that be please?"

"That's exactly four pounds," he said. John nearly died at the cost, but he gave the confectioner a £5 note.

"She's worth it! By God, she's worth it!" said John to himself as he went back to the bus station to catch the next Knaresborough-bound bus.

He got onto the 9:50 AM to Knaresborough. It stopped just opposite the trailer park and John's heart was pounding. He could hardly believe he was doing this!

"What if she's out? What if she's on holiday, oh yes, I never thought of that! What a fool I'll look if they are all sat around the caravan this morning with friends? What if she doesn't like chocolate?"

All sorts of fears came through his head as he slowly walked down 1st Avenue. He could hear his own heart beating rapidly in his ears. He clutched the flowers and breathed deeply as he turned the corner at the bottom of the avenue to where the McCauley's caravan was. He stopped dead in his tracks, dumbstruck. They had gone. The caravan was gone. He stared at the space, now empty, where the object of his desires had lived. She had gone. He dropped the flowers.

At that moment, the heavens opened on him. He could not suppress the tears. The rain kindly washed them away. He walked into the empty space and just stared at the mains facilities connections. The name 'McCauley' was still on the letter box, just to the front of the little tarmac path that lead to the caravan door.

A cheery postman cycled past him and shouted, "Good morning!" but John did not answer, he could not. He slowly walked back to the flowers, picked them up and sniffed the aroma and then he put his whole face into the blooms and cried.

He walked slowly out of the trailer park and turned left, to walk up the Knaresborough Road. Buses came past, but he kept on walking, the flowers held upside down as he held them loosely at the ends of the stalks. The chocolates were now in his fleece pocket, wet and a little crumpled and the bright red ribbon slowly started to unwind and it became limp, almost as if joining in poor John's misery and suffering.

All the way home, John said to himself, "Why have they gone? WHERE have they gone? Why did neither Lorna nor Sean say anything; not a word about moving? Maybe their mum and dad kept it a secret from them? Maybe they didn't know until the day they left? Maybe their dad was called back to Ireland at a moment's notice?"

Whatever the reason, John was gutted and broken hearted beyond words. The first cut is the deepest and this cut would stay with John for the rest of his life.

When he got home, his mum and dad were out. He was thankful of the fact, as he wondered how he could explain why he was in such a state. He filled up a vase with water and arranged the flowers into it and put them on the sideboard. Not knowing when his parents would be back, he quickly took advantage of the fact that the house was empty and he went upstairs to have a warming shower and get changed.

He got changed into a pair of jeans and a T-shirt and went into his room. He lay on his back on his bed and stared at the ceiling and he could feel the tears beginning to well up again. He tried to fight this off by putting his clock radio on and he listened to some music. He dozed off and had the strangest thoughts. He could hear Lorna's voice calling to him and saying, "Don't forget me John, always remember me fondly."

The young, love-struck boy got up from his bed and had an idea. He almost regarded this as a 'death' and he was going to treat it as such. He switched off his clock radio and went back downstairs. He grabbed another coat from the under stairs cupboard and ran back to the bus stop, to catch the next bus back into Harrogate. When he got there, he went back to the florist, who was quite surprised to see him again and thought initially that he had come back to complain about his earlier purchase.

She didn't have the time to say anything before John said, "I'd like two roses please," and he pointed to the stand that contained them. "I'd like a red one and a yellow one please."

He said it with such determination that she thought it prudent not to question why he was back or why he wanted the roses. In fairness, she could see that he was distraught and she knew it was none of her business anyway. John asked for a little greetings card and a pen. The florist obliged with both. John wrote a few words on the card and handed the pen back to the lady. He put the card into its envelope and put it into his pocket. The florist asked if he would like the roses wrapping separately or together.

"I can put either or into a clear plastic tube with an oasis at the bottom to keep them fresh?"

John said, "Will you put them both together into one tube please and some of that red ribbon around the tube."

"Of course!" said the florist and within a couple of minutes, it was done and John paid for them. Once again, John got onto the Knaresborough bus and got off at the same stop he had done earlier, not far from the trailer park. He walked purposefully to the caravan plot where Lorna's caravan had been and he stared at it for several minutes, before gently placing the roses onto the ground right in the centre of the plot.

"Goodbye, Lorna," he said with tears in his eyes. "I will never forget you for as long as I live and I will love you forever." He took the card from his pocket and placed it under the ribbon to secure it. He looked once again wistfully at the caravan plot and then turned to walk away for the last time.

The piteous words on the card read, "A red rose for my beautiful Irish rose. A yellow rose for the tears I will forever shed for you. Goodbye."

When Helen and Michael had got back home earlier, they saw the flowers that John had arranged into the vase on the sideboard. Helen smiled broadly and said, "Oh, how sweet of John to buy me some flowers!"

"Eighup, lass," said Michael, "they're probably fer ME! Don't be so presumptuous that they're fer YOU! Ha ha!"

They never did know the secret behind the blooms. John kept the secret all his life.

Past Tense, Future Perfect

In his last years of secondary school, John studied English, in all its forms, especially literature and language. He also studied Business Studies, History, Mathematics, Biology, Chemistry and Sociology. He studied Latin privately and with a passion, that both Helen and Michael thought it to be a good investment. He achieved a perfect run of 'A' in most of these subjects at GCSE.

He sat the Mathematics and English at 'A' level a year earlier than most students would normally do. With advice and counselling from both teachers and his parents and a good look at several universities on their open days, John eventually considered that law was definitely going to be his future profession. John was nobody's fool. Young as he still was, he knew that one day he would spread his wings and be independent and away from his mother's apron strings. He knew that one day he would be fending for himself.

Michael always told him that he must do what he considered to be right for him and not be pushed or bullied into a career he didn't really want to do. Both Helen and Michael did, however, try to 'influence' him away from doing just manual work, as he had far more to offer himself and a career than just using his hands. He was smart and quick witted. When they realised that John had a penchant towards studying law it made their hearts sing.

They always encouraged him to keep his dextrous skills well and truly alive though and Michael taught him everything he knew about all the practical things that he enjoyed and his father enjoyed too, building, constructing, woodworking and welding. It hadn't taken too much effort for Uncle John to persuade his nephew to join the Sealed Knot Society and Helen and Michael had many precious photographs of him in his costume!

He was still too young to do any battle scenes, but he relished being part of it all, with the other younger members in the Society. He was also much sought after as an advisor to the senior members when it came to the subject of musket problems! All in all, John had had a very happy childhood so far, apart from in love. He was still just a boy with boyish wants and cares. He was always good natured and polite, especially to his 'elders' as was the way of most decent children of the day.

More and more, John studied, slept, ate and studied. His hobbies took second place and they almost disappeared altogether as he studied with grim determination to succeed in his chosen subjects. Although he was always 'John' to his family, he seemed to become quite insular. Even at school, there was a big change in John. He stopped playing sports, which he normally loved, especially rugby and he was sadly missed by his team mates. Some actually started to resent John and called him a 'swat' and a 'bookworm'.

John shrugged off these derisive comments for what they were and paid little attention to the taunts. "Sticks and stones, mate!" he'd say to any of his so-called classmates, who used to indeed be his mates, who now saw John as someone who was 'nerdy' or a bit of a misfit all of a sudden. Since Lorna had disappeared from his life, he lost himself in his studies. If he couldn't have her, he didn't want anyone else. He often used to say to himself, "When and if it ever happens, it will happen."

Helen and Michael never knew John's heart-breaking secret. Oh, they saw a change in him alright, but they just put that down to him just growing up and recognising the fact that the 'right here and now' of his secondary school years would be the mould for his future career.

It didn't ever occur to them that he had never had a girlfriend and that he didn't really seem that interested, they just took it on face value that he was a hardworking, intelligent young man with his eyes on his future. In some respects, they were very relieved that John had such a mature attitude to his studies. Never once did they have to push him to do his homework or have to tell him off for bad reports from school.

Lorna had made such an impact on John, that he thought for a long time that there could, would never be anyone else in the whole wide world for him. Often times though, he would smile to himself as he got a little older and he would concede to himself that he was perhaps in love with her looks, rather than the 'girl' herself. In fact, she treated him appallingly really, now he looked back!

He could never forget her though and he often thought of her, as if they were a couple and he could still smell the perfume from her hair and her pleasant odour of her ever-immaculately laundered and pressed clothing. Her smile was burned into his memory, her softly waved raven black hair, her dark brown eyes and long languishing eye lashes that once he held the gaze of, he just could not look away. He often said to himself, "I wonder what may have happened if we had gotten together? Another time, another place—?"

Then came the day for the final school exam results. Every mum and dad that had a son or daughter of that age had bought a copy of the Harrogate Advertiser to see the results page as early as they possibly could. All over the town, in fact the whole country, were frantic telephone calls made to friends and family, with congratulations or commiserations on the results.

Many tears of joy as well as sadness were shed on that morning. Many hugs and kisses of congratulations as well as cuddles of consolation were shared. For John, a mass hug from his mum and dad and jumping up and down on the spot by all three of them as they punched the air, having read the news that he had passed all his subjects with top marks.

"Well done, John lad! 'Tell thi what, yer mam an' me are gonna tek yer out fer the biggest steak you've ever 'ad! Eh mam?" said Michael with such pride at John's achievements.

Helen agreed and continued, "We always knew you would do it, John, you wouldn't be your father's son with lesser results!"

John couldn't deny that he was proud of his results, but was modest enough to say to his mum and dad, "Without your help, I could not possibly have got this far! It should be ME buying YOU the steaks! Thank you so much for your support and help all these years!"

"Nowt o' t' sort lad! But if ya wanna buy the steaks like, me an' yer mam won't stop ya! ha ha!"

"No you will not!" said Helen. "Tonight will be YOUR night and you will get what you deserve!"

"Yeah, a clip rahnd t' ear-'ole!" joked Michael, to which Helen picked up a cushion from the sofa and dealt Michael several blows with it!

"Gerroff! Eighup! Eighup!" he said, trying to shield his face from a perfect volley of blows.

"Sorry, Dad," said John laughing, "as they say in the westerns, 'It's fer yer own good, boy!'"

"Eighup! Mutiny! Gerroff!" Michael said as Helen still lay on the blows. "Ah thought you were mah ally, lad! You just wait till ah—GERROFF! Ah'll be dustin' your 'ide fer this, lass!" he said laughing and grabbing the cushion from her, she ran out of the living room and out into the garden, with Michael in hot pursuit!

John smiled to himself and enjoyed the first bit of true relaxation he had had in months. He felt like a little boy again and as he watched his mum and dad running around the garden laughing and bashing each other playfully, he felt truly grateful that he had been blessed with such a caring and gentle mother and father.

Evening approached and Helen shouted up the stairs to John, "Have you any ideas of where you would like to go to eat tonight?"

John was in the bathroom having a wash and shave and he stopped for a moment to think about his mother's question.

"Oh, I don't know, Mum, is there any place that you and dad fancy?"

"Well, there is a really good steak house on Cheltenham Mount that we have never been to, they say that if you want a steak, that's the place to go!"

"Sounds good to me, Mum!" he replied as he applied his razor again.

Michael came in from his den. He'd been working on his latest project, a miniature Majorcan wind pump, the type that abound around that island and it was to be a perfect scale working model of one of these and would be about four feet high on completion. He was going to use it as a garden feature, with a small underground reservoir, to pump water to the fish pond he had made, using Yorkshire granite. Even the building around such a pump was to be constructed in miniature, using scaled down natural stone 'bricks', exactly like the real thing in Majorca.

"Eighup, lass, is our John gettin' ready ta go aht?" he said enthusiastically.

"Yep, he's just upstairs having a shave."

"'Avin' a shave—tut tut! Dun't it tek ya back, lass? Our little boy 'avin' a shave! Weren't it only last week that ah were the wind an' 'im the feather?"

Helen laughed and said, "You wouldn't be able to do it now, big lad, *he's too big! He's only three inches shorter than you and he has your build! He could pick YOU up and take YOU to bed! Ha ha!"

"Aye, that 'e could, lass! One o' these days, 'e may 'ave ta, when ah'm old an' grey like!"

"You're already grey, you daft bat! You were grey when John was born!"

"Cheeky cow! Ah'm not THAT old yet, an' ah still 'ave energy enough ta give YOU a good seein' to, 'aven't ah?"

"My God, you certainly do, Mike, I just don't know how you get the energy!"

"From Devil-red lippy an' nail polish! That's where from! Oh, an' yer little pink baby doll that ya put on fer us from time ta time!"

"You saucy bugger!" she said playfully and she wrapped her arms around him and gave him a huge hug.

"Will you always love me the way you do today, Mike? When all my 'bits' start moving south?"

He gently pulled her away from the embrace and he looked at her adoringly, at her black hair, with a few grey ones here and there and just the suggestion of 'laughter-lines' about her eyes and he cupped her face in his hands and said, "From world's end ta world's end, ah will love you! You are mah other half, mah right 'and, mah soul-mate, mah reason to live an' to go on. Without you, mah life would be over, Helen."

And he kissed her with such sincerity and in a way that he did when love was young and new to them, slowly, tenderly and with absolute love. She kissed him back, it wasn't passionate, it was so gentle and meaningful, a union of two souls, adoring each other for all time and her tears flowed with happiness. He had indeed answered her question.

The steak house was full and alive with mainly young people, but here and there were older folk, scowling at the 'youth of today' and their disregard to other diners and some of them clicking and sucking their dentures with disgust! Helen had reserved a table and when they arrived, a pretty young waitress greeted them and showed them to their table. They sat down and took in the atmosphere for a while and they all looked at each other and smiled. There was a party of 'line dancers' at one end of the restaurant, in their uniforms and cowboy boots.

"Daft buggers!" Michael shouted to his two having observed them.

"Why are they 'daft buggers', Dad?" asked John.

"Well, ah' mean, look at 'em! Silly sods! All dressed the same, doin' t' same things on a dance floor, an' tekin' themsen's so seriously like!"

"You're getting old, Dad!" laughed John. "You're obviously out of touch with what people like to do today for relaxation!"

"Humph!" said Michael. "It were bad enough wi' *yer do the 'okey kokey an' yer turn arahnd* when we used ta tek yer on 'oliday when ya' were a kid!

Ha ha! But worrever t' yanks do, WE 'ave ta bloody-well follow as a country, don't we?"

"Oh shut up, killjoy!" shouted Helen with a smile. "Don't listen to old Mr Grumpy, John!" she said smiling at him.

"Dad is entitled to his own opinion, Mum, it's just a shame that he's wrong!" said John and he grabbed his father's hand and shouted, "You're not often wrong, Dad, but you're wrong again!"

Helen and John laughed at what was obviously 'throw-away' comment, but Michael scowled at them and said, "You two never agree wi' me even when ya can!"

He stared petulantly at the menu for a while and Helen and John were still staring at him, waiting for some sort of response. Michael thought about his own last comment and he started to smile to himself but kept a stern face.

God! Am ah turnin' into a grumpy old git like? he mused to himself. *Ah'll 'ave ta be purrin' a stop ta that, startin' from right nah!"* he told himself resolutely.

After a moment of two, he lowered his menu. Helen and John were still staring at him for some kind of reaction. His face was still stern, but then his face lit up with a beaming smile and he said, "Eighup, you two, am ah the only 'un 'ere wi' an appetite like? Ah've chosen what ah'm 'avin! C'mon, get yer faces into t' menus! Ah'm starved! Ah could eat a dead 'orse between two mattresses tha knoas!" and he clapped his hands together as if giving them an order.

They both laughed as the tension they thought there had been, vanished. So, three 16oz steaks were ordered, medium rare for the men and medium to well done for Helen. The general atmosphere of the whole establishment was happily uproarious by the time their meals came and Michael let himself 'go with the flow' and they all thoroughly enjoyed what was a perfect steak dinner, over which, they all discussed John's future, his aspirations and what would be in store at university.

He had seen several universities on their open days, but was very much impressed with the University of Leeds, which seemed to have all the right sort of criterion for him. They talked for quite some time after they had finished their steaks and a huge knickerbocker-glory a piece. They really had lost the track of time, when through the hubbub, came the young waitress and very apologetically said, "Excuse me, but would you like anything else? We have lots of people waiting for tables—"

"Oh, sorry, lass, are we in t' way like?" Michael said with a sincere look of surprise. The girl was relieved that Michael had not taken umbrage at that, as many would have done and Michael continued, "Give us our bill an' we'll gerroff! Hey, we're rayt sorry abaht that!"

The girl smiled with gratitude and went off to get the bill. When it came, Michael looked at it and folded it up. He took his wallet out and gave the girl cash for the meal.

"There's an extra fiver there, lass, that's for you, an' ah mean YOU mind, fer purrin' up wi' us!"

"Oh! My goodness! That's extremely generous of you, sir!" she said as she stared at the money. "Thank you very much indeed!" And she turned away with the money and the last of their plates, smiling from ear to ear as she walked into the kitchen and out of sight.

The night was still young and they still had lots to talk about. None of them wanted to go home yet, so they decided to take a drive up to the Greyhounds at Killinghall for a couple of drinks and to continue their conversations.

"Good evening, my friends!" came the cheery welcome from the manager behind the bar, who by now knew them very well. After the Sealed Knot battle a few years before, they became good and loyal customers and they, (and the 'true' locals) liked to call themselves 'locals'. They were indeed the very next best thing to that title. Many were the times they would go there for their lunches or evening meals.

They were on first name terms with everyone they knew there and as Michael had such strong Yorkshire roots, albeit South Yorkshire, where the accent is quite distinct from that of North Yorkshire, especially Harrogate, which has always been regarded as a 'posh' town, he was regarded as 'one of the boys' and was always welcomed thus with a smile and an "Eighup lad!" from all the regulars and staff.

"Mike lad! What ya 'avin'?" said the manager. "An' you Helen, What would ya like, pet? An' you, John, gosh, if it weren't for the fact that you 'aven't got a tash, ah'd swear you were yer dad! Ha ha! What do yer fancy?"

Michael said, "Well, afore ah answer that 'un, ah just want ta point aht that we don't look THAT much alike, *AH'M* far better lookin' than 'im!" he said smiling at his son.

"Oh that's OK, Dad —age before beauty!"

"Cheeky bugger!" grinned Michael. They all got a drink and sat down and glasses were clinked in congratulations to John.

"Cheers!" said Helen.

"Bottoms up!" said John.

"Froth in yer tash!" said Michael. They were all smiling and contented. The conversation wandered from subject to subject. For a while, they discussed Uncle John, which of course lead to the subject of the Sealed Knot Society.

"Now that yer exams an' such are finished, are ya gonna go back to 'em fer a bit, John?" asked Michael.

"Oh yes, I think it's time to chill and get some relaxation in now, Dad, I do enjoy it and I've had several phone calls from friends asking me when I'm coming back! They all understand why I've not been going though."

Helen said, "Yes, I'm sure there will be others in the Society that were in a similar position as yourself with studies and exams and it would be good for you to all catch up and compare notes!"

"That's for sure!" said John sipping at his drink, "I guess it's doubly important to get back into it for a while, 'cos when I get to 'uni', it'll have to take even more of a back seat in my life than doing my A levels and God willing, when I qualify, I will be too busy getting my head round my career for the first few years. I'll bet that by the time I get back, most of the other guys I sparred with will have left!"

They all laughed and sipped at their drinks. There was silence for a minute or two then Michael asked, "How d'ya feel nowadays, John?"

"Fine! How do you mean, Dad?"

"Ah mean like wi' yer bad dreams an' such; 'ave they gone completely? It's summat we've never talked abaht since you were a nipper! Ah were just lookin' at yer like, now yer quite a man, an' the memories came floodin' back ta me! Ah remember 'avin' ta sit up wi' yer fer hours until ya fell asleep agen, ha ha!"

John thought for a moment and said, "Do you know, I DO still dream about certain things from time to time, like the squeaky shoes and the cubby-hole, but I'm so used to it that I tend just to think to myself, 'Oh, this one again, how boring'!" and he laughed, as they all did.

Michael said, "Hey, ya never know, lad, yer may 'ave bin a barrister in a previous life, wi' yer buckles on yer shoes and yer Latin, eh? Maybe you've done it all afore today!"

Helen agreed and said, "Yes! You never know, you may have changed the course of history with your sharp brain and saved noblemen from the axe or the Tower ha ha!"

John laughed and replied in a very matter of fact way, "I have often thought about that myself! True to say that I can't explain the dreams and they *are* in such detail as to be almost a true memory of something, but just a fragment of a memory. Do you know what I mean? It's difficult to describe really, it's like looking at 'snapshots' from your past, but you can't remember where they were taken! Am I making any sense?" and he laughed, a bit embarrassedly.

Helen and Michael went straight to his rescue there and agreed wholeheartedly that what he said made absolute sense to them.

"We were advised, all those years ago, by Dr Forsythe, not to 'open up Pandora's box' by asking you questions about the dreams at the time, only to talk to you if you broached the subject first," said Helen.

This seemed to open up an interesting conversation on time machines, memory genes, reincarnation, the 'time-space-continuum', the Pharaohs and a whole shebang. John was able to tell his mum and dad of other snippets of the dreams.

"Do you know, when you used to take me shopping, Mum, I often saw the man on front of a porridge oats packet and he always reminded me of one of the characters in my dreams; a similar sort of hat, a flouncy white collar and shirt front and the black clothing. When I was little, I always thought that the man in my dreams must be a porridge maker!"

They all had a good laugh at that!

"I also remember looking down a dark, smelly and moss-sided water well and feeling very uncomfortable about it. It gave me the creeps! Another one is that I'm building what can only be described as a windmill of some kind, a bit like what you're making at the moment dad."

"Oh aye? A wind-pump like?" Michael said with great interest.

"Yes, I guess so and I have the feeling that the well and the windmill have something to do with each other, but I haven't the foggiest what! Then I would often dream about lightning, as you know. There would be a flash that hits the ground, maybe 50 meters away from me, then another a bit closer, then another closer still and I just know that the next one is going to hit ME!"

"Oh dear!" said Helen.

"Cripes!" said Michael.

"Then there's an old woman, a *very* old woman, with a weather worn face, no teeth, shaking with palsy and dressed in what seems several layers of ragged old clothes. She tries to make me come closer to her. She's smiling at me and stretching out her bony hand to me, as if wanting to shake my hand. Yuck! I haven't had that dream in years, but it still makes me shiver!"

"How horrible!" said Helen.

"By the cringe!" said Michael.

John also remembered a dream, but a much newer dream, about Lorna McCauley, but he thought it was worth repeating.

"I also dream about a beautiful young woman. I can see her quite vividly. She has black hair and lovely brown eyes, a bit like you, Mum," and Helen blushed and said, "Get away with you!"

"But to continue," he said, "she is also dressed in very unusual clothing, similar to the clothes that some of the women wear in the Sealed Knot re-enactments and she is crying and stretching her arms out to me and she is begging me not to leave her. I am also crying and I try to reach to her, but I can't move my arms. Even though she is not moving, she seems to be drawn backwards, away from me and her voice becomes 'echoey' if you know what I mean and she seems to slowly disappear, as does her cries to me and the next thing I'm aware of, is that I'm flat on my back in the pitch black 'cubby-hole'! It's almost like I'm in a coffin!"

"Oh, John! What a horrid dream!" exclaimed Helen.

"Jaysus!" said Michael.

Both Helen and Michael stared worriedly at John for several seconds. John laughed out loud and said, "Hey, you two! How many times have you told ME that dreams are just dreams! I'm perfectly OK!" and he picked up his drink and took a good draught of it.

Michael copied John's example and said, "Another rahnd o' drinks ah think!" and he got up and went back to the bar.

Helen said, "You certainly DO have a vivid imagination, son, no wonder you used to wake up so distressed during the night!"

John squeezed her hand and said, "Hey, most of these dreams were years ago and of the ones I still get, it's just once in a blue moon! They don't worry me anymore! They're just dreams!"

Michael came back, still with a very concerned look on his face, but that was taken care of by Helen and John, who were laughing and joking about something and Michael joined in with the jovial conversation. The subject of the dreams never came up again and the evening was concluded with a happy and convivial atmosphere.

Bitter-Sweet

John had a few months to wait before he started university and he got a little job as a waiter at a restaurant in the centre of Harrogate, called Stage Left. It was situated on Mount Parade, just next to the Grand Opera House and the building had something of a history to it.

It had actually been a theatre as well, dating back to 1910 and had boasted the name of 'Empire Theatre' for several decades and had been well patronised in it's heyday. The restaurant was beautifully decorated and it was very obvious of its history, by the fact that there was a stage area, a stalls area and circle area above, all with tables and chairs on.

There were palm trees and exotic plants everywhere and there was always a bustling, friendly feeling to its diners, who were many and regular. The whole idea of a converted theatre-to-restaurant really worked well. The way the tables were arranged and the massive photographic portraits of actors from a bygone era adorning the walls and galleries, really gave the customer a feeling of quite literally, eating in a theatre.

Much as he found the work itself enjoyable, the owners were quite hard task masters and asked a lot for a little. As previously alluded to, John was quite gregarious and loved working and being with people, even those he had never met before. The hours were not social, as would be expected in a restaurant, but he liked to think that he gave good value for money. He was always keen to help wherever he could, even doing tasks that were not within in his normal remit, like helping in the kitchen, peeling potatoes or carrots or vacuuming the eating area before or after opening hours.

Invariably, there would be one member of staff or another off sick or on holiday, so being so flexible was a plus in the eyes of his employers. The money that he earned was harvested away for a rainy day for when he was at university. His employers, Mr and Mrs Upton, were extremely hard working themselves and had made a fortune from the restaurant over the years.

To the eyes and ears of the customer, they were the perfect restaurateurs, charming, courteous, polite, diligent and gushingly intent on the customer's pleasure and comfort. Constantly monitoring the customer's progress with their meals, so they didn't have to wait too long between courses, but mindful enough to give them just the right amount of time to let the previous courses go down.

They kept a respectful distance from the customer at all times, but on the instant a customer required anything, they would either hurry to the table themselves or with a snap of their fingers, they would dispatch one of their waiters or waitresses to attend to the customer. Because of John's polite and friendly manner, he was a favourite to be sent to the tables, especially to the more wealthy or obnoxious customers.

To the staff, Mr and Mrs Upton were classed as ogres and they did run the establishment with an iron fist, but when the mood took them, they could be extremely generous. If the takings that day had been substantial, they would often put a £5 note into the hands of each member of staff and thank them for working so hard. They intended to retire within a few years and hand the business over to their daughter, Chantelle.

She was about a year younger than John, having just turned seventeen and was something of a snob. With an effected lisp that she sometimes forgot to use, she was a mixture of attributes and horrors all at the same time. She was about five and a half feet tall, blonde and was seen more often than not in a pair of horse riding breeches and riding boots and she was in the habit of wearing a pair of sunglasses on top of her head, even if there was no sun at all.

John was very much attracted to her looks, as she did in fairness have the most superb figure, beautiful doe eyes and high cheekbones, but he detested what she was and the way she acted and treated other people, especially the staff of the restaurant, who she regarded as 'pond life'. Much as she hated to admit it to herself, Chantelle could not help but be attracted to John, who, like his father, was good looking, tall, broad shouldered and slim hipped. She did precious little when she wasn't at the private ladies college that she attended, except ride her horse, preen herself and incessantly flick her long blonde hair.

One would think that this would be a recipe for disaster and indeed, John and Chantelle had nothing whatsoever in common, apart from physical attraction, but a strange sort of 'love-hate' relationship subsisted between them. She never called him 'John', it was always 'John Twigg', which reminded him of Lorna McCauley. He just let it go over his head and never corrected her rudeness or incorrect use of address.

One Friday evening, after the last customer had gone and the restaurant locked up for the night, John was busy taking the last of the plates and glasses from the eating area into the kitchen for washing up.

The head chef, (who was as cantankerous as Mrs Upton, but was thought the world of by the Upton's and he couldn't do or say anything wrong in their eyes) had dried his hands and thrown his chef's 'whites' onto a work surface and said, "Right! That's it, I'm off! I expect to see everything cut and prepared by the time I get in tomorrow. Oh and Paula," he said looking at a tired young woman who had a streaming cold and who had just put her coat on to go home, "don't even THINK about throwing in a 'sickie' tomorrow, we have 6 bookings of 4 and 2 of 6 and a birthday party of 20, so illness is forbidden!"

She gave him a sullen look, then looked at John with a pitiful expression, as if to say 'you can't win can you?' but she didn't reply to the chef.

One by one, the staff left the building and pulled the door closed behind them. John was doing the last of the tables and just tidying odds and sods before he too went home. He walked into the small bar area, now only lit by the night-lights and there, sat up on the low bar, was Chantelle, in her riding breeches, cross legged and leaning back on her hands. As he saw her, she blew a big bubble with the gum she was chewing, which she sucked in and made it pop.

"Hello, John Twigg, I thought you'd have gone home by now."

"Hi, Chantelle, I didn't see you there, you gave me a start! What are YOU doing here?" he said.

"I asked first!" she retorted with a wry smile and then blew another bubble and swinging her booted leg back and forth.

John smiled and he dryly said, "It may have escaped your observation, Chantelle, but I work here! I'm just finishing off. Is there anything I can do for you?"

She stopped chewing her bubble gum and smiled. She thought for a moment and she said, "Yes! There IS something you can do, pull my boots off, they're killing me!" and she impertinently lifted a leg up so that the sole was right in front of him. He just looked at her, with no expression on his face at all.

"Cat got your tongue then, John Twigg?" she said cockily.

"No not at all," he replied in a disinterested manor, "I just don't get paid for taking young ladies boots off."

There was a lengthy silence and then Chantelle lowered her leg. She stared at him and said, "Does mummy and daddy pay you much money?"

"It's about average for this kind of work," he replied and he leaned against a table opposite her about six feet away and folded his arms.

"Why are you here, Chantelle?" he asked again.

"None of your business!" she said with a smug grin. She started to swing her leg again and she saw John look at it and she noticed him look higher to her thighs. She secretly delighted in this and said, "I can go wherever I please at whatever time I please! I will own all of this soon." And she looked around the place. Her eyes again came back to meet John's.

"What do your parents do then?" she asked as if almost genuinely interested.

"They are retired," he said simply.

"Oh, are they very old and grey then?"

"No, they also have a lot of money and they don't have to work."

Chantelle's whole face and demeanour changed at this and she said, "Why are you working here then?"

"Pocket money!" he said laughing, "Pure pocket money and to save me from getting bored until I go to university."

"University? You? Why?" she said mockingly. "What would *you* hope to study then?"

"I don't *hope* to study anything! I'm GOING to study law!" he said, a bit rattled by her continued snobbish taunting. "If you'll excuse me, I'd best be going home."

"Why?" she said with a bit more of a genuine sound to her voice. "I've learnt something about you today and I'm curious to know more! Besides, will you turn into a pumpkin if you don't get home by midnight? Take my boots off and I'll buy you a drink!"

"Hmm," said John. She lifted her boot up to him again slowly and she said, "Go on then!"

"What do we say first?" John said smiling.

She smiled back and said, "RIGHT NOW!"

He took the boot in his hands and said, "I repeat, what do we say?"

Her breathing was noticeable changed and she looked him straight in the eye and said, "Please."

Then he tugged at the bottom of the boot several times, almost dislodging her from the bar and certainly ruining her pose. She had to sit upright to regain her balance, but then the boot slipped off and John put it on the floor.

"Very good!" she said. "You did that as if you knew what you were doing! Don't tell me you know anything about horses, ha ha!"

"Actually, I probably know more about horses than YOU do!" he said feeling confident in his statement.

"I wouldn't have thought so!" she said with an angry look.

"Please yourself," said John, happy that he seemed to have the upper hand and he turned to walk away.

"Hey! Where do you think YOU'RE going?" shouted Chantelle, one boot off, one boot on and still sat on the bar, "Aren't you going to pull my other boot off?"

"No, I don't think so, goodnight, Chantelle."

"John Twigg! Come back here this instant, I haven't said you can go yet!"

John stormed up to her and eyed her up and down and he said to her in a deep and positive voice, "Listen here, Chantelle Upton, you are NOT my employer, you DON'T pay my wages and to be perfectly frank, I don't *need* this job and what's MORE," he said, raising his voice and putting his face very close to hers, "don't you DARE talk to me like you've just scraped me off your shoe ever again, do you understand me, you stuck up little bitch?"

There was a heart-stopping silence. John was breathing deeply with the passion of his last statement. They stared at each other. Chantelle's eyes were dewy and John expected her to dismiss him on the spot. She pursed her lips and then slapped John's face. He just stood there and didn't flinch. She was about to slap him again but instead, he caught her hand with a vice-like grip which made her wince and he slapped *her* face.

After a moment, she turned her head to face him and they stared at each other again. John realised he should not have done that and was awaiting his marching orders. She pulled her hand from John's grip and put her head in her hands and she sobbed. John was totally confused, but still expected a tirade of abuse and threats at any moment.

This will have been the very first time that Chantelle would have been spoken to like that, let alone be slapped around the face! The expected dismissal didn't come and she just sat and sobbed. John could do nothing but watch at this point and he offered no comfort or words of apology. Several minutes went by and at last she looked up at him and said, "Would you be so kind as to pull my other boot off before you go home, John?"

He looked at her and she seemed so small and helpless all of a sudden. She was, at that moment, just an ordinary young woman, beautiful and shapely, but she had lost all her previous superiority and effected high and mighty attitude.

"OK, if you would like me to," he said gently.

She lifted her leg up to him, still sobbing and he carefully pulled at the boot, which came off much more easily than the first and he put it onto the floor next to the other one. He stared at her foot, then up her legs, then her breasts and then to her face. They gazed at each other for a few seconds, her still sniffling and dewy eyed.

She lifted her arms to him and said, "May I have a cuddle? I'm sorry I've been so beastly to you."

He instinctively moved towards her and she parted her legs to allow him to get closer to her. She put her arms around the small of his back and pulled him close. Both had their eyes closed. She ran her hands slowly up his back and then cupped his face in her hands and their lips met, gently and slowly at first, then with more urgency.

John slowly unbuttoned her blouse and fondled her breasts. She didn't pull away, quite the contrary, she started to become extremely aroused, until they heard the sound of a car pulling up outside the restaurant. It was Mr and Mrs Upton, returning from personally driving a couple who were wealthy and important patrons of the restaurant, back to their home in nearby Ferrensby.

"Oh my GOD!" shouted Chantelle, "They will KILL you! They will kill ME!" she said as she pulled her bra back into position and buttoned up her blouse.

They were both still breathing quite heavily, but the recent shock of her parents coming back speeded up their efforts to resume at least some air of normality. Fortunately for them, they could hear her mother and father talking to someone outside.

"Oh, we're SO pleased you enjoyed it! We do pride ourselves in the beef wellington, Chef is a genius you know and the cinnamon apple pie is one of my own special creations! We look forward to seeing you again soon—"

They had met a gentleman who was walking his dog. He lived not far away from the restaurant and being a retired lieutenant colonel, he was well heeled and was in the habit of dining at the restaurant regularly, preferring to let someone else do the cooking and washing up. This gave John and Chantelle enough time to get her boots back on and think up a reason for them being together. At length, Mr and Mrs Upton came in through the rear door, through the kitchen area.

"COOO-EEEE darling!" shouted Mrs Upton as she came through the back door.

"What's she doing down here?" said Mr Upton to his wife. They came through the kitchen and into the eating area, where Chantelle and John were now sat at a table with a drink each in front of them. Mr Upton put his hands on his hips and said, "Hello, what's going on here then?"

Chantelle had composed herself by this time and replied in her usual manner, "Hi daddy, I saw the lights on from the office and thought that someone had forgotten to turn them off, so I came through, but who should I bump into but John Twigg here!"

"Why are you drinking with the staff?" Mrs Upton said with a scowl.

"Don't be so beastly! I had had problems with the till drawer and as John was just about to leave I asked him if he'd have a look at it for me! He fixed it and so I offered him a drink. Voila!"

"Oh, right then," said Mrs Upton with a frowning face and she eyed John narrowly. "OK, make sure you lock the door behind you! Goodnight!"

"Goodnight, Mummy; goodnight, Daddy," said Chantelle and with that, Mr and Mrs Upton walked away towards the living quarters. They waited until they heard the door to the living quarters shut. All was silence again. Chantelle and John looked at each other for a few seconds and then Chantelle started to snigger.

"Bloody hell, that was close!" she said in a hushed voice.

"Yeah, I thought I was going to have a heart attack!" said John. "Chantelle, you didn't answer my question earlier, why were you in the restaurant?"

"Silly boy! Do I have to spell it out for you?"

"Spell WHAT out?" said John with a grin.

Chantelle leaned forward so her face was only a few inches away from his and she said, "I fancy you! I know it's silly and it's a taboo to fraternise with staff, but I can't help it! Don't you fancy me? Not even a little? Don't you think I'm sweet?" she said standing up and running her hands over her breasts and stomach, then placing her hands on her hips, as if demonstrating the words.

"God yeah, who wouldn't?" said John hypnotically.

This was honey to Chantelle's ears and she pulled the table away, leaving John sat on his chair. She went up to him and straddled her legs to sit on his knee, facing him. She put her arms around his neck and said, "Do you like this?" as she nibbled his ear and kissed his neck.

John closed his eyes and said, "Mmmmm!"

She kissed him quickly on his lips and then said, "Right, you'd better go now or mummy and daddy will find you doing this and they might not be too pleased!"

"God, you're a tease!" said John, who realised that she was right and one thing may lead to another.

"Listen, John, I know what you're thinking, but you're wrong. I don't have a boyfriend and I'm NOT just using you! If you want me to back off, I will! I'm NOT a tease and I know I tend to come across a bit 'county' but I'm telling you, I'm not seeing anyone else and was hoping that you might be interested enough in me to look through my silliness. I can't help who and what I am! Will you at least try to like me?"

John smiled and said, "Let's just sleep on it and think carefully about it! Your mum and dad would hit the roof! Plus, one minute you regard me as just another member of staff and the next you want to kiss me!"

Chantelle playfully pushed John in his chest with her index finger and said, "Yes, but now I know *you* are not from a working class background, Mummy and daddy might just approve."

These words stuck like a fishbone in John's throat as he eyed this beautiful, bold, smug little snob, who he fancied like mad and he thought to himself, *If she just wants to use me, then two can play at that game!*

Union of Differences

When John got home, he went upstairs and had a cool shower and brushed his teeth, then got into bed. His mum and dad had gone to bed ages ago. He thought long and hard about what had happened at the restaurant.

What a difference a day can make! One minute I'm a skivvy and the next I'm being eaten alive by the boss's nympho daughter! Why on earth this change of heart? What does she want? Money? Sex? Just someone on her arm 'cos she's bored? What if she DOES just want sex! I'm still a virgin and wouldn't have a clue how to satisfy her. God, she'd just laugh at me! I'll bet she DOES have a string of boyfriends, all chinless Hooray-Henrys with daddy's 'Wange Wover' on a Saturday night! Why me?

He thought all these things and tried to convince himself that she was up to no good somehow. He could not help still feeling extremely aroused at what had happened and he closed his eyes and relived every moment. The soft fragrance of her perfume, having her sit on him in such a 'come-on' way, the way she invited him to unbutton her blouse and touch her breasts.

Had he dreamed it all? Would he wake up and find it was all in his head? No, it was real alright and he decided to go with the flow of it and let it take its course and onto its natural conclusion, which he suspected would be that she just felt randy or closer to the mark, it was a perfect opportunity to tease him to death! Time would tell and he resolved to play it by ear when he went to work the following day.

John couldn't wait for the next day to get back to work. He was doing the 11 AM 'til 8 PM shift. When he got to work, he was greeted by his colleagues, Pete and Steve, the other waiters, Michelle, Barbara and Lucy, the waitresses, then by Carlos, Liz, Karen and Paula in the kitchen. Poor Paula had a streaming cold and looked like death! She was confined to washing duties and anything that would not put her in contact with food or the other staff. She had to wave to John from her confinement in one corner of the kitchen, operating the dish washer.

"Goodmordig Johd!" she spluttered at him waving and with a broad smile and a little red nose.

"Hiya, Paula," he laughed back to her as he changed into his waiter's apron.

The restaurant was getting busy already and it was only 10 minutes past 11! Saturday and Sunday lunchtimes were particularly busy for them and all the waiters and waitresses were waiting for the nods and beckons from the customers to take their orders.

Mr and Mrs Upton were there, greeting customers on their arrival and those who had booked, were cordially shown to their tables and had their chairs pulled out for them, until he or she was comfortable, then they would return to the entrance, nodding and waving to left and right. John had a spring in his step and even though the restaurant was at capacity by midday, John kept a look out for Chantelle, but she didn't put in an appearance, not even from the office or the kitchen. He was very disappointed and his heart sank.

"Maybe she WAS just teasing," he thought to himself gloomily, as he re-set table after table and brought out meal after meal. He lost himself in his work and before he knew it, it was the 'quiet' period of around about 2:30 PM. A break was called by Mrs Upton for a few of the staff. There was a small staff room to the back of the building, where they could sit and relax and have their lunches. John was one of the few and he made his way past the bar and headed towards the restroom.

Mrs Upton saw him and called to him, "John, I'd like a word with you please."

She said it with an expressionless face. John thought that he was going to get his dismissal there and then and wondered if Chantelle had given her parents a sob story the he was 'awful' to her or that maybe they themselves had witnessed something the night before? He braced himself for the worst as Mrs Upton led him into the office.

"Sit down, John," she said as she closed the office door behind him. She sat at the desk and looked sternly at him.

"Chantelle has told me how kind you had been to her last night, how you fixed the till and that you said you would do the repairs to her stable door next weekend. I wanted to thank you personally, you are a good hard worker and I reflected on the way I had spoken to you last night and I just wanted to apologise. It had been a particularly vexatious day yesterday and by the time we got back here after taking a customer home, we were exhausted."

John was totally speechless and he stammered for words. Mrs Upton didn't allow him to start speaking, instead she continued, "Chantelle has told us that you have been an unsung hero around the restaurant for quite some time, with repairs generally, that has never come to our attention and you have done them without question or pause."

"Well, erm—yes, well—I—" John groped for words and he was utterly confused.

She continued, "There will be an extra £20 in your pay packet this week tax free, as a thank you and we are going to increase your wages by another £10 per week. How does that sound, John?"

John just didn't know what to say except, "Thank you! That's very generous of you!"

Mrs Upton smiled and said, "Tush! We always repay kindnesses! Chantelle tells us that your parents have no need to work? Are they self-made or have they inherited from somewhere? Oh, I'm sorry, that's none of my business, do forgive me! You seem like such a nice young chap, John and Mr Upton and I are anxious that Chantelle only associates with suitable people. Believe it or not, we are a bit old fashioned," she said chuckling, "and we want her to be happy, but with people that we can rely upon to take good care of her, do you understand what I'm saying?"

"Well, not really," said John, biting his lip, to which Mrs Upton smiled and said, "Chantelle is very much a loner. She always tries to kid people that she is bogged down with friends, but truth be told, she is really quite a lonely girl and I dare say that we have, how can I say, 'protected' her maybe a bit over zealously. She sings your praises all the time, but we have always insisted that she doesn't fraternise with staff. Familiarity breeds contempt!

But knowing you a little more now and feeling as we do that she should have more friends, especially male friends, we agree that it can't do her any harm to be friends with someone she chooses rather than us trying to pick her friends for her. An all-girl college is fine, but it does tend to make a girl a bit insular. Oh, she tries to make out that she is OK and doesn't need any more friends, but she does talk about you in such an animated way, so I wanted to check you out personally.

You are obviously well educated and have a good deal of oil in your lamp. Would you like to take Chantelle out once in a while, to the cinema or to a theatre show? She tells us that you know quite a lot about horses! We were extremely happy to hear about that and we realise now that you obviously come from a similar background to Chantelle and that pleases us! I'm glad that you have so much in common with her. Will you consider my request, John?"

John was wide eyed and totally blown away by all of this. He was speechless, which Mrs Upton construed as thoughtfulness and she liked that very much indeed. At last he said, "Yes, it would be an honour and a true pleasure to accompany Chantelle to somewhere like you have described and I thank you for considering me to be a suitable escort. I cannot deny, I do have a tremendous respect for her and hope that I can be the friend that she obviously seeks. I'm looking forward to getting to know her as a friend and not as a taboo at work."

Mrs Upton leaned towards John and squeezed his hand, "Good-oh!" she said with a smile, "I was hoping you would say something like that! But listen, I want you to keep this to yourself whilst you're at work. I don't want there to be any suggestion to the other staff that Chantelle and you have anything but a professional relationship, do you understand?"

John thought for a moment and then replied, "Yes. I do understand, but what if we we're seen out together by a member of staff?"

"You would say that it was pure coincidence and that you were both there at the same time by accident, so you decided to sit next to each other."

John nodded in comprehension, but inwardly, he detested all of this. He was being used and he knew it, but having been given such a golden egg, he wasn't going to shoot the goose that laid it!

If I'm going to be used, what a hell of a way to be used! he thought to himself.

"Now then, Chantelle's horse is always kicking his stable door and a couple of the wooden panels have come loose. They may need replacing. I have pre-empted your answer just now and have told Chantelle that we will take you up to the paddock next Saturday to do the repairs. You don't mind, do you? We will just drop you off and then Chantelle and you can set to and do whatever's necessary for the repairs. Chantelle has one of these new fangled 'mobile phones' you know and she can get hold of us if you need any materials or tools to help you. Will that be alright?"

John nodded assent, but even though his head was a jumble, he said to himself, "I didn't agree to fix any stable doors? What the hell's she talking about?" but he feigned a look of deepest thanks to Mrs Upton.

"Now, you'd best be on with your duties. If anyone asks why I was speaking to you, just tell them that I was reprimanding you for a dirty fork or something. Oh and not a word to anyone else about the pay rise!" she said pointing her finger at him.

With that, she got up and went back into the restaurant. John watched her erect and dignified frame as she swanned into the reception area. He eyed her up and down and thought to himself, "What a nasty, conniving, scheming cow you are!"

Saturday came. It was John's Saturday off, so he was up with the lark, showered and brushed and had gone downstairs to make some breakfast. Helen and Michael wandered down as the last of the toast was popping out of the toaster.

"Eighup, lad!" said Michael, "Sleep well?"

"Like a log, Dad!" John replied with a huge grin, which told his dad there was something special on today.

"Ya smell good enough ta eat! Mmm, got yer best poo-foo on an' all! It must be a lass? Eighup, Helen," he shouted to her as she came through from the living room, "John's got a date! Tell us abaht it then, lad! What's 'er name like?" and Helen joined in the joke taunt.

"I hope you've vetted her carefully! We don't want any old date for our boy, do we, Mike?"

"That's fer sure! Aren't ya gonna tell us 'er name at least?"

John laughed and said, "Whoa you two, you're putting a lot of two and two's together and I can't deny, you're coming up with the correct answer! Dad, brace yourself, you will not care for her name, I know you so well, but she is the most beautiful girl and I'm a very lucky lad to even be noticed by her, let alone be seeing her!"

Michael stared at John for a few seconds and then said, "Well? Go on then, ya daft ha'porth, what's 'er name?"

"She's called Chantelle," he said.

There was a bit of a wide eyed pause from Michael, who then said, "Mmm! Mum an' dad loaded, are they? Hang abaht! It's not that piggin' Chantelle who's the snotty daughter of yer boss, is it?"

"Well, er, yes it is," said a very embarrassed John.

Michael was completely taken aback by this, as he had often had a good rant about Chantelle in the past and how she acted and the way she treated other people.

"Bugger me! What the 'eck ya doin' wi' a bit o' nowt like 'er?" quizzed Michael, but Helen could see that John was embarrassed and said, "Come on now, Mike, enough. John, has she had a change of heart towards you then?"

"She needs a change of brain—and parents—AND name!" said Michael sarcastically.

"Michael! That's quite enough! John, don't listen to old Mr Grumpy! Tell me what you're planning to do today? Has she really changed her ways?"

John dealt his father a bitter look then he turned to his mother, who was smiling sweetly at him.

"Yes mum, I don't really know how it happened, but you are right, we seemed to hate each other at one stage, in fact everybody hated her, but lately, I have seen another side to her. She is really quite soft and almost pathetic in the true sense of the word. There really is a human being under the surface."

"How did ya discover that then? Wi' dynamite?" sneered Michael.

John continued without retaliation, "Her mum and dad have given me a pay rise too, I'm not sure why, I guess I must be doing the job right or something."

"You'll need a pay rise ta pamper to t' whims o' that over privileged little bint!"

"DAD, just SHUT UP!" shouted John and he slammed his tea cup down on the breakfast table and stormed out of the kitchen. He grabbed his coat and stomped out of the house, slamming the door behind him.

"Well! You asked for that, Mike! Why the hell did you go off on one at the poor lad?"

"SHE'S askin' fer one, ya mean! Ah can't stand t' likes o' them sort o' folk, ya *know* that!"

"Yes, Mike, but how's it hurting YOU? In fact, what's it got to DO with you? Let John be young! Goodness me, he's worked so hard on his studies, let the poor kid have some time off and a bit of fun! What's the worst that can come from it?" Helen said angrily.

"Getting' 'er up the stick?" he said raising his voice a little.

"Oh come on! It's a first date for God's sake! Credit your own son with a bit more sense and besides, there ARE such things as condoms nowadays you know, I'm sure if it ever came to that, he would be sensible. Do you know you can be such a hypocrite sometimes! How long were WE going out before we made love? You should feel pleased that John has a girlfriend after all this time! How would you feel if he came home with a BOY in tow?"

"Now yer just bein' daft! John is a chip off the old block! 'Es as red blooded as me!"

"Then shut up and let him be a man then! Let him discover himself and have some fun! Heavens above, stop being so judgemental to things that don't suit YOU!"

Michael thought for a moment and then said, "Fair do's. Ah can only 'ope 'e gets what 'e wants from 'er an' then gets shut of 'er. If they DO get serious like, I'd want nowt to do wi' 'er family, do ya 'ear me?"

Helen was lost for words and she shook her head in despair. She put her cup down and walked out of the kitchen and left Michael to brood.

John arrived at the restaurant at just before 9 o'clock. He went in through the 'Pit Entrance' door at the side of the building and met Mrs Upton coming out of the office. She was in jeans and a T-shirt, which he stared at, as he had always seen her dressed like she had just stepped out of a shop window! There was no other staff around at that time and Mrs Upton greeted him in a bright and chipper manner, "Good morning, John, nice to see you. How are you today?"

"Oh, fine thanks," he said, still trying hard to lighten his face after his spat with his dad. "I've brought a bag of tools with me," and he looked down at a bag of tools that he had taken from the garage at home, when he had left the house. "I just put together what I thought I may need, from the way you described the damage to the stable door. Where's Chantelle?" he asked, looking round to see if she was there.

"Oh, she's not here. She has an appointment this morning. Besides, you don't want a girl around whilst you're doing manual work, do you?"

John's heart sank like a lead weight. He knew there would be something like this and he reproached himself for taking the bait, but Mrs Upton continued, "She will be going up to the stables in an hour or two. She's just recently passed her driving test and we have bought her a little car, so she's quite independent now!"

The look of relief on John's face must have been very obvious, as Mrs Upton laughed and said, "Oh! Did you think that she wasn't coming at all? Ha ha! She's very much looking forward to seeing you! Right, come along, let's get you up there. I've got to get back here soon, as chef is poorly so I have to do the cooking today."

"Oh dear!" said John, who inwardly said to himself, "nothing trivial I hope!"

They climbed into Mrs Upton's Jaguar and John admired the classy looks. The smell of faux leather and the walnut dashboard! He was well impressed! It drove silently and as if they were in an aircraft, just riding the road effortlessly.

Mrs Upton drove John to the stables that were situated just behind a public house called 'The Black Bull' near Kettlesing, about 5 miles west of Harrogate. It was a beautiful morning and surprisingly warm for the early hour. Mrs Upton pulled up at the gate to the paddock. John could see the stables, about 50 metres away, surrounded by a little coppice of trees.

His heart was thumping and he had to think carefully about what he was saying to Mrs Upton, who had said to him, "Here we are, John, can I drop you here? The gate is not locked. You can let yourself in, is that OK?"

"Oh that's fine, Mrs Upton, I'll be alright from here!"

Mrs Upton smiled at John and said, "John, seeing as you are a little closer to the family now, when you address me privately, do call me Jenny!"

"OK—Jenny," said John with a bit of a blush and they shook hands. Mrs Upton then drove away, back to Harrogate.

High in a tree, the sound of a lone meadow pipit was singing its creator's praise and John breathed in the fresh, clean air of the countryside that was there within his sight. What a gorgeous day! He stared at the dew on the cobwebs on a nearby bush and he could hear the distant mooing of cows. He walked towards the stable and all of a sudden, he heard the whinny of a horse. It was Chantelle's horse, who had seen John walking towards him and was instinctively thinking that here was someone who was going to give him his breakfast!

John approached the stable door and the friendly horse whinnied again in greeting. John stroked the horse's muzzle and it responded with a powerful lift of its huge head two or three times. John loved horses, having worked with them with the Sealed Knot Society for so long and he had stowed some food in his tool bag, especially for the horse. He first took a couple of carrots and the horse made short shrift of them! Then an apple and that went in the blink of an eye too.

John stroked the horse's muzzle all the while and could feel the loud crunching through the horse's chin as he stroked it there. Next, a few sugar lumps that he had taken from the restaurant. The horse once again whinnied in appreciation and John admired the creature for a moment, a beautiful chestnut gelding, with intelligent eyes and ever alert ears. The horse nosed John for more food and he smile at the horse's personality.

"You are a good boy, I can see we're going to be friends," he said gently.

After a few minutes petting the eager animal, John thought it prudent to get on with his appointed task. He examined the stable door and sure enough, three of the boards had been kicked outwards. He looked at the workmanship and tutted. The good news was that it was a very easy repair to do. He vaulted the stable door, much to the delight of the horse, who nuzzled him expectantly and he considered the damage from the inside.

"Yes, a few 2 inch screws and wood-glue to the transoms should do the trick," he said to himself. He vaulted the stable door again and got the things he needed to do the repair. The horse looked wistfully at John, as he vaulted the gate again with his things. The horse nosed John again and he smiled, knowing what the horse was hoping for and he delivered the horse's wish, with another large apple. The horse munched away and John got on with the repair to the door.

Within 10 minutes, all was done and John put his tools back into his tool bag. He vaulted the gate once more and sat on a patch of grass near to the stable.

I wonder when Chantelle will get here? he thought to himself and he got up to admire a nearby bush, laden with blackberries. He picked a few and ate them, savouring their gorgeous flavour. Next to the blackberry bush, were yet more fruit bushes and John sampled a few of the berries. There were Logan berries, raspberries and gooseberries. As he was screwing his face up at a sour gooseberry, a pair of hands covered his eyes from behind and a voice said, "Guess who?"

John's heart missed a beat and he turned around to see Chantelle, who was almost unrecognisable in a pretty little peasant blouse with puffed shoulders and little pink flowers down the buttoned front. She had a peasant-style skirt on and a pair of simple trainers on her feet. Her long blonde hair was tousled and had a few little ribbons here and there, making her look absolutely beautiful.

John just stared her up and down and said, "My God, Chantelle, you look divine! Why are you dressed like this, just to repair a stable door?"

"Ah!" she said with a smile. "You have repaired my stable door and I thought it was about time I repaired the way I have treated you all these months!"

With that, she took John's hand and led him back up to the now open gate and said, "Help me with these things. I thought you might like a spot of brunch with me, seeing as you have been so kind and come here to help me."

She opened the small boot of her Rover Mini and there, was a big wicker picnic basket. John instantly picked it up out of the boot and said, "My God, why all this?"

Chantelle smiled and kissed him tenderly on his cheek and replied, "I told you, I am not the person you have always thought I was, I just want you to know how much I appreciate what you have done for me this morning!"

They walked back through the gate and Chantelle locked it behind her.

"Would you like to take a walk around my fields?" said Chantelle, with a really happy and relaxed smile.

"Oh, yes please!" said John, still admiring her from the riding breeches that she would normally wear. Chantelle offered her hand to him and he took it. They walked away from the stable and down the field towards a stream. It was the most evocative spot, the brook babbling away, huge trees dipping their heavy load of leaves close to the water. A more perfect aspect could not have been hoped for and John's heart melted.

"Do you like what you see, John?" said Chantelle.

"Hell, yeah!" he replied, staring at her.

"No, silly, I meant the view!"

"Hell, yeah!" he repeated and he tried to lean towards her to kiss her.

"John, no, I mean what I say! I love this spot and when I feel lonely or blue, I often come here and have a good cry or just get my head around things. Do you know what I mean?"

"Chantelle, how could you EVER feel lonely, you are young, beautiful, intelligent and sexy! Why on earth should you be unhappy? You have the world at your feet!"

Chantelle smiled sadly and said, "I told you the other day that I didn't have a boyfriend? Well, I honestly don't. I have always been steered away from boys by mummy and daddy, saying to me that they are horrid, money grabbing creatures who only want gain. That's why, when we spoke the other night and you told me that you didn't really need the money, my heart jumped for joy! I told my mummy and she took a bit of convincing, but she thought you would be good for me and not just use me like a lot of guys would."

John's thoughts went back to the fact that HE thought he was being used at that time and he tried hard to believe her.

"Chantelle," he said softly and taking her hand, "What is it that you really want? What have I got that you could possibly want?"

She turned to him with a sincere look and said, "Exactly this! You are good and honest and you seem to want me for what I am and not for what I seem to be to everyone else. I know I've been brought up as a snob and when I was little, it amused me to think I was better than everyone else—I was taught that lesson every day by mummy and daddy.

They want me to marry into money and they don't have a regard as to whether or not I will be happy! Then you came along and I fancied you, but knew I couldn't have you because you seemed to be below me, then you told me about your mum and dad and that they were reasonably wealthy and the fact that mummy and daddy knew you as such an honest and hardworking boy, they acceded to letting me see you from time to time."

John's heart was boiling! What snobs! What prejudice! Horrid, horrid people! Especially stifling their daughter, who it seemed was not of the same mould as them, she was being manipulated into something they wanted her to be! All of this went through his mind as he faced Chantelle, took her hands and tenderly kissed her.

"Come along, 'John Twigg'!" she said in a jocular way, "let me show you what I have brought you in repayment for your hard work!"

John's mind reeled! They walked slowly up the field, hand in hand, until they reached the stable. The horse whinnied as it saw Chantelle. She opened a door to a room immediately next to the stable, where there were provisions kept for the horse. She grabbed a huge bag of oats and took them through to the stable.

The horse whinnied excitedly to see Chantelle and she put the oats into a trough in front of him. John knew exactly what to do, with his training with the Sealed Knot Society and he brought through some fresh straw and put it into the feeder. Having done that, they both walked out into the sunshine. They stared at the beautiful aspect around them and she took his hand.

"Hungry?" she said smiling at him.

"Starved!" he said with an impish grin and she went into the adjoining room to get the picnic hamper. There was a small, grassy hillock about 20 feet away from the stable that was a lovely vantage point for the whole of the fields around them and the magnificent view across Nidderdale, all the way to Brimham rocks. Chantelle opened the hamper and there was a veritable feast inside! Fresh crusty bread and butter, a beautiful duck-liver pâté, scones with fresh strawberry jam, croissants and a bottle of Chardonnay, straight from the restaurant's cellar.

Once again, Chantelle smiled and said, "Do you like what you see?"

John was famished and said, "Hell yeah!" and they took out the plates and cutlery from the hamper basket and set to the food.

"Cheers!" John said as he poured Chantelle a glass of the wine. They clinked their glasses and Chantelle said, "Here's to us! A strange and extraordinary mixture of differences! Here's to mingling our differences even further!"

She looked John in the eye as she said this. There was no mistaking what she meant.

It wasn't long before the food was all gone and the wine had had a mellowing effect on both of them. They weren't drunk, but they were happily silly.

"I've always fancied you, you know!" John said with a grin.

"And I've always fancied YOU, you gorgeous hunk of spunk!" she said.

John smiled at the compliment and said, "Do you know, you sound completely different now, you sound just like a normal human being, you gorgeous upper class beauty!"

Chantelle span round to John and said, "Do you really think that I'm beautiful, John? I think I'm ugly! I know that my manner needs addressing and that I hurt people with my attitude, including YOU in the past!"

She got up and walked away a little. John responded tenderly, saying, "Chantelle, the fact that you realise your shortcomings proves how beautiful you really are and that you are not of the same mindset as your mum and dad."

She still had her back to him, but she paused and thought for a moment and then stretched out her hand behind herself. John was there in an instant and she led him into the room beside the stable. Not a word was said. In one corner of the room was a huge pile of straw, pulled from the hay bales. Chantelle grabbed a large tartan blanket, usually used for keeping her horse warm after riding him and spread it onto the straw and she flopped herself onto it. John just gazed at her. His thoughts were on fire and his heart raced. She lay on the blanket and smiled timidly at him.

"Come here beside me and let your lunch go down," she said. John was lost for words and just stared at her.

"Do you like what you see?" she asked simply, as she seductively ran her hands from her hair down to her breasts, then to her hips.

John slowly lay on the blanket next to her and said, "Chantelle, you are the most beautiful girl I have ever seen in my life!"

He got up onto his knees and positioned himself between her legs. There was a moment's pause as they stared at each other, then she pulled him down by his shirt front and she kissed him. Instantly, the kissing became more passionate and Chantelle tugged at the top button of John's jeans. He responded and helped her to undo it. His mind was wild with desire. He unbuttoned her peasant blouse. She had nothing underneath it. Her skirt had an elasticised waist and as they kissed, she slipped it effortlessly over her hips and off her legs.

John gazed at her now naked body. He kissed her breasts and they both panted with mounting passion. John took off the rest of his clothing and he stood over her, she looking up at him with the same dewy eyes he had seen at the restaurant a few days before. She raised her arms to him and he slowly and tremblingly came down on top of her. As their bodies met, she tremulously said, "Please be gentle, John, I truly AM still a virgin."

"So am I," said John. They kissed passionately for a few moments and then he said, "I can't believe this is happening, Chantelle," as he positioned himself.

"Ouch!—ouch!" Chantelle said. John didn't reply.

"You're hurting me, you're—" and then she stopped talking and she breathed heavily.

"I'm sorry," said John, panting into her ear, "I'm trying to be gentle!"

"It's—OK—John—just—keep—doing—that—YES—you're—OH GOD, yes—do that to me—" And the last moments of innocent childhood for two young people were allowed to go free.

The Final Straw

They both lay on their backs, exhausted and smiling at each other.

"I never imagined it could be like that! That was amazing!" said Chantelle.

"Bloody hell yeah!" said John and they cuddled up while they regained their breath. It was a truly magical moment. The meadow pipits and skylarks were chirping their songs and the sun was streaming through a high window of the stable, making shafts of light from the dust of the hay that they had kicked up during their love making. The afterglow was overwhelming and they both felt sleepy, especially after the effects of the wine too.

They dozed and would probably have gone into a deeper sleep, but they were disturbed by the sound of a dog barking. Chantelle got up and ran the door. Walking towards them was the farmer who owned the land adjacent to theirs. He had been given permission to graze his sheep there by Mr and Mrs Upton and it was actually doing them a favour, as it did help to keep the grass of their meadow trimmed.

He was a true, dyed-in-the-wool Yorkshire farmer, of about 50 years of age. He always wore green corduroy trousers, an old tweed jacket with elbow patches and an old, well-thumbed flat hat, that he wore slightly to the right side of his head, a collarless shirt of heavy cotton and a big green pair of gum boots with straps at the top and a shepherd's crook made up the appearance of this rustic. Rustic maybe, but truth be known, he was worth a fortune and even though in vernacular and deportment, he was a million miles away from the Uptons, in money, he probably equalled or bettered them and this is why the Uptons liked to keep on his good side.

His dog barked again with excitement at seeing the horse. Chantelle told John to hide behind the hay bales, so he grabbed his clothes and ran to where he was told. Chantelle had just enough time to put on her skirt and blouse and then she nonchalantly walked out of the stable door.

"Oh, hello, Mr Whittles, how are you today?"

"Eighup, Chantelle! Ah didn't recognise ya, lass! Ha ha! I ain't seen yer in lasses clothes afore! What ya doin' up 'ere? Is that your car parked up by t' gate like?"

"Yes, it is!" she said putting on her effected lisp again, which John cringed at as he heard it! "I was showing my horse to a friend of mine. She's gone now, but it was such a nice morning, I decided to stay for a while."

While they were talking, John was able to get dressed and he tidied his hair and got all the bits of straw from his clothes. He opened a side door to the stable, which was secured by a latch to the inside and he closed the door silently behind himself.

He could see Mr Whittles' back, as he was talking to Chantelle. She saw John over Mr Whittles' shoulder and could see him gesturing that he would go up to the gate and pretend to come in again. He was at the gate in a few seconds and opened it gently then he banged it deliberately, whistling loudly as if to himself. This had the desired effect and Mr Whittles turned and squinted into the sunshine, where the noise had come from.

"Oh, John sweetie! Hiya, Glad you were able to make it!" and John came bounding down the grassy path towards the stable. The horse whinnied again, with perfect timing, as it seemed that it had recognised him and that suited their secret ruse perfectly.

John came up to Chantelle and put his arm around her waist and feigned being one of the 'in set' that Chantelle liked to aspire to and he said, "Hiya, babe, who's the dude?"

Mr Whittles just gawped at John and raised his flat hat as Chantelle said, "Oh yes, sugar, this is Mr Whittles who has land adjoining ours and we let him graze his sheep here. Mr Whittles, this is my boyfriend, John!"

John held out his hand and there was a pregnant pause as Mr Whittles scowled at it. John held the pose for some seconds and then dropped his hand and laughed and said, "It's a shame his manners aren't as quaint as his looks!"

To which Mr Whittles turned on his heels and muttered to himself as he trudged away back to the gate. He latched the gate and stared back at the two of them, still muttering to himself, then walked down the lane and out of sight. Chantelle and John laughed out loud and fell into each other's arms.

"Thank God, you had that idea, my 'knight in shining armour' you! Because I wasn't dressed as I would usually be when I come up here, Mr Whittles was getting quite amorous with me and was trying to give me unwelcome compliments. He was leering at my breasts and eyeing me up and down!"

"Why did he come here in the first place?" asked John.

"Oh, he saw my Mini and he trusts nobody and when he saw the stable door open and, knowing him, he was hoping to give someone a good threatening with the police for trespassing. I guess we should be grateful, as he IS a good watchdog for us!"

They packed all their things away and took them back to the car.

"Must you go home just yet, John?" she asked sincerely.

"Of course not! What made you think I had to go home? I won't turn into a pumpkin, you know!" She remembered the instance of those words and she let go of the gear stick and held his hand.

"Would you like to go for a stroll through the woods with me?" she asked.

"Yes, that would be lovely! Where had you in mind?"

"Well, Mummy and Daddy loved to take me through a forest of pines not far from here, when I was a little girl in my pram. That was when they spent a bit less time on making money. Money is their golden idol you know, John."

"Yes, I HAD gathered that, Chantelle," he said with a hint of sarcasm in his voice. They drove along the Skipton road and past Menwith Hill station which was situated to their left. She took the next turning right, which took them onto the Otley road. In the near distance, John could see a large transmitter tower on top of an outcrop of rocks.

"It's not far from here now, not too far away from that tower," she said.

Another left turn took them onto Broad Dubb Lane, towards Beckwithshaw. Within a couple of miles, they noticed a rock outcrop just off the main road to their right. John stared at it and seemed to remember it from somewhere, but he'd never been there, that he could recall. It seemed to have distant memories for him, but he couldn't put a finger on it. They came to a bend in the road, where there was a car park to the right.

She went into the car park and pulled up. They looked at each other again and they smiled and kissed each other. Out they climbed and walked to a large wooden gate, with a pedestrian gate to the left of it. Beyond, was a footpath, cutting its way through huge pine trees, leading to who knew where! It was a beautiful day, warm, bees humming and the sound of all kinds of birds echoing through the dense forest cap.

The breeze softly rustled the treetops and the new couple took each other's hands and they strolled along the footpath. There was not another soul in sight and it was truly peaceful and away from the hustle and bustle.

Chantelle was staring at John and at length she said, "John, please forgive me for the way I have treated you over the last few weeks, I was so desperate to talk to you but I thought you would not take me seriously and that you would think me a snob or a stuck up bimbo. I thought I had to impress you with an air of independence and couldn't-care-lessness, do you know what I'm trying to say?"

John smiled and said, "If you recall, that is exactly what I DID call you!"

"Don't mock me, John, I'm trying to be honest with you! Yes, I know I come across a bit county, but it's been drilled into me from a child, both at home and at college! There has been another me, deep inside, bursting to get out and I have never had anybody to call a true friend. No one to release my desires. Nobody cared for me even though they were drowning me in lavish gifts, education and holidays.

Then you came along! As soon as I saw you, I wanted you. But I didn't know any different. I thought I was acting the way I should act to someone I fancied. My mum and dad always told me to keep boys at arm's length and to keep them begging at my feet, *"That's the way to get what you want in life, darling!"* is what they would tell me time after time. But then I knew what I wanted but didn't know how to get it.

When you slapped my face, my immediate reaction was to shout for the police and do you as much damage as I could, but I thought, *I have been a total bitch, just take it and be damned for your own impudence!* When you slapped me, you changed my whole life and I adore you for it! Yes, I was a bit scheming wasn't I, but you DO fancy me, don't you, John?"

She looked at him and he had tears rolling down his cheeks at this speech.

"Chantelle, I am NOT an animal! Do you really think I would have done what we have just done if I didn't fancy you? The dumb animals have sex, we made love! It was my first time and I am truly thankful it was you that took my virginity away from me. You are a tremendous girl and I can't believe how fast we went from enemies to lovers."

"I was NEVER your enemy, John, I just didn't know how to get to you! We seemed to live completely different lives and I knew or at least thought it could never happen. I care for you, 'John Twigg'! I want you to know that I wanted

YOU to make me a woman at last and not some drunken champagne guzzling suit in the passenger seat of his Porsche, having got me drunk first!"

They eventually came to another wooden gate. Beyond that was a road that disappeared to left and right, presumably to farms. They leaned on the gate and could see, to their left, aircraft coming and going into Leeds Bradford airport, some 9 or 10 miles away.

They could distinguish the planes companies from there and it was quite a mesmerising sight. 'Spanair, Jet2, Ryanair, they all came and went to and from their far away destinations, carrying happy, holidaying people to their sunny holidays or returning them to good old 'Blighty' with sombrero, tan and screaming kids. John was looking at Chantelle all the while, as she was watching the 'planes coming and going. He placed his hands on her buttocks and she span round immediately.

"Do you want me again?" she said with an urgency in her voice,

"God yes! I do, I really do, Chantelle!" and she led him away from the gate, back up the path that they had come down.

The forest was very dense and dark. Within 20 feet of leaving the path, it was as if it were dusk. The ground was covered in years of pine needles that had mulched into a bed of soft carpet-like consistency. They vaulted an irrigation ditch and were in the quiet and darkness. It was warm and had a strange sort of 'greeting' feel to it. They found a dry, branch-free hillock and they sat down on it. At once they embraced and took each other's clothing off. They used the clothing as blankets and they once again made love, this time, with a little more understanding and control.

Exhausted, John said, "Chantelle, I want to make love to you until I die!" She said pretty much the same to him and then her face dropped. He said, "What's wrong love? Did I say something wrong just there? Did I hurt you?"

"No," she said, "I'm just thinking to myself that I hope I'm on my 'safe' period."

"WHAT?" shouted John. "Aren't you on the pill?"

"No, not yet," she said sobbing.

"Oh, my GOD! Chantelle! What have you DONE?" he screamed as he put his jeans back on. "What the hell do you think you are playing at? Why did you let us get this far and not say something? Jesus Christ! I have a bloody CONDOM in my pocket, why did you let me go all the way? TWICE?"

Chantelle was in floods of tears and couldn't respond. He left her there, semi naked and he ran all the way up the path to the car park. He could hear her shouting, "John—John—" behind him, but he didn't turn around.

"John—please—" he could hear her plead, now in the distance. He ran all the way home, about 7 miles. All the way down Norwood Lane he kept looking behind himself to make sure that Chantelle's car wasn't coming, but at last, he saw it and he vaulted a wall and hid until she had gone past. He ran and walked the rest of the way and when he eventually arrived home, he burst through the door. Helen and Michael heard the front door open with a thump and immediately knew something was wrong.

"JUST LEAVE ME ALONE!" shouted John. He was bawling his eyes out.

"John lad! Talk ta yer old dad! It's OK, lad!"

"Just leave me ALONE!" he screamed as he thundered upstairs. Below, Helen and Michael could hear John breaking his heart and realised that he could not possibly be consoled. They left him to it.

"Ah'll bet it's that bloody Chantelle Upton at t' bottom o' this, mark mah words, it is!" said Michael with a grim face.

"Oh, they've probably just had a spat like you and I used to have all those years ago!" she said, trying to lighten the mood a little.

"Ah bloody TOLD 'im ta leave t' likes o' 'er alone, but would 'e listen? Would 'e buggery!"

Helen got up from her chair and put her tea cup down. She went to Michael's chair and sat on her knees beside him. She took his hand and said, "John's a sensible boy, but he's new to girls! He'll be OK, love, it will be a trivial thing that will be forgotten in the morning." And she stretched up and kissed him on his cheek. She thought for a moment or two and then still trying to lighten the mood, she said, "Shall I go upstairs and put on some devil red lippy and nail polish on for you—?"

Michael thought for a moment and said, "Maybe," with a little boy look.

"Come and take me tiger!" she said as she pulled at his hand.

"Only if ya put on the pink baby doll too!" he said, now with a smile on his face.

"Give me 10 minutes, you sex-god!" she said pouting at him.

Michael smiled and said to himself, "Fer what ah am abaht ta receive, may ah be given the strength ta enjoy it!" and he went up the stairs to brush his teeth.

During the night, Helen and Michael heard John getting out of bed and going into the bathroom. He seemed to be suppressing sobs still and they heard him vomiting from time to time. It was a broken night for all of them. In the morning, John was last down to breakfast and he looked pale and drawn.

"Are you OK, son?" said Helen, putting her arm around his shoulder.

"Yes. I'm fine," he said, with red eyes and subdued manner.

"Would you like some breakfast, I have done a grill. Bacon, eggs, mushrooms, beans—"

"Oh please shut up, Mum!" he said nearly retching at the thought.

"OK, son. Have it your way—" she stared at him and then Michael with a confused look. John walked to the cubby-hole and got a coat and walked towards the front door.

"I need some fresh air," he said, "I'll see you both later."

Helen stood there like a statue, with a pair of tongs in her hand and at last looked at Michael, who too, was looking dumbfounded. After a minute or two, Michael said, "OK, lass, all's the more fer you an' me then! Gerrit served up!"

John would not go to work all the following week, despite many a phone call from the restaurant. On their answer machine were calls from Mrs Upton, Mr Upton and Chantelle, who was always tearful. John just deleted them as soon as recognised. This went on for a week. John decided to listen to a few of the recordings that he hadn't deleted.

Firstly Mrs Upton, who sounded very concerned at John's absence, then increasingly angry that he hadn't responded to her calls. Then Mr Upton, who told him, in no uncertain manner, that he was dismissed. Then there was a recording from Chantelle, who had a very resigned sound to her voice and she said, "Hi John, I've tried to contact you many times now, but you won't answer me! Please, please will you answer me? I need to tell you—" John deleted the message.

Poor Helen and Michael hardly got a word out of John that whole week and they didn't know what to do for the best. They thought the best thing to do was to just leave him alone and let him come out of it naturally. The postman delivered the mail early on the Thursday morning and amongst the bills and junk mail, was a pale pink envelope, with a pretty design on the left hand corner. It was hand-written, in beautiful writing and addressed to John. Helen picked it up and realised it was a letter from Chantelle. She put it to her nose and it had the aroma of a lovely perfume.

"Here it is!" she said to herself. She made a pot of tea and let it brew. She went into see Michael, who was reading his newspaper in the living room. She whispered, "Guess what!" to him and pointed at the letter.

Michael smiled and said quietly, "Eighup, put yer tin-'at on!"

Helen poured John a cup of tea and took it and the letter to John's room. She tapped at his bedroom door. After a few seconds, a very grumpy John said, "Come in."

In she went.

"Good morning, son," she said and she looked at him still in bed, hands behind his head and staring at the ceiling. "I thought you might like a cup of tea," she said gently. She looked at him expectantly, waiting for some kind of response. It didn't come.

"Thanks," he said as she had given up and was just about to walk out of the door. She went back downstairs and joined Michael to drink their tea. John was oblivious of the letter and he lay there brooding. After about five minutes, he propped himself up on his pillows and reached for the tea. He saw the letter next to the tea cup and his heart nearly stopped! He stared at it. His heart was beating out of his chest.

Part of him desperately wanted to rip it open and read what she had to say and part of him wanted to throw it away and tell her to go to hell! The former prevailed and he picked it up. He closed his eyes and put it to his lips and he could smell her perfume. He had complimented her on it on several occasions and she had told him it was called 'Angel' which at the time, he thought suited her, not necessarily in name, but its delicate fragrance did and would forever remind him of her.

He went into his bedside cabinet drawer and took out a Swiss army knife. He opened the main blade and carefully sliced the envelope open, taking great care no to cut the letter. It had been written in fountain pen and he could see that there were tear stains on it. It read:

"My Dear John, please don't tear this letter up. Just read what I have to say and then if you wish to forget me forever, then so be it. I cannot tell you how much you mean to me and I'm so, so sorry I seem to have hurt you so deeply. I can understand why and I can only hope that you can forgive me. Meeting you has changed my life. YOU have changed my life and I can't thank you enough.

For a few precious moments, you and I were as one and I can never forget it for as long as I live. Oh, the times I have been 'with you' and telling you how much meeting you and being with you has meant to me, words truly fail me. Can you forgive me for the terrible thing that I have done? I also wanted to give you peace of mind on two accounts. Firstly, I am NOT pregnant! I came on two days later. All is well on that account.

I have since visited my doctor and I am now on the pill, so within a month, we would never have to worry about that again. I have not gone on the pill for anybody but you. You are the boy I want. Oh John, PLEASE forgive me? My heart is breaking for you. For once in my life, I have found someone I care for, truly care for and I can't bear the thought of losing you in the same week as finding you.

We gave something special to each other, a precious thing that can only be offered once. For the sake of what we felt on the blanket in my stable, I beg you to give me another chance. I am truly sorry. If there is another way to prove my sincerity, I swear I don't know what it is. Secondly, I swear on my life that I didn't and never will, use you. I can make up the differences between you and my parents. I can assure you your job back and at the same terms that my mother had offered you.

Do you remember where we were parked at Stainburn Forest? There is an outcrop of rocks called Little Almscliff about 200 meters up the hill from there? I will be there next Saturday at 1 o'clock, rain or shine. If you come, I am yours, if you don't, then I want you to know that I understand why and that the fault is all mine. I can only hope that you will be there." And it was signed "Your Chantelle. Xxx".

John cried and hugged the letter to his chest. The relief of it all was just too much for him. He read the letter again and then he told himself off for being so selfish himself!

"You silly sod! She had more to lose than you! Yes, she should have taken precautions, but so should YOU! You can't paint yourself white! You were desperate for her weren't you? Did you ask her if she was protected? No you damn well didn't! You couldn't see past your own zip could you! How DARE you judge her when you've done exactly the same thing? You should be begging HER for forgiveness!"

John instantly changed his tune. He shot up out of bed and took a quick mouthful of his now cooling tea. He was in the shower and singing to himself in no time at all. Meanwhile, Helen and Michael could hear this from downstairs and they smiled at each other.

"Put yer tin 'at away, it seems like that letter were what 'e were 'opin' for!"

Helen laughed and said, "Yeah, youth is truly wasted on the young, isn't it!"

John came bounding down the stairs smelling like a Jasmine tree. He grabbed a slice of toast from his dad's plate that was sat on the armrest of his chair and said, "Cheers dad!" with a cocky smile.

"Cheeky bugger!" said his Michael smiling.

"Oh don't fuss so, Dad, I'll put you some more toast in the toaster you poor old gimmer!"

"Eighup! Cheek o' t' highest degree, Helen! Gerrim aht o' here!" he said, playfully smacking John on his backside with his now rolled up newspaper. John got his coat from the cubby hole and walked towards the front door. He paused to check his teeth in the hallway mirror and smoothed his hair on one side.

"Where ya goin', lad? Can we expect ya back fer tea?"

"Oh, just out, nowhere in particular, I just want to get out and enjoy the day and yes, I will be back in time for tea! 'Bye you guys!" he said as he closed the door behind himself.

"Well!" said Helen, "Things DO happen quickly around here, don't they?"

"Ha ha, they sure do, lass!" said Michael, "I were never as flippant as that when I were a nipper! Never! Not once!" he said with mock sincerity.

"No, I'll bet you weren't!" laughed Helen! "You were just perfect, weren't you?"

"Yep! That ah was, lass, that ah was!"

The Strange Occurrence at Little Almscliff

John knew that Chantelle would be at college and he knew that trying to contact her was futile. He went along to a telephone kiosk and phoned the restaurant. He hoped that Chef or one of the waiters would answer, but he knew there was a good chance that Mr or Mrs Upton would answer the phone, so he prepared to disguise his own voice. *'brrr brrr—brrr brrr—brrr brrr'*

"Hello, Stage Left Restaurant, how may I help you?" It was Mrs Upton, putting on her best 'Queen's English' voice.

"Och, ah'm sorreh, ah appear tae hev the wrang number!" said John and he put the phone down. He waited a few minutes and tried again. *'brrr brrr—brrr brrr—brrr brrr'*

"Stage Left," came a voice he knew to be Pete, his fellow waiter.

"Pete! Hiya, it's John!"

"John? What the—why—why are you phoning here? Where have you been? Mr and Mrs Face-ache aren't too pleased with YOU y'know! Ha! It's good to hear from you! What do you want?"

John said, "Listen, I've only got a couple of 10 pence pieces. Do you think you can get me Chantelle's mobile phone number from the back of the bookings diary in the office?"

"What the hell do you want HER bloody phone number for? I'd phone the SAMARITANS first! I'd be doubting my own sanity!"

"Look, I don't have much time! Can you get it for me?"

Pete was a good friend of John's and he said, "OK, I think I can swing it, give me your number and stay where you are, I'll buzz you back in a minute!"

"Cheers Pete, you're a star!" and he gave Pete the number of the booth, then put the phone down.

Meanwhile, outside the phone booth, a little old woman was waiting patiently to use it. Then another lady came. Then a man. John tried to pretend he was having problems with the phone, as he could see them getting impatient. At last, the phone rang and John picked it up in an instant.

"Hello? Pete? Did you get it?"

"Yes! Have you got a pen?" and the people outside could see John scribbling down something on the back of the Yellow Pages, then ripping off the piece that had he'd been writing on. He put the phone down and opened the booth door.

"Bloody vandal!" shouted an angry man. John paid him no heed, but walked swiftly up the street to the taxi rank. He had decided to go up to Little Almscliff crag as a kind of pre-pilgrimage to the place he knew that Chantelle and he would make up their differences. He resolved to surprise her by phoning her on her mobile, after college hours.

He felt sure she would be thinking about him, come about 7 o'clock that evening and by then, she would hopefully had enough time to have eaten her tea and time to get changed and settled for the evening, plus the fact that if he phoned the restaurant's number, Mr or Mrs Upton would undoubtedly answer it! He got a taxi to take him up to Little Almscliff. Not a word was said between John and the taxi driver all the way there.

"Nature lover are you, lad? Like looking at wild birds?" enquired the taxi driver as he took John's fare.

"In a manner of speaking," said John with a wry smile, as he took his change.

"None of my business like, but do you want a lift back to Harrogate?"

"No, I'll be OK, thanks," said John as he turned to step over the wooden stile and towards the rocks, that were 30 or 40 meters away. He walked up the inclining, grassy path towards the stones and as he did so, he had the strangest feeling again, that he had seen them before—sometime long ago? He couldn't quite place when or why, he just sort of 'knew' he'd been there before. Maybe as a baby? Maybe his mum and dad brought him there on a picnic as a little boy? He didn't know.

It may be that he'd seen something similar somewhere and he was getting that confused with these rocks. But no, he KNEW that there was something about these stones that made him very happy and also gave him a feeling of immense longing for something or someone he once knew. Lorna? No, they had never been near the place. Had he dreamed something like this and it's just a fragment of that dream? But he definitely knew its distinctive profile from the path.

He started to feel a little uneasy and remembered bits of his dreams from all those years ago. The squeaking shoes, some fragments of Latin—and a woman, vague; vague but there, in the very depths of his memory. He reached the stones and climbed to the highest point. He took a deep breath of the clean fresh air and looked at the transmitter tower to the south-west, about 900 meters away from him. He wondered what it was for, as he looked at the transceiver dishes on its pylon-like frame.

He looked down at the rocks that had all sorts of carvings of names and dates from people over the decades. Some of them were quite old, going back a hundred years or so. But his heart stopped as he looked just behind himself, at a carving into the rock beneath his feet, that he recognised instantly and he shouted out, "Ohh! Oh my GOD!"

He stared at the carving which was centuries old, worn by countless sheep walking over it and of many hands that had felt it over the years and of people who had wondered at it and run their fingers around the grooves of the carving or just walked over it as they rambled or picnicked obliviously on it. It was a carving of what he 'knew' to be, to the left, the moon, with moonbeams coming from it and to the right, the radiant sun and in the middle, the veil of life, death and time itself separating the two. He was frightened and fascinated at seeing this ancient carving and he got onto his knees and stared at it more closely.

"I know about this!" he said out loud, "I just can't remember what?" and he put his hand, instinctively right in the middle of the carving, on the 'veil'. Instantly, he experienced what could only be described as being hit by a thunderbolt! It was as if he felt a terrific concussion. And he heard a loud voice in his head—a woman's voice—"JOHN!" it said and it echoed around the area, as if he and the rocks were in a huge cavernous space. "Oh my God—JENNY! JENNY!" he cried before he lost consciousness.

He slowly became conscious of a cold feeling on his lips, then his cheeks, then a licking sort of sensation on his eyes and forehead. He slowly opened his eyes, to see a big Mastiff dog above him, looking very concerned in its own little way at John and it was trying to revive him.

The dog's breath was enough to revive him and he spluttered and wiped the dog's saliva from his mouth and cheeks! The poor thing had only tried to help and it wagged a stump of a tail at him as it realised that John was regaining consciousness. Its huge head was only inches from his and it was panting into his face.

"OK, OK! I'm OK, Lazarus-breath!" he spluttered. "Jesus! OK! Get off, I'm OK!" And as he spoke, the dog's owner came bounding up the path from the road.

"Hello there! Are you alright?"

It was a very energetic woman of about perhaps 70 years of age, spritely, hale and hearty and striding towards him with vigour that belied her years. She was dressed in Tweed jacket and trousers and a big flat cap of the same material.

"It's OK, my dear!" she shouted as she approached John, who was still pinned down by 120lbs of dog. "I saw you from the road as I pulled up just now! You seemed to just faint there! I sent Billy to see if you were alright, he's such a wonderful dog you know—" and as she approached the summit of the stones, a little out of breath, she continued, "He loves a challenge and he's almost human you know, one word from me and he just bounds to the rescue!"

"I'm much obliged I'm sure!" John said as he rose slowly to his feet and patted the dog's head and removed the slobber from his own face.

"Are you alright, dear?" said the woman.

"Yes, I'm fine," he replied, but his head was thumping and he was recalling flashes of memories that he had whilst unconscious. He had seen a beautiful young woman's face, which he knew or *thought* he knew as being Lorna McCauley, but not quite her somehow. She was dressed in peasants clothing from a distant and bygone era, but he knew her somehow.

He put his hand to his forehead and said, "I just felt faint for a moment for some reason! I don't know why!"

The woman pulled out a hip flask from her pocket and unscrewed the cap. She offered it to John and said, "Go on, have a sip! Best Napoleon brandy! I always keep a drop with me in case of a cold spell up here on the moors! You never know when the weather may change you know!" and she prompted John to take a sip from the flask.

He took it with gratitude and he took several sips, probably constituting half of the flask.

"Goodness me! Yes, you DID seem to need that, didn't you!" she said as she examined the remainder of the flask.

John wiped his lips and said, "Thank you, I appreciate that! I have had some unhappy news just recently and I always come up here to think things through," he said lying through his teeth, but couldn't think of what else to say.

"Oh my dear young man!" she said, "When my dear departed husband shook off this mortal coil, he said to me, 'Dymphna,' he said, 'always remember me at this spot!' Ha ha!" and she looked dewy eyed around the stones. "We plighted our troth here to each other in 1940 and I lost him five years ago this very day!"

"Oh, I'm so sorry!" said John with sincere condolence.

"Oh, don't worry about that, we will be together again one day, I just know it! These stones are quite unique you know! It is said that they have the power to allow information to come and go from the past to the present! A bit like a telephone you know! A load of rubbish I'm quite sure, but it gives an old woman like me a degree of comfort that I just may get a whisper from Douglas if he's there somewhere, ha ha!"

John shuddered at her words, given the frightening experience he'd just had.

"Are you feeling better now, my dear?" the woman asked sincerely as she grabbed hold of John's elbow. "Can I give you a lift home?"

"No thank you, but I DO appreciate your kind offer!" he replied.

"Are you sure you haven't broken anything, young man?" she said.

"No, I'm fine, but thank you again!" he said smiling at her. He offered his hand and she took it.

"I do hope you hear from Douglas, in the nicest possible way I mean!" he said a little embarrassedly as the words left his lips.

"Oh, you can be sure that if anyone can do it, my Douglas can!" she said with pride in her old eyes. "Well, if you're sure you're alright, then goodbye and good luck, young man. I hope that your problem will resolve itself, I feel quite sure that it will! Good day to you!" she said with a flourish of her floppy flat hat and John patted the dog on its head and it licked its drooling jowls.

He then made his way back to the road. He vaulted the stile, onto Broad Dubb Road and headed right, to where the road became Norwood Lane and then walked unsteadily back down towards Beckwithshaw.

His mind was buzzing with the recent events up on the rocks.

"What the hell was all that about? What in God's name are these flashbacks? Who is this Jenny? I seem to know someone called Jenny, but who is she? I've only ever known two people called Jenny, one is my employer and the other was at primary school and she had bright ginger hair and freckles!"

All the way back to Beckwithshaw, he pondered the mysterious event and what the old lady had alluded to, about the rocks having some ancient legend about them.

"When people are dead, they are dead! There are no such things as spirits or ghosts!" he said out loud to himself, but he just could not dispel the horrible feeling or the experience he had witnessed up there on that rock. Everything he had tried to convince himself about since becoming a smart and responsible young adult was now being challenged about his scepticism on supernatural issues.

He started to doubt himself and his own sanity. Those bad dreams years ago, the inexplicable way he spoke in Latin in his sleep, the citrine stone that really DID seem to help him to sleep and the way it seemed to keep the nightmares at bay. He tried to rationalise the situation.

"Suggestion! That's it or even autosuggestion! No other explanation for it! Mystery and imagination! Déjà vu! All just thoughts and ideas conjured up at the time!"

But then he thought about so called 'crank' myths, like water divining, that for centuries was mocked and pooh-poohed by science, but now, was accepted as a genuine method of finding underground steams. Indeed, his own father used to show him how to divine for water back at home, using two welding rods, bent at one end to make handles. When they were held parallel to each other, about six inches apart and one walked along, if there was water underground, the rods would cross irresistibly, almost like magnetism.

"Magnetism!" he thought to himself, "That's another one that can't be explained! You can't see it, but it's there! Gravity too! The thing that holds us onto the earth and the earth to the rest of the solar system and it keeps the universe together!"

By the time he reached the bus stop at Beckwithshaw, he felt quite gloomy.

Rendezvous

When he got back home, he had adopted a happier frame of mind. Helen and Michael were happy to see him and they asked him about his day. He told them the truth, inasmuch as he admitted that he'd been up to Little Almscliff crag. He omitted to tell them the whole story of why he went there or the strange experience he had had there.

"Tell me, Mum and Dad, did you ever take me up there when I was very little? I just seem to remember it."

"Where d'ya say it was again, John?" said Michael.

"Oh, you know if you go up the Otley Road to Beckwithshaw, turn left, then the next turning right, up Norwood Lane—?" Helen and Michael looked blankly at each other.

"Nope, never 'eard of it, lad!" said Michael.

"I can't say as I've heard of it either!" said Helen. "Why did you decide to go up there in the first place?"

John coloured up a bit because he hadn't thought of an excuse as to why he should go to a place nine miles away, to an outcrop of wind-ravaged rocks.

"Oh, well, I remember reading about them in geography lessons. They were part of a geology project that we did. The stones are the result of millennia of erosion, leaving behind Almscliff crag, Brimham rocks and Little Almscliff crag. I always thought to myself how evocative they looked in the text books, so I decided to take a trip up there to see them for myself."

"Oh aye?" said a very sceptical Michael. "Why didn't ya ask us fer a lift up there like? Yer mam an' me would maybe like ta 'ave seen 'em too! At very least, we could've saved yer t' cost o' t' bus fare!"

"Yes John, why not share your interest with us?" said Helen quite innocently, "I love places like that! We could have had a bit of a picnic like we used to do!"

John bit his lip and felt awful that he was lying and for the fact that his mum and dad always took HIM to such interesting places when he was little, but he could not tell the truth.

"It's a bit wild and windy, but there's a car park and there seems to be some lovely walks up there. Why don't we go there sometime then?" said John in a cheerful voice, but deep down, he did NOT want to go there, especially with them, as it was a bit of a 'sacred' place for Chantelle and him and he had definite reservations about going to the rocks again! He didn't fancy the idea of a repeat of what he had experienced there.

"Eighup, that's settled then! D'ya fancy that, lass?" Michael said to Helen and patted her on her bottom.

"Yes, that would be really nice! I love it out in the countryside! When can we go?"

John couldn't help but smile because his mum and dad sounded just like HE would have done when he was little.

"Ah'll tek me camera, an' we can get some snaps o' us up on those rocks yer describin' to us, lad!" John smiled outwardly. Inwardly, he cringed.

John went up to his bedroom and got changed into a comfy track suit. He shouted to his mum and dad, "Would you two like a cup of tea?"

"Y'wot! 'Ang around while I 'ave an 'eart attack! YOU gonna mek us a cup' o' tea!" shouted Michael in mock surprise.

"Don't be so nasty! John often makes us tea, don't you, love?" Helen shouted towards the living room door and in John's direction.

"Aye, yer right, lass," Michael said, "An' a couple o' buttered crumpets wouldn't go amiss just while yer boilin' t' kettle, would it, mam?" Michael shouted.

John smiled and bounded down the stairs. On went the kettle and he went into the bread bin and took out the crumpets and popped them into the toaster.

"Would my lord and master require anything else?" said John mockingly, "Shall I peel you a grape?"

"No, no," said Michael, "that won't be necessary, just gi'e us a merest whim to go wi' me crumpet, knave," laughed Michael.

"What did your last one die of?" John teased his dad.

"A severe case o' smacked arse!" Michael joked back.

John was happily compliant with all of this because he knew it would keep his mum and dad occupied whilst he rehearsed what he was going to say to Chantelle later. In came the tea and buttered crumpets on a tray.

"Mmmm! That looks alright!" said Helen as it was set before them. "Aren't you having some, John?"

"No, I'm OK for now, plus the fact I know that dad's going to cook me a HUGE sumptuous dinner tonight as a thank-you for these crumpets!" laughed John.

"Cheeky bugger!" spluttered Michael, as he chewed at a buttered crumpet.

"Just going to make a quick telephone call, I'll use the phone in my room, is that OK?" said John.

"Yeah, that's fine love, off you go!" said Helen, who secretly smiled at Michael and he to her. Off John went, up the stairs two at a time and they heard the door slam behind him. Helen and Michael held each other's gaze and smiled.

"Silly sod!" said Michael, "he forgets that WE were his age once, but at least we got some tea an' buttered crumpets out o' 'im afore he buggered off t' phone 'is little bit 'o nowt!" he smiled.

"Don't be cruel, Mike, he's just a boy! Let him be a boy!"

Upstairs, John was nervously rehearsing what he was going to say to Chantelle. He had chickened out of phoning her after 7 that evening, he knew that he would just clam up and make a fool of himself if he talked to her, so he considered that leaving a message on her mobile's answer machine was the next best thing to do. He went through his speech again and again. He realised he didn't have long to do this and he took a deep breath, closed his eyes and thought to himself.

"Right! This is it!" He took the scrap of the Yellow Pages that he had written her number on and tried to read his own scribbled writing. He dialled the number. *'brrr brrr—brrr brrr—brrr brrr'*

"Hello, you're through to the voicemail of Chantelle Upton, I'm sorry I can't take your call, but please leave your name and number after the tone and I'll get back to you. Thank you." *'BEEEEP'* John's heart was pounding.

"Hi Chantelle, it's me. I just wanted to surprise you—I mean I just thought I'd give you a buzz on your mobile to see how you were. I wanted to thank you for your letter and wanted you to know that I'm sorry too. It was—I mean you are—erm—I'd love to meet you, but I was wondering if we could change the rendezvous place? It's just a bit far away for me and my parents will be busy and I—I just thought of somewhere else a bit closer to home that would be nice?

Will you meet me at Spruisty Bridge at the bottom of Knox Lane? Do you know where I mean? It's the little packhorse bridge where the road runs out, where the ford used to be? I will be there at 1 o'clock, rain or shine! See you!" and he put the phone down, cursing himself at his imperfect message that was nothing remotely like what he'd rehearsed! It was too late though, the message was what it was and he couldn't delete it now!

He half hoped that Chantelle would phone him that evening, on the other hand, he knew he would be talking to her for some considerable time if she did and he knew that she wasn't exactly flavour of the month with his dad. He lay on his bed and contemplated the fact that Chantelle was everything that his dad detested and he wondered how he could convince him that she wasn't like that at all!

On the other hand, he knew Chantelle well enough to know that if they DID meet, which they would eventually have to do if they were going to have any kind of relationship, she would automatically put on her lisp which would be like a red rag to a bull to his dad! She would undoubtedly put on her 'stage show' voice and air and he just knew it would be a disaster. His mind wandered to Mr and Mrs Upton. His blood ran cold for a moment.

What if Chantelle and he had to have a clandestine relationship? What would they say if they found out? How could Chantelle say that he could get his job back? And if he DID get his job back then on what terms and at what price? He couldn't help feeling a tang of uneasiness.

The more he thought about their strange relationship, how it started and how fiery it had been in just a short space of time, the more uncomfortable he got; in fact, everything about Chantelle frightened him slightly. He always got a tingle up and down his spine when thinking of her or anything to do with her, so why was he so fascinated by her or she by him?

Chantelle did not contact John as he had hoped she would do and he found himself worrying that for some reason she had changed her mind. Saturday couldn't come quick enough and when it did, it was a dark, miserable day. The rain was coming down very heavily and as there was no wind, it seemed like it was set in for the day. John's spirits sank at the gloomy aspect from his bedroom window. No birds were singing and the leaves on the trees hung down as if deploring the weather too.

He opened his bedroom window and he listened to the steady drum of the rain and the sound of the rainwater as it gushed down the drain-pipes and in to the drains around the house. Helen and Michael were still sound asleep and John would have turned over and had another hour or two's sleep himself, but he had been wide awake for several hours, thinking about Chantelle and what may happen at 1 o'clock. He looked at his alarm clock, 7:20 AM.

He yawned and got out of bed. He went downstairs and into the front room, where he sat by the window and looked at the torrents of water gushing down the gutters of the footpaths and away down the foaming drains. An elderly gentleman walked down the street in a waterproof gabardine mackintosh and a cowboy-style rain hat. His collars were up against the elements and he had a small dog on a lead, plodding along after him. The poor thing looked like a drowned rat as it walked along, shivering with cold.

She won't turn up on a day like today I'm sure! I wonder if she'll ring me instead? he thought to himself. The morning dragged on and eventually a sleepy Helen and Michael came downstairs in their dressing gowns and slippers.

"Eighup, John, where's the tea then, ya good fer nowt wazzock!"

"Oh, 'morning dad, yeah, sorry, I was going to make a cuppa, but I just got to watching the rotten weather."

Michael looked out of the window too and sighed, "Yer right, lad, it's a bit grim aht there today ain't it! What yer got planned fer today like?"

"Well, nothing at the moment, in fact I think the whole day will be governed by this weather, don't you?"

"Yep, yer dead right there lad, a good day fer tidyin' yer bedroom!" said Michael with a hopeful smile.

"Oh, goodness me! Bless my cotton socks! It appears to be miraculously clearing up, Dad, look!" said John laughing.

"Well, bugger my old boots!" said Michael with equal mock jocularity, "Ah'll tell yer what, if it stops piggin', well rainin' afore lunchtime, ah'll clean yer room up FOR ya!"

"It's a deal!" said John who fell to his knees and clasped his hands together and with screwed up eyes said, "PLEASE, PLEASE make it stop raining before lunchtime!" and they both had a good laugh.

Michael went into the kitchen to put the kettle on and said, "You'd better get thissen ready ta clean yer room up lad, ah don't think there's anyone up there payin' any heed to THEE! Ha ha!"

The rain poured all morning. It was dismal and drab. It was so gloomy that it had an almost ghostly feeling to it. John was down-hearted.

She's not going to come out in this weather. I wonder why she hasn't phoned? Should I phone her? he thought. Helen had made a light lunch of a continental style breakfast of sliced salami and cheeses, ham and crusty bread and butter and a variety of delicious side dishes like guacamole and coleslaw. The victuals were lovely, but not the weather. It still poured with rain and the light was almost nonexistent. The sky was a sort of dark grey, but tinged with an amber sort of look. Michael commented,

"Ah can remember when ah worked dahn't pit, gerrin' up of a mornin' an' looking at skies like this! The air were so full o' coal dust, an' everyone were burnin' coal fires, you could almost taste the air! It 'ad a sort o' dark amber-gold look to it. Everythin' were allus silent on days like that and there were no birds singing, nor cats or dogs moochin' arahnd. It were almost as if ya were in another world like!"

Michael's recollections did nothing to pacify the gloom and even he succumbed to the general feeling of despondency.

As it got closer to 1 o'clock, John knew that he had to keep his promise and be at the bridge by 1 o'clock. He made the excuse that he needed some fresh air and went to get his coat and a huge fisherman's umbrella that his grandpa had given to him years ago.

"Where ya goin', lad? It's such a filthy afternoon! Ya won't be gerrin' any fresh air out there!"

Helen agreed and said, "Why not stay and play a game of scrabble with us, John?"

John said, "Yes, I should I guess, but I just need to get out for a while, you know what I mean? I know that you know I have had a bit of a rough time lately."

Michael looked up at John and said kindly, "It's alreet lad, ya can bring 'er back 'ere if ya want to, ah promise ah won't say owt ta embarrass ya." And his eyes met his son's and John stopped for a moment, then went up to his dad and, just like the little boy his dad loved so much, he kissed his dad on his cheek and gave him a hug.

"You are the best dad in the world!" John said with dewy eyes, but with a smile on his face. Reinforced by his dad's statement, he went to the front door, brolly in hand and went out into the murky afternoon.

He walked out of Hill Top Way and onto Crab Lane, then down Knox Lane towards the packhorse bridge. He passed the popular Knox Arms to his right, where his mum and dad often enjoyed a relaxing drink of a Sunday afternoon in its welcoming beer garden. The road gradually became narrower and more remote and it was almost like going back in time, from modern, swanky new-build houses, to a lane that time had forgotten.

He walked by where a railway bridge had once crossed the road, now dismantled, but the huge buttress sides of it were testimony to its once impressive past. Down the lane further, he came past some old and quaint little stone cottages that marked the very end of Knox Lane. Ahead of him some 20 meters away, was the packhorse bridge, spanning over Oak Beck. He shuddered and pulled his collar up.

Hidden under his huge umbrella, he made his way to the centre of the bridge and stared into the swollen water below him. He was mesmerised at the torrent. The rain steadily poured above his umbrella, but he was quite dry and was of a strange opinion that Chantelle would not turn up. He just had to do this silly thing, he thought, to exact a deal or at least a bargain to her if not to himself. 1 o'clock came and went.

10 past the hour and he thought that he was a fool to have contemplated such a stupid idea as to come out on such a horrid afternoon. Above the noise of the torrent, came the sound of a car. He looked up Knox Lane and saw a car's headlights coming down towards him. His heart jumped! Yes! He recognised the car, it was indeed Chantelle's Mini and she pulled up just before the blocked-off ford. John was just about to run to the car to greet her, but she was out of the car like a gazelle and ran to John with her arms open wide.

"John, oh John!" she cried as she ran towards him, "Oh my GOD, I've missed you!" she sobbed as she ran into his arms. He dropped the umbrella as she ran into him and nearly took him off his feet. John sobbed back.

"Oh Chantelle, I didn't think you'd come, it's such a horrid—"

"Not come? Oh my God, I'd have come here with my last breath, John!" and they kissed each other as if it would be their very last; a kiss that said everything and lasted for a long, long time.

They hugged each other and said not a word. The silence said more than words could have done. Soaking wet by this time, John picked up the umbrella and placed it up over their heads. They both looked into the foaming torrent below them, as it roared its way to the right, against a huge stone wall, then left to eventually join its forces with the river Nidd a mile or two away. Then they stared into each other's eyes and gently kissed again.

"You're wet!" John said simply.

"Damned right, I am!" she replied with an impish grin and she took a condom from her back pocket and held it up to his face. She tugged at his arm and pulled him back to her Mini. John dropped the umbrella and they both climbed into the back seat of her car. Instantly, she tugged at his clothing. He needed no encouragement and as the car rapidly steamed up and as the rain poured even heavier than before, drumming on the car roof, they found out, to their delight, that it was indeed possible to 'do it' in a Mini.

A short while later, they were sat in their respective seats, laughing and panting and what clothing they did have on was in total chaos. They giggled as they clambered about trying to put wet underclothes and jeans on. John buttoned his shirt up all wrong and Chantelle laughed as she undid the buttons and did them up correctly for him and he pouted at her like a naughty little boy would to his mother. At last, they were dressed and still smiling at each other. The interior windows of the car were dripping wet with the condensation from their wet clothing and their body heat from their love making.

"What should we do now?" said Chantelle.

"What CAN we do now?" replied John.

They both thought for a moment then Chantelle said, "Look, we can't get any wetter, why don't we go up to Little Almscliff crag and run about the rocks?"

John shuddered at the thought of those stones, but couldn't think of a good enough excuse to say 'no' without sounding like a wimp, so he put on a brave face and said, "Yeah! Why not? It'll be a bit like Gene Kelly in his 'Singing in the Rain' film ha ha!"

The car engine burst into life and Chantelle turned her car around and sped up the deserted lane to Knox Avenue, which led onto the Skipton Road. There were hardly any other vehicles around, except a few juggernauts thundering past, leaving huge plumes of dirty water mist behind them. Up the Skipton

Road they went, then Otley Road and onto Beckwithshaw then at last onto Norwood Lane and up to the rocks.

John stared at them with trepidation. He could discern the foreboding outline of the rocks through the rain and gloom. A slight mist had formed around the area, making the appearance of the rocks even more hideous to John. Chantelle switched the engine off and said, "Right, come on, I'll race you!" and she got out of the car and vaulted the stile.

John was hot on her heels and shouted, "Oh no, you don't!" and he pulled at her clothing to arrest her progress.

This childish behaviour lasted all the way up to the rocks. They hadn't reckoned with the state of the boggy terrain, mixed up with myriads of sheep-droppings! The ground was awash with mud. They just laughed and slithered up to the rocks, laughing and acting like two infants in a ball-pool. Dragging themselves up to the highest rock, they sat down to capture their breath.

The rain had eased slightly, but it still came down steadily and persistently. Chantelle lay on her back. Her clothing was absolutely soaking. Her blouse was transparent and as she breathed heavily, John watched her bosom heaving up and down. He lay beside her and got up onto one elbow to look at her more closely. Her blonde hair was drenched and some of it was stuck across her face. He removed it and caressed her cheek.

"You truly are the most beautiful girl, Chantelle," he said tenderly as he looked into her big blue-violet doe eyes. She smiled sweetly at him, showing her perfect teeth and thanked him. They kissed again and she started to fumble with his belt.

He stopped her dead in her tracks and said, "NO!" to which she looked up at him with alarm.

"What's wrong, John? What have I done wrong?"

John was still looking at her body, but as he stared at the area where her bottom was, he had noticed that she was directly on top of the ancient carving of the sun, moon and veil of life. He shuddered and said, "We've got to get away from this place!" and he looked around wildly as he tried to pull her to her feet.

"John! What's wrong with you? You look like you've seen a ghost!"

"Just get up!" he shouted at her. He heard a deep boom of menacing thunder, like he'd heard in his dreams as a child.

"Did you hear that?" he said looking up to the clouds.

"Hear what?" said Chantelle, who was becoming a bit frightened by the change in John's demeanour.

"That thunder!" he said.

"I can't hear anything but the rain!" she said, straining her ears to hear what John could obviously hear. He stared at the carving again and Chantelle followed his gaze to it.

"What's that?" she asked, looking at it more closely.

"Don't touch it!" he snapped at her with a commanding tone. "Come away from it, Chantelle."

She did as he asked. She could see that John wasn't fooling and that he wasn't to be gainsaid. She took his hand and gently pulled him towards her. She took his face in her hands and forced him to look away from the carving and into her eyes.

"John, please don't be afraid of this place, it's just a pile of old rocks." Whilst saying this, she took both his arms and placed them around her back. She wrapped her arms around him and said, "OK, John, let's go then, I'm getting chilly now."

John still had a wild and excited look in his eyes, as they walked down from the rocks and he kept looking back and staring at them. Only when they got to the stile, did he look forward to negotiate himself over it. He helped Chantelle over the stile and they got back into the car. There was a full minute's silence and then Chantelle said, "What's wrong? You seemed to be afraid of something up there. What was it? Can you share it with me?"

John thought for a moment and then replied, "I honestly don't know WHAT spooks me about that place. It scares me, but at the same time, I get that strangest feeling of longing for something or someone and I just don't know who or what it is."

Chantelle looked a little blank at the thought that he may have been alluding to another girl. He realised his faux pas and took her hand in reassurance.

"There's nobody in my life but YOU, Chantelle, I didn't mean it like that, honestly!" Chantelle smiled and leaned over to kiss him on his cheek.

"What do you think we should do now?" she said, looking at the state of them both.

"Yeah—we're in shit state, aren't we? YOU can't go home like that and neither can I without pleading insanity to my mum and dad!"

They both thought for a moment as to what to do next for the best. Chantelle started the car's engine and it wasn't long before the heater kicked in and they could feel the warmth. With the heat came the steamy windows again! It was so bad, that Chantelle couldn't wipe the condensation away fast enough! They both laughed at the silly situation and held each other's hands. Chantelle put the radio on.

There we had the sensational Carpenter's with Rainy Days and Mondays, hope it's not raining where you are pop-fans, now let's take a look at the rest of the charts in the stupendous year of 1971 pop-pickers!—They just looked at each other and howled with laughter!

As the radio drivelled on, John said at last, "I know! Let's go back to my place! It's about time I showed my beautiful girlfriend off to my parents!" Chantelle's face hit the deck.

"WHAT? I thought you said to me that we were a taboo?"

"Did I? I don't recall saying that, but if I did, I must have said it in jest! Come on, let's get going, I'm eager to show my mum and dad just what taste I truly have in women!"

Chantelle looked at him with a puzzled expression, but did as she was asked. Off they went back down Norwood Lane, with the windows still steaming up in front of them. As they approached Bilton, Chantelle said, "John, I don't think this is such a good idea? Shouldn't I just drop you off and get off home? I look like shit and I don't want to meet your mum and dad looking like something the cat rejected!"

John looked at her as she bit her bottom lip with anxiety. He said, "Chantelle, my mum and dad will adore you more just as you are, rather than in your riding breeches and sunspecs on your head! They will see that you are NOT what they would have expected!"

"Oh. Do you really think so?" she asked. "If I took YOU home to MY mum and dad like this, it would be your one and only visit to 'come to call'!"

"Ah, but MY mum and dad are completely different to yours! Chantelle, just be your TRUE self! Do you know what I mean? Talk to them as you do to me! Don't talk to them as you would to a stranger that you feel that you have to impress! Just be my girlfriend, smile and be yourself, you don't have to impress anybody, your charm and beauty will do the rest!"

"Oh John, you say such wonderful things to me, I DO hope I won't let you down! I'm nervous though!" she said as they pulled up outside John's house. A kiss from John and a squeeze of her hand told her that things would be alright.

"Chantelle," he said, "without sounding patronising, try NOT to lisp!"

"I DON'T."

"You DO—I promise—just don't do it and my dad will be putty in your hands!"

She didn't get the time for further discourse and he got out of the car. He waited for her to nervously get out of the car and lock it, then she sheepishly walked towards him and she took his hand.

The Colours of an Actress

As John opened the front door, he heard his mum and dad shouting from the living room.

"Eighup, lad, where the 'ell 'ave ya been?" and Helen joined in Michael's concern, as she got out of her chair and walked into the hallway.

"We were getting worried—" and she stopped dead in her tracks as she laid eyes on Chantelle. What with the sound of the pouring rain outside the still open front door and the sight of her bedraggled son hand in hand with this girl, she was totally stunned.

"Oh, Mum, may I introduce you to Chantelle—Chantelle, my wonderful mother Helen!"

Michael had heard this and was out of his chair and next to Helen in a second. Helen regarded Chantelle, soaked to the skin and covered with mud and sheep poo, her hair all covered with bits of gorse bush and moss, eye makeup smudged and running and looking at Helen with such a pathetically sweet look, as she offered her soaked hand in greeting. Helen took it and her heart melted.

She placed her other hand on Chantelle's shoulder and said, "You are very welcome to our home, Chantelle! Welcome, welcome!" and Michael, bowled over by the sight of this extremely attractive but sodden wet young woman, couldn't help to agree with Helen and he said, "Ah've heard a lot abaht you, Chantelle, ah'm so pleased ta mek yer acquaintance at long last! Eighup, Helen, get this lass up the stairs an' into a nice warm shower right this minute!" and he shook her hand cordially too.

Helen smiled—so did John! So did Chantelle!

"Rayt then, get yer mucky shoes off an' ah'll get 'em cleaned up for ya!" Helen led Chantelle up the stairs and Michael gave John a significant look, then he winked at him.

"Ah'll expect a full report on this in t' mornin', lad!" he whispered with a broad grin. "Get thissen up the stairs and get aht o' those wet things ya daft bat!"

John closed his eyes as his dad went into the kitchen with the muddy shoes and put them onto a newspaper and then put the kettle on. Michael smiled, but had a knowing look on his face and his eyes sparkled with an inner knowledge of things to come—perhaps. John heard his mum chatting animatedly to Chantelle upstairs.

"Now then, let's get you out of these wet things and you can have a nice warm shower! I'll wash your clothes and pop them into the tumble dryer; they'll be done in no time at all!"

As John went into his bedroom to get undressed, he couldn't help but shed a tear of happiness that at least the first hurdle of prejudice had been overcome—on both sides.

Helen took a big, warm and fluffy white dressing gown into Chantelle, who had just finished her shower. She also had a pair of jeans over her arm and said, "I think that these may just fit you, Chantelle. What size are you?"

Chantelle replied, "Oh, I'm a ten!"

"Good!" said Helen with a smile; "Try these—they should fit you I think! I just thought that your skirt looked very creased and I thought that you may be a bit more comfy in these?"

Chantelle thanked her very much and then asked if there was somewhere she could dry her hair. Helen obliged straight away and showed Chantelle into their bedroom and took out a hair dryer.

"There you are, my dear! Just come downstairs when you're ready. We'll have something nice and warming for you when you come down!" and she turned to go downstairs.

As she passed John's bedroom door, she said, "You now, John, get a good shower and don't forget to give me your wet things!" and then she went downstairs.

John jumped into the shower and after Chantelle had dried her hair, she could hear him singing to himself, *Hey—if you happen to see the most beautiful girl in the world—and if you did—was she cry—in'—cry—in'—*and she couldn't help but to brush away a quiet tear as she sat on the top step of the stairs. She didn't want to go downstairs alone, so she waited for John to come out. At length, he opened the bathroom door with a fog of warm steam billowing out behind him and he was startled to see her sat there.

"Hiya! Why are you sat there? I mean, why didn't you just go downstairs?" he said.

"Because I wanted to see you first you great lummox!" she said smiling at him. He stared at her, in her dressing gown and smelling of baby powder. Her hair was beautifully blow dried and she looked an absolute picture. No pretentiousness, no airs or graces, no horsiness, just a lovely, beautiful girl. He bent down to give her a quick kiss and then told her to go downstairs.

"No, I can't, not without you! I don't know them!"

She was right, of course and John said he would get dried in a moment. They could hear Michael and Helen talking away to each other downstairs, which made Chantelle feel more at ease. Two minutes later, John was with her at the top of the stairs. He kissed her, then they linked arms and went downstairs.

As Helen and Michael heard them coming down the stairs, chatting to each other, Michael snapped his fingers to Helen to get her attention and he whispered, "Ah'm tellin' ya, don't get yer 'opes up! She's lyin', ah swear it, an' she's after summat!"

There was some soft music playing on the stereo when they entered the living room and Helen and Michael got up out of their chairs to greet them.

"Sit yersen down an' mek yersen comfy, lass!" said Michael in the most friendly way to Chantelle and he gestured to the huge soft leather sofa. She did as she was asked and John sat down beside her.

Helen shouted through from the kitchen, "Would you like tea or coffee, Chantelle?"

"Oh, a cup of tea would be very welcome, thank you!" she replied eagerly.

She immediately turned to Michael and said, "I've been looking forward to meeting you, Mr Twigg, I rather had hoped that my first meeting with you would have been a little less dramatic than this! I'm SO sorry I brought John back in such a state, it's all my fault I promise," she said smiling at John, "but we went for a spin up to the stable to feed my horse and there was a problem with the stable door, so John fixed it for me, didn't you, John?" she said.

She looked at John significantly, then she continued, "It was a bit boggy, but John fixed it while I tried to hold his umbrella over him to keep him dry! I lost my footing and slid onto my backside and John tried to catch me as I went down, bless him and all of a sudden, we were soaked and we started to laugh, didn't we, John? We couldn't get any wetter so after John fixed the stable door, we went for a walk down the meadow to see how much the stream had flooded, oh, yes, there's a stream at the bottom of our meadow? And then JOHN fell near the bank of the stream and I didn't have the strength to help him to get up out of the mud! Ha ha! I know it sounds crazy, but it was such fun, wasn't it, John?"

John instantly picked up on the 'reason' for them coming back in such a state and he looked at Chantelle with such gratitude in his eyes.

"Yes, it was all a bit daft," he said feigning a laugh at a situation that never existed, "but it was a good giggle, wasn't it, Chantelle?"

Michael joined in the laugh. Chantelle's lucid description of what happened had been swallowed hook, line and sinker—or so she thought. Even Helen was laughing as she came in with a tray with tea and hot buttered muffins.

"Oh, that looks LOVELY, Mrs Twigg!" said Chantelle as she eyed the muffins.

"Do call me Helen!" she said kindly,

"And call ME Mike!" said Michael with a smile.

Chantelle rejoiced in the thought that she had won John's mum and dad. Not once did she come across the high and mighty young yuppie, nor did she feign her lisp or talk about anything remotely 'upper-class' or 'county'. She was what John had hoped and prayed for, a lovely ordinary, gorgeous girl! His girlfriend! His Chantelle.

The conversations went back and forth between the four of them. There was much laughter and a wonderful, relaxed feeling subsisted all afternoon. Helen popped out into the garage to collect all the clothing from the tumble dryer and offered Chantelle's to her.

"They are remarkably un-creased Chantelle, will they be OK as they are or would you like me to run an iron over them for you?"

"Goodness me, no!" said Chantelle. "I'm very grateful you have gone to so much trouble on my behalf!" she said smiling sweetly at her and Michael.

"Not at all! It's the least I could do after such an afternoon's entertainment! You really are a down to earth young lady and it's so refreshing to hear someone of your age with such a sense of humour and with such a wonderful and gentle personality!"

This was music to Chantelle's ears and she blushed crimson.

"Yes, you do 'ave a very mature and positive outlook on things—apart from getting' clatted up wi' muck this afty, ha ha!" said Michael and they all laughed. Michael looked at the clock on the wall, which read 4:50 PM. He looked at Helen and pre-empted what he knew Helen would say anyway.

"Do ya fancy stayin' fer tea wi' us, Chantelle? It seems a bit daft fer ya to be leavin' now, rayt on tea-time?"

They all stared at each other for a second, not knowing what to say for the best. Michael continued, "Better still, why don't we all go aht fer tea? Ah could do wi' getting' aht o' t' 'ouse fer a bit, we've been cooped up in 'ere all day! What do ya say?"

Chantelle looked at them all in amazement, her mouth open with excitement. Helen said, "Well, Mike, Chantelle may have to go home for tea?" looking at Chantelle.

"Oh, no, the restaurant will be in full swing by now, I'm usually all on my own on Saturday nights, I usually just get a burger or something, to eat on my own!" she said looking to the floor and wringing her hands together.

"That would be lovely, Mr Twigg!" she said renewing her smile.

"MIKE!" said Michael.

"Oh, yes—Mike," said Chantelle, looking downwards demurely.

"Will you have to tell your parents where you're going, Chantelle?" asked Helen.

"I'll just give reception a buzz and let them know that I won't be back until later on, they'll be OK with that, they're not usually bothered where I go or what time I return, within reason," Chantelle replied, rolling her eyes to the floor and looking forlorn. Helen offered Chantelle the use of their phone and she left the message with reception to give to her parents.

Chantelle and John went upstairs and got changed into their dry clothes, then came back down to the living room where Michael was discussing with Helen where the best place to eat would be.

"Yer mam an' me were talkin' abaht goin' up to t' Greyhounds; they're doin' a great Barnsley chop at t' moment! Do you two fancy goin' there like? It reminds me o' bein' back 'ome!"

"Sounds fine with me, Dad!" said John and Chantelle said, "Oh yes, I've never been there and I've heard of a Barnsley chop, but never tried one!"

That all agreed, they all got into Michael's car and they headed off to Killinghall. The rain had all but stopped by now and in the distance, there was the promise of better weather. The clouds on the western horizon had given way to shafts of light from the maturing sun and it appeared to be heading towards them. They chatted animatedly all the way to the Greyhounds Inn and when they parked, the pub manager was just going in through the back door.

"Eighup, Mike lad! How are you doing? And you Helen and John! Nice to see you!"

"Hiya Les, nice ta see ya too! We thought we'd all come up an' sample yer superb Barnsley chops a piece!" said Michael.

"Oh, they're on song alright! I'd better make sure we have some in for you, they're so popular that we sell them like hot cakes!" and he walked ahead of them into the lounge, carrying some kindling and logs for the open fires.

Even though it wasn't very chilly yet, the manager liked to keep the fires alight, apart from anything else, it did give the place a very welcoming atmosphere and many a tale and legend had been shared by locals and strangers alike around the Greyhounds' cheery fires, deep into the autumn and winter evenings. Michael went to the bar and ordered their usual drinks. He asked Chantelle what she would like.

"Oh, just a lemonade, thanks," she replied.

Michael and the manager had a bit of a chat, as they hadn't seen each other for several days, meanwhile John and the two girls were getting along like a house on fire. As Michael waited for his pint to be pulled, he looked at Chantelle discreetly and admired her beauty. He smiled to himself as he remembered all the things he'd said about her, what a snooty upstart she was and that John should steer well clear of her and yet here was the most delightfully polite and charming girl, who yes, was very well educated, but without the pretensions that he had been led to believe or at least he had made his own mind up on or so it may have seemed.

But to keep an open mind, he whispered, "God, ah wish ah were 40 years younger!" to the manager, who smiled in agreement as he looked at Chantelle too.

"She's a real head-turner isn't she, Mike! Has John been seeing her long like?"

"No, just a few days!"

"Wow! He's a lucky lad, eh? He'll need to be watching over his shoulder with *her* I would imagine! Ha ha!"

"There's no doubt on that, lad! No doubt at all!" replied Michael, with a forced smile, as he turned away from the bar.

Michael brought the round of drinks over to the table and they all took theirs and they clinked glasses.

"Cheers!" they all said to each other. They all read the menu that was on a blackboard on the wall, next to the bar. There were indeed some scrumptious sounding dishes, but the Barnsley chop was the thing that was on all of their minds!

Les, the manager, said from behind the bar to them, "Have you decided what you fancy then, my friends?"

"Yep! Ah think we're all goin' fer t' Barnsley chop," said Michael.

"It comes with peas and chips or mashed potato," said Les. They looked at each other and Helen said, "Ooh, I think I'll have mash!"

"Me too!" said Chantelle. Michael and John opted for the chips. The order was taken and Les went into the kitchen to give the order to his wife Carol, who was doing the cooking. The pub started to fill up and the atmosphere became very convivial.

After such a terrible day, people were glad to get out and let their hair down for a while! Michael and John waved here and there to regulars they knew. John's younger acquaintances especially, were unusually friendly and made sure to come over to greet him—and of course, his new 'friend' who had been studied surreptitiously by all the men folk in the pub from the onset and discussed with admiration, to say the least! Their attentions were not lost on Chantelle, who secretly smiled here and there at one or two of the better looking young men and that wasn't lost on John—or his father!

Their meals came out and were set before them. A young waitress followed Les from the kitchen with a gravy boat and that too was put on the table.

"Would you like anything else? Sauces or anything?" asked Les. Nobody required anything more, so they were left to enjoy their meals in peace. The chops were delicious! They all discussed them with relish.

"Mmmm! It's absolutely gorgeous!" said Chantelle, "thank you so much for inviting me and your recommendation of this chop was spot on! I must tell mummy and daddy about these chops, they should be included into our restaurants menu!" she said, with a voice that was designed to carry further than the ears of her hosts.

John detected a bit of her 'old' self in her voice, he didn't like the 'mummy and daddy' bit and her voice had risen a little when she alluded to 'our restaurant'. It wasn't lost on Michael either, who secretly eyed Chantelle, who was secretly eyeing a tall, rough but handsome young chap in working clothes, who was stood at the bar having a pint and who was overtly staring at her. Chantelle saw Michael looking directly at her as her eyes came back to her food.

Her body language proved that she knew she had been seen and she embarrassedly continued with her food. John saw this too and dealt the young man a look that could not have been misunderstood. The young man just sneered at John in a defiant and cocky way and turned to talk to another man in similar working clothes.

Michael saw this and followed John's gaze to the young man. He knew him and his name, but only as someone who occasionally came into the pub with the man he was stood at the bar with, but by no means were they on talking terms. The conversation at the table cooled and Helen, who had not witnessed any of this, was bewildered at why there now seemed to be an 'atmosphere'.

"Well! That was delicious! Anyone for a pudding?" she said happily and still smacking her lips. There was a sullen silence from Michael and John and Chantelle looked over to Helen and timidly said, "Oh, that was lovely, but I think I've had quite enough now, thank you."

"So have we!" Michael muttered under his breath, but Chantelle caught it and quickly responded, "I beg your pardon, I missed that, Mike?"

"Oh, nowt, lass, ah were just talkin' to missen, Bill behind me 'ere were sayin' that 'ed just booked his 'oliday, didn't ya Bill?" and he said leaning back on his chair to speak to a portly man who was enjoying a drink with another regular and who indeed had been talking about booking his holiday to Santa Ponsa in Majorca.

"Aye, Mike! Ah can't wait! Only 198 days to go and we'll be on that big silver bird!"

The logs on the fire near to them crackled and sparked. So did the mood. It was obvious that things were drawing to a close and that conversation had all but dried up. Chantelle excused herself and went to the ladies toilet. Michael, John and Helen just stared at each other.

"Ah warned ya, lad!" said Michael with a sympathetic look to his son, who was shredding a beer mat and had a very unhappy look on his face. Several minutes went by and then Helen noticed that the young man who was stood at the bar and ogling Chantelle had gone too. She put two and two together and excused herself too, to go to the ladies. As she came into the small corridor that led to the toilets, she saw Chantelle taking a scrap of paper from the young man. He looked at Helen and smirked at her. Chantelle tried to act as if nothing had happened.

"Oh, this corridor is very narrow, isn't it? I had to squeeze past that grubby chap in the overalls! I hope he hasn't soiled my clothes! Ha ha!" she said, trying to be as natural as possible. Helen noticed the scrap of paper was pushed hastily into the back pocket of her jeans and was nearly falling out. Helen said nothing, but went to the ladies. When she got back to her chair there were four more drinks at the table. Helen was bemused.

"Hiya, pet!" said Michael, "Chantelle 'as bought us all a drink! She asked us what we all fancied, so we got a pint a piece. She weren't sure what you fancied, so ah said a double vodka an' tonic, is that alright?" and he gave her a significant look.

"Oh, thank you, Chantelle, that's very generous of you!"

"No, not at all! It's my pleasure I'm sure!" said Chantelle, trying to lighten the mood. They all took a sip of their drinks, but John was still moody and went back to shredding his beer mat.

A few moments went by and Michael said, "Ee lass, ya DID get wet through this afty, an' ya DO suit me wife's jeans!" to Chantelle, who stopped sipping at her drinking straw and replied, "Goodness me, yes we did! But we did enjoy it, didn't we, John?" and she turned to John as she said it, to which he just replied, "Yeah."

The atmosphere was charged and Chantelle knew why. Michael held his pint in both hands, his elbows on the armrests; he leaned back in his chair and said, "Strange thing, rain, innit? Gets all yer clothes soaked, an' it meks the leather of yer wallet sticky like, don't it? You 'ave a wallet, rather than a purse, like a lot o' other lasses do, don't ya? Ah guess ya 'ad it in yer 'andbag an' it got piss-wet through? Ah saw ya tek it out o' yer back pocket ta pay fer t' drinks like! Ha ha!"

Chantelle knew something was very wrong and wondered if Helen had seen her talking to the young man in the corridor. Chantelle looked dumbstruck for a second, then hurriedly said, "Oh, excuse me, I think I've left something in the ladies! I won't be a moment!" and she shot out of her chair, fumbling around at the back pockets of her jeans, then disappeared down the corridor.

As the firelight flickered between the three of them, Michael held up a scrap of paper between his index and middle finger. It was the scrap of paper that Chantelle had been given by the young man. It had dropped out of Chantelle's back pocket as she was buying the drinks and Michael had leaned over behind her and picked it up. Helen looked with concern and said, "I just saw the young man who was stood just there giving her that bit of paper!"

"Aye! I'll bet ya did! Wet leather is sticky tha' knoas, an' it'll pull owt that's in yer pocket wi' it!" He opened it up, looked at it and with a knowing look on his face, he said, "Graham Fairchild—" and he read out a telephone number that was written on it as well.

John had to excuse himself and went to the gents. The young man in question had left the pub with his workmate. Helen was mortified and said, "Poor, poor John! I hope there is a genuine reason for this? Maybe she knows this chap as a builder or joiner? Maybe they need repairs doing to the restaurant? Let's not jump to too many conclusions yet, pet!"

"Mmm!" said Michael. "We shall see! Do ya remember when they were up 'avin' a shower, ah TOLD ya that she were still poison despite 'er class act o' bein' sweetness an' light? A wolf is allus a wolf even if it ain't eaten yer sheep! That she's bonny can't be denied, but she's still nowt but a flirt an' a little tart. Our John's just brought 'er to life, that's all! She'll be like a bee 'rahnd flowers, tekkin' worrever she can from t' likes o' poor John!"

Chantelle came back at this point. Her face was red and she had obviously been crying.

"Summat up, lass?" Michael asked dryly,

"Oh, no, I just thought that I had done or said something wrong after such a wonderful time with all of you! I could sense that you somehow didn't like me anymore and it made me so unhappy!"

"Dear, dear, dear! What sort o' thing could ya possible mean, lass? Tell us what would mek YOU so un'appy like? Hasn't our John done all sorts o' things for ya? 'Elped ya, an' tekken care o' ya? Scivvied for ya? An' 'aven't WE tekken yer into our 'ome an' bathed ya an' warmed ya an' fed ya, as if ya were one o' our own? Why should YOU feel so bloody un'appy, *Miss Upton*?" he snapped.

Chantelle couldn't answer. At that moment, John returned, quite calm and collected.

"Hi everybody, everything OK? Chantelle, are you OK?"

"Oh, she's just fine and dandy, lad!" interjected Michael. "Sit yersen down! Ah think she 'as summat ta say to ya."

Chantelle's eyes opened to their extremities. She looked from one to the other of the three of them, as they stared at her and she bit her bottom lip.

"What have you got to tell me, Chantelle?" John asked with his heart in his mouth. There was a long silence as Chantelle looked down at her knees.

"I don't know what to say," she said meekly.

"Well, my pretty little spider, shall ah speak *for* ya then?" Michael said, producing the scrap of paper. He opened it and placed it in front of her.

"Yer cousin, is it? A brother ya didn't know you 'ad until toneet maybe? Uncle Tom bloody Cobbly? Maybe just a fan o' the great Chantelle Upton, who 'as a soddin' great 'orse too, that 'e fancied showin' ta ya like!"

A pin could have been heard dropping by the whole pub, who by this time, were all staring at them, motionless and silent. Michael opened his wallet and took out a £5 note.

"Here ya go lass, get yersen a taxi, wi' our compliments!" he said as he slapped the note next to the scrap of paper.

"Pick yer car up anytime ya like. Ya don't 'ave ta come to t' door, just tek it away when yer ready."

By this time, Chantelle was in floods of tears. Her nose was running and she had to use a serviette to dab her eyes.

"You've got it all wrong! I can explain! I'm so sorry!"

Every eye in the pub was on Chantelle. Michael put his hands on his hips and said, "Ah'm SURE yer sorry—'*poppet*'! Go on then, *sweet'eart,* here's yer big chance before the curtain comes dahn! EXPLAIN IT TO US THEN!" he barked at her.

She couldn't, of course and she was left, sobbing uncontrollably, in the middle of the pub, as the three of them walked out to the car park. John had his handkerchief over his face and was also inconsolable. Helen put her arm around her son's shoulder as she led him out of the back door.

When they got back home, John was still very distraught, but was putting on as brave a face as he could.

"Dad?" he said, walking up to him; "Forgive me, I was wrong and you were right. I'm sorry I made such a fool of myself and of YOU two." Michael put his arms around his son and hugged him.

"Don't say that, lad, we all 'ave ta go through such sweetness an' pain, such beauty an' ugliness."

John bawled into his dad's chest and Michael hugged him all the closer.

"Consider it as a test of yer character, John and you came aht on top. Don't be too upset, you'll find someone else soon enough, an' *she'll* be 'istory. You 'old the moral high-ground, son. She will be 'urtin' a damned sight more than you before too long. Ah promise ya, she'll remember you fer what you are and you'll do t' same abaht 'er. Don't ya see lad, she's done yer a favour? 'Ow would ya feel if you'd been goin' aht fer a long time like, an' she buggered off wi' someone else then?"

John was still sobbing, "She's so beautiful!"

"Aye, that she is, an' she knows it! She'll brek many an 'eart afore she's through, lad, but as sure as eggs is eggs, she'll end up a lonely old lass wi' a rake o' money in t' bank, an' no one ta share it wi'."

"I just can't believe it!" said John. "She seemed so genuine! So lovely!"

"Ahh, it 'appens, lad, when t' likes o' 'er set their sights on summat they want, they'll stop at nowt until they gerrit!"

John thought about that and remembered the instance in the restaurant, where Chantelle told John to take her riding boots off and how snotty and arrogant she was then.

"What the hell did she want from me, Dad?" John said still sobbing.

"Exactly what you gev 'er lad, exactly what you gev 'er, an' nowt more."

John went up to his bedroom and opened up the drawer of his bedside cabinet. He took out the tear stained letter that she had written to him. He sniffed at the perfume still on the pages and then he tore it up and put it into the waste paper bin next to his bed. The rain had cleared away and the last glows of red could be seen on the western horizon. The sun was going down too on a bitter-sweet interlude for John.

He would never forget Chantelle, for good and bad, but at least they had shared the sweetest thing that two young people could possibly share and that could never be taken away from him. He would remember her for that at least, for the rest of his days. He thought to himself, *If I really had to be used, then what a way to have been used—by a beautiful, elegant, educated, upper class, gold-mining useless bloody bitch.*

No sooner had the thought passed through his head, then he saw a taxi pull up outside their house and Chantelle climbed out of the back seat. She fumbled in her pocket and got her car keys. She looked up at the bedroom window and even though still crying, she smiled a hollow, vindictive smile at John, then got into her car, slammed the door and raced off into the evening, to go back to the theatre-restaurant. How fitting.

University

Before John knew it, October had arrived and it was time to go to university. He had packed his things and his mum and dad had taken him through to Leeds. There were no feelings of sadness for any of them, quite the contrary, they were all in tremendous spirits and laughing and joking all the 16 miles to the campus. It wasn't as if John was moving to the other end of the country and they all knew that they were all just a short ride away from each other, so especially for Helen, the knowledge that they would be back together at weekends from time to time was a comfort.

They arrived at the main university, a huge, imposing building, with a distinct American 1940's sort of flavour. It was constructed in white stone blocks, that stood out a mile away in the sunshine and it was somewhat out of place from all the other buildings around it, aesthetically speaking, with two 19th century churches right next to it and many little old terraced dwellings, dating back to the early 20th century and recalling a pre WW2 feeling, with their red-bricks and grey Yorkshire slate roofs. But it truly was a magnificent structure and it impressed the feeling as soon as seen, of what it was.

It stamped its mark on the Leeds skyline and stood proudly and imposingly to the glory of the thousands of students who had come to it, in the same way as these dozens of young people milling around, to the caps and gowns that launched them into their respective careers at the end of their studies.

Helen and Michael helped John with his bags into the main entrance area and as soon as John walked through the main portal, he closed his eyes for a second and took a deep breath. He smiled with satisfaction and he just knew that from this moment onwards, his life would change forever. How right he was and how little he knew what truly lay in store for him!

Helen and Michael said their goodbyes to John and hugs and kisses were being exchange, not just by them, but by many people just like them, parting with their 'little boys and girls'.

"Tek care o' yersen, son!" said Michael, "Gi'e us a buzz when yer settled in won't ya?"

"Of course, I will, Dad, you can count on it!" replied John.

Helen needed another hug and whispered into John's ear, "My little boy, grown to young manhood! Weren't you born yesterday?" she said laughing tearfully.

"Hey, Mum, don't you know that when I leave this place in a few years' time, I will make you proud to call me 'son'!"

"I'm already proud of you, John, SO very proud of you! Take care, son, enjoy yourself and keep in touch with us, won't you?" and she took her hanky from her pocket and dabbed her eyes.

"Stop it, Mum, you'll have me in floods of tears in a minute!" John said smiling at her and trying to give her a bit of encouragement to say their last goodbye. A stout handshake from his dad and one or two wistful looks over Helen's shoulder and they went back to the car, leaving John with hundreds of other new freshers, just like himself, with their bags and waiting for instructions from tutors and older students, who were all more than happy to direct them all to their destinations in the Halls of Residence.

John made friends from the first moment. Everyone was smiling and couldn't do enough for each other. A year 2 student came up to John to greet him.

"Hello, my friend! Welcome to Leeds! My name's Jeff, Jeff Rogerson," and he held out his hand, which John instantly took and replied, "Hi! John Twigg."

"It's a bit daunting at first, but I promise you, you'll settle in within the first day or two! What's your subjects?"

"Law first and foremost, how about you?"

"Languages; I want to major in Spanish, but I'm kind of neck and neck with French and I don't know which way to go, I love them both! There are so many opportunities and they are all offered to you with such enthusiasm and gusto from older students and tutors alike. It's a fabulous place, John, I'm sure you'll be very happy here. Do you know where you're staying?"

"No, not really, it's on a sheet here, but where it is in relationship to this building—"

"Let me see," said Jeff. "Ah yes, you're in the same building as me! That's handy eh?"

With that, he helped John with his bags and took him to the main entrance, where there was a registry and John signed in. Jeff took John to the main entrance and pointed up the road to some buildings on the other side.

"It's just up there. Give me a few minutes and I'll walk up with you! You'll be able to meet some of my cronies, they'll all be coming back today, in fact some are already here and have been here for a few days, because of the way some of their studies have been structured."

"Cheers for that!" said John and he sat on a huge leather sofa not far from the main exit.

Ten minutes later, Jeff came back, with some more new students, three girls and two boys. They all looked pretty nervous and John stood up and introduced himself to them. They eagerly took John's lead and they all shook hands and gave each other their names. Instantly, the ice was broken. They were all to be in the same part of the Halls and they realised right from the onset, there was a tremendous amount in common between them all!

They all arrived at the 'digs' and were shown to their respective rooms. John was sharing with a real pair of true comics, who saw the bright side to everything, one of them was to become one of John's truest and most loyal friends, Ian Priestley, who was about to study law too. They were to become not just friends and confidants to each other, but in the future, they were to cement a working relationship.

The other chap in with them was of Indian parents, but he was born and raised in the U.K. What would become a constant amusement to John was that he could put on the true 'Indian' accent at will, but his hometown was Birmingham and he had a true 'Brummie' accent that just creased John up! He would swing from one accent to the other for the amusement of his friends and he was the heart and soul of the party, with a tremendous sense of humour! He would often joke that he was the only Indian that he knew that didn't like curry, far preferring egg beans and sausage!

Pritesh Gupta was a real clown and hadn't the slightest qualms about any racist jibes, he was more than able to give and take any joke, from Irish to Mexican and from Indian to Scottish. He was a true diplomat and a genuine young gentleman. He had come to Leeds to study mathematics and he aspired to work one day, for NASA. After they had all unpacked, Jeff had come back with yet more new students.

He popped his head around the door of their room and said, "Everything alright, you guys?" They all gave the thumbs up to that.

"Meet me downstairs in the lounge at 5 o'clock; a few of the 1st and 2nd year students and I will show you around a bit. I know you've all seen the campus, but you might like to see where we all go to relax, you know, the local student's drinking holes and places to get some good, but inexpensive grub!"

"Sounds great!" said John.

"Oh, blimey! Nat to be going to curry houses please!" said Pritesh in a thick Asian accent and wobbling his head gently from side to side, then instantly continued with, "But a few beers and a pizza sounds bloody great!" he said in the strongest Brummie accent.

They all howled with laughter and Jeff said, "Steady on! I LOVE a good curry!"

"Ha ha! You're welcome to MY share then!" said Pritesh with a huge smile that displayed two rows of pure white teeth.

5 o'clock came and there were several new students in the TV lounge. Some were just chatting to each other and others were watching the TV. John, Pritesh and Ian walked in and they said a sheepish 'Hi' to the others. They sat in some old and worn, but comfortable armchairs and waited to see what was going to happen next. Another few students came in, chatting animatedly to each other, all of them girls and one of them looked straight at John and came across to him.

"Hiya, aren't you John Twigg?" she asked in a very friendly and excited way.

"Well, yes, I am!" he replied and looked at her, searching his memory for her face. She offered her hand and said, "Amanda Parry? Bilton Grange?" she said hoping John would remember her.

"Well, I'll be!" he said and he stood up to shake her hand with enthusiasm. She was always smaller than the other girls in her class and even now, if she was 5 feet tall, she was doing well! John towered over her at 6 foot 2 inches.

"How wonderful to see you again, Amanda, crikey, YOU'VE grown! And all in the right places, if I may be so bold!" he said admiring her now petite, but perfectly formed little figure.

"You were in Miss Blake's class, weren't you?" he said.

"That's right, then I went into Mrs Scrafton's class, but then I moved schools and went to Woodland's Primary because my mum and dad moved to that part of Harrogate."

"Now you come to mention it, I DO remember thinking what had become of you, all those years ago! God, how time flies by, Amanda! It's really great to see you! We really must have a sit down and a natter!"

"Oh that would be great, John, I look forward to that!" she enthused. With that she nodded and said, "See you soon!" and she rejoined her friends, who were all giggling and staring at John and saying quietly to Amanda, "Who's the eye-candy then?"

At length, Jeff came through the lounge door and said in a loud voice, "Evening everybody, welcome to the 'digs' walk! They're basic but comfy and I hope you'll all be happy here! You all know me and I know you as individuals, but I hope you'll all take the time to get to know each other tonight, 'cos you're gonna be spending a lot of time together ha ha! What I hope to do is show you around a bit. I'd like to introduce you to my fellow students—" and he proceeded to introduce three young people of 1st and 2nd year, "Martin Valentine, Michelle Day and Alpana Kapoor."

The latter was a beautiful Indian girl and Pritesh leaned towards his roommates and said, "I'm loving this already, guys, keep your mitts off THAT one!"

"Hell, she IS a stunner, isn't she?" said John with genuine approval. "See anything *you* fancy then, Ian?" smiled John.

"Oh hell YEAH!" said Ian, "Dozens of 'em so far!"

"Right then, if you want to tag along, then please do, if not, I hope you settle in and we'll see you later," said Jeff.

There was a hubbub of excitement. Some of the girls had brought coats and light bags, the boys were more optimistic of the warm and salubrious weather outside and put their faith in Lady Luck for not getting a soaking later. Off they all went and they split into three groups, naturally enough, with the three 'hosts' of the evening, but they all stayed within a hundred yards of so from the next group.

They walked past the main University complex, with its imposing white tower, now ruddy in the evening sun, then down towards the centre of Leeds. They were shown all of the student's local pubs and sandwich bars as they went along. All three of the hosts were chatting animatedly to their respective group, about this building or that aspect, as they were walking along.

After about 20 minutes, Jeff said, "Right! This is where a vast amount of the world's most prolific decisions and mathematical breakthroughs have been contemplated!" and they all looked at a small, but very inviting pub-come-eatery called 'The Cat's Whiskers' and Jeff recommended that they all take a short stay there for some refreshment.

They all agreed, apart from anything else, nobody wanted to be split up from the rest, on this first evening. Inside, it was very comfortable and deceptively larger than the outside would have you believe. Jeff took the lead and went to the bar, where he ordered a large cola. They all piled in behind him. John followed Amanda, no particular reason why, it was just that way it happened. When they arrived at the bar, John asked her what she would like to drink.

"Oh, that's kind of you, John, may I have an orange?"

"Still orange?" asked John.

"Yeah, I haven't changed my mind!" she said and they creased into laughter at her joke. The drinks and a few bags of crisps were bought and they all sat down in a lovely, cosy and convivial area, designed to be attractive to working students, for peace and quiet or relaxing people, out for a quiet drink. John and Amanda sat next to each other, it wasn't intentional, but just the way that everyone just sat down.

"What are you going to study, John?" Amanda asked as she sipped at her orange juice.

"Law," said John, "I know it sounds a bit stuffy and boring, but I've always had a sort of 'calling' to it! I don't know why!"

"Law! Mmm, that's a BIG earner! But it's a tremendous amount of effort and training! I DO admire your pluck!"

John smiled and looked at his fingernails in mock satisfaction and said, "Oh, it's nothing really, I'll probably only use one eye and one hand y' know!" They both laughed. "What about you, Amanda?"

She smiled with pride and said, "I hope to qualify as a paediatrician! When my little sister Karen died of a rare infantile problem, it haunted me all my life and I swore on her tiny grave that I would one day help to find a cure for it."

John's memory flew back to the episode she was alluding to and he remembered it, now with a vivid detail.

"Yes, I DO remember Karen! She was only about three years old? I'm so, so sorry!" and he looked down with genuine sadness at her loss.

"Don't be so silly!" said Amanda, "Little Karen is not worrying about me! She's quite happy now! But I just know that I will be able to cure or help to cure little children like my sister, who didn't stand a chance all those years ago." And she sipped at her drink. John couldn't help but feel a tremendous respect and compassion for her.

It was only a short stop and Jeff rallied them all together again.

"Come on everyone, we'll show you some other places of interest. Those who'd prefer to stay here, that's up to you. We'll see you back at the digs!" and with that, he and his student assistants moved towards the front door. They all got up and followed Jeff, as they all busily chatted to each other.

John and Amanda had sort of 'paired up' for these perambulations and Pritesh had made it his business to sidle up to Alpana and steal most of her attention away from the other new students! They all walked down into the busy shopping areas, past Merrion Centre and along The Headrow, then right, onto Briggate. Jeff and his colleagues were busy showing this and that place to them, good bars, coffee shops, restaurants and the like.

They eventually made their way to the train station and for many of them, who came in by train, the geography of where they now were made more sense as they got their bearings. Michelle Day, who was a 2nd year student and studying to one day become an Occupational Therapist, said that she was going back to the Halls and that anyone wanting to come with her were welcome to do so, otherwise, she'd see them all later. She smiled and waved to the crowd and she and several of the others headed back.

"Do you want to go back now Amanda or would you like to have another quick drink somewhere?"

"Well, if it's OK with Jeff, are *you* OK with that?" she asked him. John also turned to Jeff and repeated the question.

"Yeah, that's fine with me guys, how about you, Martin?" He was also fine with that and so Jeff said, "See you later!" and Jeff winked at John, then turned to go back to the remainder of the group and they all slowly walked up Park Row and back towards the university.

"See you two later!" came a voice from the receding group and it was Ian, who had too made instant friends with several of the group and who all the while had been engrossed in conversation with them.

"Yeah, see you, Ian!" shouted John. John and Amanda sauntered behind the main group and they chatted about Bilton Grange School and what had happened to them respectively in the intervening years. They walked past a little theme pub called 'The Jack in the Box', which looked very inviting and there were hardly any customers in there, so they went in.

"What do you fancy?" asked John,

"Oh, a half a sweet cider, thanks very much!" John ordered that and a pint of lager for himself. They sat in a cosy, high backed leather sofa that was designed in a semi-circular way, so that people could sit opposite each other and chat. There was a static table, anchored to the floor. They squeezed round it to sit in the middle of the sofa.

"Cheers!" they both said and clinked their glasses together. Amanda looked at John and said, "I'm sure we'll enjoy it here, John, I'm told it's a fantastic place to study, many of my friends are here and they all say the same thing! Everyone is so enthusiastic and friendly and nothing is too much trouble with the majority of the tutors."

"I don't doubt it! I felt very comfortable when I came here on the open day last year. My roommates seem to be loonies and I'm happy about that, it's nice to be with people with a good sense of humour and don't take themselves too seriously!" Amanda smiled.

"Do you have a girlfriend, John? I'm not fishing, I'm just curious."

"No, I don't, I've always been too busy studying to have time for the opposite sex! How about you?"

"Pretty much the same, Oh, I've had one or two 'crushes', but nobody I could call special, I think that most boys considered me a swot and a bit boring, nobody ever really looked at me twice at school and in some respects, that suited me just fine!"

"Yeah, same here, all the girls I fancied couldn't stick me and of the one's that fancied me, I couldn't stick them! Ha ha!"

Amanda wasn't classically 'gorgeous', but she was by no means unattractive. As mentioned, she was 5 foot in her stocking feet, elfin-cut mousy brown hair; she was narrow hipped and broad shouldered, at least for one so tiny. She almost could have been taken for a gymnast, as her limbs were very well toned and there wasn't an ounce of fat on her. She had certainly blossomed since John had known her as a little girl and as she excused herself to go to the ladies, he was able to take a good look at her and he really did like what he saw.

She was nothing like Chantelle, with her airs and graces, Amanda was a genuine, likable girl and John just knew instinctively that they were going to be good friends, reinforced by their own history at Bilton Grange. When she came back, she sat next to him again and smiled. As she sat down, he noticed that she had put a fragrance on, which he recognised instantly as the one worn by Chantelle, 'Angel' and he just loved it! It suited her somehow and he said, "By God, you smell edible! Is that Angel?"

"Why, yes, it is!" she answered slightly embarrassed and slightly surprised at his knowledge of perfumes.

"It's absolutely my favourite ladies fragrance; it *'does things to me'!*" he laughed and acted the fool by raising his hands menacingly, as if he were Mr Hyde from the old movie.

"I'm SO pleased you like it, it's my favourite too! I hope this is the first of many things that we have in common, John!" she said with a gentle smile. "Can I get you another drink? It's my round and then I guess we'd better be off," she said.

"Thank you, Amanda, same again for me, would you like me to go to the bar for you?" he asked like the gentleman he was.

"Don't be silly! Women are emancipated today, didn't you know that?" she said laughing, but secretly thought to herself as she went to the bar, "What a lovely, gentle young man! I do hope that he will like me and we can be good friends."

After their second drink, they decided to stroll back and as they did, they talked as if they'd known each other for years. They arrived back at the campus and in the dusk and in the poor light of one of the street lights before mentioned, which was about 20 feet from them, they said their goodbyes. Amanda had to go one way to her digs and John the other to his. John smiled and offered his hand.

"It's been a true pleasure, Amanda; I'm really looking forward to seeing you around the campus." She took his hand and smiled back.

"Likewise! You'll be snowed under for a few days, just like me, so I probably won't see you for a while." Her eyes sparkled in the imperfect light and John felt comfortable with her.

"Look, that's my room!" she said pointing to a second storey bedroom, where the silhouette of another girl with a towel on her head could be seen against the curtains. As they still had their hands clasped, their eyes met and for a second or two longer than would have been usual under the circumstances. She pulled his hand towards her to pull him to her and pecked him on his cheek and then smiled broadly.

"Adios amigo!" she said with a happy, chirpy voice and with that, she span round, not letting John respond and ran towards her digs. One last glance and a wave to him and she was gone. Her perfume lingered by John, who was tired but happy and he sniffed at the air and closed his eyes for a moment. He smiled to himself, looked up at her window and repeated her sentiment, "Adios, mi amigo especial!"

John's new found friends proved to be all he had hoped for and more besides! He settled into his studies very quickly and absorbed his tuition like a sponge. At the end of a hard day's study, he would come back to the digs, which would invariably be in a state of complete disarray and it was their new custom, that unless previously arranged or discussed, the first back to the digs would cook the tea. On this particular occasion, Pritesh was back first and he hadn't had a good day!

"Hi Pritesh! How's it going?" said John.

"Humph!" said Pritesh. John smiled to himself. Pritesh was raking around in the food cupboard and muttering and cursing from time to time.

"Do you want anything to eat?" said Pritesh,

"Not half! What are the choices?" queried John.

"Yes or bloody no!" said Pritesh, who couldn't help but chuckle to himself. He popped his head around the cupboard door and gave John a beaming smile and putting on his Asian accent, he said, "So sorry, old fruitie, mother hubbard's nat gat much in today, it's eggs, eggs, corned beef or eggs! Oh or a packet of sage and onion stuffing!" he said blowing the dust off it.

"Mmm, what about your world acclaimed boeuf a corneau, avec oeufs a la scrambuels, et le stuffeaux de la sage et onion, Môn Amie?" Pritesh howled at the description and picked up on it and continued, "'Ow's about l'oef au toast, avec le boeuf a corneau sarnaise, et grossamant sauce de la tamat, splodgeau all oveur, avec stuffeau boulles?"

Pritesh came down from the chair he'd been stood on and sat on the chair next to John, who was busy sorting out his books from the day's studies. They both had a good laugh and as they were enjoying it, in walked Ian and that made them laugh all the more! Ian smiled, but with a quizzical look.

"Did I miss something, lads?" he asked and they both, as one, said, "Oh, no no, nothing—"

So Ian made the mistake of saying, "Hey! What's for tea? I'm starved!" and the other two laughed until they cried! Eventually, they calmed down, Pritesh said in a pseudo-French accent, "Zair iz buggeur-all, Môn Amie, ze cubbeurd, she is bare, ah'm soh sorrie!" and he threw the stuffing at him.

Ian joined in with the joke and caught the stuffing as it came towards him.

"Ah, oui bien! Le boit de la stuffuea! Ah sink zees ees not eneurf to sustehn uhrs, mah friends, ah guess we 'ave to mek ze decision most large! What seh we gur aht for dinneur?" and of course, they all heartily agreed, apart from anything else, they didn't have much choice if they were going to get some food!

Ian then thought for a moment and said, "Listen, can I leave you guys to that, I've just remembered that I was going to talk to a tutor tonight about one of my essays that I'm struggling with. But I can get along to the supermarket after that and get some grub?"

They agreed and John and Pritesh took some money out of their wallets and gave it to Ian. They put the kettle on for a cup of tea, only to discover that it was the last tea-bag too! Ian busied himself with writing a shopping list. John sat reading the paper for a minute or two then said to Pritesh, "Hey, shall we see if Amanda and Alpana fancy coming too? I've got the house number?"

Pritesh's eyes lit up and said, "What a good idea! Why didn't YOU think of that, John?" to which John smiled and said, "Oh, I don't know, I guess I'm just stupid?"

"Get on that bloody phone!" said Pritesh.

John went downstairs to the lobby, to where the telephone was. He dialled the number and one of the girls from the downstairs rooms answered the phone.

"Hello?" she said.

"Oh Hi, could I speak with Amanda Parry in room 4?" he asked.

"Oh, just a moment—" and he heard her shouting at the top of her voice.

"AMANDA—IT'S FOR YOU-HOOO!" There was some mumbling in the background then John heard someone thundering down the stairs and noisily pick up the phone.

"Hello?" said a breathless voice, "Amanda Parry speaking."

"Oh, hi, Amanda, it's John!"

"Oh hiya, John! How nice to hear from you! What can I do for you?" she said still panting.

"Am I disturbing something?" he asked genuinely,

"Oh, hell no! I was just about to cook myself something to eat! I've just jumped out of the shower!" John got a mental image of her wrapped in a towel, with a frying pan in her hand and he smiled.

"You don't cook in the shower do you? You have better facilities than WE do!" he said with a laugh.

"Silly, I didn't mean that!" she said, realising her error.

"I was just wondering if you would like to come out for tea with Pritesh and me?" he said and the answer came back in a flash, "YES YES YES! Oh YES! When do you want me? What time? Where are we going?" she said excitedly.

"Steady, steady!" said John with a laugh, "We've run out of grub and thought it was a good idea to just find somewhere nice and cosy, nice and romantic, with a couple of beautiful senoritas to flatter us, after a hard, hard day at the knowledge-box, to enjoy an exquisite, candle-lit meal and an excellent bottle of Chateau D'arbanville '42—"

"OK, OK—shut up, you smooth talking sod! You've sold it to me! Now serve it up!" she said with a voice that didn't betray her happiness at the offer.

"Seriously, when and where? I will be there!"

"Don't be daft!" he said, "We will come by your place and pick you up! Shall we say 7:30? Will that give you enough time to do your, erm, ablutions?"

"Oh hell yes! Give me 20 minutes and I'm all yours!" she said excitedly.

"Well, shall we say an hour, I still need a shower and a change!" then he said with a sincere voice, "It'll be just great to see you again, Amanda, I'm really looking forward to the privilege."

There was a silence and then she responded, "The privilege is mine, I do assure you. Thank you for thinking of me." And then she lightened the tone by continuing, "John, you're a star and you're also psychic! We were going to have cardboard boxes in gravy, with a little bit of dust mash for tea!"

John laughed and told her the similar story about their hunger-department! Then he continued, "No, 7:30, that will give us both time to get ready and put us in the mood!"

"I'm already in the bloody mood," she howled with laughter.

"OK, see you at 7:30, John! I'm so looking forward to it! Bye!" she said and John put the phone down.

"EEEYESSS!" he said as he punched the air in front of Pritesh, who had just come out of the bathroom, having had a shower.

"Hey, you seem to be happy!" he said looking at John.

"I bloody well am! I'm gonna get some food!" he said.

"Bugger off!" said Pritesh, "I was alluding to the fact that you've got a date!"

John feigned indifference and said, "Oh, yeah—there is that I suppose."

Pritesh said, "Hell! I'd better try and get hold of Alpana and see if she can come out!" and he went downstairs to the telephone. He arrived back at their room a few minutes later with a face that told John the tidings.

"Nope, she's already out with another Indian guy. Apparently, he's a hot-shot businessman from Leeds. I guess I'm sunk on that one, lad!" he said with a very forlorn face.

"Good luck, old chap, do keep the British end up for me won't you?" he said still trying to be the clown and took John's hand.

"If I don't hear from you by 23 hundred hours, then I know you're lost too!" he said with a sad face. John said,

"You daft sod, do you really think I would desert a comrade? Come with us anyway! We're all pals together, aren't we?" John pleaded.

"Hey man, two's company and with a cute chick on your arm like YOU will have, you won't want a good-looking dude like ME in tow will you? I just might steal your date away!" and he punched John on his shoulder.

"Thanks, Pritesh, you're a true mate!" said John and punched him back on his shoulder. "Make sure you get something to eat though, you daft bat!" he said, as he went to get changed.

"Oh yes, I'm gonna do boeuf a corneau, avec oeufs a la scrambuels, et le stuffeaux de la sage et onion!" said Pritesh with a laugh.

7:30 arrived and John was waiting outside Amanda's digs. She came out dead on time and greeted John with a beaming smile and a kiss on his cheek.

"Hiya John! It's good to see you!" John smiled back and returned the compliment. She put her handbag onto her shoulder and she carried a light coat, in case it got chilly later on. They walked down Woodhouse Lane and into the city and they chatted about their respective week's work and studies.

After slowly walking down The Headrow, Amanda asked, "Where are we going?"

"Do you know, I haven't got the foggiest!" he said, "Let's keep our eyes peeled!"

They looked here and there and had passed many pubs along the way, but they didn't look particularly inviting. They both got a whiff on the air of oriental food and they looked at each other.

"Mmm, fancy a Chinese?" said Amanda.

"Yeah! I never really thought of that, but that smell is gorgeous, isn't it?" and they both looked left and right, to see if they could find where the delicious aroma was coming from.

By chance, John noticed the green-slated roof of a pagoda style entrance to a large Chinese restaurant, called the Dynasty Restaurant, on Gower Street. It did look welcoming and they could see people coming and going; the one's leaving, looking quite satisfied with what they had had to eat. They both agreed that this was the place and they walked in and stopped at a little counter and waited to be shown to a table. A very pleasant Chinese lady, dressed in a black mandarin outfit, piped with reds and golds came up to them and asked how many would be eating with them.

"Oh, just the two of us!" said John and the lady showed them to a table for two in a cosy little area against one of the innermost walls, which was lit by beautiful red Chinese lanterns and a huge picture of the Great wall of China right next to their table. The lady asked if they wanted set meals or the buffet. They had already agreed that the buffet sounded great and thanked the lady, who showed them where to go to choose their meals.

"Would you like drinks?" she politely asked.

"Oh, yeah, a couple of colas please!" said John and then she went to get their order of drinks. Amanda put her coat behind her chair and her handbag back over her shoulder and they both eagerly went to the buffet servery.

They came back to their table with plates piled high with all sorts of delicious food and they both attacked their meals. Amanda had got a pair of chopsticks for each of them from the utensils bar and after starting with knives and forks, they ripped open the chopsticks from their paper wrappers and giggled at each other as they both attempted to impress the other with their chopstick skills, which in both cases, was not too good, much to the amusement of the Chinese lady, who had brought their drinks for them.

The meal was sumptuous! Chicken dishes and pork in hoi sin sauce, spare ribs, crispy roast duckling, pancake rolls, omelette, king prawns, several types of fried rice and meats on skewers, that they weren't sure what they were, but God, they were good! Having been around the servery three times each and having sampled just about all the dishes on offer, they were getting full and they agreed that it was time to pay and leave. John called the waitress over and asked for the bill.

"That was just perfect!" said John rubbing his stomach at the waitress, who smiled courteously and placed their bill in front of John on a little dish and started to take their empty plates.

"God, yes, I can't move now!" said Amanda.

John got his wallet out and was about to get the correct cash, when Amanda said, "How much was it?"

John smiled and said, "It's OK, it's my treat!"

"Not on your Nelly!" she said with a determined look on her face, "We're going 50-50 with this, I pay my way, buster!" she said smiling at him.

"OK, I'll tell you what then, I'll pay for this and you can pay for the next one, how's that?" he said broadening his smile.

"Oh, I see, do I take it, sir, that you intend to ask me out for another meal in the not too distant future?"

"Well," he said looking sheepishly at her, "I was rather hoping that you may just agree to accompany me to some other equally tasty venue, but—if you don't want—"

"Oh, I want, I want very much!" she laughed. "OK, it's a deal, but I insist on buying the drinks on the way back! Deal?" she said.

He thought, *two can play at this game* and he repeated to her, "Oh, I see, do I take it, madam, that you intend to pay for the next meal and I to pay for the drinks thereafter?"

"Uh-huh!" she said grinning.

"It's a DEAL!" he said and they shook hands and smiled at each other. The bill was paid and they thanked the staff for such an excellent meal, then they left the restaurant.

The evening was cool but dry. Amanda put her jacket on and they strolled slowly back towards the campus and they passed one of the pubs that Jeff had recommended on that first day. There was a happy hubbub of voices and laughter coming from inside and they noticed several students from the university whom they recognised, sat on wooden benches outside, next to the entrance. John would rather have walked by, preferring to have found somewhere a little quieter, but Amanda saw some of her friends and shouted hello to them. Instantly, they came over to her and started to chat enthusiastically about this and that.

"Where have you been tonight?" asked one.

"Come in and have a drink with us!" said another. John thought that the evening was over and that Amanda's friends had commandeered her, as they dragged her into the pub. John stared after her for a moment, then decided to let her enjoy some time with her friends. After all, he didn't own her. He decided to stroll back to the campus. He hadn't got more than 100 metres, when he heard Amanda, running up behind him and shouting,

"Wait on! Wait for me!" and he turned to see her running towards him. She caught up with him and panted, "Where do you think YOU'RE going?"

"Oh, sorry, I thought you had been whisked away by your friends and I thought I'd leave you to chat with them."

"Ha ha, *you* are my date tonight, young man! Did you think that I am so fickle as to just leave you in the lurch? No way!" she said and she took his arm and hugged it.

John smiled and felt a kind of 'electricity' at her simple embrace. They strolled on together and Amanda did not let go of John's arm, which made him very happy, that she obviously felt comfortable enough to do it.

"So! I've got a drink to buy you! Where are we going then?" she said.

John laughed and said, "Hey, I know Leeds about as well as you do! Let's just walk until we find another watering hole!" So they crossed the road and walked down a street they had never been down before. Sure enough, within a half a mile there was a large, family pub, which looked inviting. They walked in and straight to the bar.

"What you fancy, John?"

"Oh, a pint of lager for me!" he said.

"A pint and a half of lager please," said Amanda to the barman. There wasn't many people in the pub and they had pretty much a choice of seats.

They chose a nice cosy corner to enjoy their drinks and they sat next to each other.

"Cheers!" they said and they both took a sip. Amanda looked admiringly at John and said, "I've had a wonderful evening, John, thank you so much for inviting me out. I look forward to reciprocating!" and again, she linked arms with him.

John coyly said, "The pleasure was all mine, Amanda, It's I who should be thanking you! You are quite a girl and you are fabulous company." He continued without thinking what he was saying, "You smell divine with your Angel on and you LOOK divine and I—" he paused, slightly embarrassed at his own words and shuddered at how she might react; he thought that that was a bit premature and that it was a silly thing to say.

"And you—what?" she asked looking into his eyes and slowly coming closer to him.

"And—I think—" he mumbled, losing his train of thought;

"And you think what?" she whispered, her head slowly getting closer to his, her smile had gone and she was looking at his lips.

"And I think you're gorgeous."

He just had enough time to whisper back, before their lips met. A slow and gentle kiss that said everything to each other. John's heart was beating fast and his head was reeling. Then she tenderly placed her hand on his cheek and looked at him, her eyes sparkled and she smiled sweetly at him.

"I think you're gorgeous too!" she said softly.

Time was pushing on and they decided that they had better make a move. They walked back to the campus, hand in hand and it felt very comfortable, very natural and nothing rushed. What had happened had happened by itself and they both instinctively knew that their relationship would be honest and meaningful to them both.

Once again, they were outside her digs and again, like time was repeating itself, they stood facing each other in the imperfect light of the old street light, a little down the street from them. Once again, Amanda looked up to the bedroom and saw one of her girlfriends' silhouettes on the closed curtain and once again, her eyes shone. This time, however, they gently hugged each other for several minutes and said not a word, then they kissed as before, in a meaningful and caring way, before they said goodnight.

As they parted, they were both smiling happily, full of good food and feeling very positive. One last wave to each other and she went into her digs. John walked on air back to his. He knew that this girl was going to be special and he swore to himself that he would never ruin it by 'trying it on' or ever alluding to sex, unless it was mutual and happened completely naturally.

Back in the digs, there was the aroma of curry! John saw Pritesh sat watching the TV and said, "Hiya, I thought you hated curries!"

Pritesh scowled and said, "Don't blame ME for that rotten pong man, blame HIM!" and in walked Ian, with a beaming smile and a satisfied look.

"Yeah, I can't deny it, I couldn't resist it! I had some mushroom pakora, then a tandoori murgh nirali and a naan! Yumski!" he said.

"Ha ha, yes, the aroma is still competing with the boeuf a corneau, avec oeufs a la scrambuels, et le stuffeaux de la sage et onion!" said John.

"Har bloody har!" said Pritesh, but he couldn't help but crack a smile at the repeated 'pigeon' description of his own 'bottom of the barrel' tea!

John said, "Well, I had the most incredible Chinese!"

"Oh yeah—" said Pritesh with a wry smile and "what *else* was on tonight's menu then?"

"Ah, jealous, huh?" said John, looking at his nails in a satisfied way.

"To be frank, yeah!" said Pritesh. "At least you got a date, I didn't—anyway, who'd have wanted to share my bowl of gruel, as the cold wind whistled cruelly over these bare floorboards and my fingerless gloves singed as I warmed my fingers around this feeble candle on my tea-chest here?"

All the while, Ian was playing an air-violin and whistling Hearts and Flowers. They all had a good laugh.

"Next time, we'll all go out together eh? Just the three of us? Sound good?" said John.

"Yeah, right, Athos, Porthos and Arijit!" grinned Pritesh.

"Misery-guts!" laughed Ian, "Good idea, John, count me in, I look forward to it."

"OK, OK, count me in too, It's obvious that you both need someone mature and in control to chaperone you both and lead you not into temptation on curries or women, unless of course I get one too! Woman, that is, you can stick the curry!" said Pritesh.

Ian ruffled Pritesh's hair and said, "Great! It wouldn't be the same without YOU looking after our welfare and stealing all the limelight now would it!"

As the months rolled by, the three of them had many a good night out on their own, a few beers and a burger; or sometimes with some girlfriends, but John always took Amanda, who was almost 'one of the lads' and it would never have been the same without her. This enduring team of young people would be the best of friends, right the way through their university years and beyond.

Success

The study was hard. It was more so than John had expected. But with such good friends as previously described and with such support from the tutors and of course from his dear mum and dad, he excelled. His determination and dedication to his chosen subjects took shape. But many was the night that he burned the midnight oil with his friend Ian, who shared John's passion for law and they indeed helped each other on countless occasions with their complex tutorials, projects and essays.

John's year out took him to France and he studied law in its oldest forms, much of which is still used, including some of its law-terms and phrases, dating back many hundreds of years. Pritesh was a rock to both Ian and John, with his endless humour, support and seemingly limitless resistance to stress and pressure to his equally difficult subject of mathematics.

John and Ian could help each other, but Pritesh stood alone and studied relentlessly and without moan or groan to anyone. Only rarely would they witness a book being hurled from one side of the room to the other. A huge support to Pritesh, was eventually winning the heart of the beautiful Indian girl he admired from day one, Alpana Kapoor, who eventually succumbed to Pritesh's good looks and zany sense of humour.

John went home for the summer that year and had a good brain cool-off. His mum and dad just could not do enough for him and one day, his now very elderly Nanna and Grandpa came for Sunday lunch. John was so excited to see them again and when they arrived, John hugged them, just the way he did when he was a little boy, although this time, he towered over their diminished heights, his Nanna just about coming up to his chest!

Michael, on the other hand, now in his 63rd year, was still well built, tall, still good looking and although his hair and moustache were pure white, one wouldn't have liked to have argued with him in a brawl! The chances are that he would still have come out best! Helen was also very 'well preserved' at 54 years old, she still looked at least ten years younger and with a little pampering to the colour of her hair and regular gym work-outs, the devil-red nail varnish and lipstick still worked its magic for Michael and she had a figure that most women of 25 would be envious of!

The Sunday in question, was a replay of the Sunday they had had all those years ago, just in reverse! The men were sat in the garden with a cold lager and the women were in the kitchen putting the last touches to the roast beef and trimmings and they were chatting away happily to each other. Nanna was getting a little slow in her ways and her words and Helen noticed this with a sad smile.

The birds were singing and the butterflies were flitting around Michael's miniature Majorcan wind-pump that he'd created all those years before. Oh, the smell of the roast was divine and every mouth was drooling, including their old next door neighbour, Neville, who was plodding away cutting his grass.

"Ee Mike, that smells great! If yer got any spare, remember that I'm a registered charity y' know!"

Nanna heard this and replied, "OK, lad, I'll save you a Yorkshire pudding!"

To which he responded, "God bless ya! I'm surprised that a slip o' a lass like you knows how to make *real* Yorkshire puddin's!" but then instantly looked at Michael's dad, realising his faux pas and said, "Oh, oh sorry mate, ah weren't bein' rude like, but eee, that cookin' smells gorgeous!" with a hearty laugh.

Grandpa laughed and goaded the old next door neighbour by saying, "Eighup, lad, It'll be as good as it smells, but my missus is spoken for!"

Neville smiled and said, "Ah haven't tasted a true Yorkshire pud since me lass deed some twenty years ago, I just do a sarny of a night nowadays or a tin o' beans on toast! Ha ha!"

Then he continued with cutting his lawn. Dinner was served and the men were called into the house. They didn't take any persuading and were at the table in an instant. As they were watching the food being served, Nanna had sneaked out of the back door, with a huge Yorkshire pudding and a slice of the roast beef, smothered in gravy on a side plate and caught the eye of Neville, who stopped the engine of his grass cutter and came across to her.

"Eighup! Is this fer me?" he said, his old eyes lighting up.

"Shhh, just a bit of a nibble! Enjoy!" she said looking furtively around her, then went back into the kitchen.

As she disappeared, Neville smiled to himself and said, "Ahh, she wants my babies!" and he tucked into it and closed his eyes with relish at the fabulous taste of the food.

Nanna looked at him through the back window, smiled and secretly put her index finger to her lips at him. It was the best Sunday lunch, small as it was, that poor Neville had tasted since his dear wife was carried aloft.

As can be imagined, the roast and the sweet afterwards were stupendous! Helen put the dishes into the dish washer and they all came out into the sunshine with their glasses of wine. Michael had put all his garden furniture out, including a comfy swing-seat for two people, in a gaily upholstered yellow gingham design. Helen and Nanna sat in this and gently rocked to and fro, whilst the men sat in some upholstered recliners.

"Ah, that were just fabulous, Helen!" said Michael.

"Yes it certainly was!" they all agreed and applauded her.

Helen smiled and said, "Good! I'm glad you all enjoyed it, thanks for helping me, Nanna," to which Nanna smiled and noticed Neville smiling too from the other side of the privet hedge.

"Tell me, John," said his Grandpa, "How's all this study coming along? How much longer do you have before you qualify?"

"Oh, it's just fine, thanks, Grandpa, I hope to qualify next year. I found my gap year in France very helpful indeed and the Faculté de Droit was just amazing! I learned such a tremendous amount there and I feel sure that will help me when it comes to my exams. Hey, one thing I don't think I told you mum and dad, but whilst I was in France, I had some of the nuttiest dreams I think I have ever had in my life ha ha!"

"Eighup! They *must* 'ave been nutty then, John! You've 'ad some 'umdingers in your time, ain't ya, ha ha ha!"

They all laughed—all except Helen, who instantly remembered those awful days of sleeplessness and worry and she said, "John? What sort of dreams were they, love? Nasty ones? Scary ones?"

John smiled and replied, "Oh, a bit of everything really—hey, I'm not paranoid about them though—I just thought I'd tell you? They were all probably just brought on by the fact that I was working so hard and I was in a comparatively unfamiliar place?"

Helen still wanted to know more and she said, "Give me an example John—" and Michael added, "Aye, lad—gi'e us all a grin like!"

John had no qualms in giving them all a huge grin as he searched his memory for a good dream to relate, that would indeed give them the best laugh.

"Do you remember that dream I used to have about walking swiftly along and I'm staring at my shoes? And the shoes were old fashioned things—black, with a square buckles and square toes? Well, I had that one quite often, but this time, I look up and see a young girl of maybe 20 years old and she is—is—"

"Yeah?" encouraged his dad.

"She's very beautiful, but absolutely filthy! She has the most amazingly green eyes. She looks like a peasant. The scary bit is that standing behind her, is a huge black 'thing' that I can't quite make out the features of. It is almost as if it is a guardian to her of some kind—and yet, it has huge, tallonned fingers, almost like it was some kind of demon—am I boring you all?"

"Hell no, lad—we're all agog, ain't we?" said Michael looking at the others who were all nodding with the same interest of what he was telling them.

"Well—" continued John a bit nervously, "I feel pity for the girl and she holds her arms out to me, presumably for help. I raise my left hand towards her, when suddenly, she is naked and laughing and this 'demon' thing is laughing too. They both raise their arms and fingers towards me, as if they would 'go' for me, but I raise up my right hand, in which, I am amazed to see that I am holding a blazing torch!"

His face dropped as he said this and he was obviously uncomfortable now, but he continued, "I lift the torch up and hold it between them and myself and I remember peering though the flames. The demon seems to descend into the earth, leaving the girl, who now seems to be trapped in the flames and crying pitifully. I feel such compassion for her but somehow I feel disgust and 'hate' at the same time! I feel like I am 'free' from something as I watch this poor girl writhing in the flames—"

There was total silence. Helen said, "Don't upset yourself, John, it's only a dream?"

Michael looked positively embarrassed and toyed with his moustache as he looked at the grass.

John said, "A bit gruesome, eh?" and he laughed to lighten the atmosphere.

Nobody asked anything else about his dreams, but John seemed none the worse for his recollection of it, in fact he said with a grin, "Oh and I have often dreamed that I have invented the flintlock musket, ha ha! That must be something to do with *you,* granddad—that must be *your* influence, ha ha ha!"

Nobody smiled except his granddad, who tried to look like he wasn't perturbed by John's earlier dream.

Throughout his final months at university, John studied hard. He became almost reclusive in his room in the evenings and he fell into a routine of eat, sleep and study. He didn't have much time to spend with his friends. Ian and Pritesh too got their heads into their respective studies. Only Amanda got anything like 'time' alone with John and they would occasionally go out for a drink or a meal, but never like within their first 'freshers' year, that was so relaxed and carefree. There was urgency now amongst all of these young people, to achieve what they were all there for, to get their degrees.

When that day came for John, it was truly a dream come true. All the study, the hopes and fears all came to a head, when capped and gowned, he walked up to the podium to receive his diploma. It was surreal as he shook the hand of the Head of the university and received the parchment, tied with a red ribbon, that bore the words 'LLB (HONS) LAW'

Fate and Human Falter

John sent many applications to firms of solicitors and lawyers. He had superb foundation knowledge in the field of personal injuries, so his applications were focussed on that subject. As an NQ solicitor, there were literally hundreds of opportunities as that time and it took a bit of time and research to narrow his targets down.

He was offered interviews with 10 firms, of the 30 or so that he had approached and he decided to narrow this further to 6 of them and arranged times and dates to attend. The first 3 were not suitable for various reasons, either accessibility to and from work or the 'salary negotiable', as is advertised with many situations, was a joke, something his father had previously warned him on many occasions to steer clear of.

"If a job's worth its salt, they won't be shy in showin' what the reward is! 'Salary negotiable', is an embarrassed way o' sayin' 'ow little can we give ya'?" he would say.

John was anxious to start his chosen career, but he wanted to make sure that wherever he went, it was the correct move right from the start, so he took his time and eventually chose an opening at a firm in Leeds, called Roland Peterman and Co. Mr Peterman (senior) was a jolly and fun-loving gentleman of some 70 years of age, but with bright eye and sharp wits, he was still the Chairman of the company and oversaw his firm with care and diligence.

His son, Giles, was about 40 years old and a bit of 'clever dick'. He took no prisoners, both within the firm or with his clients, which lost the firm favour on many occasions and many was the time that he had to be 'carpeted' by his father, who was in turn invariably undermined by his own son. Nobody really liked Giles, including the rest of the associate solicitors, of which there were 6.

All of them had specialist talents and they were second to none as a firm. John had done his homework on them prior to interview and was able to make a good impression as a consequence whilst in the interview chair. John's talents as an NQ solicitor, coupled with his truly winning personality, had secured this position, albeit probationary and John intended to make sure that by the end of his probation, they could not do without him.

On day one, John proved to be exactly what they had been looking for. He was assigned several clients with various legal problems. He was 'shadowed' by one of the more senior associates, who listened very carefully to how John conducted himself and the way he advised his clients. Everything went John's way. Even John had to smile to himself at the fact that at every juncture, he was able to give perfect counsel and advice.

His wonderful advisory service, learned from the brilliant tutors at Leeds University, came back to him and he just knew that he would be able to get through his probation with ease. It wasn't long before he was called into Mr Peterman's office, where there were assembled, the senior associates and directors of the firm and he was cordially invited to accept the post as permanent and what was more, that he would be awarded a pay increase of 15%.

Even Giles smiled at John and said, "Congratulations, John and welcome to our successful and forward-looking firm! Your 15% salary raise is well earned, John! However, nothing comes from nothing, I will be observing you over the next few months, you will need to spread your wings and attract new business and clientele by that proportionate amount! We will then review your remuneration again. Bottom line, earn us a fortune and we will give you a proportionate cut of the pie, ha ha!"

John smiled and thanked Giles. The rest of the directors applauded John, but one or two eyed Giles narrowly, as they knew him to be exactly what he was—out for any way he could do a little less work at the expense of someone else, so that he could spend more time on his private yacht, currently moored for the winter in a little port on the island of Menorca.

John was a latecomer as far as taking driving lessons was concerned and he had struggled, at university, to eventually pass his test, after 20 lessons. His dad had taken him out on countless occasions when he was 17 and prior to university, in the hope that he would have passed his test before he went to Leeds. John was so wrapped up in his studies, that driving became very much a secondary consideration, relying, rightly or wrongly, on his mum and dad or friends to taxi him here and there.

Having passed his test, he bought an old, but beautifully restored Hillman Imp. He loved it and it was in fairness, immaculate and a real head-turner.

Everybody was so pleased and proud of John when they heard of his good news at being appointed a position at the law firm! All his friends, including Ian, Pritesh, Alpana and, his most precious friend, Amanda, were all so happy for his success. They all agreed to meet up and have a good 'bash' in the near future! His mum and dad, Nanna and Grandpa had been at his graduation ceremony and saw him, capped and gowned, receiving his scroll of qualification.

Here he was now, earning his living for real! They were so proud of him, Helen had cried out loud at the moment he received his hand shake. Amanda, of course, had been there too and applauded louder than anyone else in the auditorium, with a tear of pride in her eye for him.

One evening, specifically, the evening of 21 May, when John was at home with his mum and dad, he was watching the TV, when the phone rang. Helen was just coming down the stairs at the time and intercepted it before Michael or John could.

It was Amanda and Helen said, "Oh, hi Amanda, how are you, love, it's so good to hear from you!...Yes, John's just here...bye," she said and smiling, handed the phone to John.

"Hi Amanda! How are you?"

"Oh just fine John, are YOU OK? I was just sat watching the telly and all of a sudden I just got a severe attack of the 'blues'! I haven't the foggiest idea why! I just got the feeling something was very wrong! Are you OK?" she asked anxiously.

"Whoa! I'm just fine and dandy, pet, you don't need to worry on my account, I'm just sat in front of the goggle-box and vegetating just like you!"

"Oh, thank God for that! I don't usually get feelings like that, but on the rare occasions that I do, I obey my instincts, as they're not usually wrong! I don't suppose you're free to go for a drink? Have you eaten yet?"

"Well, actually no! As it happens, we haven't really considered tea, we went out for an all-day breakfast about 10 this morning and we were all full—until now! Now I come to think of it, some food wouldn't be such a bad idea! What 'you got in mind?"

"Anything, so long as I can just be with you big-boy!" she said with a laugh.

"Just a moment," he said to her and put the phone to his chest as he shouted through to his mum and dad, "Have you any plans for tea this evening? Amanda was wondering if I'd like to go out for a bite to eat."

Helen and Michael had no problems with that at all and Michael said, "Eighup! Y'ad better be shovin' off sharpish then lad, it's quart' t' six nah! Ya won't get owt to eat, all t' restaurants 'll be full!" he said light heartedly.

John spoke to Amanda again, "OK poppet, shall I pick you up in my super-dooper fantastic girl-magnet new car then?"

"Great! What time can you get to me?"

"For you, in the blink of an eye! Your merest whim is my iron law!" he said laughing.

"You are too kind sir! But make it 10 blinks while I have a quick shower, my hair looks like I've just been hit by a bolt of lightning!" and as the words left her lips, she took a deep intake of breath, almost as if in pain and John heard it and said,

"You OK, love? What's wrong?—Amanda, what's wrong?" After a moment, Amanda replied,

"I don't know John, I just felt a—a sort of feeling like I had just joked about just now, it was almost like I HAD been hit by something! Honest! I'm not losing my marbles; it was the most horrid feeling!"

"It's OK, love, I'm sure it was nothing! There isn't a drop of rain out there, let alone a storm! Get yourself showered; I'll be with you at 7? Will that be OK?"

"Yes, that should be fine love, see you then," she replied, trying to compose herself as she put the phone down. The feeling was real alright and it truly frightened her! She got undressed and into the shower. It felt good and it quickly eased the feeling. She started to sing to herself and eventually, she dispelled the feeling altogether and told herself that she had just imagined it.

John was at her house at exactly 7 o'clock. Mr Parry opened the door to John and greeted him.

"Well, hello, young John, come on in!" and he showed John into the living room, where Mrs Parry and Susan and Eileen, Amanda's sisters, were all watching TV. They all smiled at him and said a polite 'hello'. At that moment, Amanda came running down the stairs and into the living room.

"Sorry, I'm 30 seconds late," she said, "but I couldn't find the handbag I wanted!"

John smiled and looked at her admiringly. She usually wore jeans and a blouse or T shirt, but here she was, in a lovely black pair of snug-fitting velvet trousers and a little matching bolero jacket, a pretty white blouse and a little pair of black suede boots that had small heels and were buttoned to the sides. She had put on some red lipstick and some makeup that accentuated her deep brown eyes.

All her family wished them a pleasant evening and they made their way to the door. A last wave from Mr and Mrs Parry and they got into John's car. John was still reeling at how lovely Amanda looked and he was not backward in telling her so.

"Amanda! You're beautiful!" he said in the most sincere tone.

She went a bit coy and replied, "Oh, I just thought I'd make the effort for my hunky date tonight!"

"No, you truly are gorgeous! I've never seen you looking so lovely!" he continued with absolute resolve and admiration.

Amanda looked at him with equal feelings and said, "Thank you, John, I don't know what to say!" and she blushed crimson.

"Don't say anything, you look wonderful and I'm so proud that you are with me tonight! Where would you like to go?" he asked.

Amanda was still a bit speechless and said, "Oh, I really don't mind, you decide."

John thought for a moment then said, "There's only one place in Harrogate that would be so fitting for such a stunningly attractive young woman as you! Let's go to Stage Left!"

"Oh, isn't that where that Chantelle Upton was at?" Amanda asked curiously,

"Yep, it sure is!" John replied. "It's time that that place saw a TRUE beauty. I don't care if she's there or not, I really don't, but the food and service there is second to none and this time, I will be going through that door as a customer! What are they going to do? Throw me out, in front of all their snooty patrons? I wouldn't have thought so, ha ha!"

Amanda saw the humour and felt flattered that John was prepared for the possibility of seeing Chantelle again. It didn't bother him in the slightest; in fact he welcomed it, should it happen at all. They parked right outside the restaurant, more by luck than judgement. John got out of the car and ran round to Amanda's side and opened her door for her.

"Well, thank you!" she said, a little taken aback by the gentlemanly gesture.

"My pleasure indeed!" he said and took her hand as she got out the car. She felt very special. John knew she was special and couldn't wait to show her off to his ex-colleagues if they were still there!

They went into the foyer and to the reception desk. The young woman on the desk was new to John; she had obviously been employed after his departure.

"Good evening, Sir, Madam," she said politely, "is it a table for two?"

"Yes, thank you," said John, feeling quite pleased at not being recognised thus far.

"David, show the lady and gentleman to table 21," she said to a waiter who John didn't recognise. John kept a lookout for Mr and Mrs Upton and of course, Chantelle, but there was no sign of any of them.

"Here we are," said David, "Will this be suitable? If not, I can escort you to another table?"

"No, this is fine!" said John. They were sat on the stage of the old theatre and had a good view into what were once the stalls and up into the circle. This vantage point suited John admirably. They both sat down and after making sure that they were comfortable, David left them to peruse the menu. They both looked at each other and their eyes shone.

"My goodness, it's a bit posh, isn't it, John?" Amanda said looking about herself and admiring the huge black and white photographs of long dead actors and actresses on the walls.

"A wee bit," he replied, "but the food is superb and you'd have to travel a long way to get a better meal, I assure you!" he said smiling at her. They studied the menu.

"What do you fancy then, Amanda?" John asked.

"Gosh, there are so many scrumptious looking things here, aren't there? Mmmm, I think I fancy the garlic mushrooms, then the salmon fishcakes—yes, that's what I fancy, how about you?"

John studied the menu a little longer, after all, it had been some considerable time since he had worked there, some five years in fact and the menu bore no real resemblance to the one he knew so well as a waiter under that same roof!

"Oh, it's got to be the mushrooms too, then the Porterhouse steak with all the trimmings for me!"

"Ooh, that sounds scrummy! Do you think I might just have an iddy-biddy samplette of that when it comes? It does sound fantastic!" said Amanda.

David was with them again and asked if they would like some drinks. They had already thought about that and decided on a lager each. It was with them in less than a minute and their order for food was taken by David. "Cheers!" they said to each other, as they clinked their glasses.

"John, do you remember that first meal we ever had in Leeds?"

"Hell yeah, of course I do! I will never forget it!" he said, linking his fingers with hers. "But tonight, Amanda, you are not that university student, tonight, you are the star of the show, the main attraction, the head-turner of the theatre!"

Her eyes sparkled with delight and she leaned across the table and gave him a peck on his lips. In about 20 minutes, out came the starters and they set to them with a vengeance! Absolutely delicious!

"They certainly haven't lost their touch!" John said smacking his lips.

"Goodness me, no, that was absolutely wonderful!" said Amanda.

No sooner had they polished the starter off, then along came the main courses. John's steak was sizzling as it was presented to him, with the fries and side dishes set next to this majestic cut. As they eyed their main courses and were just about to set about them, a familiar face walked towards them, with a silver tray in his hand. It was his old colleague Pete, who welcomed John with such enthusiasm! John stood up and gave Pete a hug.

"It's good to see you, Pete! God, I didn't think you'd still be here after all this time, you old rogue!"

"Good to see you too, my old friend!" said Pete.

"May I introduce you to positively my best friend in the world, Amanda! Amanda, Pete!" and they shook hands.

"Ah!" said Pete, picking up the silver tray that he had put onto an empty table next to them, whilst he was greeting them. There was a large bottle of champagne on the tray, with two glasses.

"Here we go!" said Pete with a smile.

"Just a moment!" said John. "I didn't order that!"

"Yes, I know you didn't!" said Pete with a knowing smile to John. "It's with the compliments of the house!" he continued.

"What? Compliments of whom?" John asked dryly. Pete shrugged his shoulders and feigned ignorance, but when Amanda was reading the label of the champagne bottle, Pete gestured with his eyes up to the circle of the old theatre and there, staring down at them and looking absolutely impeccable in dress and demeanour, was Chantelle, who smiled at John, then majestically walked away to one of the exits from the circle and out of sight.

Pete whispered, "You're looking at the new boss, of about the last two years! You wouldn't know her today! She's hard, but fair and since her horse died, she has lost herself in the business. Mr and Mrs Upton moved to Cyprus and left all of this to her. She raised all salaries and increased our holiday entitlements! What a transformation!"

Amanda looked up at that moment, but in the hubbub, hadn't heard a word that had passed between John and Pete.

"Oh, bon appetite, mes amis!" said Pete, who bowed courteously to them and then left them to enjoy their meal.

John was not expecting this. Not one damned bit of it and his head was a jumble. They started on their meals. Amanda's eyes shone with happiness. John's thoughts were in turmoil. Little did John know though, that Amanda had secretly seen John looking up into the circle, followed his gaze and had seen the beautiful young woman he was staring at with Pete. She had put two and two together as to who this woman was, but she trusted John and knew that she was the special one in John's eyes. It had to be true, it just had to be because he had said so himself.

The meal was truly fantastic! They had ordered a sweet each and that had complimented and finished the rest of the food perfectly. Pete came to the table and asked if they would like anything else. As they were considering coffees, Pete picked up the champagne bottle to uncork it.

John instantly put his hand up and said, "No Pete, the champagne is NOT required!" to which Pete looked at the pair of them bemused and Amanda widened her eyes and said, "Why on earth not?" She smiled at John and said, "I thought I was your special date for tonight? Would you not pamper me and finish off a perfect evening with a little champagne?"

Pete agreed and interjected, "Yes, John, this is a Dom Perignon! It's not an Asti Spumante you know!" and he leaned closer to John and continued, "It's the best in the house! It's worth a bomb!"

"Yes, I know!" said John with a scowl, "I used to work here remember?"

"Oh, sorry, John, just trying to be of assistance," said Pete meekly.

Amanda was listening to all of this and looked like how she felt, left out. She said, "Look, sorry to interrupt, boys, but I'm sure you can discuss 'old times' some other time? Hello, John? Remember me?" and she looked at John with watery eyes.

"Oh Amanda, I'm so, so sorry! I can't tell you how wretched I feel! I will explain all later, it's just that I—"

"It's OK, John, you don't need to explain anything to me, I'm not stupid and I have eyes in my head."

John stammered for words and Pete looked very awkward. Amanda smiled and said to John, "As the old song goes, Tell me on a Sunday, please," and clapped her hands and said to Pete, "Garcon, the champagne if you please! I'm having such a good time! Champagne is the only thing that is fitting right here and now after such a fabulous meal! Uncork it I say!" and she snapped her fingers.

John and Pete's eyes met for an instant in puzzlement, but Pete rose to it and said in a jovial voice, "Of course, mademoiselle!" and he popped the champagne, the noise of which attracted the whole of the surrounding diners and they all clapped, suspecting that the champagne was for some very special occasion.

The foaming flutes settled and Amanda raised hers to John and said, "Here's to my best friend at the start of a long and illustrious career! May he find health, wealth and true happiness—and his heart's desire!" and she lifted her glass to her lips and looked at him over the rim of the glass.

Pete was sensitive enough to move away from their table and titivated and pampered to other diners. All the while, Chantelle had been observing this from the shadows of the outer walkway of the stalls area. John did his very best to lighten up and he returned all sorts of compliments and toasts, but he could see that Amanda's heart was dying in her bosom. She truly loved John, but never ever told him as much. She had always wanted John to be happy and she considered that if this was the only thing she had left to offer him, she would give it with all her heart.

John had a couple of flutes of champagne, then said, "I'm driving, love, I'd better not have any more!" to which Amanda agreed and said, "Well, you'll excuse me if I finish the bottle, won't you? It's far too good to waste! Besides, it's making me a bit tipsy and you never know, you might just get lucky with me tonight!" to which John's gut was turning with anguish and embarrassment at the whole situation.

She finished the champagne and presently, grabbed a passing waiter by his shirt sleeve and said, "Cognac! Bring me a cognac, would you?"

John looked a bit worried and said, "Steady on, love, that's strong stuff, especially on top of strong champagne!"

She smiled and looked back at the waiter, "Make it a double!" she said insistently. "I feel wonderful tonight and I want to remember this moment for a very long time. You wouldn't deny me that, would you, John?"

"No—of course not, love," he said looking down, then he nodded assent to the waiter, who instantly went to get the cognac.

"Amanda, I just wanted to say—"

"Ah, John, don't say anything!" she said, in a voice that betrayed her slight intoxication, "I've had a wonderful evening and I wouldn't have it spoiled for the world!" Then her whole demeanour changed and she looked him in the eyes, as if searching his soul and said, "You really DO care for me, don't you, John? I know you do and I care for you, like I have never cared for anyone else. Let me go with a little grace and dignity, that's all I ask of you," and she held his hand and continued, "I will love you for always, unconditionally and truly. Now, you must go where your destiny leads you."

John just didn't know what to say for the best. He loved Amanda, but wasn't *in* love with her. He had promised himself that after what Chantelle had done, he would never forgive her and thought he hated her, but here, he was being hypocritical to the last degree, his eyes were drawn to Chantelle and he couldn't take them away. Amanda truly cared for him and Chantelle did not! Amanda only had eyes for John! The cognac came and Amanda applied herself to it and took a large mouthful.

"Steady on, Amanda, you'll make yourself sick!"

"Oh no, I won't, I feel just fine! I won't have any more after this, I promise. Would you be a real sweetie and take me home after this, unless you would like to take me somewhere and make love to me? It'll give me something else to remember a truly memorable evening with the guy I adore!" and she giggled like a schoolgirl as the alcohol took greater effect.

John started to feel a little agitated by this now and felt it could only get worse than it was. He caught the eye of a waitress and asked for the bill. The waitress went to get it and was only gone a moment then returned with a piece of paper on a small silver salver. John opened it up expecting to find the bill, but instead, it had a short note in Chantelle's handwriting and it said, "Paid in full, with thanks. Please call again. Chantelle."

Amanda finished her drink and by this time was decidedly squiffy. As she got up from her chair, she smiled at John and said, "I'd better go to the loo. I won't be long," and she walked with unsteady steps in the direction of the toilets.

John hated himself and he watched her petite frame heading off to the ladies toilet, but his eyes burned as they met Chantelle's as Amanda passed her unwittingly. They held each other's gaze and neither of them could look away. They both felt that same passion and breathless excitement as they did on that afternoon at her stables. The sounds of the restaurant seemed to disappear and it was as if there were only Chantelle and himself in the whole place. Amanda reappeared and John dropped his eyes from Chantelle's.

"OK, John, I'm ready when you are! Have we paid the bill? How much do I owe you? HIC!" and she put her hand to her mouth and giggled. "Oh, pardon me!" she said.

John took her hand and led her to the main doorway to leave. John stopped for a moment to thank Pete and Pete shook his hand and they chatted for a few seconds. This was just enough time for Amanda to walk up to Chantelle.

She took her hand as if in a cordial farewell and as soberly as a judge, she looked her straight in the eye and said, "Take care of him. You break his heart again, just once and I'll break your jaw! Do you hear me, my pretty one?" then she smiled at Chantelle as if they'd had a pleasant parting, then walked towards John and took his arm, then they both left the restaurant and into a gloomy night that threatened a storm.

Amanda was quite drunk, but not as drunk as she made out to John. She joked and giggled as they got into the car. John was sober in mind and spirit and his face told a tale. He knew he couldn't worm out of the situation and he detested what he had seen, said and done, especially to poor, poor Amanda. He got into the car mechanically.

Amanda said, as she opened her door, "Will my knight in shining armour not open my door for me then?"

John didn't answer and proceeded to fasten his seat belt. He started the engine and revved it loudly as if in annoyance. Amanda got in and tried to kiss John on his cheek, but he pulled away as she was trying to say what a lovely time she had had. He sped off, making Amanda's head jerk backwards, but she giggled and said, "My! You are a fast boy tonight, aren't you?"

As they got out of the town centre, he slackened his pace a little. Soon, they had to go down a quiet lane towards her house that was poorly lit by the streetlights. It reminded him of the poorly lit street outside her digs in Leeds, on that very first date.

"John, love, stop the car?" she asked.

He paid no attention. She giggled again and repeated, "Please John, stop the car before we get back to my place? Please?"

John did as he was asked. He pulled up in a dark area of the lane and switched off the engine. He looked straight ahead and said nothing. Amanda waited for a moment and then said in a chirpy voice, "That was just fabulous, John! Thank you so much for taking me out tonight! I just adored the food, you were right, it is the most wonderful place to eat, isn't it?"

He didn't reply. She paused; then continued, "What a novel idea, to make a restaurant out of a theatre! I thought it was really cleverly decorated! I'm so happy I got to see it! I guess that you'll be seeing a lot more of it in the future?" John still didn't reply. Amanda took his hand and said, "I haven't paid my share of the bill! Will you tell me know how much I owe you?"

There was still silence for a few seconds then he looked at her with his heart nigh bursting and eyes brimming and he said, "You owe me nothing Amanda, nothing at all. I, on the other hand owe you everything."

As he looked at her, he could only see half of her face, the other half was in shadow from the dim light of the street lamp and he could see a tear rolling down her cheek, it sparkled as it slowly fell. She was still smiling sweetly at him and had nothing else about her that suggested that her heart was breaking for him. She leaned over and kissed him, gently and slowly.

She said, "If you won't let me give you any money, would you like to have *me* instead? I'm not bad looking under these clothes if you would like to see? Just once? Pretend that you're in love with me for a little while and imagine that our futures were to be with each other, forever entwined. Make love to me, John—please? Whisper to me that you love me, even if you don't mean it, then go and leave me forever if that's what must be?"

John could stand no more and he completely broke down.

"Get out! Get out! Go home, Amanda! Forget me forever and never come looking for me, do you hear! I'm rotten to the core and I don't deserve to breathe the same air as you! For God's sake, just go!" and he sobbed his heart out, with his head in his hands for several minutes.

All the while, Amanda looked on at him, clutching her handkerchief and occasionally dabbing her eyes. At last, she tenderly kissed him on his cheek and said, "Goodbye, my love, always think fondly of me, as I will of you. Goodbye—goodbye," and she opened the car door and slowly walked down the lane in the direction of her house.

John was still crying uncontrollably as he heard her sobs and the little heels of her ankle boots on the footpath. Click, click, click went the little heels and the sound became fainter and fainter, until at last, the only sounds left were of his own pounding heart and his own sobbing. All John wanted at that moment, was to close his eyes and die. He knew now why Amanda had had such a fatalistic experience earlier that evening. She was right, there WAS something wrong; it was HIM.

He cursed himself for his own weaknesses and for the fact that he had suggested going to Stage Left! Why did he do that? Of all the places they could have gone to, why there and risk seeing Chantelle? He HATED Chantelle—no, he didn't, he adored her—he hated HIMSELF and for so many good reasons. He stared up at the side of Amanda's house, at where her bedroom was and his eyes tried to pierce the brickwork to see her crying her heart out on her bed.

Oh GOD! What a mess! He wanted both these girls, for completely different reasons. He knew he couldn't have both. He knew he was the loser, a total loser and he knew that he had at least done the right thing in the end for his once-closest friend, Amanda. He had to get away, right away, as far as he could get. He started his car and sped off home, with a breaking heart and the Devil in his soul. The sky took on an eerie, dirty look and a deep, menacing growl of thunder was heard all over the neighbourhood.

"You just bring it on, you bastard!" said John to the impending storm.

Cruel Transportation

John arrived back home at 11 o'clock. He could see his mother and father's bedroom curtains were shut and the whole house was in darkness. He got out of his car and closed the door as quietly as he could and did the same with the front door of the house, closing it without a sound. He had stopped crying by this time and he had adopted a much calmer, if not self-militant approach to his own deeds.

He was really quite numb and self-denial seemed to be coursing his recent thoughts. He knew he hated himself, but he almost felt that fate had taken a hand and this horrid situation somehow just had to be and that perhaps it wasn't his entire fault after all? He didn't know and he didn't really care. He just knew that everything he cared for and truly loved had been screwed up by his own doing.

He went upstairs mechanically and went into the bathroom. He poured some cold water into the washbasin and threw it over his burning cheeks. A flash of lightning lit the dark bathroom up and it startled him for a second. The thunder reverberated around the house as he dried his face. He faced the bathroom mirror over the basin as he did this and another, more fearsome flash revealed his own image in the mirror.

Was it just his heated brain or was the image staring back at him really himself? The reflection was certainly him, but much, much older, with greying hair and traces of age-lines about the eyes. He recoiled from the mirror and turned on the bathroom light. He hardly dared to look back into the mirror, but when he did, all he saw was his own reflection, with tired, red eyes and the start of beard stubble growing.

The storm grew in intensity and the eerie light became a horrid mustard colour, from the light of Harrogate's sodium lights reflecting in the sky. John staggered into his bedroom and fell onto his bed. The thunder outside rattled around the house. He cried and cried, until his tears soaked into his pillow. He slipped in and out of sleep and his thoughts and dreams became awful, they became almost horrific, with grotesque faces looming up to him and ghostly visions menacing him.

He saw his own father's face but with almost fantastical evil in its expression, screaming at him, "I warned ya, lad—you'll rue this now!" He saw his Grandpa too, with equally horrid expression saying, "Sorry son, you've shot you're last round with me and your Nanna!"

Squealing sounds were all around him and he saw vague shapes and menacing demons shaking bony fists at him and laughing, displaying terrifying fang-like teeth as they laughed. He awoke with a start as a deafening crash of thunder reverberated around the house. He was sweating and terrified. He instinctively opened his bedside cabinet drawer and reached for the citrine stone that he had kept there for years. He grasped it in his right hand and put his fist to his lips.

He said out loud, "If there is the remotest truth about the power of this ancient stone, then I invoke that power now!"

A flash of lightning, lasting several seconds, lit up his bedroom and the resulting thunder was so deafening that he had to clasp his hands to his ears. As a result, he dropped the stone. In the imperfect light of his bedroom the stone seemed to be pulsing a feeble orange glow, on the floor where it had fallen.

He picked it up again and redoubled his breathless invocation, "By the power of this ancient stone, I curse myself and my unforgivable actions. Amanda, forgive me for the wrongs I have done you! Chantelle, haunt me no more! You have totally possessed me, now leave me! Let me go to a place that you can't ever get to me again! If there is a wish in this stone, my wish is—that I never forget this moment! I wish to be a better person in the future by re-living this day, forever, never let me forget the pain I have given Amanda. May I re-live this day forever in my mind!" and he kissed the stone, as if it really could help or curse him.

In that instant, the storm stopped. It just stopped! John, still sobbing, pulled his bedroom curtains to one side. The clouds were just as threatening as before, but they seemed to just swirl around. He could see them all around, turning slowly around Harrogate, almost as if Harrogate was an epicentre of something very ungodly. Silence though, deathly silence now. No rain, no sound, just a huge, swirling grey-mustard coloured cloud, low in the sky.

John shuddered at the result of his 'invocation' and he tried to convince himself that it was pure fantasy and coincidence. No, he wasn't dreaming, this was for real! It was now very humid and John went back into the bathroom to wash his face. He couldn't understand why the terrific noise from the previous thunder hadn't woken up his mum and dad. Notwithstanding, he dried his face and decided to go back downstairs and into the back garden, to look more closely at the eerie sky.

He stood in the middle of the garden and looked straight up into the sky. Sure enough, the immense swirl of cloud was still circling overhead. He realised that he was still holding the citrine stone and he looked at it, now sparkling in the unnatural light. Suddenly, he was aware that his mum and dad were calling to him. Their bedroom light was on, although he hadn't noticed it until now. He heard his mother calling his name with fear and concern.

He looked at the stone one more time and he felt a surge of courage and defiance, then held the stone skywards and said in a loud voice, "I mean what I say! Never let me escape this day! Make me truly regret it for the pain I have caused Amanda!"

No sooner were the words from his lips, then a bolt of lightning came from the very centre of the cloud and struck the stone with such ferocity that it knocked Michael, who was now not within six feet of him, completely off his feet and as he fell backwards, was knocked unconscious as his head hit the garden. John fell like a stone. Helen screamed at the sight as the rain once again hammered down. She was totally incensed as to what to do, having just witnessed this fantastic spectacle, her husband unconscious at her feet, her son, seemingly dead in the middle of the garden.

John was all but dead. His mother was above him now, he could see her through closed eyes, crying and calling his name. She screamed for help and John could hear, as if in the distance, other voices, as neighbours came running into the garden to offer assistance. Poor Helen fell to her knees and cradled John's head to her bosom, as the rain lashed down and the thunder roared all around her.

Her cries were just as echoes to John; he felt comfortable and warm. He was slipping away from life. He saw his Nanna and Grandpa, now smiling at him, his mum and dad doing the same. He saw Lorna smiling at him and saying, "Silly boy Twigg! Why did you want to do a silly thing like that for?"

Suddenly, the noises he heard were mixed. He heard his mother calling to him, "John! John darling—hold on, son—" He heard his father, who had regained consciousness.

"John lad—fer God's sake, lad, don't leave us—we love ya, lad—" and he heard his father sobbing.

John felt peace and total calm. He could see all sorts of happy and comforting images, Amanda, University, Nanna, Grandpa—all was peaceful. He vaguely heard the sound of an ambulance siren, but it was oh, so far away and meant nothing to him really. He felt his shirt being torn open and through closed eyes, he looked at strangers in ambulance uniforms, looking at him with very worried faces.

He had forgotten about his invocation, the citrine stone and the whole evening's incident. All he was vaguely conscious of was the feeling of rain on his chest. Then, he was conscious of other noises and sensations. He heard summer birds. He could smell beautiful fragrances of flowers, but he could also smell the pungent smell of horse manure; strange voices and unfamiliar sounds; dogs barking, horses neighing, the smell of hay.

He just couldn't open his eyes though, he felt sleepy and as if he was a little boy again whose mummy was trying to wake him up after a wonderful night's sleep. He felt sunshine on his face and something cold being held to his forehead. Very odd, strangely phrased Yorkshire accents now rang in his ears, "What 'appenned loike?"

"Oi dunno, 'e jus' fell off 'is cart loike a stoan!"

"Are yo' alreet, lad? Can yo' 'ear meh loike?" John opened his eyes, to see a rustic young man in a russet serge outfit, a leather jerkin and knee length breeches and a large floppy brimmed hat with a feather to one side of it. Next to him was an older man, in a similar type of outfit and supporting himself on a staff.

"What happened?" said John.

The young man replied, "Can't roitly say, mate, but I spoid yo' fallin' from yer 'ay-cart loike! Lewks loike yo'd been struck about yer heod! Are yo' feelin' alreet?"

John looked more closely at his two saviours.

"What's going on? Are you from the Sealed Knot?" he asked.

"Sealed Knot? What yo' talkin' on, lad?" the young man said with a laugh.

"Who are you?" asked John.

"Ah, oi'm Ralph Stockdale and this is Ruchot Watkins o' Knaresborough! Who moit you be, lad?" John pulled a cold compress from his forehead that had been applied by Ralph and he struggled to sit up.

Ralph helped him get into a sitting position. John looked around himself. All around were trees and tall grasses. He was sat in the middle of a narrow path of dried mud. There was a hay-cart next to him, with 10 or 15 bales of hay stowed on it. Two powerful shire horses were yoked up to the cart and were grazing at the grass and were just stood quietly, as if awaiting their next instruction from their owner.

"Can yo' 'ear meh? 'Oo are yo' lad?" asked Ralph again.

"Oh, my name's John—John Twigg? Where am I?"

The two men looked at each other and Richard replied, "Yo' mun ha' tekken a thwack o' yer bonce young feller, canna yo' remember nowt loike?"

John screwed his eyes up then opened them again, in the hope that he would find himself once again in a familiar place. No, the two men looked at him with obvious concern on their faces.

Ralph said, "Yo'd best be comin' along wi' us, lad, we'll tek yer up to t' Killin' Hall, where we can get yo' sorted out wi' a doctor or summat! Ruchot, help me gerrim back onto 'is cart, an' we can go wi' 'im up to t' Inn. C'mon, lad, we'll 'elp yo' up, one, two, three—up ya get!" and they got John to his feet and helped him onto the cart.

They both climbed up next to him and with a slap of the reins, the horses strained their huge, powerful shoulders and legs to the task.

John was dazed and totally confused. He vaguely remembered being in his back garden and the lightning and thunder, but he couldn't really remember much else. His head ached and he started to feel frightened. The two men chatted jovially to each other and occasionally spoke to John, to make sure he was alright and hadn't slipped back into unconsciousness. They made their way to a slightly wider path and turned right, to a gentle downhill incline. The path took them to a ford along a small stream.

John mused that it looked similar to Knox ford and said in a befuddled voice, "Is this the Knox ford?"

"Whoi yeigh! Yer memory is comin' back to yo', is it lad?" said Ralph.

"This cannot be Knox ford! There are no cottages! There are far too many trees and the pack horse bridge isn't there!" John said pointing in the direction that the bridge should be.

"What bridge do yo' allude to, lad?" said Ralph,

"There used to be a wooden bridge o'er yonder fer pedlars an' sich jus' there—" and he pointed to the same spot that John was staring at; "burrit were washed away some two years agone boi a 'uge torrent ha ha!"

"No!" cried John, "This is impossible! There should be a farm up there on the hill and there are too many trees! What the hell's going on around here!" he said and he tried to get up from the wooden seat, only being restrained by great effort from Ralph.

"Sit yo' down at once, lad, do yo' 'ear meh? Thou wilt do thissen more of a mischief! Be still oi say!" and he pulled John back into the seat between them.

John just sat dumbfounded and did as he was told. He stared around himself and at the two rustics that now appeared to John as being his captors rather than saviours. His eyes alighted onto his own arm and he realised that all his clothes were changed. He was dressed in a similar sort of material to the two men he was with, although of a slightly richer material.

He had a deep brown leather jerkin on, a white rough cotton shirt with puffed sleeves, a baldric and broad leather belt, with a dagger in a scabbard attached to it. There was a small leather purse containing coins on the belt that tied with a drawstring. He had a hat next to him, which he took to be part of his own strange apparel, which was made of a thick black felt and a peacock feather tied to one side of it. He had rough tights and a pair of well made, soft leather boots that stopped at his knees.

John shouted aloud, "I am dreaming this! This is not real! John, WAKE UP NOW!" to which Ralph and Richard laughed heartily and thought John was having a joke, as he was feeling better. John slapped his own face, to which the other two just stared.

"Calm thissen, lad, thou'lst be alreet!" said Richard, giving Ralph a significant look. Realisation started to hit John. He now seemed to recall the citrine stone and saying some kind of invocation—but what? He just couldn't quite recall. He calmed himself and feigned being a lot more in control.

"I'm sorry, gentlemen, I feel a lot better now! Tell me, just to reassure myself, after my fall, ha ha—humour me and remind me what year this is?"

"Ha ha ha!" laughed Ralph. "Boi the saints, yo' do 'ave 'umour returnin' wi' t' colour o' yer cheeks, lad! Boi moi faith, but ah'll tell thee that thou art aloive an' kickin' in t' year o' our Lort, fifteen hundert an' forty four, just as it were yesterday an' t' day afore! But hist! In what manner do'st thew speak?

Thou hast a strange an' well spoke tongue lad, the loike ah've ne'er 'eard! Wherefore come'st thou?"

"Oh, I'm from—well—from right here! Yes, Harrogate is where I was born and raised!" The two men glared at each other.

"Arrogut? Arrogut?" said Ralph with his eyes widening, "Art thou a lawmun or a glergymun lad? Ah've 'eard talk o' that manner o' speak, but thou must be o' noble birth? Or at t' least, a monk o' travel or a laird? Boi our leady, if yo' be ony o' t' list oi allude to, oi would be obloiged if yo' wad forgive moi uncouthness squoire!" and he took off his hat and bowed his head in deep apology and reverence to John.

"Don't be silly, Ralph!" said John, "I don't know any other name for Harrogate? Do you?"

Ralph and Richard cowered to John and Richard, seeing John was genuine and he was indeed not a nobleman, said, "If it please yo', lad, oi mean, sir, the folk 'ereabouts call this li'l pleace 'Arlow Gata! It were once a strong 'old o' t' Romans tha' knoas! Has't thew been livin' in a far country squoire? What age hast thou?"

John realised that his accent was a far cry from theirs and they looked petrified at his obvious education and deportment. He tried to 'dumb it down' for their peace of mind.

"Ah, sorry, lads, oi'm feelin' a lot better, sorry for moi accent, oi was taught in Italy and France as a lawyer and it's hard to drop the pure Oxford English ha ha!"

"Oxford English?" roared Ralph, "Oxford be many days journey! Boi our Leady, thou hast travelled, lad! Thou must be ravenous boi now? What say yo' to a flagon o' ale at Libby's ale 'ouse at t' Killin' 'all an' a few cakes? Elspeth does rare cakes tha knoas!"

John pretended to know what and where they were talking about and joined in the general chat. They turned right at the end of Knox Mill Lane and onto a slightly larger road, leading up a steep hill. John took his bearings and recognised the terrain as being the junction to the Ripon Road, up to Killinghall, although his head was still reeling!

No houses, no cars, hardly any noises, save the hooves of the horses and the sound of the summer birds and the humming of more bees that he had ever heard in his life. As they slowly climbed the hill, John once again tried to join in and not appear too out of place.

He said, "Ah, the Greyhounds Inn is just up ahead! I'm ready for a pint!"

Once again, the two men looked at each other with a puzzled look. Richard said, "Beggin' pardon squoire, where is this 'Grey'ounds Inn' thou hast alluded to? Do'st thou mean Libby's ale 'ouse? 'Tis t' only ale 'ouse oi recollects 'round these parts, an' it's just at t' top o' t' 'ill 'ere!" and as they trundled onto a flat area of the road, they could see the tiny village of Killinghall and John could see that roughly in the same place that the Greyhounds Inn stood or *would* stand, several centuries in the future, was the little ale house of Libby's.

About a dozen small dwellings surrounded the ale house and to the rear and looming above all the other buildings, was a large, imposing building, with a fortified appearance. It was quadrangular, with battlements all around, giving it an almost military look.

"Tell me, erm, Richard and Ralph, what is that place?" Again, the two men looked at each other.

"Yo' say yo' comes fra 'Arlow Gata? How comes yo' dunna knoa this pleace squoire? 'Tis t' Killin' 'all! By our Leady, it's where all t' local magistrut courts be 'eld, an' if a soul be found guilty, an' if they canna be tekken t' Gallows 'ill at Ripon or to t' York Tyburn fer what e'er reason or if t' judge sees fit, they wad swing in t' courtyard o' that edifice! That's whoi this pleace be called t' Killin' 'all! Most folk 'ere abahts is afreared o' t' pleace, an' say there be ghosts o' t' souls that were hongt fer no real reason!"

John smiled a strange smile of recognition. *Of course!* he thought to himself, *The Killing Hall—Killinghall! I often wondered how it got its name!* They approached the little alehouse and John just stared with open mouth and reeling head. Could this truly be happening? Was he really in the year 1544?

A few moments went by and Ralph again asked, "If it pleases yo' squoire, may oi enqoires as t' yer age? Yo' seems t' 'ave fair set speech an' education?"

John looked sheepishly at him and said, trying to emulate the vernacular again, "I am four and twenty years of age, sir."

What on earth is happening? Is this all just a dream? Has John gone mad or did he actually die from the terrific blast from the thunderbolt? And if he is dead, is this an afterlife of his own making?

All will be revealed, gentle reader...